SUCH A WINTER'S DAY

SUCH A WINTER'S DAY

Carlene Thompson

**SEVERN
HOUSE**

First world edition published in Great Britain in 2021 and the USA in 2022
by Severn House, an imprint of Canongate Books Ltd,
14 High Street, Edinburgh EH1 1TE.

Trade paperback edition first published in Great Britain and the USA in 2022
by Severn House, an imprint of Canongate Books Ltd.

severnhouse.com

British Library Cataloguing-in-Publication Data
A CIP catalogue record for this title is available from the British Library.

ISBN-13: 978-0-7278-5087-4 (cased)
ISBN-13: 978-1-4483-0724-1 (trade paper)
ISBN-13: 978-1-4483-0725-8 (e-book)

All Severn House titles are printed on acid-free paper.

Typeset by Palimpsest Book Production Ltd.,
Falkirk, Stirlingshire, Scotland.
Printed and bound in Great Britain by
TJ Books, Padstow, Cornwall.

To my husband Keith

PROLOGUE

Nine and a half years ago

'Juliet, your brother should have been home over an hour ago. Dinner is almost ready.'

Fifteen-year-old Juliet Reid looked up from the Kindle she was reading at the kitchen table. 'He's probably at play rehearsal.'

'He's usually not this late,' her mother, Sera, said.

'Have you called him?'

'Twice. Went to voicemail both times. I'm sure he forgot to turn on his phone again after rehearsal. Most likely he's on his way home. Will you go and hurry him along?'

Juliet sighed. If she came home over an hour late, she'd be in trouble. Because it was Fin, her mother merely looked annoyed. 'Can't Alec do it?'

'I sent Alec to the grocery store for brown sugar and it's taking him forever. I don't know what can be keeping him.' Nineteen-year-old Alec Wainwright had lived with the Reids since he was sixteen. His family had been killed in a car wreck and he had no other living relatives. Now he attended Ohio State University and had come back for Christmas break.

Sera, her long blonde-and-silver hair pulled back into a neat French braid, looked at Juliet with patient, slightly amused blue eyes. 'Please, honey. Surely you can tear yourself away from your reading for twenty minutes. You know Fin – he has no sense of time.'

'He has a watch,' Juliet groused. 'It's snowing.'

'It's just beginning. Hurry and you'll catch him before the snow really starts.'

Juliet took her puffer coat down from the rack in the kitchen, went out the front door, and started north on Evening Star Lane. The houses were fairly large and each set on nearly an acre of land that sloped down to a patch of woods surrounding a narrow stream called Argent Creek. Some people questioned how her father could afford such a large house on a deputy policeman's salary, but her mother had once explained to her that they were able to live in such a nice neighborhood because she'd inherited money from her father, who had been a physician. 'My mother died when I was your age. Dad died five years later and I was his only heir. When I married your father, I was able to buy us a pretty home.'

Juliet loved the spacious neighborhood and most of the neighbors except for the Booth family, who lived six houses away from the Reids. Micah Booth was a foreman at Tresswell Metal Fabrications, which was owned by Fin's friend Jon's family. Mr Booth stood on his front lawn giving Juliet a hard look. Juliet ignored him. She had more on her mind than a man who didn't like her parents.

Juliet thought about Fin. Her parents said he'd first started trying to play the guitar when he was three and he'd shown enormous musical talent – both with instruments and vocally – ever since. Now her eighteen-year-old brother had not only written but was starring in the school Christmas musical and he'd been acting like a movie star who didn't have to abide by any household rules. Neither her father nor mother ever got really mad at him. At least it seemed that way to Juliet. They rarely had a harsh word for her, either, but then she always did as expected. She kept her bedroom neat, made good grades, and practiced the piano endlessly. Also, at fifteen she was a good cook like her mother. Still, she wasn't the spectacular presence that was Finian Reid.

Now Juliet plunged her hands in her pockets and looked at the surrounding mountains turning dusky blue in the evening. She'd been born here and loved the hills and the nearby wide Ohio River that formed the eastern border between Ohio and West Virginia. She thought the land was beautiful and she couldn't imagine living anywhere other than the city of Parrish, Ohio. On this December evening, though, the snow was growing heavier and she felt an unaccustomed loneliness descending with the coming twilight. The hills seemed higher, pressing closer, and darkness was falling faster than usual. Juliet wasn't a timid girl – her parents often said she wasn't as cautious as she should be – but a strange uneasiness crept over her. She pulled her cellphone out of her pocket and called Fin. He still didn't answer. Damn! He was really being so inconsiderate lately. Oh well, maybe she couldn't blame him. Fin was handsome, wrote music, played lead guitar and keyboards, had a strong, fantastic voice, and at six feet with his wavy golden blond hair, vibrant blue eyes, and electric personality, was nearly every girl's dream. Juliet had always adored and admired her big brother and forgave him for his recent inflated ego. If she'd been in his place, she'd probably be even worse, she admitted to herself.

She phoned him again but still with no luck. She jammed her cellphone back in her pocket. Now snow fell steadily. She pulled her hood over her long dark blonde hair and wiped snowflakes off the lashes curling above her blue eyes. Ahead was the tree-covered knoll she and Fin always used as a shortcut to the high school. She crossed the intersecting street and started up the incline, following the path that wound between shedding maple trees. She scuffed through fallen leaves and jumped when a chattering gray squirrel ran in front of her. 'Hey, don't you know you're supposed to be in your den watching TV?' she called. The squirrel raced up a tree and disappeared. *I wish I were home watching TV*, Juliet thought and in a burst of frustration, yelled, 'Finian Reid, where *are* you?'

As the path continued, the woods grew denser. Juliet trudged on, thinking that if Fin missed dinner, their mother would be really unhappy. She was fixing pork roast with twice-baked potatoes and carrots in brown sugar sauce, Fin's favorite meal. This was so bad of him, she fumed inwardly. He knew their mother was preparing something special for him and Juliet didn't like to see her disappointed.

She heard a soft 'whooo' and looked up to see a small, long-eared owl sitting on a bare branch. 'Are you searching for dinner or sightseeing?' she asked. 'You haven't seen my brother, have you? Blond hair, big ego?'

The owl hooted again, apparently unfazed by her presence as it gazed steadily at her with golden eyes.

Juliet walked on, her head down as she got madder and

madder at Fin. Her mother called. 'Haven't you found him *yet?*'

'No. I'm afraid he's still at school.'

'Oh, he *couldn't* be so forgetful,' Sera fretted. *Yes, he could,* Juliet thought. *Or he's hanging around with his girlfriend Carole Tresswell.* 'Dinner will be ruined!'

'Don't wait on him, Mom. Having overcooked food will serve Fin right.'

'But you don't deserve it.'

'Oh, well, never mind me,' Juliet said with the right amount of weary forbearance in her voice to spark her mother's pity. Fin wasn't the only actor in the family, she told herself. 'Besides, the chocolate pound cake I made will be good with warm chocolate sauce.'

'Yes, it will. You did a really good job with it.'

'Thanks.'

'Keep looking for another ten minutes. If you don't find him, come home. I don't want you to miss dinner.'

Juliet put her phone back in her pocket again, took a deep breath and continued along the path. A mouse darted from under a moss-covered log, then quickly ran beneath it again. Darkness had almost fallen and angry at the thought of missing dinner, Juliet kicked a pinecone and sent it soaring. It landed about fifteen feet ahead and rolled a couple of times. When it came to rest, Juliet looked at it then raised her head and froze. She felt as if all the air gusted out of her body. She couldn't move. She couldn't make a sound. She couldn't breathe.

All she could do was stare at the body of her brother sitting on the ground, legs splayed, a rope tied around his upper body and holding it to the base of a pine tree. His head was bowed and bright red blood drenched the front of his white wool sweater.

ONE

Present Day

Juliet Reid hoisted the last piece of her luggage into the trunk of her six-year-old white Ford Focus and slammed the trunk lid. It was nine a.m. The trip from Columbus to Parrish took two-and-a-half hours and Juliet planned on arriving at eleven so she could spend most of the day with her parents and Alec Wainwright, who had arrived yesterday from New York City, before her birthday celebrations the following day.

The late June day was glorious – a baby blue sky, clouds as fluffy as cotton candy, and a butter-colored sun. She got behind the steering wheel, fastened her seat belt, and after a quick mental check to see if she'd left anything behind, she pulled out of her apartment complex parking lot near Ohio State University and headed east toward home.

Juliet's parents had come in May to see her graduate with a master's degree in Music. She'd remained in Columbus, playing the piano five evenings a week at an upscale restaurant as she had the entire year before. In April, she'd begun sending out curricula vitae to high schools for a full-time teaching job. She'd had two interviews but didn't feel she'd be happy at either school, both having extremely strict, old-fashioned programs. She had three more interviews lined up for late July and early August. She hoped the schools were more to her liking and they liked her in return. In the meantime, the restaurant had given her a week off to visit home for her birthday.

As Juliet left the heavy traffic of Columbus and sailed along the calmer stretches of Interstate 70, she flipped on the radio. Usually she brought her own music, but she decided on a change. She chose a station playing vintage sixties and seventies music and sang along with 'Ricky Don't Lose That Number' by Steely Dan, 'Gloria' by Van Morrison, and 'I Think I Love You' by David Cassidy. Her mood soared with the music and the sound of her own voice, which was in good form today. And then she heard the opening notes of 'California Dreamin''.

Fin's face flashed in front of her. She closed her eyes for five seconds, her car swerved, and another car's horn jolted her back to the present. How many times had she heard Fin play the guitar and sing that song? Before he could play the guitar well, he'd listened to it over and over. He loved the song. He loved the idea of California. Loved? No, he was obsessed. The family had started jokingly calling him 'California' when he was fourteen. By the time he was seventeen, they were worried. Fin planned on graduating from high school and going straight to California to start a rock group. They'd taken the announcement of his plan lightly at first. When he was eighteen, though, they realized he wasn't fantasizing – he was determined. He knew no one in California. He had no plans to go to college in California. He was extremely talented, but he had no contacts in the professional music business. He'd spent his whole life in an Ohio town of thirteen thousand people, yet he was hell-bent on going to Los Angeles and becoming a rock star. He'd always been confident – overconfident, really – but this course of action was reckless, possibly dangerous. When his parents told him he couldn't go, he reminded them that at eighteen, he could do as he pleased. And they knew that after he'd graduated from high school, they would not be able to stop him.

On the radio, The Mamas and the Papas sang about dreaming of California on a winter's day. Juliet's stomach clenched. Was Fin dreaming of California on that awful winter day when she'd found him, tied to a pine tree, his head crushed by multiple blows with a rock? No doubt he'd dreamed of California within hours of his death, not knowing that he'd never see the place. And Juliet would never be able to listen to her brother's favorite song without feeling the sharp, unrelenting pain of losing him.

She quickly reached for her CD case and pulled out a disc at random. In a moment, she was listening to Andrea Bocelli. After a few minutes, her heartbeat slowed down, but the image of Fin wouldn't fade. That day long ago as dusk had closed in and she'd seen Fin roped to the tree trunk, she'd rushed to him and felt his pulseless wrist. She'd looked up into his dulling, open blue eyes. 'Fin! *Fin! No!*' The air seemed to roar around her and the world darkened.

Juliet was slumped against the base of another tree, covered with a thin layer of snow, when Alec had finally found her. Dimly, she'd heard his voice shouting, 'Juliet! You haven't answered your phone. Your mother's worried sick' – as he rushed toward her. Then he'd shifted his gaze to the tree and seen Fin. 'My God!' he'd gasped. Suddenly he was beside her, grasping her shoulders. 'Are you hurt?' he'd shouted urgently.

She'd said faintly, 'No. I just can't stand up.'

After Alec had felt Fin's wrists and neck for a pulse, he'd called home. Juliet could tell her father had answered and Alec told him there was trouble in clipped words she didn't remember. 'We're halfway up the knoll in front of that big white pine.'

Alec had then tried to pull her up, but she was limp. He gave up and sat down beside her, drawing her close to his strong body, rubbing his hands over her arms and murmuring in a rasping voice, 'Oh my God. Little Juliet. My God.'

'Alec,' she'd quavered. 'He's dead.'

'I know.'

'He's not wearing his coat. He looks so cold.'

Juliet had heard the rustle of leaves and looked up the hill and to her left. She'd turned and spotted a bulky form wearing a plaid jacket and blue toboggan staring back at them. 'That's Wendell Booth.'

Alec's arms had tightened around her. The figure looked at them for a moment, ducked, took a few halting steps bent over as if he could sneak away, then stood and ran. 'It's Booth,' Alec had confirmed, referring to the tall, muscular son of the Booths.

'He hates Fin.' She'd reached for Alec's hand and squeezed it. 'I'm scared. I've never been so scared in my life.'

'Look at me.' She'd gazed into Alec's intense eyes so darkly brown they looked almost black. 'I won't leave you. You're safe with me and help will be here soon.'

In less than fifteen minutes, Owen Reid, still in his deputy police uniform and coatless, had run toward them, his usually ruddy face ashen, his big hands shaking. Juliet remembered her father looking at Fin in disbelief for a few seconds before emitting a loud wail that sounded more animal than human.

Juliet shuddered and Alec held her closer. 'We saw Wendell Booth right over there. He looked at us then ran off.'

'All right,' her father had said tonelessly. 'I've already called nine-one-one. Take Juliet home. I'll stay.'

'We don't want to leave you alone—'

'I have a gun. I can take care of myself. Juliet looks like she's going into shock. Get her home. My car's at the foot of the hill.'

Alec helped Juliet up. Although she was wobbly, she could walk now with his help.

'Tell Sera as little as possible,' Owen had said.

'Not that Fin's dead?' Juliet asked.

'That he's hurt. That's all.'

When they arrived home, Sera demanded, 'What's happened to Fin?'

Juliet murmured, 'He's hurt . . .'

Sera's gaze searched her face. Juliet knew their bond was too strong for her to hide anything important from her mother and she looked down.

'He's dead,' Sera said. Alec had tried to hug Sera but she'd shaken him off. 'How?'

Alec's straight black brows had drawn together. 'He was beaten. But maybe—'

'He's still alive?' Sera had sat down with a thud on a kitchen chair. 'Will you fix me a brandy, Alec? You need one too and so does Juliet. Her lips are blue.'

They sat in the kitchen sipping brandy. No one spoke. The regulator clock on the wall had ticked away the minutes until it chimed on the hour. Then Owen came home. Sera rushed to him and broke down into shaking sobs in the safety of his arms.

By eleven p.m., when Juliet later knew dozens of crime scene photos had been taken before Fin's body was gently freed from the tree and transported to the morgue, cars crept by the Reid home, people peering from windows, some taking pictures, and a crowd lingered at the base of the knoll where Fin had been found. Police stood guard, keeping the curiosity-seekers at bay so they couldn't disturb any evidence that hadn't already been discovered. The sheriff had ordered Owen home, where he paced silently, staring out windows, chain-smoking cigarettes, occasionally cursing the world at large. A doctor had prescribed a tranquilizer for Sera, who lay in bed, curled into a fetal position in a drug-induced haze. It was Alec who sat beside Juliet on the couch, his arm wrapped protectively around her shoulders. He didn't burden her with clichés about how God worked in mysterious ways and Fin was in a better place. He offered nothing except his strong, comforting presence and she was more grateful than she could have told him.

Two days later, twenty-three-year-old Wendell Booth was arrested. Booth was six foot seven, two hundred and forty pounds, and was known for his strength and his temper. He had an IQ of seventy-eight and irrational parents who would not acknowledge that their son had mental challenges or address them in any way. They had refused to have him evaluated and without an evaluation, he couldn't be placed in special education. He remained in general education, and as a result Wendell couldn't keep up with his classmates and often suffered their jeers and scorn that heightened his emotional problems, most notably his constant frustration and fury.

When Wendell was twelve, his beloved younger brother died and Wendell's behavioral problems worsened. By age fourteen, he'd accumulated several misdemeanors that ranged from shoplifting to joyriding in his father's car, which ended doing major damage to his and another car. In a fit of fury, he'd destroyed a neighbor's flower garden and hurled a rock through the picture window of the house opposite. He had altercations with other boys, one of which had ended with Wendell breaking a boy's arm. He had been tried in juvenile court and the broken arm deemed an accident but while in custody, he was diagnosed with borderline personality disorder manifesting in lack of impulse and anger control. Doctors said the problem could easily be treated with medication and therapy, but Wendell's parents would not allow neither. Almost everyone knew the Booths were their son's worst enemies, nothing could be done about it without removing Wendell from the home, which the law prohibited.

Wendell had dropped out of school at age sixteen, having reached no further than the eighth grade. Afterward, he frequently loitered in the area of the high school and shouted insults at the students who were his age. He still lived with his parents and did lawn work, although he had few customers.

For years, Wendell and his parents had harassed the Reids because Sera read tarot cards and conducted informal classes on identifying and avoiding poisonous herbs, plants, and mushrooms. She never charged for her tarot readings. Both her mother and her grandmother had read the tarot and Sera always stressed that the cards merely revealed alternatives for the future rather than predicting the future and were open to interpretation. She never claimed to have extrasensory perception. Her lessons about what flora was safe and what was not sprang from her aunt dying when an uninformed cook had accidently served her poisonous mushrooms in a stew. The Booths, nevertheless, labeled Sera a witch and told everyone she dispensed potions – some love potions, but mostly those causing illness and death. A small number of people in the city agreed with the Booths, although none of them were as vocal. Wendell, in particular, had a long-running verbal feud with Finian Reid and two days before the murder of Fin, Wendell had been seen arguing with him and shouting, 'I'm sick of you, Reid! You think you're better than everybody but you're a witch's spawn and I'm gonna fix you for good!'

Still, if Juliet and Alec hadn't seen Wendell in the area of Fin's body, police attention wouldn't have been directed at him so quickly. Once it was, though, pieces easily fell into place. Near Fin's body were three shoe prints that exactly matched Wendell's. Traces of skin belonging to Wendell were found on the rope that tied Fin to the tree. Fin's black wool pea coat, tossed aside from the body, bore no trace evidence of Wendell, although blood matching Fin's type was found on Wendell's corduroy jacket cuffs. Finally, a serrated-edged knife supposedly used to slash Fin's throat and caked with Fin's blood was found buried in the Booths' lawn, but Fin's initialed gold keychain was never located.

The trial was held in the summer and although Sera couldn't bear to go, Juliet had attended every day. At first, she could barely take her gaze off Wendell. He towered over every other man in the courtroom. Once, before Wendell had begun to hate Fin and they'd been on speaking terms, Fin had said that Wendell maintained his impressive build by working out at least an hour a day on equipment his parents had bought for him. For the trial, he wore a dark blue suit that strained over his muscular shoulders and his thick neck rose above a tight white shirt collar.

Throughout the expert testimony about blood types and DNA results, Wendell fidgeted and drummed his fingers. Once in a while he turned completely around and looked at the courtroom full of spectators in confusion, in tears, and sometimes in anger although he never said a word. His heavy-set, red-faced father took care of that for him, several times standing and bursting out with accusations of 'Objection!' and 'Filthy lies!' until the judge threatened to have him removed. Wendell's towering mother Hannah sat stone still, her broad face mottled, her lips pressed together, her bulging blue eyes burning with loathing. Juliet felt that if you touched her, her skin would literally scorch you. Her eerily motionless, seething hatred made her more frightening to Juliet than either Wendell or his vociferous father.

She remembered when Fin's best friend, Jonathan Tresswell, had taken the stand. Darkly good-looking like his Italian grand-father, poised, and from one of the city's wealthiest families, he clearly and concisely described the day before the murder when he and Fin had been walking home from school. He was so composed, Juliet felt as if he was addressing the court from behind thick, protective glass. He said on the knoll not far from where Fin was found, he'd seen Wendell Booth. He was carrying a rope, striding toward Fin and yelling, 'Hey, Reid! Hey, Reid!' Jon had been running to catch up with Fin and had just reached him when Fin called back, 'What do you want, Booth?' Wendell had stood uncertainly for a few moments, looking from Fin to Jon, then turned and ran in the direction of the school, disappearing in the woods. When asked what he'd thought at the time, Jon said, 'Nothing. It was Booth being Booth.' 'And later?' A thick, protective glass seemed to shatter and Jon's composure cracked. He'd looked almost sick as he said in a slightly shaky voice, 'When I heard Fin had been tied to a tree with a rope . . . well, sir, I wondered if Booth had meant to kill him the day before but stopped because Fin wasn't alone. I didn't walk home with Fin the day he . . . died.'

There had been objections to Jon being unable to know Booth's state of mind the day he'd seen Wendell with the rope. Another student was called who on that day and time had also seen Wendell carrying a rope as he walked toward Fin, and finally Kyle Hollister, a third student and friend of Fin's, attested to seeing Wendell pacing on the knoll with a rope. The point had been made. It indicated premeditation on Wendell's part and the jurors had taken it seriously. Micah Booth had stood and shouted, 'They're rich, dirty liars! They're all going to hell!' Suddenly, Wendell had burst into a startling fit of shuddering and crying.

In the end, Wendell Booth had been charged guilty of aggravated murder and sentenced to twenty years in prison with a fine of $25,000. When Owen Reid heard the sentence, he'd said quietly, 'Twenty years isn't nearly long enough.'

But luck was on Wendell's side. Nine years into his sentence, a woman who had been on the jury that convicted Wendell Booth came forward with a confession. She was dying and wanted to go 'with a clear conscience' she said. While on the jury, she'd hadn't understood much about DNA evidence and didn't trust it. She also felt sorry for Wendell. She hadn't believed he was intelligent enough to premeditate a crime and his tears had half-convinced her he didn't have the soul of a murderer. She was on the fence about finding him guilty. Also, she'd struck up a romantic liaison with a male member of the jury. When she was approached with a $50,000 bribe to find Wendell guilty, she'd talked it over with her secret love. He'd persuaded her they could take that money and start a wonderful life together. So she'd accepted. She had no idea from whom the bribe came. There had been someone who described himself as the 'middle man,' a man she claimed kept his face covered and she couldn't describe. The money had been paid in cash and she and her lover had voted guilty. Her lover had disappeared from her life after a year the trial and authorities had confirmed he'd died in a plane crash two years later. Because of the woman's confession, the trial was declared invalid because of jury tampering. The conviction was over-turned and Wendell Booth had walked out of prison on March 15 and returned to his parents' house in Parrish.

Juliet's mother had been stunned and her father livid. He'd taken his two-week vacation time early and they'd gone to Charleston, South Carolina, for a much-needed break from their hometown and the site of Fin's murder. Juliet's heart broke. She remembered the flabby-faced woman who'd stared almost unflinchingly at Wendell. Juliet didn't believe the woman had felt sympathy for Wendell as she now claimed. She was merely fascinated by him and the handsome man who sat beside her, giving her small, encouraging smiles. Someone had sensed her weakness, and probably her avari-cious nature, not that Juliet had realized it at the time. But that was almost ten years ago. She was a woman now and she was as angry as her parents.

Juliet's phone rang. She realized that her hands had started sweating with the memories of Fin's death when she clicked the 'connect' button on her steering wheel and said, 'Hello.'

'It's Tommy,' whispered Juliet's best friend Leslie's just-turned five-year-old son. 'Are you comin' home?'

'Yes, I am. I'm on my way. Does your mother know you're using her phone?'

'No. I'm not s'posed to but this is important.'

'Oh. What's so important?'

'That you come home.'

'For my birthday? Why? Is there a party?'

Tommy had stopped whispering. 'I'm not a blabbermouth but you need to come home. *Everyone* wants you to come home. You should hurry.'

Juliet felt an odd flutter in her stomach. Usually Tommy's voice was light and full of laughter. Today it sounded almost urgent. 'Can I speak to your mother?'

'No. She's in another room and besides, like I said, I'm not s'posed to use her phone. I wanna make sure you're comin' home.'

'I am. Tommy—'

'Here comes somebody. Bye.'

Tommy clicked off. She immediately returned the call, but no one answered. No doubt Tommy had shut off the cellphone so Juliet couldn't call back on Leslie's number and nobody would know he'd called her. She could call someone else, but she didn't want to get Tommy in trouble. Oh well, she thought. Tommy was merely going to spill details about her surprise party, which she was already expecting. She grinned. In less than an hour she'd be home and she wouldn't let on that Tommy had called her.

Later, Juliet passed the sign proclaiming she was entering the city limits of Parrish, population 13,260. She hadn't been home since Christmas. Juliet headed down the wide Main Street lined on the west side with brick sidewalks lined with old-fashioned lamp posts and stone tubs blossoming with petunias of every color. To her left was Hollisters' restaurant. To the north of Hollisters' was In Tune Music, Pauline's Flower Garden where her mother worked part-time, Ohio One Bank, a high-end women's clothing store Longworth Style, Townsend Jewelers, and the small, elegant Parrish Hotel. In the summer, most people who came to Parrish for the boat shows on the Ohio River chose The Heritage Inn two miles north of town and managed by Juliet's father's closest friend, Frank Greenlee, but the Parrish Hotel managed to hold its own.

Farther up the street was the impressive courthouse with its marble columns and clock tower with bells that rang on the hour, and the Regal Cinema, a once-beautiful movie theater that had been closed for seven years. Juliet remembered going there with her family when she was a child. Wendell Booth usually sat in the front row, laughing and whooping and having such a grand time he sometimes had to be removed. Later, after Wendell was in prison, she and her friend Leslie had double dated with Leslie's steady, Jon Tresswell, and Kyle Hollister, Juliet's casual boyfriend.

To her right the Parrish Park's four bright green acres sloped down to the Ohio River whose smooth water reflected the cerulean sky and golden sun. At the end of Main Street stood the three-story brick Episcopal church with its tall steeple. The street forked in front of the church and Juliet took the right road, heading up the slope to her neighborhood.

She shut off the music, her heart lifting as she turned onto Evening Star Lane. Juniper trees shaded the sidewalks. A few children played on their large front lawns and a man washed a car in his driveway. As she neared home, she saw four cars parked in front of her parents' slate blue ranch style house with its white door and shutters. She also spotted a police cruiser and instinctively slowed down.

Oh no, a tiny voice inside her cried. Something's wrong. Tommy's unusual call telling her to hurry home. All of these people. *Please. Please. No.*

Juliet pulled into the driveway, turned off the car and simply sat, gazing at the house. She could not make herself get out and go to the door. But she didn't have to. Within a minute, Alec Wainwright came outside and strode to her car. He opened the driver's door and stooped to his knees, his handsome face grim, his dark eyes bloodshot and sad.

'W-what is it?' she murmured. 'What's wrong?'

He took her hand and held it tight. 'Juliet, I'm so very sorry.' He swallowed hard. 'Your father committed suicide last night.'

TWO

'Suicide?'

Alec nodded.

Juliet gaped at him. 'That's crazy!'

'I know it sounds that way—'

'I don't believe it!'

'I couldn't either at first.'

'He's *dead*?' Alec nodded again. 'He *killed* himself? No!'

'He did, Juliet.'

'Last *night*?' Fury washed over her. 'Why are you just telling me *now*?'

'We didn't know he was dead until after midnight. Your mother insisted that we not call you. She was afraid you'd immediately head for home.'

'Of course I would have!'

'Please listen and stop shouting. You would have been shattered. You were coming back early today – you'd know soon enough and she didn't want you to be upset while you were driving and maybe have a wreck. She's terrified of losing you, too.'

'Maybe, but—' Juliet had a swift feeling of being underestimated. 'Dammit, I'm not a little girl. You should have told me, Alec!'

'I promised her. Forgive me, Juliet, but . . . well, I halfway agreed with her.'

'I hate when people make decisions for me.'

'I'm sorry.'

Juliet searched the face she'd always thought so handsome. The depthless, nearly black eyes that could seem so coldly appraising now looked vulnerable and he had new lines on either side of his perfectly sculpted lips. His skin was so pale she could see the black shadow of stubble beneath his high cheekbones. She took a deep breath. 'How did he do it?'

'With his service weapon – the Smith & Wesson. He did it in Fin's tree house when your mother wasn't home.'

'Where was she?'

'At a party. Your father didn't want to go so I went with her.' Alec paused. 'Please come in the house. Your mother wants to see you.'

Juliet unfastened her seat belt, stepped from the car. Alec touched her arm. 'Are you all right?'

'No, I am not,' she snapped. 'I need a minute.' She closed her eyes and drew two deep, shuddering breaths. 'OK.'

They headed to the front door and climbed three steps up to the long porch lined with neatly trimmed box hedges and edged with white wrought iron. As they reached the front door, Juliet balked for a moment, not knowing if she could bear to walk inside. But the door opened and her mother, Sera, flung herself at Juliet, hugging her hard and crying.

'Oh, honey, I'm so glad you're home.' Her body shook. 'I don't know what to say.'

'There's nothing to say,' Juliet replied mechanically. 'Daddy's dead.'

'Yes. I never thought he'd leave me – us.' Sera pulled back and looked at her. Her delicate, fair skin, naked of make-up, showed a fine cobweb of wrinkles Juliet had never seen. 'Come inside, sweetheart. You look like you're going to faint.'

Juliet's mother clutched her as they stepped into the entrance hall. 'Juliet's here!'

A dog raced to her. 'Hello, Hutch.' Juliet stooped to hug the sixty-five-pound black-and-white beagle-basset hound mix her father had rescued from the pound three years ago. The dog licked her face ecstatically.

Juliet stood as her friend Leslie approached, her long, golden-brown wavy hair pulled back, her amber brown eyes red-rimmed. Even in her heart-felt grief, Leslie's delicate features were still lovely. 'Juliet, I'm *so* sorry. I loved your father.' She hugged Juliet. 'I'm shocked. Everyone is. You must be, especially. You and Owen were so close. It's awful. Terrible. Heartbreaking. In a way, it's worse than when Dad died. Well, Mom and I knew for months he was dying – we had time to prepare. But you and Sera . . . oh, I'm saying all the wrong things!'

'There is no right thing to say.' Juliet hugged Leslie, who'd been her closest friend since they'd met at Leslie's fifth birthday party. 'I know how you feel. You don't have to tell me.'

Sera pushed Juliet ahead of her. 'Come in and sit down, sweetheart. You must be tired. Are you hungry? Thirsty?'

'I'll have some coffee.' Juliet slowly walked into the sunny living room. Her mahogany Essex upright piano dominated one wall and above it hung a rectangular mirror in a bronze frame. Several people sat around speaking softly, all looking stiff and uncomfortable.

Frank Greenlee, their next-door neighbor and Owen's closest friend, came toward her, arms outstretched. The two men had been through so much together – both having sons die within three months of each other, Juliet thought. Fin's death had come so soon after Gary's. Now here was yet another blow for Frank. 'Juliet, dear, I'm so sorry.'

Frank, who'd been strikingly handsome in his twenties and thirties, now stood with stooped shoulders and paunchy body. Sympathy and love shone in his dark eyes with their drooping lids and puffy pads caused by alcohol. His once-thick brown hair was thinner and streaked with more white than the last time she'd seen him and his skin looked slightly gray. 'Thank you, Frank,' Juliet said woodenly. 'I'm . . . surprised.'

'Of course you are. We all are, but you . . . well, I can't imagine what you're feeling. If you ever need me . . . to talk or, well, anything . . .'

Juliet tried unsuccessfully to smile at Frank and was relieved when Tommy ran to her. 'Juliet!' He had light golden-brown hair and amber eyes like his mother.

'Hello, Master Thomas,' Juliet said with genuine warmth. 'How very nice to see you. You've grown a foot since Christmas.'

He looked relieved that she hadn't mentioned his phone call to her. 'Dad says I'm going to be tall like him. I'm awful sorry about Uncle Owen. I sure did love him.'

'I know you did. And he loved you.'

'Then why did he kill himself?'

'Tommy!' Leslie cried.

Tommy looked confused. 'Well, I heard you say he did.'

'Yes, he did,' Juliet said calmly to the child, looking into his eyes. 'Not saying it won't change it. We don't know why he did it, Tommy, but we'll all miss him.'

Leslie hustled Tommy to the kitchen as Kyle Hollister, Fin's former bandmate and her former sometimes boyfriend, walked toward her. With his wavy dark brown hair, deep blue eyes and perfect features, he had barely changed since they'd casually dated nine years ago. 'Juliet, I'm sorry. Mom and Dad and my brother were here for a while earlier. We all really liked Owen and we feel terrible for you.'

'Thank you, Kyle.'

Sheriff Davis Dawson set his cup and saucer on the coffee table and rose from the couch. At fifty-two, he was tall and trim with short, curly black hair laced with silver, a narrow face, and piercing gray eyes. Juliet had always thought he was attractive. 'Hello, Juliet.' He held out his hands. 'You know how I felt about your father. We'll really miss him on the force and in the community.'

'Thank you, Sheriff. He loved being a police officer.'

Sera hurried in with a cup of coffee for Juliet, trailed by Tommy, and urged her to sit in the recliner that Owen had favored. Tommy planted himself on the wide arm of the chair and Hutch lay at her feet. For the next twenty minutes, conversation limped along. Juliet heard herself adding comments, managing smiles, shaking hands. Everything external seemed far away and dreamlike while inside she roiled with emotions.

The doorbell rang. 'I'll get it!' Juliet jumped up, unable to sit still a minute longer. She hurried to the front door and opened it to face a skinny boy of thirteen or fourteen with tousled sandy hair and startlingly beautiful green eyes. He wore loose jeans, a baggy once-red T-shirt, and held a glass bowl topped with aluminum foil.

'Hello, ma'am,' he said in a soft voice that cracked. 'My mother wanted me to bring this for Mrs Reid.' He held out the bowl. 'I sure am sorry.'

Sera appeared behind Juliet. 'Eddie! Juliet, this is Eddie Maddox. Eddie, my daughter Juliet. Come in, honey.'

Eddie's face colored. 'Oh, I don't want to be a bother. I just brought some food Mom made for you.'

'You're not a bother. Please come in. Tommy's in the living room. He'll be disappointed if you leave without saying hello.'

'Well . . . if you're sure.' Eddie sounded uncertain. 'I really just brought the food.'

Sera handed the bowl to Juliet and hustled a reluctant Eddie inside, leading him to the living room. Juliet noticed Eddie looking around almost warily before Sera said, 'Tommy, look who's here!'

The child looked up and brightened. 'Eddie! Hi! Hutch is here, too, but he's sad like me.'

Eddie immediately focused on Tommy, sitting down on the floor to pet Hutch while he smiled and said, 'Hi, fella,' to the little boy.

Juliet took the bowl into the kitchen. Along the way, she passed the hall mirror. This morning she'd added shadow and mascara to her blue eyes so much like her mother's. She'd also brightened her face with coral blush and lipstick. Now her skin was ashen beneath the make-up and her eyes looked huge, staring.

She set the bowl on a counter. In a moment, her mother hurried in. 'That poor boy,' Sera whispered. 'His father died four years ago. The mother, Belle, works nights at that dump of a bar Rocco's – I've heard they sell drugs there – and lives with one lowlife man after another. I think half the time forgets she has a son. Belle has an older sister – a very nice lady – who tried to take Eddie away a while ago, but the court said he belonged with his mother. I can't believe Belle sent food.' Sera took the foil off the bowl to reveal canned mixed fruit topped with some dried-out miniature marshmallows. 'Oh.' Her mother frowned. 'I guess she meant well.'

'You and Dad mentioned Eddie Maddox, but you didn't tell me much about him.'

'He turned up in January asking if he could shovel the snow in our driveway. Owen likes to do that but Eddie's jacket was *so* thin and he didn't have gloves. I knew he needed money so I gave him the job. Afterward he began helping with lawn work and outside work – the kind of thing Wendell Booth used to do.' Sera's face tightened at the mention of Booth and she swallowed. 'Anyway, Eddie's sweet and diligent. He works for Davis Dawson and his new wife. She's pregnant. He works for Leslie, too. Tommy loves him. Oh, and Danielle Tresswell! He also does work for a couple of other families, but he and Owen took a real shine to each other. Eddie was like a surrogate son or grandson, I guess, and I could tell Eddie genuinely liked and admired Owen.' Her mother talked too fast and her hands trembled. 'Eddie was here two or three times a week, so keen about learning everything Owen could teach him and that I could teach him about plants and flowers. He talked about becoming a police officer someday. Owen was encouraging, offering to help him get in the police academy when the time came.' Sera looked at Juliet and her eyes filled with tears. 'Oh, what are we going to do without your daddy?'

Juliet's throat tightened. She hugged her mother, patting her back. 'Everything will be all right, Mom. I promise.'

But she wasn't at all certain she was telling the truth.

Juliet went back to the living room. Eddie was still talking quietly to Tommy and stroking Hutch. After less than five minutes, the boy slowly backed out of the room as if trying to be invisible and she heard the front door closing behind him. Meanwhile, conversation ebbed on, everyone trying to say the correct thing. Juliet resumed her seat wondering how much longer she could keep up a pretense of graciousness. She glanced at her mother, worried. Sera looked shattered and kept chattering in a high, brittle voice. Juliet knew she desperately needed to go to bed to rest and be alone with her misery.

Finally, Davis Dawson looked around at everyone and said, 'I have a job to do. I've been gone from headquarters long enough.' He stood and went to Sera. 'Once again, my deepest condolences.'

'Thank you.' Sera teared up again. 'That means a lot.'

He directed a few words of sympathy to Juliet and Alec before Sera saw him to the door. Juliet jumped up and followed them.

'Sheriff Dawson, may I speak with you for a few minutes?'

'Sweetheart, Sheriff Dawson has to go,' Sera began, clearly

knowing that Juliet wanted to learn more about her father's suicide.

'I've known both of you for years. I'd be more comfortable if you call me Davis.' He smiled at Juliet. 'Of course we can speak.'

'Mom, I'd like to talk to him alone.'

'Oh, well, if it's all right with the sheriff . . . Davis, I mean.' Sera looked back and forth at them.

'It's all right, Mrs Reid,' Davis said gently and the woman retreated into the house. 'How can I help, Juliet?'

'Had my father been let go?'

'Fired? Good God, no! He was our best officer.'

'Do you know of anything having to do with the job that could have sent him spiraling like this? After all, even his son's murder—'

'Devastated him but didn't make him suicidal. I've thought about that. He was a strong man. I certainly don't know of anything in his professional life that could have resulted in this.'

'All right. Then can you tell me the circumstances? How he did it? My mother and Alec will give me a sanitized version but I want the truth. I'm not a child. I'm old enough to handle the details, even if they're grisly.'

A furrow appeared between his eyebrows. 'You've just gotten home. Maybe you need to rest before we go into it.'

'I don't need to rest. I rested last night because I didn't know my father was dead. Please tell me.'

'OK. You're right – you're not a child. Let's sit down for a minute.' They sat on two white wicker porch chairs. 'Danielle Tresswell had a party last night. Alec took your mother but your father didn't go. Neither did Marcy and I – she didn't feel well. Anyway, Alec called nine-one-one around twelve-twenty. He said he'd found Owen Reid dead at his home. It looked like suicide. Two patrolmen were dispatched and Alec led them to the tree house. When they saw there was no mistake – it really was Reid and he was dead – the patrolmen called me. Your father was slumped over a small table with a low-light lantern turned on. We found his forty caliber Smith & Wesson pistol . . . well, he'd shot himself in the head.'

Juliet winced.

'I'm sorry.'

'I'm all right. Go on.'

'There was blood on the wall behind him and a lot of blood on the table. The medical examiner said he'd been dead for at least an hour.'

'None of the neighbors heard anything?'

'The people living on the right are on vacation. Frank Greenlee on the left was watching a movie and had the sound up high.' Davis hesitated. 'I also think he'd been drinking.'

'Was there a note?'

'I don't know of one. Maybe he was sick, Juliet. Cancer. Something else. The autopsy is being done today. Perhaps it will show something we don't know. I'm afraid that's all I can tell you right now.'

'You said maybe he was sick. Had you noticed a physical difference in him at work?'

'No. Not physical, but he was quieter. Preoccupied, although it didn't affect his work.'

'Preoccupied. I wonder if Mom noticed.'

'I couldn't say.'

'I want to see the tree house.'

Davis looked surprised. 'You can see the outside—'

'I want to see the inside.'

He shook his head. 'It's officially a crime scene. Maybe in a couple of days.' Juliet was silent. 'I mean it. Stay out.'

'All right, although if Dad committed suicide, I don't know why it's a crime scene.'

'Because a violent death occurred there. You know that.'

'Yes, I do, but I'm having trouble accepting this.'

'I understand,' Davis said patiently.

'You know, the tree house was Dad's idea and he and Frank built it for Fin and Gary and their friends. Even after both boys died, they maintained it. Dad hoped that someday I'd have a child who loved it.'

'Maybe you will. Or maybe you'll want to tear it down after what's happened.'

'That decision is Mom's, but I can't imagine her wanting to get rid of it. It's not an ordinary tree house. Dad and Frank put so much work and love into it.'

Davis smiled. 'They did a great job.'

'Frank has been Dad's best friend since they were kids. Fin and Gary were the same age and just as close. Dad was there for Frank when Gary overdosed and then after Nancy left him, and Frank was there for Dad when Fin was murdered. I'm sure Dad would have told him what was wrong or at least given him a hint.'

Davis frowned. 'Maybe. You can't be certain of that.'

Juliet glanced over at the house across the street where she could see people peering out their front windows. 'I suppose we'll be getting a lot of attention for the next few days.'

'Try not to let it bother you.'

'I'll try.' Abruptly she came to herself. 'I forgot to ask about your wife! How is she?'

For the first time, Davis's smile was quick and sincere. 'Great. Marcy's eight months along now. It's a boy! She gave up her job at the bank this week. She's getting really uncomfortable, although she's not one to complain, especially because she'd wanted children for so long. She said that at thirty-six she'd given up hope.'

Quite a few people in Parrish had disapproved when Sheriff Davis Dawson – whom every available woman in town had thrown herself at since his first, brief marriage dissolved over twenty years earlier – finally married a woman sixteen years his junior, but Owen and Sera had been happy for him. Now, a year later, Davis and Marcy were close to having a child.

'Marcy is a lovely woman. You're a lucky man. You're both lucky!'

Davis grinned. 'Leave it to you to say something kind and completely unselfish at a time like this. You're a good person, Juliet Reid. Your father was very proud of you.'

A silver Dodge Durango SUV pulled up behind the police cruiser and Jonathan Tresswell emerged from the car. Leslie's husband, Jon, wore dark wash jeans and a tailored light green button-down collar shirt with long sleeves rolled up. *I've never seen him look sloppy*, Juliet thought distantly as he approached them, tall, smiling, confidence in his every step. His dark brown hair shone in the sunlight and he was lightly tanned.

'Juliet.' He came up on the porch and hugged her, then drew back and searched her face with his hazel eyes, which looked tired and bloodshot. 'How're you doin', kiddo?'

He'd called her 'kiddo' since he turned thirteen and thought he was a man. 'So far I'm holding up fairly well. I guess the reality will hit me later.'

'Probably. At least Alec is here for both you and your mother.'

'I'm glad he's stayed close, although he isn't really family.'

'He's the same as family.'

'Oh, Jon . . .'

He hugged her. 'I know. I know, kiddo. I'm sorry.'

'New car?' Davis asked Jon, who nodded. 'A Hellcat. That's a fast one.'

'I know. Leslie was against it. She doesn't want Tommy to ride in it, but she has her own car.'

'As I remember, you've always liked fast cars. Well, I have to be on my way,' Davis said. 'Nice seeing you, Juliet.' Then he looked stricken. 'That was an awful thing to say under the circumstances.'

'No, it wasn't. Say hello to Marcy for me.' As Davis headed toward his car, Juliet looked at Jon. 'Your wife and son are inside.'

'I hope Tommy has been behaving himself.'

'Beautifully. You and Leslie are bringing him up well.'

'I give the credit to Leslie. I spend a lot of time at work.'

Jonathan's great-grandfather, Albert Tresswell, had started Tresswell Metal Fabrications, Inc. in the late forties. After his death, his son Andrew took over and eventually Jon's father, Nathaniel, became President and CEO. Nathaniel got cancer. He had treatment and lived with it for years but died when Jon was sixteen. His mother, Danielle Bellini Tresswell, served as head of the company until Jon turned twenty-two and finished his degree in engineering at Massachusetts Institute of Technology. Within an astonishingly fast two years, he'd married Leslie, had a son, and taken over the reins of Tresswell

Metal, which over the last ten years had opened branches in Pennsylvania, Kentucky, and Tennessee and was one of the twenty largest metal fabrication companies in the United States. Juliet knew Jon worked long hours and put his soul into the business, often to Leslie's frustration. 'I wanted to marry a man. Instead, I married a company,' she sometimes complained to Juliet. 'I love him *so* much and I admire his dedication, but it's like an obsession. He talks about it all the time. He doesn't sleep well; he's edgy. Sometimes I wish he'd give it back to Danielle to run.'

'Daddy!' Tommy exploded out of the house and wrapped himself around Jon. 'I saw you through the window.'

'You did?' Jon picked him up and groaned. 'You're getting *so* heavy!'

'Juliet said I've grown a foot since Christmas. Mommy's waitin' for you. She's been waitin' for hours.'

'*Hours?* I think you're exaggerating.' He shifted Tommy to his left arm and reached out his right to Juliet. 'Ready to head back in?'

'As ready as I'll ever be, especially with you and Tommy escorting me.'

That night Juliet tossed in bed, tired but unable to sleep. She'd been smiling, reassuring people of her emotional well-being, thanking them for their visits, their offerings of food, and their condolences for most of the day. She'd nibbled at a piece of cake for dinner although her mother, who'd barely sat down since Juliet arrived, tried to force servings of several casseroles on her. At last Sera had given up, turning her nervous agitation to cleaning an already spotless kitchen, and Juliet retreated to her pretty coral-and-white bedroom at eleven o'clock for peace.

Now it was one a.m. She knew she could lie here for two more hours and still not sleep. She felt as if everything inside her were churning, demanding to be set free. She got up and put on a robe and rubber-soled slippers. She stuffed several tissues in her pocket and opened her top dresser drawer, felt for a small box at the back, and removed a key. Then she left her room and walked down the hall.

In the living room, Hutch slept in his doggie bed beside Owen's recliner. The dog raised his head. 'Want to go out for a breath of fresh air?' Juliet asked quietly. She found his leash curled beside his bed. He stood patiently and quietly as she attached it to his collar. 'Good boy.' She rubbed his ears. 'Right now I need a friend who'll listen and not talk. I think you're the perfect guy.'

She went out the sliding glass doors into the soft warmth of the late June night and stepped onto the terrace. Decorated with blue-cushioned synthetic rattan furniture – a long couch, three blue-cushioned chairs and a glass-topped rectangular serving table. Above was a wicker arbor covered with yellow-bloomed jasmine vines dangling in the moonlight. When they were children, their father had taught Fin and Juliet about the phases of the moon. To the west she saw the waxing crescent moon and judged that it was emitting only about twenty percent light. The lawn would have been fairly dark if not for a dusk-to-dawn light glowing about twenty feet away from the house, a safety precaution Sera had demanded although Owen said its 'glaring' light ruined the ambience of the new terrace decorated with six flickering solar torches. Her parents didn't often argue, but Juliet remembered the great 'dusk-to-dawn light' dispute going on for months. Fin said their father had finally given in out of sheer exhaustion.

Dew dampened, the newly mown grass and the night was quiet except for the sound of Hutch huffing along as if he were diligently tracking prey. Juliet smiled. He always seemed bent on showing he'd been worth saving from the animal shelter. 'You never had a thing to prove,' she said to him now as he gazed up at her. 'Dad, Mom, Alec and I loved you from the first time you looked at us.'

They'd passed the dusk-to-dawn light but Juliet didn't slow down. Their backyard, like most in the neighborhood, was enclosed with a vinyl picket fence that shone cleanly white in the moonlight. She walked the dog to the back of the fenced-in lot, opened the gate and passed through. They took three steps into the shadowy woods, passed the prominent *No Trespassing* sign and stopped at the bottom of the stairway leading up to Fin's tree house.

High above the ground, it stretched fifteen feet between two parallel oaks. The tree house had a peaked roof, shielded deck, windows, cedar shingles, strong posts that secured each end to the two trees as well as one in the middle, and an angled stairway. Owen Reid had spent months building the structure that Fin loved and his friends envied.

Oh, Daddy, when you built the house did you ever dream it would be the site of your death? Juliet thought. *Why here? Was it because this was a place that brought your son so much happiness?*

She clutched the key. She remembered a month after her father had finished the fairy-tale tree house for Fin and she'd stood gazing up at it, tears dripping down her face because the wonderful place was *his*. She didn't have anything so magnificent. It was all for him. Suddenly he'd appeared, walking toward her purposefully. She'd stiffened when he stopped in front of her.

'Hold out your hand,' he'd ordered.

'Why?'

'Just do it.' Suspiciously, she'd extended her hand. Fin had turned it over and placed the key in her palm. 'It's a spare key to the tree house. You can go in it when I'm not there. *Only* then. Understand?' She'd nodded. 'Leslie can go in with you. Now stop crying like a baby.'

Fin hadn't smiled, he hadn't spoken in a sweet voice, he could hardly have been less gracious. Yet he'd made a kind gesture toward his hurt little sister by sharing his precious tree house and she'd always been thankful because it meant he cared about her.

'I used to come here when my brother wasn't around,' Juliet now said to Hutch. 'Let's look at it.'

Hutch panted as they slowly began climbing the wooden stairs. When they reached the top, Juliet realized her hands were sweating although it was seventy degrees. She clasped the key in damp fingers, slipped it into the lock, and turned it. The lock clicked and she pushed the door open, reaching to the right and flipping on the overhead light. Hesitating, she took a deep breath and stepped into the tree house.

After Fin's death, his parents had removed most of the items he'd kept here. A few things remained the same, though. Fin had loved – and played only – classic and hard rock. On the walls were posters of Pearl Jam, Foo Fighters, Jimi Hendrix, Radiohead, and the famous 'airplane' poster of Led Zeppelin. Two folding canvas chairs and a wicker loveseat with a green cushion sat at one end of the house. Nearby was a two-shelf wicker bookcase with a few magazines on the top shelf. Juliet went to it and flipped through issues of *Revolver*, *Car and Driver*, *Premier Guitar*, *Rolling Stone,* and six Marvel Superhero Comics, all dated before Fin's death.

'Not much has changed,' she said to Hutch, mostly to hear a voice. He made a chuffing sound. She walked to a small table and chair pushed against a wall. Looking at the wall, she saw a framed photo of Fin with their collie Sarge, another with Fin and Gary waving American flags from the top of the tree house stairs. She vaguely remembered a framed photo of Fin and some of the guys who'd played in his band over the years. In it had been Jonathan Tresswell, Frank's son Gary Greenlee, Kyle Hollister, and a scruffy, long-haired young man who looked older and more worn than the others but whose name she couldn't remember. She didn't see the picture – only a hook where it might have hung. A hook and—

Blood spatter. She looked down at the little, wobbly table placed directly below the spots on the pine wall and a couple of the photos. The table was made of wicker, old and rough and coarse. Bending closer, she saw reddish smears in the wood fibers. A wicker chair sat a foot away from the table.

Her vision blurred. The room seemed to be swimming, slowly, then faster. She thought she heard whispers, soft and insidious at first, then louder and louder: *'Juliet, Juliet, Juliet help me, dear God, help me . . .'*

This is where her father had sat, leaning over the table, placing his service revolver to his head, pulling the trigger—

'*No!*' she wailed, startling Hutch. 'Daddy, *no!*' She could almost see him, looking at her with an inscrutable expression, before the room shuddered with a gunshot that sounded like an explosion.

Juliet whirled, flipped off the glaring overhead light and, dragging Hutch behind her, slammed the door and ran as fast as she could down the staircase. At the bottom, she looked up at the quiet, empty darkness behind her. Breathless, she sat on the first step and let tears overwhelm her. They had been churning in her, demanding to be set free since she'd arrived home. Sobs came in deep heaves, shaking her entire body. Hutch whined and put his big paw on her thigh. She leaned over and buried her face in his neck, wrapping her arms around him. 'You were home when he did it,' she said. 'Do you know why? Did he talk to you the way I'm talking now, knowing you couldn't repeat anything?'

She pulled tissues from her pocket and wiped her face. Hutch looked at her with his big, sad eyes and her tears poured again. She wadded the tissues and cried into them until they were sodden, then wrathfully tossed them on the grass. Juliet's voice went sharp. 'I don't care that you'd hate me messing up your lawn, Dad. You killed yourself in Fin's tree house. Why did you do it at *all*? What could have been so bad that you'd shoot yourself in the *head*, for God's sake? Fin's been dead for almost ten years – it wasn't grief over him. Didn't you think about Mom? Or me? And what about Alec? He loved you like a father. He's already lost one father. Did you have to take another one away from him? Oh, damn it, Dad! I'm so mad at you! I'm so . . .' Her voice broke before she sobbed, 'I'm so sad. So terribly *sad.*'

Her only answer was the sound of frogs jumping into Argent Creek, the hooting of an owl, the light-pitched hum of katydids and crickets, the occasional plop of a toad hopping into the water. She was reaching for another tissue when Hutch's head shot up and he looked behind them. Then he began growling long and low. 'What is it? A squirrel? A rabbit?'

Hutch's body stiffened. Juliet's hand tightened on his leash. 'Is someone out there?' she called. No one answered except a yellow warbler singing out its heart. She relaxed a fraction. 'It's OK, Hutch.'

But the dog pulled on his leash. Then the growling grew louder and finally he burst into sharp, constant barking. Juliet's heart speeded up as she peered into the darkness. Hutch stopped barking and snarled. Juliet heard a twig snap about ten feet away. She stood up and turned toward the house to see Alec sprinting barefoot across the back lawn to her. Holding tight to Hutch's leash, she ran away from the tree house, breathless and almost blind from her swollen eyes and fear. In a moment, Alec clutched her in his arms.

'Someone's out there,' she managed. 'They wouldn't answer me.'

Alec took Hutch's leash and hurried them both back to the house. Inside the living room, he closed the sliding glass doors, locked them, and drew the draperies shut. Then he shushed the still-growling dog, gently eased Juliet down on the couch, and turned on a table lamp. 'Sit still and catch your breath, Juliet. You're safe now,' he said soothingly. 'I'll get you something to drink.'

'I don't want anything.'

'Yes, you do. So does Hutch. You two hold on.'

Juliet sat on the couch trembling while she rubbed Hutch's ears with her right hand. 'It's OK, boy. I wish you could tell me who – or what – set you off.'

The dog looked at her and whined.

'Hutch woke me up,' Alec said five minutes later as he walked back into the room holding a bowl in one hand and two brandy snifters in the other. 'Here you go, boy. Nice cool water.' The dog immediately began lapping. 'And for you, miss, a healthy dose of brandy.'

'Ah, brandy, like we had after we found Fin.'

'Oh, sorry.' Alec sat down near her on the couch. 'At least it's a different brand.'

Juliet took a sip. 'It's good. And strong.' She sipped again. 'Who do you think was in the woods?'

'It might have been an animal – a stray dog or cat. A raccoon.'

Juliet shook her head. 'An animal would have run away when Hutch started raising hell. Besides, he's used to animals in the woods. He doesn't go nuts over them. It was a person. I know it.'

Hutch let out a groan and lay down on Juliet's feet. His barking fit seemed to have completely exhausted him.

'It could have been some random person who wanted to see the tree house or maybe even go inside it.' Alec frowned.

'Or it could have been Wendell Booth. About a month ago your father told me that Wendell prowls a lot at night. Walking beside Argent Creek past here seems to be one of his favorite routes.'

'Wendell!' Juliet was shocked. 'He's allowed to roam around at night? He's a convicted felon!'

'That's just it, Juliet. The conviction was overturned and a psychological evaluation deemed him fit to return to society. He's not a felon. Owen said the police strongly encouraged the Booths to keep him indoors, but as usual, they won't cooperate. As long as Wendell hasn't broken the law, there's nothing the authorities can do. I'm sorry that in all the hubbub today, everyone forgot to tell you about him coming near this house.'

'Maybe, but how stupid of me to go out there at night! I remember how fascinated he always was with the tree house!' Juliet took a gulp of brandy. 'I wasn't thinking about Wendell Booth being a free man.'

'He was in prison for nine years and he's been free for less than four months. You haven't been home since he came back.'

'I haven't been home since Christmas. I deserted my parents.'

'You didn't desert them, Juliet. You came home on every school break. You even delayed going to college for two years after high school so you wouldn't have to leave them too soon.'

'I haven't visited as often as I should, though, especially after Wendell was released. My parents were so upset. They needed me and it's not like I lived hundreds of miles away. But everything got so hectic during my last year and I had my job entertaining at the restaurant. Still—'

'No *still*. You couldn't have done anything to make your parents feel better about Booth. Besides, they knew you were throwing yourself into finishing school, with a four-point average, no less. They were thrilled.'

'I hope so. But if I'd come home, maybe I could have figured out what was wrong with Dad.'

'I doubt it. Your mother didn't have a clue what was wrong,

so stop feeling guilty,' Alec said calmly. 'Now tell me why you and Hutch were at the tree house past midnight.'

'I went inside for a minute.'

'You found a key?'

'I have one that Fin gave me a long time ago. I only stayed a few minutes. It was creepy. Oh, God!' She pulled the key out of her robe pocket. 'I didn't lock the door when I left!'

'It's all right. I'll lock it in the morning.'

'Thanks. I can't go back there – not even tomorrow. It was so awful, Alec.' She took another sip of brandy. 'Anyway, after I came out, I sat on the bottom step crying. Crying for Dad because I love him so much and I can't imagine life without him. And bitching at him. I hate being mad at him, but I am – I'm mad that he's hurt so many people, mad that he's hurt *me*. I'm bereft but I also feel betrayed. And baffled, Alec. He seemed all right when he came to my graduation in May. What could have happened since then to make him *kill* himself?'

Alec slowly shook his head. 'I know I FaceTime you pretty much every week but I only do the same with your parents every two or three weeks. Lately, he's been usually busy when I call, until last weekend when I talked to Owen about coming home for your birthday. I thought he sounded different than usual. He even looked different.'

'Different how?'

'Not as upbeat. Sort of distracted. Thin.'

'That's what Davis Dawson told me today. That lately he's acted distracted. *Preoccupied* was the word he used.'

'Any other differences at work?'

'No. He said Dad was doing his job as diligently as usual. I talk to Mom and Dad every week and he always sounded the same. He seemed really happy at my graduation. You got here yesterday. Was he different then?'

Alec frowned. 'He seemed glad to see me but at the same time sort of distant. He asked questions about my life, told me I looked good, said how happy he was that I was home, but . . .'

'But?'

'Well, he seemed like a house with all the curtains drawn and the door locked. Does that make sense? I got the feeling he was using all of his will to keep something hidden inside.'

'I do understand what you mean and it's so different for Dad. He was outgoing, gregarious.'

'I know, but he was different yesterday. After I'd been home a couple of hours, he told me Danielle Tresswell was having a party at her home, but he didn't feel like going. He asked me to take your mother. Hollisters' restaurant handled the catering and the decorations. They even put up two outdoor party tents. It was a big affair – at least fifty people ambling in and out of the house and around the terrace and back lawn.'

'Jon's mother gave a party? For what?'

'Her fifty-fifth birthday.'

'Oh. She's always loved giving parties.'

'When Owen said he had a headache and wasn't in the mood for a party, your mother said she wouldn't go, but he insisted and that I take her – she'd already bought a new dress. I know now that he was trying to get us both out of the house. If I'd refused and stayed with him . . .'

'You told me not to feel guilty, Alec. You shouldn't, either. How could you have possibly known what he had in mind? Did Mom mention anything?'

'She said he hadn't seemed to feel well the past week. Nothing serious, just tired. But I knew something wasn't right with him.' He swallowed. 'Anyway, the party was fun. Your mother had a good time although she felt a little guilty for leaving Owen. Leslie and Jon were there, dancing, visiting. Danielle's daughter Carole is back, minus her second husband. She seemed to be having fun with Kyle Hollister. Leslie danced several times with Kyle – Jon won't dance and Carole didn't seem to mind. Sera and I came home about midnight. Owen wasn't around and when we found Hutch shut in the bathroom, we knew something was wrong. Your mother ran all over the house calling for Owen. Finally, she opened the glass doors and Hutch ran to the tree house. I took a flashlight and insisted that *I* go up and look inside.' His voice became a rough whisper. 'Thank God your mother didn't see him . . . like that.'

Juliet almost asked 'like what?' She caught herself and drained her snifter of brandy. 'More please?' she asked, handing the glass to Alec.

'Certainly.' He looked down at Hutch. 'Can I get you anything?' The dog had begun to snore. 'I guess not.'

When Alec returned, he seemed determined not to talk anymore about her father and said, 'I like your hair.'

She smiled. 'To celebrate my graduation I added some honey-blonde highlights.'

'Honey blonde as opposed to . . .'

'Golden blonde, strawberry blonde, platinum blonde.'

'You made a good choice.' He reached out and gently lifted a blonde strand. 'It suits you.'

'Thanks.' She took a sip of brandy. 'Are you still enjoying life in New York City? I've barely visited you there.'

'Not because you haven't been invited often.'

'Mom and Dad like for me to come home on holidays.'

'Make that both of us. Anyway, New York is fine. The place is so busy, day and night. And crowded. But I've been there almost two years now. It's beginning to feel like home.'

'As much as this house?'

Alec was quiet for a moment. 'At first I didn't feel like this was home. Your family knew my family but only our fathers were close. I was surprised when Owen and your mother wanted me to move in.'

'You had no blood relatives. Besides, Mom and Dad cared about you.'

'Fin didn't.'

'Fin was fourteen and wrapped up in himself and his music.'

'And he looked at me as an interloper.'

Juliet put her hand on Alec's bare, warm arm. 'Maybe at first. But the rest of us didn't. I was glad when you came here.' She stopped. 'I don't mean *because* of why you came here!'

Alec smiled at her. 'I know. You made me feel welcome. So did Owen and Sera. And Fin and I eventually became semi-friends.'

'I know you had a rocky start with him. He could be difficult, but he did like you, Alec.' She paused. 'How's your job in New York?'

'It's good. I was afraid I'd bitten off more than I could chew at first. Bernard-Widmere is one of the biggest stock investment houses in the world.'

'But you became the assistant chief of security.'

'How flattering! I'm only one of several assistants. Yes, I seem to be doing all right.'

'Do you like it better than being in Afghanistan?'

Alec exhaled. 'I knew this would come up again.'

'We were so worried about you.'

'Yes. I'm sorry.'

'You have a degree in criminal justice and we thought you were going into politics. You've never said why you joined the army instead.'

'I'd thought about it for months during my senior year of college, but I didn't tell anyone.'

'You deployed to Afghanistan *twice,* Alec. The second time when you were wounded, we thought you were going to die!' She tried not to sound accusatory, but she was suddenly angry. 'I'm sure you went because of the wreck, but you've never talked about your parents or sister. Why not?'

'The wreck devastated me,' Alec said quietly. 'I didn't want to talk about it with *anyone.* Can't you leave it at that?'

'I could when I was a kid, but I can't now. Did you go to Afghanistan – did you do something so dangerous – out of guilt because your parents and Brenda were killed in the car wreck and you escaped with a broken leg and two broken ribs? Or was it something else?'

He drew a deep breath and looked at her with his grave, steady eyes. 'I felt compelled to go.'

'*Why?*'

'I just explained.'

'No, you didn't. You *won't* explain.' He looked at her unflinchingly. 'Oh, Alec, I thought I'd never see you again.'

'Yet here I am.'

'Yes, you are and thank God. But what a risk you took! If something had happened to you . . .'

'What?'

Juliet looked down and said frankly, 'I can't imagine a world without you.'

'You don't have to.' He abruptly set his glass on the table and stood. She knew he didn't want to go further with the conversation or with her emotions. 'I'm worn out. So are you.'

'You mean I'm getting maudlin.'

'And mad. Anyway, we're both desperate for sleep.' He leaned down and kissed her forehead. 'Don't stay up too late, little Juliet.'

Juliet's bleak gaze followed his back down the hall. She had always been 'little Juliet' to Alec and she still was, even though she would be twenty-five tomorrow – just one year younger than Leslie. She had sinking feelings of disappointment and frustration. She wished Alec saw her as a woman – a woman who cared for him in the way a woman would, not a young girl. Unfortunately, she couldn't change Alec's perspective when it came to her any more than she could bring back her father.

Juliet walked to the sliding glass doors and peeped through the draperies. The lawn looked still and harmless in the glow from the dusk-to-dawn light. She peered farther back to the woods, wishing she had binoculars. Alec said Hutch could have been startled by an animal, but she didn't believe it. She knew someone had been out there watching her, coming close to her. She'd felt it.

Almost an hour later, Hutch, who lay beside Juliet's bed, went to the window, nosed apart the curtains and whined. Without turning on a light, Juliet crept to the window. In the darkness and between the tree limbs, she saw a small light in the tree house. It was dim and slowly moved the length of the house. A flashlight. After around ten minutes, it disappeared from the tree house and she saw it moving down the steps to the ground before vanishing toward Argent Creek.

So someone *had* been out there, waiting in the undergrowth until she came back inside and the house lights had gone off for a while. She'd known she hadn't heard a harmless animal in the brush. She'd heard someone with a mission – to get into the tree house. Why? To search for something? What? And would the searcher come again, this time not letting a crying woman get in the way?

Alec moaned softly and kicked off his bedsheet. Although the room was cool, he was drenched with perspiration, dreaming of his second tour of duty in Afghanistan. He had been stationed

at a small base that almost every night was battered with
rockets and mortars and he'd always awakened confused and
terrified, flailing in panic. During the days, his platoon climbed
the steep mountains in the east near the Pakistan border
looking for caches of enemy ammunition. Now, in the dream,
he was climbing one almost 8,000 feet high. After his first
climb, he'd thought he was dying. Every muscle in his body
burned with strain, he was dehydrated, his feet that had worn
heavy boots all day swelled until he was sure the skin would
split, and he'd had a blinding headache that forced him to
keep his eyes closed. After three months, he'd built up his
stamina. He was instantly awake and on the move at the first
sound of a night attack. After a climb, on one of the rare, quiet
nights at the base, he could actually stay up and play cards,
laugh, write some letters to the Reids or call them, always
downplaying the danger while acting upbeat, almost cheerful
even though he felt his world had reduced to little more than
sand and unrelenting sun.

The dream shifted to the day when he'd been walking on
flat ground next to a stone wall with soldiers in front and
behind him. Suddenly guns had begun firing. The men around
him had jerked down to their knees, firing back and throwing
grenades at the hidden enemies. Machine gun fire from army
Humvees filled the air as a full-fledged fight escalated. Staying
low, Alec and other soldiers crept past the wall into a wheat
field, searching for the enemy. Sweat dripped into Alec's eyes
and as he'd reached up to wipe it away, a shot rang out and the
soldier beside him fell. Alec dropped to his knees and looked
at the man – his closest friend, Hopper. The left side of his
head was blown away. 'God no, Hopper,' Alec heard himself
crying. 'Medic! *Medic!*' In shock, he'd half-stood before pain
seared his abdomen. Then his helmet slammed against the back
of his head. He'd collapsed, hearing groaning, slowly realizing
it was his own.

Dobbs had shouted, 'Got him! Shooter down!' Then voices
surrounded Alec. 'You're gonna be OK. Hang on, Wainwright.'
He'd felt himself being moved gently, men yelling at each
other to take it easy. 'How's his head?' 'Bullet didn't go
through the helmet.' 'Damn, that's lucky.' A face in front of

his grinned and said, 'That hard noggin of yours is fine, buddy.'
His abdomen hurt unbearably. 'My gut,' he'd rasped. 'Yeah,
we've got it, guy. We're takin' care of it.' Someone was holding
up a plastic bag of fluid with tubing, picking up his arm and
inserting a needle. Another voice asked a man working on
him, 'Is it bad? It looks bad.' 'I tell you he's *OK*!' Then a
furious whisper, 'Stop talking so damned loud. He can hear
you.' *I'm dying*, Alec had thought. *This is the end.*

Then he'd heard a helicopter. Dobb's face appeared above
his. 'That's the Medevac, Wainwright. They're takin' you outta
this hellhole. You're gonna be all right, fella.'

Men were lifting him for evacuation. During the process,
Alec felt as if he were floating far away. The world around him
began to dim. As he was being loaded into the helicopter, he'd
finally closed his eyes for what he thought would be the last
time. Through a haze of pain and dust beneath his eyelids, he'd
seen his sister in front of a wall of flame, her tortured blue eyes
imploring him to save her after the car wreck 'I'm sorry, Brenda,'
he'd murmured. 'It should have been me. I'm so sorry.'

THREE

'Juliet! Wake up!'

Juliet felt someone shaking her out of a dream of flowers – acres of vividly beautiful flowers on a warm sunny day and her walking among them in a long, flowing white dress.

'Sweetheart, wake up!'

Juliet didn't want to leave the sea of flowers but someone was shaking her, pulling her back to reality. She forced her eyes open. 'Mom?'

'Yes! It's important!'

Sera's long hair floated loose around her shoulders and she wore only her pale pink nightgown. Her face was almost incandescent.

'Mom, what is it?'

'Sit up and look at this.' Sera waved a piece of paper sealed in a Ziplock bag in front of her. '*Look* at this!'

Juliet closed her eyes briefly then reluctantly pulled herself up. Sera pushed a piece of note paper with red roses across the top and message written in shaky script:

Dear Sere,

I know you won't understand but its something I must do. Don't think to badly of me I love you.

Owen

After a brief silence, Juliet said, 'It's Dad's suicide note. Davis Dawson said he didn't leave one.'

'I didn't find it until late last night lying in Hutch's doggie bed and partly covered with a toy. I picked it up with a tissue so I wouldn't disturb fingerprints. That's why it's in the bag, but I brought rubber gloves so you can take it out and read it. Since when did your father *ever* call me *Sere*? And you know he was a stickler for grammar and punctuation. He writes "*its* something I must do" not "*it is*" or "*it's*" something I must do. And "don't think *to* badly of me," not *too*. And *badly*. It should be *bad*!' Sera ended triumphantly.

Juliet blinked at her. 'I don't get it.'

'You don't get it?' Sera looked at her in shock. 'The mistakes. Your father wouldn't call me "Sere" or write "its" or "to" or leave out a period before he writes "I love you." *I love you* would be a separate sentence.'

Juliet waited a beat then said gently, 'Mom, Dad must have been so distraught, he wasn't thinking about punctuation.'

'Right! He was distraught so he would have written without thinking, which means he would write naturally, and you know writing naturally to him meant writing correctly. Making mistakes took thought.'

'Are you saying he didn't write the note?'

'Of course he wrote the note. The handwriting is messy but it's his.' Juliet looked at the note and back at her mother's hopeful face. 'Oh, Juliet, don't you see? He was sending me a message!'

'A message?'

'It's like code for *something isn't right!*'

'Something *wasn't* right. He killed himself.'

Sera drew back and looked exasperated. 'You're too sleepy to understand what I'm saying. You'll see what I mean later.' She jumped up from the bed, clutching the note. 'In the meantime, I have to show this to Davis Dawson!'

'Sheriff Dawson! Mom, you need to show it to Alec first.' Sera was clearly nearly hysterically joyful. Juliet knew it was all part of the extreme shock the woman felt over the suicide of her husband, but she desperately didn't want her mother to make a fool of herself. 'Maybe Alec will think the same as you.'

But her mother was already flying down the hall to her bedroom, maybe to get dressed, maybe to call Davis Dawson.

Juliet pulled on her robe, stood in front of the dresser mirror running a brush through her long hair and looking at her eyes, which seemed sunken in dark circles. No wonder, she thought. She'd only slept about four hours. She walked barefoot into the kitchen, where Alec sat at the table sipping coffee from a mug while Hutch ate his breakfast.

'Good morning,' Alec said. 'Sleep well?'

'You're not serious.'

'No, I'm not.'

She wanted to tell him about the light in the tree house, but she didn't want to take time to explain. She was too worried about her mother. She poured a bit of milk into a mug, filled it with coffee and sat down opposite Alec. 'Did Mom show you the note?'

He raised a slightly haggard face. 'Yes. I asked her to wait an hour before she woke you, but she couldn't. She thought you'd be as delighted as she is. Are you?'

Juliet shook her head. 'I think she's grasping at straws. She thinks bad grammar is a code.'

'That sounds farfetched.' He frowned. 'Still, he did call her *Sere*. How do you explain that?'

'Nerves? Fear?'

'If he was so afraid of killing himself, then why did he do it?'

'Oh, God, I don't know. Maybe he was losing his mind.'

'Did he seem like he was losing his mind when you saw him less than two months ago?'

'No. He seemed fine. Did he seem crazy when you saw him two *days* ago?'

'No. Different but not suicidal.'

Juliet took a sip of coffee. 'Davis suggested maybe he was sick. Something that would be painful, something he couldn't face.'

'There'll be an autopsy. I guess we'll find out.'

'I guess.'

Alec gave her a steely look. 'I think there's more to the note your mother found than might seem at first. I don't think your father committed suicide. I never have – not really. And I know you, Juliet. You don't believe your father committed suicide, either, even if he was sick.'

She had no answer and was glad when Sera rushed into the room. She'd put on a long, flowered robe and she was waving the Ziplocked note from Owen. She sat down and smacked it on the table. 'I called Davis and caught him before he went to work. I told him about Owen's note and said I'd bring it down to headquarters in about an hour, but he said he'd stop here to see it before he goes in. He should be here in about fifteen minutes.'

Sera jumped and headed back through the house, no doubt to dress. Juliet and Alec looked at each other. 'I'm afraid she's in for a letdown,' Juliet said.

She didn't bother dressing and in ten minutes the doorbell rang. Alec answered and ushered Davis Dawson into the kitchen. 'Would you like some coffee?'

'No, thanks. I had two cups with breakfast before I left home. Marcy always insists on fixing me breakfast, although I'd rather she got an extra hour's sleep.' He smiled at Juliet. 'How are you this morning?'

'Not much better than yesterday. Have a seat. Mom will be back in a minute.'

Almost immediately Sera appeared in tan pants and an embroidered peasant top. Her hair still hung loose. 'Dawson! How kind of you to come so quickly. I hated to bother you so early, but I couldn't wait.'

'I understand. You found a note from Owen?'

'His suicide note. I thought he hadn't left one, but it had gotten knocked off a table into Hutch's doggie bed. Have a seat.' Sera sat down at the table beside him and pushed the note forward. 'This is it. You can read it through the bag.'

'Well, that's smart.' Creases appeared between Davis's eyes as he read the note once, then again. Finally he looked up. 'It's brief. And vague.'

'Yes, but you're not getting it!' Sera said impatiently.

'Getting what?'

'The *mistakes*! They're the key to the code!' Juliet's and Alec's gazes met. She closed her eyes as her mother rushed on. 'First, he spelled my name *Sere*. Owen Reid never in his life called me *Sere*. And "its" with no apostrophe. And "to" when it should be "too." And "badly" when it should be "bad" and "Don't think to badly of me I love you" is a *run-on sentence*! Don't you see?'

Davis smiled uncomfortably. 'Well . . .'

Sera leaned toward him. 'You've read dozens of police reports written by Owen. You must have noticed that they were always well-written, grammatically and mechanically perfect. That's how Owen always wrote. These mistakes are a *signal*!'

Davis stared at her.

'Oh, for God's sake, it was written under *duress*!'

Davis's black gaze sharpened. Finally, Sera had caught his serious consideration of her claim. He read the note again.

'I'm very glad you found this—'

'You do believe me, don't you?' Sera implored.

'Would you mind if I take it to headquarters and think about it for a few hours? I mean, if what you're saying is true—'

'Oh, it is. I know it!'

Davis seemed to be taking her mother at least half-seriously. Juliet was stunned. Could her mother be right and not simply reaching for an explanation for Owen's inconceivable act? If so, that meant someone had wanted her father dead. Who? And why?

Alec rushed back in with an 8 x 10 manila envelope. 'I got something big so you wouldn't have to fold the note.' His words were rapid and slightly breathless.

'Thanks.' Davis carefully slipped the note into the envelope. Then he looked into Sera's eyes. 'I'll give this careful scrutiny, I promise you. For the rest of the day, try not to worry about it. You need to rest your mind, Sera.'

'That's a tall order, but I'll try. Davis?'

He raised his eyebrows.

'Thank you for not laughing at me.'

After Davis left, Juliet gently held her mother's slender arms. 'Mom, did you think Alec and I were laughing at you?'

'A bit.'

'Oh, Mom.' Juliet hugged the woman. 'We were just surprised. It takes a little while to sink in, you know.' She smiled. 'Especially when we just woke up!'

'I know, dear. I understand completely. You two are my rocks, the people I love most in the world and who love me. Now I'm going to take my shower and change clothes. You have a second cup of coffee with Alec. And some toast, at least. Maybe you could fix an omelet. Neither of you ate dinner.'

'Mom, I called Leslie and she's free this afternoon. I think I'll drop by and visit for a while. Do you mind?'

Sera smiled at Juliet. 'I think that's a fine idea. You haven't seen her since Christmas. I'm sure you've talked on the phone, but that's not the same.'

'No, it isn't. I won't be gone for long.'

'Stay as long as you like, dear. I'm fine.'

Juliet drove less than half a mile to Leslie's two-story brick home that they would soon be leaving for a new, modern farmhouse-style house. 'Danielle cringes when Jon and I call it a farmhouse,' she'd said when they bought it two months ago. 'I believe she thinks we'll have a haystack in front and a chicken coop in the side yard.'

Juliet smiled as she pulled into the circular driveway of the house. She climbed three steps to the front porch and rang the bell. In a moment, Leslie answered and her face lit up. 'Juliet!'

'I should have called first. If you're busy, I can come another time.'

'Oh, don't be silly!' Leslie drew her into a hug. 'I'm *so* glad to see you! Yesterday was awkward and we didn't get a chance to talk.'

Tommy appeared behind Leslie. 'Hi, Juliet! Did you bring Hutch?'

'Not today,' she said as Leslie pulled her into the entrance hall. 'He was having his afternoon nap when I left.'

'Come into the family room,' Leslie said. 'Do you want iced tea, lemonade, or coffee?'

'I'll take lemonade. I haven't had any for months.'

'I made a pitcher this morning.'

They walked into a narrow room with beige carpet, leather furniture, and a brick wall with a fireplace and a television mounted above it.

'The family room in the new house is larger and brighter with sky lights. It'll be good for my plants.' Leslie nodded at the five-tier rack holding various greenery springing from painted pots. 'I took your mother's horticulture course *again* before I chose those herbs. I didn't want anything that might hurt Tommy or a dog.' She smiled. 'I'll get the lemonade. Be right back.'

'We have the right plants but we still don't have a dog.' Tommy had sat down on the couch beside Juliet and looked at her plaintively. 'Don't you think everyone should have a dog?'

'Well . . .'

Leslie arrived just in time to rescue Juliet from having to answer. She carried a tray with a pitcher of lemonade and two glasses. She looked young and happy in her tight jeans and pink-and-white striped knit top with her long, curly light brown hair pulled back in a ponytail. She poured a glass of lemonade and handed it to Juliet and then another for herself.

'Where's mine?' Tommy asked.

'You've already had two glasses. How about waiting until evening for another? You can have it with your dad. In the meantime, why don't you go in the back yard and pick up your toys? They're scattered everywhere.'

'All right.' Tommy turned to Juliet. 'She wants me out of the way so she can have grown-up talk with you, but I'm a big boy and I understand.'

As he left through the sliding glass doors, Juliet smiled. 'He's so great, Leslie.'

'Jon and I try.' Leslie paused. 'After my miscarriage two years ago, we were devastated, but . . .'

Juliet's instincts quickened. 'But?'

'I'm pregnant again.'

'Oh, Leslie, I'm so happy for you!'

'You're not supposed to tell people until after the first trimester. The last time we told people after ten weeks and . . . well, you know what happened. This time we're being more careful. I'm a little more than twelve weeks along but I haven't told anyone, not even Mom.'

'She's still happy with the new husband?'

'Extremely happy with him and her new house in Atlanta. I miss her.'

'She'll probably come to visit more during your pregnancy and certainly afterward. Have you told Danielle?'

'No, not even her.'

'Will Jon be mad that you told me?'

'I won't tell him that I told you, but I knew you'd be glad for me and you can certainly use some good news.'

Juliet closed her eyes, smiling. 'It's wonderful news, Les. Thanks for telling me.'

'We'll be settled in the new house when the baby arrives. It's almost twice the size of this one with four big bedrooms and no stairs. I've already begun some light packing.'

'Don't overdo it.'

'I won't. Not after last time. I was depressed for months after the miscarriage.' Leslie looked at her sympathetically. 'I don't want to dwell on this, but how are things at home?'

'Sad.' Juliet decided to not tell Leslie about Sera's theory concerning the suicide note. 'If it had to happen, I'm relieved Alec is here. He's so strong and reliable. But I'm bewildered. My father is the last person I could imagine committing suicide.'

'I know. Our fathers weren't friends – I don't think your father even liked mine – but after Dad died, Owen got closer to me. He agreed to walk me down the aisle at my wedding as if it were the most natural request in the world. I loved Owen. And so does Tommy. And Jon, of course.'

Juliet sipped her lemonade. 'Davis Dawson suggested that Dad was sick – physically, I mean, with something incurable. I wonder if he was sick mentally. If something sent him off the rails.'

'I know he was livid when Wendell Booth was released from prison. But that was months ago. And when I saw him last week he didn't look as healthy as usual. He was thinner and quieter. Maybe he *was* ill.' Leslie shook her head. 'Still, if it were cancer or heart trouble, it doesn't seem like your father to end his life without a fight. Jon's father had cancer and he struggled with it for years before it became a lost cause. No one knew he was sick until he had to step down at Tresswell Metals.'

Leslie fell silent for a moment before she burst out, 'I'm being a terrible hostess! I didn't even offer you a snack. I've been baking like crazy and we have cookies and muffins – I crave sweets when I'm pregnant – and you're all out of lemonade. Maybe you'd like coffee, instead.'

'I'd like more lemonade but I'm not at all hungry,' Juliet said as Leslie refilled her glass. 'We have an unbelievable amount of food at home.'

'Casseroles, I'll bet.'

'Lots of casseroles.' Juliet smiled. 'Now, if you don't mind, I'd like to ask a question about the next Tresswell heir. Are you and Jon hoping for a boy or a girl?'

Leslie laughed. 'I don't care although I think it would be fun to have a baby girl I could dress up in ribbons and bows. I think Jon would like another boy. He hasn't said so, but I know he'd be happy if Tommy had a brother like Nate,' she said, referring to Jon's older brother, who'd died at fourteen. 'Jon idolized his big brother.'

'I was only eight when Nate died and barely knew him, but I remember he was a good swimmer.'

'Jon and Carole look like Danielle but Nate looked like Nathaniel. He was a *great* swimmer. Some people thought he was headed for the Olympics, him especially. But he got overconfident and tried dives he should never have done when he was alone.'

'Alone? I thought he and Jon were swimming together in the family pool.'

'They were, but Jon got tired and quit. He showered off the chlorine water like his father insisted he always do and left the house. That's when Nate dived and hit his head on the side of the pool.'

'And cracked his skull.'

'Well, he was knocked unconscious but the blow didn't kill him. He was dead when his father found him, but the autopsy showed water in his lungs. He drowned. Don't you remember?'

Juliet rubbed her forehead. 'I haven't thought of it for years and my memory isn't great right now.'

'Of course it isn't. Anyway, Jon still blames himself for leaving Nate, but Nate was fourteen and Jon only eleven and wanted to go play with his friends. Nate didn't want to stop swimming but promised he wouldn't dive anymore. Nate broke his promise and he died for it.'

'God, what a tragedy.'

'Especially because Nathaniel never completely forgave Jon for leaving. He changed toward Jon afterward.'

'That was unfair.'

'I know. It still bothers Jon, too. Although we'll have almost two acres of land at the new house, Jon refuses to have a pool. He's afraid to even let Tommy learn to swim.'

'I didn't know.'

'Oh, yes. Nate's death traumatized Jon forever. Oh, I don't know why I'm running on about Nate. Anyway, it would be nice if this baby's a boy so it will be relatively close to Tommy's age. But if it's a girl, we'll be delighted. And there can always be another boy later.'

Tommy pushed open the sliding glass door and came in, shutting the door behind him. 'I'm *all* done,' he announced in a weary voice. 'Anything else you want me to do?'

'No, poor you.' Leslie laughed, then she whooped. 'Oh! Birthday presents! Tommy, get your birthday present for Juliet and I'll get Jon and mine.'

'It's not necessary—'

'It definitely is! It's your birthday!' Leslie and Tommy ran upstairs to the bedrooms. In a couple of minutes, they both descended holding wrapped gifts and smiling. 'From us with love.'

Juliet looked at Tommy. 'I've known your mom longest, so I'll open hers first.'

He grinned and nodded.

She took the flat, square box, carefully removed the pink bow and paper and lifted the lid to reveal a three-inch-long pin in the shape of a treble clef with a pink pearl in the swirl at the base.

'It's white gold so it won't tarnish. I chose a nine-millimeter freshwater pearl.'

'How beautiful!' Juliet exclaimed. 'You shouldn't have been so extravagant!'

They laughed and hugged before Tommy, looking as if he were ready to explode with anticipation, said, 'Now mine! I wrapped it myself!'

'Did you now?' Juliet smiled as she carefully removed at least two feet of violently blue foil paper and a huge glitter bow to reveal an insulated lunch box decorated with a hippopotamus, a zebra, a camel, and other wild animals. 'Wow! It's just . . . wow!'

'Mommy says you're going to teach school and that means

you'll need a lunchbox so I picked out one like mine, only mine has sharks on it, but it's the same kind.'

'It's wonderful, Tommy.' She opened it and they inspected the thermos and mesh pocket. 'I can take a lot of food with me to school.' She hugged him. 'Thank you so much.'

'You're real welcome, Juliet. And Mommy told me not to ask you . . .' he cast a guilty glance at Leslie, '. . . but you're comin' to watch the Fourth of July fireworks at Parrish Park with us, aren't you?'

'Tommy, I *did* tell you not to ask because Juliet is too busy,' Leslie said in mild annoyance.

'But she always does! I look forward to it!' The last thing on Juliet's mind was an Independence Day celebration, but she'd been going with Tommy since he was less than a year old. 'You're not busy at night, are you? *Please*,' Tommy begged.

Juliet hesitated, wondering if it seemed proper for her to be going to a celebration so soon after her father's death, but she knew Owen wouldn't want her to disappoint Tommy. 'OK. Some traditions should never be broken.'

'You don't *really* have to go,' Leslie said. 'We'll all understand.'

'I want to go,' Juliet half-lied.

'Yes!' Tommy beamed, then leaned forward and gave her a kiss. 'Thanks a lot, Juliet.'

'All right, young man,' Leslie told him. 'I think it's time you go to your room to watch cartoons before you think of anything else to cajole from Juliet.'

'What's cajole?'

'Never mind. Go watch TV.'

After Tommy had gone up the stairs and back the hallway to his room, Leslie said, 'You don't have to go to the park if you're not up to it.'

'I don't want to break his heart.'

'Five-year-old hearts mend easily.' Leslie smiled, leaned over and whispered, 'And by the way, we're getting him a dog for his birthday in two months but it's a secret.'

Juliet grinned. 'Your secret is safe with me.'

*   *   *

When Juliet got home at three o'clock, Alec's car was gone and Eddie Maddox was weeding a bed of petunias in the front yard.

'Hi, Eddie,' Juliet called, then walked over and stopped beside him. 'I see Mom put you in charge of her prized petunias.'

Eddie looked up, a sheen of perspiration on his tanned face. 'These are caramel yellow with a bronze center. I'd never seen anything like them, but your mother thought they'd look pretty in front of your yellow house. She sure has a way with plants.'

'She certainly does. She taught me so much about them that, when I took off a year between high school and college, I worked for almost two years at Pauline's Flower Garden downtown.'

'Why did you skip two years before college?'

'Well, my brother had died. I knew my parents would like having me around longer.' She paused. 'And I wasn't ready to leave home, either.'

'It was nice that you stayed. Did you like working at Pauline's?'

'A lot. But I liked music better. I also wanted to go to college. Are you going to college?'

Eddie shrugged. 'I don't think about it. After I graduate from high school, I have to get a full-time job so I can help out Mom.'

'Oh. Well, you seem to enjoy working with flowers.'

'When I started doing lawn work, I thought I'd just be mowing grass and it was only for the money. But Sera's taught me a lot and I found out I really like making things grow.' He tossed a handful of weeds into a wicker basket. 'She says I have a talent for it.'

'I'm sure you do. Mom thinks the world of you.'

Eddie blushed but didn't look up from his weeding. 'She's really nice to me. She reminds me of my Aunt Pamela, only Pamela's younger.'

'Is she your mother's sister?'

'Yes. She lives in Cincinnati and I don't see much of her but she calls me a lot. Anyway, your dad was terrific, too. I'm gonna miss him. We'd just started working on the basement.'

'The basement? Is something wrong with the basement?'

'About a month ago we had a big rain – it lasted two days – and there were leaks. He said it had something to do with the roof gutters being old. He had new ones installed. That basement meant a lot to your dad. He said that's where your brother practiced his music.'

'Yes. Fin spent a lot of time there.'

'Well, your dad was only going to patch where the leaks had caused damage and then he decided to renovate it.'

'Renovate the whole basement?'

'Well, part of it. And maybe renovate is too big of a word. Fix it up. He asked me to help. I learned a lot in just two weeks. Then he slowed down. He didn't want to work on it so often even though it wasn't finished.'

'Why?'

Eddie shrugged. 'I don't know. Maybe he was tired. He didn't act as peppy as usual. But he said he wasn't quitting. We'd make the place nice again.'

So Dad had begun acting different two weeks before he died, Juliet thought. Even Eddie noticed it. But what caused the change? What had happened that he hadn't confided even in her mother?

'Are you OK? I didn't mean to upset you,' Eddie said.

'Oh, I'm fine. Just thinking.' She looked around. 'Where's Alec? His car's gone.'

'He took your mother to do errands. I don't know what kind of errands. That's all they said.'

'Hey, what're you doing?' a voice thundered. 'Get away from there!'

Juliet looked across the street to see Wendell Booth standing on the curb in baggy jeans and a tight T-shirt that showed his massive chest. She turned back to Eddie.

'Where did *he* come from?'

'He's done that a few times when he thinks I'm here alone,' Eddie said quietly.

'Why?'

Eddie shrugged. 'He says I'm his little brother and I shouldn't be here.'

'He had a younger brother, but he died when Wendell was twelve.'

'I know. I don't know if Wendell really thinks I'm him or he's only pretending I am.'

'Hey, I'm talkin' to you!' Wendell yelled. 'Don't listen to her. Her brother got murdered because he deserved it. He was a devil. People told me about him and they were right. Her mother's a *witch*. A *witch* lives in that house. The girl's probably a witch. They'll do somethin' to you, little brother – somethin' bad!'

Juliet pulled her cell phone from her purse. 'I'm calling the police.'

'Oh, no, please don't, ma'am.' Eddie's voice sounded distressed. 'It'll only make things worse.'

'But Wendell shouldn't be allowed to get away with this!'

'I don't think he'd hurt me.'

'We don't know what he's capable of, Eddie. Remember that he served nine years in prison for the murder of my brother.'

'But Deke wouldn't like it. Besides, I can take care of myself. Really, I can. I'm a lot tougher than I seem.' Eddie looked trapped and Juliet knew she'd cause more trouble and decided to back down rather than add to his misery. 'How about I pay you for today's work and take you home?'

'Oh, Miss Reid, I don't want to put you out.' By now he looked like he was going to cry. 'I can walk home.'

'No, you can't. I'm taking you and that's that.'

'All right, I guess.'

'Eddie, I want you to be safe. Allow me to drive you as a favor.'

He seemed to relax slightly. 'OK, ma'am. Thank you.'

'Good. And call me Juliet. You're nearly one of the family.'

Eddie finally gave her a weak smile. Then Wendell began to yell again and his smile faded.

'Let's go, Eddie.'

'I'm leaving a mess on the lawn.'

'The lawn isn't important. *You* are, and I'm getting you to safety.'

Safety wasn't the word the popped into Juliet's mind when she turned onto a dirt road and saw a dilapidated trailer surrounded by weeds and Eddie said, 'That's where I live.'

Juliet pulled up to the trailer. Two people sat in front of it at a card table with cans of beer in front of them. The woman immediately stood when Eddie jumped out of the car. Juliet felt obligated to get out, also.

'You bringin' him home because he did somethin' wrong?' the woman called.

'No, not at all. I just offered him a ride home. I'm Juliet Reid.' She walked toward the woman, hand extended. 'We're all fond of Eddie. I'm pleased to meet you.'

The woman, dressed in jeans cut off as short as possible, rubber flip-flops, and a thin gauze tank top that showed her black lace bra, shook Juliet's hand. 'You're the one that's been at Ohio State studyin' music.'

'That's right. I graduated two months ago.'

'Well, how nice. I'm Belle Maddox.' She smiled with thin lips. Her over-bleached, straw-like hair blew in the breeze. She had refined features and fair skin, prematurely aged and coarsened, perhaps by drug and alcohol abuse. Her eyes – green like Eddie's – must have once been beautiful, but now they were bloodshot, careworn, and circled with fine lines and a thick rim of black eyeliner. 'This is Deke Nevins.'

A tall, lanky man wearing torn jeans, old canvas sneakers, and a faded Black Sabbath T-shirt lolled to his feet and grinned, showing a badly chipped left front tooth. His dark, dirty hair laced with gray hung to his shoulders and his eyes were cold silver coins surrounded by wrinkles. Something about him seemed vaguely familiar. 'Howdy.'

'Hello, Mr Nevins. Nice to meet you.'

'Aw, now, it's Deke to pretty women. Besides, we met a *long* time ago.'

'We did? I don't remember . . .'

'It doesn't matter. I'm the man of the house.' He reached out and roughly tousled Eddie's hair. 'Aren't I, Eddie?'

'Yes, sir,' Eddie said softly, his eyes downcast.

'Sure you didn't get hauled home because you were causin' trouble over at the Reid's place?'

'No, sir, I wasn't. It was Wendell Booth who was causing the trouble. He was standing across the street yelling at me.'

'Yellin'? Is that all?'

'Yes, Mr Nevins. Deke,' Juliet said. 'I'm sure you know Booth's history. I don't think he should be free to roam around and certainly not to pester Eddie. After all, he was convicted of murdering my brother.'

Deke stared at her, expressionless.

'Anyway, my mother was gone and Eddie was alone. I was afraid of what Booth might do.'

Dekes cold eyes narrowed. 'I understand why you don't like Booth, but Eddie had a job to do and money to earn—'

'Would you like a glass of iced tea, Juliet?' Belle interrupted nervously. 'I put lots of sugar in it, so it's real good.'

'Belle, I was talkin'!' Deke snapped, glaring at her.

'Sorry, Deke.' Belle looked cowed. 'I was tryin' to be hospitable.'

'I just had two glasses of lemonade,' Juliet said quickly. 'Thank you anyway, Belle. And thank you for the food you sent yesterday.'

'Food?' Deke barked.

'My fruit surprise because Mr Reid died.'

'We'll get the bowl back to you in a couple of days, Belle.'

'So does this mean you don't want Eddie workin' for you anymore?' Deke asked Juliet. ''Cause you're scared of Wendell Booth?'

She met Deke's unnerving eyes. His straggly hair blew back to reveal a thin silver hoop in his right ear and a not-too-clean neck. 'Eddie has been paid for the full day. It's not his fault I insisted he come home now. He's an excellent worker and I'm sure we'll have plenty for him to do all year long.'

Deke still looked angry. She knew he was skeptical.

'We'll need him tomorrow, in fact. If that works with your schedule, Eddie.'

'He doesn't make his own schedule,' Deke said firmly. 'He'll be there bright and early.'

Juliet took a few steps backward toward her car. 'It was nice meeting you and Belle. I really must get back, now. My mother has some things planned for me. Goodbye, Eddie. See you tomorrow.'

'Bye, Miss Reid,' he said listlessly, hopelessly, as his mother shooed him into the trailer. Juliet felt Deke's stony gaze on her as she turned the car around. She headed down the dirt lane away from the trailer feeling an overwhelming wave of compassion for Eddie Maddox.

FOUR

When Juliet got home, Wendell Booth had apparently moved on and Alec's car was still gone. She went inside and locked the door behind her in case Wendell returned. Hutch rushed to meet her.

'I'll bet you need to go outside, don't you, boy?' She rubbed his ears and he made playful, growly noises. She hooked him to his leash and they made two laps around the back yard, Juliet giving him time to sniff the vivid zinnias in a flower bed and find one of his many tennis balls beneath a shrub. She avoided looking into the woods at the tree house. Even on a beautiful, sunny day like this one, the sight filled her with darkness and grief. She concentrated on Hutch's pure joy with the outdoors. Finally she took him to the house, locked the back doors, fixed him fresh water and gave him a handful of treats. 'Dinner isn't for two hours,' she said as he noisily lapped water then began crunching a treat. 'We don't want you fainting from hunger.'

Juliet wandered into the living room and picked up a magazine, flipping through it without really seeing the pages. She kept thinking about Eddie's home, his mother and Deke Nevins. That man was trouble and Eddie was afraid of him. So was Belle. Why did she keep him around? He didn't look like the type to bring in a good income. Did she love him? She seemed more frightened of him than in love with him. Maybe she was one of those women who couldn't imagine life without a man, no matter how poor a specimen.

Then Juliet's thoughts moved to what Eddie had said about the basement. There had been leaks and her father was renovating it, which no one had mentioned to her. Maybe the renovation was too minor for her parents to consider noteworthy, but Juliet was interested.

When Fin was thirteen, her father had converted it into a makeshift recording studio. Fin and his friends had spent a lot of time there and she hadn't looked at it for at least three years. Maybe now, while her mother was gone, was the time. She went to the basement door and opened it slowly, flipping on the lights and starting down the sturdy wooden staircase to the concrete floor. Her mother had wanted to put down indoor/outdoor carpet but Fin had told her they couldn't because it would absorb high frequencies. He barely knew what he was talking about, but he always sounded convincing.

Juliet remembered the ruckus he made when her father and his friend Frank soundproofed the basement ceiling incorrectly. After everything had been removed – even pictures – and stored, acoustic panels had been arranged in irregular patterns, once again because Fin said studios must have irregular walls. Then the equipment had been moved in – a little at first, then more as the budget allowed additional purchases for Fin's passion. By the time he was fifteen, he had a decent studio – at least one that impressed his friends who'd never seen a real recording studio. And he had sincerely and profusely thanked his father and Frank, making up for any previous arguments.

Juliet roamed around, looking at the two guitars mounted on the wall, microphone stands, the dark blue couch where his 'audience' had sat. On the far right wall, several acoustic panels were missing and some of the grout between the concrete block walls was moldy. That must have been where the leaks started. She was certain her father had replaced the gutters along the roof. She also noticed damage along the tops of other acoustic panels. Across the room, she spotted plastic-covered stacks of new gray foam panels.

Juliet sat down on the couch. How long had it been since this room had been filled with people and music? At least nine years, yet except for the one damaged section, it looked nearly the same.

The doorbell rang. Juliet sat still for a moment. Her mother and Alec wouldn't ring the bell. She wished she could ignore it, but her car was sitting in the driveway. Whoever it was knew someone was home.

She climbed the stairs and pushed Hutch out of the way,

leaving on the chain as she opened the door slightly in case it was Wendell. She was surprised to see Carole Tresswell.

Juliet took off the chain and opened the door. 'Carole!'

'I know I should have called instead of dropping by but I hadn't planned on coming.' Hutch let out a bark. 'Hello, there. Do you bite?'

'No, he doesn't. And please come in. I'm a little on edge because Wendell Booth was outside yelling so much I had to take our lawn boy home.'

'Eddie Maddox? Leslie and Mom use him, too.' She smiled, her eyes the exact shade of hazel as her brother Jon's. She was tall and wore white tailored pants, a burgundy flutter sleeve top, and gold hoop earrings. Her glossy dark brown hair fell in waves below her shoulders and the beautiful, classic lines of her face looked almost the same as they had when she'd been Fin's girlfriend.

'Oh, don't get me started on Wendell Booth,' Carole said in her slightly husky voice, bending over to pet Hutch's head. 'The fact that he's walking around here free as a bird literally makes me sick.'

'I'm going to talk to Davis Dawson about doing something to keep him at home. He was here today yelling at Eddie. He thinks Eddie is his little brother.'

'*What?* Oh my lord.' Carole raised herself up, abandoning Hutch, and smiled. 'I haven't seen you since you were fifteen. You're lovely, Juliet. And a piano virtuoso to boot. Fin would be delighted.'

'Do you really think so?'

Carole looked surprised. 'Well, of course! Why would you ask such a thing?' Before Juliet could answer, Carole laughed. 'Because Fin made it seem like he always wanted to be the star and didn't want any competition, but he wasn't as egotistical as most people thought. He thought you were extremely talented. He just wasn't lavish with praise.'

'Gee, why didn't I know this?'

'Most people didn't. I only did because once in a while he confided in me.'

Juliet hadn't been close to Carole when she was going out with Fin. Carole had never been unkind or dismissive of her, but she hadn't been warm, either. The Carole standing in front of her seemed completely different.

'I was down in the basement looking at Fin's old studio,' Juliet said. 'Hardly anything has changed. Remember when you and Leslie and I used to gather down there and listen to Fin and Jon and the other guys?'

'Sure I do.' Carole looked at her brightly. 'May I see it?'

'Well . . . sure. Right this way. Eddie told me there'd been some damage due to gutter leakage so Dad had started fixing the damaged spots, then he decided to revamp the place. I don't know why.'

Carole followed her down the basement stairs. 'Do you ever record down here?'

'Me? No. My piano is upstairs and the little recording I've done has been at school. Besides, I don't want to be a professional.' Juliet stopped at the foot of the stairs. 'Here it is!'

'Oh, does this bring back memories! It's just like it used to be.' Carole's gaze traveled over the room. 'The soundproofing curtains are pulled apart at the windows. Can we close them and turn on the lights? Remember how Fin loved recording with red and blue glowing everywhere – lava lamps, lanterns with red and blue bulbs? He thought it was mystical.'

'They're in the corner. I saw them when I came down a while ago. Dad must have moved them.'

She and Carole placed the lights on the three aluminum folding tables in the sparsely furnished studio, plugged them in and turned them on.

'There!' Carole said gleefully. 'I can almost believe it's years ago and Fin was singing, Jon was playing bass guitar, and Kyle Hollister was on keyboards. You dated Kyle when you were older, didn't you?'

Juliet thought of the kind, handsome boy she'd dated casually for about three months. 'We went out a few times when I was sixteen. Nothing serious.'

'God, he's gorgeous! He's a cop. Still single. His parents were disappointed that he didn't go into the family businesses, especially with his looks and charisma. His older brother, Beau, is now assistant manager at Hollisters' restaurant. Well, you probably know all that. I'm rambling.' Carole walked slowly around the room. 'Sometimes you played keyboards when Kyle's parents made him work a shift at the restaurant and he couldn't show up. You were better than him. *Much* better. And Gary Greenlee played the drums until the last few months before he died.'

'Poor Gary,' Juliet murmured. 'I was only fifteen when he overdosed. He'd been Fin's closest friend for so long and I had no idea he was doing drugs.'

'Fin suspected it. Sometimes during that last year Gary's playing was . . . well, bad. He was never great, but he'd never been bad. And his personality changed. He was moody and sullen one day and volatile the next.'

'Fin wouldn't talk about the overdose. If anyone mentioned it, he'd go silent. And I didn't really know Gary. Jon was always friendlier with me.'

'I didn't know Gary well, either. He was closer to Fin and Kyle. I don't even know who Gary dated and keeping up with everyone's social calendar was a big deal for me back then.' Carole frowned. 'Let's see . . . Deacon was the sound engineer for a while. He wanted to be called just Deacon. His last name was Newsome, Neville, Nevins . . .'

'Deacon? Deke Nevins?'

'Yes, that's it.'

'I saw him this afternoon! I didn't remember him.'

'You were only around twelve when Fin got rid of him.'

'Fin fired him?'

'No one in the band got paid so he wasn't really fired. But Fin wouldn't let him come back.'

'He looks awful.'

'He was at least six years older than Fin and Jon and he never looked good. Always rough and dissipated.'

Deacon had been the tall, scruffy guy in the photo missing from the tree house, Juliet thought. 'You should see him now. He lives with Eddie Maddox's mother, Belle.'

'My God, she must be desperate.'

'He gave me the creeps.'

'I didn't like him back in the day. He drank a lot, and I mean *a lot*. I think he was into drugs, too.' Her gaze grew distant. 'When Fin kicked Deacon out of the band Deke was enraged, but Fin wasn't afraid of him.' She smiled. 'Fin wasn't afraid of anyone.' Then her smile faded. 'I guess he should have been.'

'He should have been afraid of Wendell Booth.'

'I don't know why Wendell hated Fin so much. He didn't always. They weren't friends, but Fin was nice to him. He never made fun of him like a lot of the other guys did. Then, like you flipped a switch, Wendell did a 180. I mean, he suddenly detested Fin. Fin didn't know what had happened, but he didn't worry about it. He just let things slide.'

'I don't remember Fin saying anything about it.'

'No, he probably didn't. He wouldn't have wanted to worry your mother. And I didn't think much about why Wendell was mad – I didn't pay much attention to anyone except Fin. I adored him.' Carole grinned. 'And Leslie adored Jon.'

'You remember so much more than I do.'

'You were younger and didn't spend a lot of time with most of us.'

'Except for Leslie. She was barely a year older than I was. As for the rest of you . . .' Juliet shrugged. 'I felt out of place. I didn't think any of you wanted to be bothered with me.'

Carole laughed. 'We probably acted that way. We were fairly full of ourselves, to put it nicely. I'm sorry if we hurt you.'

Juliet was confused. Carole had never talked to her so much or so openly. She sounded as if they'd always been good friends. Juliet smiled and motioned to the couch. 'Let's sit down.' They did and she looked seriously at Carole. 'You and Fin were so close.'

Carole smiled sadly. 'I might have only been a teenager, but I loved him. I truly loved him.' She sighed. 'Do you mind if I smoke?'

'Not at all.' She picked up an old plastic ashtray from the floor. 'It's seen better days.'

'An antique.' Carole lit her cigarette and seemed to drift away for a minute. When she spoke again, her voice was wistful. 'My mother didn't want me to date Fin. She liked your parents and thought Fin was good-looking and charming. He could make her laugh. But he wanted to be a rock star, of all things. He wasn't what she pictured for me – she wanted me to settle down with a guy with a degree from an Ivy League university and family money. But twice I've married men of her choice. I'm only twenty-seven now and trying to get my second divorce.'

'I'm sorry.'

'I'm not. The first time I was unhappy. The second time was a disaster. I was miserable and it's not over yet. I came home to distance myself from him and also get my bearings again. And so I wouldn't be alone. Mom and I don't always get along, but she's been supportive of the divorce.'

'Do you think if you hadn't listened to your mother, you and Fin would probably have ended up together?'

Carole shook her head. 'I don't think so. If he'd made it to California, he would have found someone prettier and talented, someone in the music business who could have really shared his world. And I don't think I would have been bitter. Honestly. I loved him enough to want him to have his best life, and that wouldn't have been with me. After all, Fin was the only *real* talent in the group. I believe he would have made it in show business.' She looked at Juliet. 'You should see your face! Either you didn't know how much I cared for your brother or you think I'm lying.'

'I didn't know how much you cared for him,' Juliet nearly whispered, feeling her throat tighten.

'I've spent my lifetime underplaying my feelings.' Carole blew out smoke then asked bluntly, 'Were you jealous of Fin?'

'Jealous?'

'Everyone made such a big deal about him. You were extremely talented, too, but I don't remember anyone singing your praises except for your brother when he'd had too much to drink. He said maybe when you were older you could join him in California, be part of his band. He admired you. He loved you, although I'm sure he never told you.'

'I didn't know. No one my age acted like I was anything special. It was hard to measure up to Fin. He wasn't just a great musician – he was a true performer. Charismatic. I was shy. I was in awe of him, but I don't remember feeling jealous.' Juliet paused. 'Well, maybe time and the way Fin died have made me whitewash my feelings. I'm sure I was jealous of him to a certain extent. Envious.' She smiled weakly. 'I'm not perfect or unselfish.'

'No one is. I was very jealous of my brothers and I admit it although I never showed it when I was young. Dad doted on Nate, who thought I was a pest. Mom was crazy about Jon. I was only sixteen months younger than Jon. We should have been close, but we weren't. I wasn't ignored or neglected at home, but often I felt lost in the shuffle. I was resentful.'

'I barely knew Nate. I know his death was horrible for your family. As for Jon, I guess I thought of him almost as Fin's brother. They were both so talented—'

'Jon wasn't as talented as Fin. He knew it although he'd never admit it.'

'Oh. Well, Fin never said that . . .'

'He didn't have to. He played guitar well but not great. Not too long before Fin died, Jon wrote a couple of good songs. But the band wasn't important except that he always wanted to be the best at everything he did. His passion was Tresswell Metal, though, not being part of a rock band, which is good because he wouldn't have made it.'

Juliet bristled. Jon had always been good to her and he was Leslie's husband. 'Carole, you've never claimed to have musical talent so are you sure you're the best judge of Jon?'

Carole laughed. 'You're right – I'm not a music expert and I spoke out of turn. Maybe that was just my jealousy talking. I'm sorry if I offended you.'

Carole's laughter and her words sounded so genuine that Juliet couldn't be annoyed although she knew Leslie would have been flamingly angry. Since she was thirteen years old, Leslie had been crazy about Jon and she still was. Crazy and protective.

'Just don't say what you said to me to Leslie.' Juliet grinned.

'Oh my God! Do you think I'm insane? She'd claw out my eyes!' Carole smiled at her then grew serious. 'Maybe I shouldn't tell you this, but I think you need to know.' She rubbed out her cigarette. 'Last week your father called me.'

Juliet was startled. 'Oh? Why?'

'That's what I wondered at first. He said he'd heard I was

back in town and he was sorry about my divorce and . . . well, just meaningless stuff. Then he asked me about Fin.'

'What about him?'

'He wanted to know if something had been bothering Fin before he . . . died. He said Fin had been acting a bit different and he wondered if I'd noticed.'

'And had you?'

'Yes. It was nothing drastic. At least I don't think so. He didn't say a word to me about being troubled. But he was distant. Preoccupied.'

Preoccupied, Juliet thought. That's what Davis Dawson had said about Owen.

'Did you tell Dad that Fin was acting different?'

'Yes. I said something was troubling Fin and it wasn't just Gary Greenlee's death, although that took the wind out of him. He was never quite the same after Gary overdosed, but he wasn't as different as he was that last week. Or maybe two. He canceled half of our dates. He didn't want to be with me as much, but I don't think his feelings for me had changed. It was more like . . .' She closed her eyes, frowning. 'It was like he thought he was protecting me.'

'Protecting you from what?'

'I have no idea, Juliet. But I told your father all this. Maybe I shouldn't have, but Fin's been gone over nine years and I didn't know anything was wrong with your dad. No one has said that he acted *really* upset. But he must have been.'

'Yes, he must have been,' Juliet echoed flatly. 'I don't know what it could have been. Mom doesn't know what it was—'

'Please don't tell your mother he called me,' Carole interrupted earnestly. 'I don't want her to think I said something that pushed him over the edge.'

'I'm sure you didn't say anything to drive him to suicide, Carole. You shouldn't be worried.'

'But I am. I interfered. I said things I shouldn't have said. And there's something else. I know it seems strange, but between my marriages, I got closer to Kyle Hollister – not romantically, just as friends – and we've stayed in touch. When my present husband found out I talk to and text Kyle, he was furious. Anyway, after your dad called me about Fin, I had lunch with Kyle and he asked questions, too.'

'What kind of questions?'

'Had Fin seemed afraid of anyone? Did he talk to me about Gary's overdose? Did I have any idea who Gary's dealer was? That kind of thing.'

'Why was he suddenly so interested in the two deaths?'

'He said your father had asked him about them a few days earlier. Owen had never talked about Fin's death with Kyle. He didn't say much of anything to Kyle – ever. Kyle thought your dad didn't like him.'

'All he would say is that he didn't think Kyle was a good match for me.'

'Why?'

'I don't know, but Dad didn't dislike Kyle. I'm sure of that. Maybe it was just that my father thought of me as a child.'

'Anyway, Kyle said he gave your father the little information he had about Fin, which wasn't much. But Kyle was distressed. Your dad wasn't acting like himself at work – detached, moody – and that phone call came out of the blue nearly ten years after Fin's death. Juliet, I should have said something to your mother and I didn't. I told myself I was minding my own business, but now I think maybe if I'd talked to Sera, given her an idea of what was going on, I could have prevented Owen's death.'

Juliet shook her head. 'Dad was obviously determined that Mom not know *anything*. He would have brushed it off—'

'Juliet, are you down there?' her mother called from the top of the stairs.

Carole looked alarmed but Juliet touched her hand and whispered, 'I won't say a word and don't you, either.' Then she called, 'Yes, I'm with Carole. We were reminiscing.'

Sera came downstairs. 'Hi, Carole.' She glanced around. 'That terrible storm did a lot of damage and I was upset until Owen decided to renovate the room.' She looked at Juliet. 'He said, "It's time we stopped making this a shrine to Fin. I'm going to fix it up for Juliet. It should have been done years ago."'

Juliet's eyes widened. 'Really? Is that why neither of you mentioned it to me?'

'Oh yes. It was going to be a surprise for your birthday. But then he stopped working on it . . .' Sera seemed to catch herself. 'Ready to go upstairs, girls?'

'Sure,' Carole said. 'I stopped by to see all of you.'

They trooped upstairs and Carole hugged Sera.

'Where have the two of you been all afternoon?' Juliet asked, looking at Alec.

'The cemetery, Hollisters' restaurant, the bakery, the florist, Ohio One Bank to empty the safety deposit box, you name it,' Alec said with a meaningful look at Juliet, which she immediately understood. Her mother couldn't stand being in the house without Owen.

'I thought you'd be overwhelmed with people yesterday, so I waited until today to pay my condolences,' Carole said. 'Owen was a wonderful man.'

'Thank you, dear,' Sera answered. 'He *was* wonderful. I'll always miss him.'

Sera's eyes filled with tears, but Carole had turned her attention to Alec. She embraced him a few seconds longer than was necessary. Then she pulled back, her gaze searching his face. 'My God, you're even better looking than you were years ago.'

'Thanks, Carole, but I think time has taken its toll on me.'

'You mean your time in Afghanistan? What on earth were you thinking running off to that sand pit?'

'I was thinking that I was in the army and that was my job,' he said smoothly. 'It's late in the afternoon. Would anyone else like a drink?'

'That sounds wonderful if it's not too much trouble,' Carole said.

Alec looked around. 'Sera? Juliet?'

Fifteen minutes later as everyone sat around the living room sipping their drinks and talking about anything except Owen's death, the doorbell rang.

'I'll bet that's my watchdog,' Carole muttered.

'I'll get it,' Juliet said and opened the door to see Danielle Tresswell standing on the porch and dressed as stylishly as her daughter, shining brown hair lifting from her shoulders in the breeze. With her trim body and clear hazel eyes, she looked closer to forty than fifty-five.

'Juliet! How are you, dear?'

'All right.'

'I was coming by to pay my respects to Sera and saw Carole's car here. I hope you don't mind that I stopped by unannounced.'

Sera appeared behind Juliet. 'Danielle. How nice to see you.'

'And you. I'm sorry I didn't come by yesterday but—'

'There's no need to apologize. We were flooded with guests. Please come in.'

'If you're sure I'm not bothering you.'

'I'm sure.'

'Can I get you something to drink?' Alec asked.

'Thank you. Just a glass of water.' She entered the living room. 'Carole! I've been looking everywhere for you.'

'Why?' Carole asked with a smile.

'You disappeared for so long. You could have left me a note.'

'I didn't think I needed to leave a note. I'm twenty-seven, Mom.'

The banter sounded lighthearted, but Juliet detected a note of tension underneath it. Was Danielle trying to keep a tight leash on Carole? Was Carole trying to escape her mother's sharp eyes? To do what?

'Oh, thank you.' Danielle took the glass Alec offered. 'It's been ages since I've seen you, Alec.'

'You saw me night before last at your party.'

'Briefly. I mean to really visit with you.' She sat down on a blue wing chair. 'You look wonderful. New York City must agree with you.'

'It does.'

'And your job?'

'Security. I like it.'

'It sounds very important.' Danielle glanced out the sliding glass doors. Her eyes narrowed slightly and Juliet knew she was looking at the tree house. After it was finished, she'd insisted on a tour to make sure the structure was solid and stable before she would allow Jon to spend time there. She quickly shifted her gaze. 'I know this must be a very rough time for all of you. Is there anything I can do? Just name it.'

'That's kind of you, Danielle, but I think we have everything under control,' Sera said.

Juliet saw the muscles in her mother's face tighten as she fought for calm but heard the slight quiver in her voice and knew Danielle did, too. 'I mean it, Sera,' she said compassionately. 'I know we haven't been close over the years but I've been through this twice with Nate and then Nathaniel. I know that no one can make you feel better, but if you ever need someone to talk to, a shoulder to cry on or someone to help with Owen's funeral, please don't hesitate to call on me. Really.'

Sera's face softened. 'Thank you, Danielle. That means a lot to me.'

'And now I think Carole and I have taken up enough of your time.' She drained her glass of water in one gulp, set the empty glass on a coaster, and stood. 'Carole, have you forgotten that Jon and Leslie are coming to dinner? We should go home and get ready.'

'It's four-thirty,' Carole protested.

'Tommy is coming, too, and he goes to bed early.' Danielle looked around the room. 'I'm so glad I had a few minutes alone with all of you and please accept my deepest sympathy. I'll be seeing you soon.'

At my father's funeral, Juliet thought. *At the burial of a man who shot himself in the head while you were at your birthday party.*

They'd just finished dinner when Sera suddenly brought up the bakery, the Sweet Shoppe. 'It's really lovely. You should stop by, Juliet.'

'Alec said you went by there today.'

Her mother grinned. 'We certainly did!' She jumped up from the table, opened the refrigerator and pulled out a three-tiered cake. 'Your father always said I can't keep a secret, but I did! We didn't forget today is your birthday, sweetheart. I had such a lovely party planned but . . .' Her eyes filled with tears. 'Anyway, we can still celebrate. It's strawberry almond with cream cheese icing.'

'Oh, Mom, my favorite cake!' Juliet cried. 'It's beautiful!'

Sera set the tall cake on the table and got tiny pink candles from the cabinet. 'How many do you want?'

'Ummm . . . five. One for you, me, Alec, Dad, and Fin.'

Alec lit the candles, he and Sera sang 'Happy Birthday' to her, then she blew out the flickering flames. 'This is wonderful. Mom, you cut the pieces. You're the most deft with the cake server.'

Once again, the doorbell rang and Hutch jumped up, barking. 'He doesn't do that during the day,' Juliet said, rising from the table.

'Only in the evening. It's as if he goes on duty at six o'clock,' Sera laughed. 'Maybe it's Leslie.'

But Sheriff Davis Dawson stood on the porch, still in uniform. 'Hello, Juliet. I hope I'm not interrupting dinner.'

Juliet felt a ripple of apprehension at the unexpected sight of him but tried to look unfazed. 'Come in. We were just about to have some of my birthday cake.'

'Oh! Happy birthday, Juliet. Marcy and I were invited to the party—' He broke off awkwardly.

Juliet smiled. 'I'm twenty-five. I don't need a party.' She raised her voice. 'Mom, look who's here.'

'Davis! How nice to see you.' Juliet saw the same hesitation in her mother's eyes she knew shone in hers. 'Welcome. We're celebrating. I hope you like red velvet cake.'

'I love it, but I don't want to intrude—'

'You're not intruding. Let me fix you a slice. Would you like coffee?'

'Sure. With milk, if you don't mind.' He looked at Alec. 'Hello there. How are you this evening?'

'Especially good now that I'll be having cake. I try to stay in shape when I'm in New York, but I'm on vacation. I'll take off the pounds later.'

'They come off easier when you're thirty like you rather than fifty-two like me.' Sera set a china cake plate in front on him.

'Good lord, this looks scrumptious!' He glanced up and grinned. 'Scrumptious is one of Marcy's words. I'm starting to talk like her.'

'There's nothing wrong with that,' Sera said. 'She's charming.'

'I think so, too.' Davis took a bite of cake and rolled his eyes. 'Wonderful.'

They all ate and drank coffee for nearly twenty minutes, talking about everything except Owen's death before Davis said, 'I guess I should get to why I came by tonight.' He leaned back from the table. 'I managed to get Owen's autopsy rushed through because he was a police officer. I have the results.' Juliet saw her mother sag slightly, Alec tensed, and she held her breath. 'I'll make this as simple and painless as possible.'

Everyone nodded. No one said anything.

'Owen didn't have a disease. In fact, he was in extremely good health – healthier than most men his age. He died of a gunshot wound to the right side of his head that fractured his skull and severely injured his brain. The bullet was still in his head. I'm sorry, Sera,' Davis said as she flinched. 'However, there was very little gunshot residue on his right hand.'

'What does that mean?' Juliet asked.

'There was a circular burn pattern surrounding the wound on the side of his head. That means the gun barrel was pressed against his temple and there was enough gunpowder to cause that burn. That leaves the question of why was there so little on the hand that held that gun. Also, they found two tiny slivers of latex – one on the gun grip, and another under Owen's right middle finger.'

After a moment, Alec said in a flat, dry voice, 'He wasn't the only person holding the gun. Someone's hand was covering his and that hand was wearing a latex glove.'

'Maybe, Alec.'

'Maybe? I *found* Owen. He wasn't wearing a latex glove. Don't you mean *probably*?'

Davis lowered his gaze. 'For now, that's speculation.'

'Speculation?' Sera looked close to fainting. 'Is it speculation that someone *murdered* my husband?'

'I . . . I don't know. There was no sign of a struggle. We have a suicide note. There was trace GSR on Owen's hand and Owen's fingerprints on the gun meaning he held it.'

'Along with someone else – someone wearing a latex glove,' Alec said. 'Isn't that what you think?'

'I believe the circumstances of Owen's death are open to question.'

'I don't,' Sera murmured. 'I knew Owen wouldn't leave Juliet and me.'

'Sera, I'd like for our forensics team to go over the tree house again.'

'Yes! We haven't been in it – nothing's been moved or even touched.'

'Uh, I went in the night I got home,' Juliet said reluctantly and looked at her mother. 'I had to see it. I can't really explain why.' She turned her gaze to Davis. 'I had Hutch with me. I know I touched the light switch but I don't think I touched anything else.'

'We'll get your fingerprints and a sample of your DNA so we can eliminate any of your trace evidence we find. Alec, have you been inside the tree house since you found Owen?'

'No. I've only been around the bottom step of the staircase.'

'Sera?'

'Have I been in that place? *No!*'

But someone was, Juliet thought, feeling a chill as she remembered the light in the treehouse she'd seen after Alec went to bed.

'Good,' Davis said. 'Listen, everyone, I know this has been a shock and I'm sorry—'

'Sorry you've told us maybe Owen didn't commit suicide?' Sera burst out. 'Short of telling me he's come back to life, it's the best news you could have brought!'

Davis looked both puzzled and relieved. 'I didn't wait until tomorrow to tell you because I'd like to get started processing the tree house before noon. I appreciate the way you've taken the news, Sera, but I don't want you to get your hopes up in case there's another explanation for the GSR and the latex.'

'There isn't, Davis. I know it.'

'We'll know for sure soon enough, Sera.' Davis stood up. 'And now I need to get home to my wife.'

'Take her a piece of birthday cake,' Sera said, grabbing a cake plate.

'Oh, I don't want to take Juliet's cake from her.'

'But you must. Marcy will want it.'

'I *know* she'll want it.' Davis smiled. 'But she's afraid she's putting on too much weight. And I don't want to take one of your china plates.'

Sera dashed to a cabinet, opened it and pulled out a sturdy paper plate and some cling wrap. 'I saw her last week and she looks fine,' she said, cutting a large slice of cake. 'She should indulge herself *now*. She can lose weight *after* the baby comes!'

As Davis left, Juliet said, 'I'll open your car door, so you don't drop the cake.' Outside, she told him about coming home from Leslie's to find Wendell Booth standing across the street yelling at Eddie Maddox. 'He thinks Eddie is his brother. He said this is a witch's house and Eddie needs to stay away. Eddie told me Wendell has done that other times. I got worried and took him home. Isn't there something you can do about Wendell?'

'I can have another talk with his parents and tell them that if Wendell does this again, we'll arrest him.'

'Can you really arrest him?'

'Not unless he's threatened Eddie. Did you hear a threat of bodily harm to Eddie or did Eddie say Wendell threatens him?'

'Only with what might happen to him if he comes around our house. At the hands of me or my mother.'

'That doesn't really count, but the Booths don't know that, and in this case, if he has threatened to hurt Eddie, it would be considered stalking a minor. That's serious and Wendell could go to prison. Maybe the Booths will listen if they think their son is in danger of getting in trouble again.'

'That would be great. And there's something else I didn't want to mention in front of Mom. Less than two hours after I went in the tree house, I saw a light moving around in there, as if someone was searching it with a flashlight.'

'Why didn't you call me?'

'It had been an awful day and night. I couldn't take any more upheaval. Besides, I saw the light moving down the stairs to the ground. Whoever it was would have been gone by the time you got here.'

'Was the door to the tree house locked?'

'No. I didn't lock it after I left.'

'Then it could have been a curiosity-seeker. But it might not have been. Your mother certainly doesn't think your father committed suicide.' Davis looked uncomfortable. 'You don't think the possibility that Owen was murdered worries her? The way she was acting . . .'

'She seemed happy. I know. But she won't stay that way, believe me. She was so demoralized thinking that he'd voluntarily left us that the idea him being murdered – of a murderer being on the loose – hasn't hit her yet.'

'I see, but it seems unusual . . .'

'Mom is unusual, Davis. But she's not crazy. She has a point about the note not sounding like Dad. Maybe that was accidental because of the circumstances, but maybe not. It shouldn't be dismissed.'

'I didn't say—'

'I know.' She smiled. 'And I don't mean to be a pest about Eddie, but when I took him home, I found out his mother is living with a man named Deacon Nevins. Apparently my brother knew him and didn't like him. I could tell he's hard on Eddie. The boy is afraid of him.'

'I know who Deke Nevins is. He's been in his share of trouble. He's behaved himself for the last couple of years, but I don't trust him. We're keeping an eye on him.'

'Thank you, Davis. I'd better get inside now before Mom thinks something's wrong. Tell Marcy hello for me.'

'I sure will. And thank you for the cake.'

When Juliet went back in the house, Hutch was downing a sliver of cake in his bowl while Alec rinsed dishes. 'Need some help?' Juliet asked.

'No. I'm good at this. Besides, your mother wants to see you in her bedroom.'

'Is something wrong? Is she all right?'

'She's fine for now.' He grinned at her. 'Run along with you.'

'Yes, sir.' Juliet hurried back the hall, still not certain her mother wasn't shaken by the news Davis had given them. Her bedroom door was shut and Juliet tapped lightly. 'Mom?'

'Come in, sweetheart.' Sera sat on the side of the double bed holding a small black leather box with a gold crest stamped on top. She patted the bed beside her and Juliet sat down. 'Do you remember this box?'

Juliet looked at it closely. 'Vaguely, but I haven't seen it for a long time.'

'Not since you were twelve. That's when your father got a safety deposit box and we stored it in there. He didn't take it out until four days ago.' Her voice shook slightly. 'We'd agreed it should be yours when you turned twenty-five. Do you remember what's inside?'

A distant memory tingled in Juliet's mind and her heartbeat quickened. 'The Lady.'

'That's right! That's what you christened her.' Sera opened the box to reveal a large cameo set in gold filigree, decorated with small iridescent pearls. The ivory relief image of a woman with upswept curls wore a gold necklace with a diamond set in the pendant resting on her bosom. 'This belonged to my great-great-grandmother Cecily. The diamond is real.'

'It's so beautiful,' Juliet breathed.

'That's why it's yours now. She would want you to have it.'

'Mom, you don't know that she'd want me to have it. She died long before you were born.'

'I know a lot about her. She was from England and married your great-great-grandfather, an American millionaire, when she was very young. Her father was a duke. I've seen a painting of her. Also' – Sera opened a large brown envelope and pulled out a vintage photograph of an elegant, blonde young woman – 'this picture of her is for you, too. Look at her. The resemblance is amazing. And she was an excellent pianist and singer. So the cameo is yours and I hope you wear it occasionally when you give concerts.'

'Concerts! Mom, I'm going to be a schoolteacher.'

'For now, maybe. But not always.' Sera stroked Juliet's long hair. 'You know I'm supposed to be a witch. At the very least, a seer.' She winked. 'Concerts are in your future, darling. With my sixth sense, I *know* it.'

'I love it, Mom. It's wonderful.'

'I'm glad.' Sera yawned. 'It's been a long day. I think I'll take a sleeping pill and go to bed.'

*   *   *

When Juliet walked back to the living room, Alec was sat on the couch, smiling at her. 'Did your mother give you the cameo?'

'If she hadn't, you've ruined the surprise.' Juliet grinned then looked at a package wrapped in pink sitting on the coffee table. 'Not another gift!'

'Did you think I'd forget your twenty-fifth birthday? Come sit by me and open it.'

Juliet sat down close to Alec and removed the layers of pink tissue paper and big pink bow. She opened a Styrofoam box and removed an antique rosewood music box with white iridescent mother of pearl marquetry in the shape of orchids on the lid. 'It's Swiss and has an eight-tune cylinder.'

'Alec, it's exquisite,' Juliet breathed. 'How did you know I wanted an antique music box?'

'When you were a teenager, I used to see you looking longingly at pictures of them.'

She looked at him in surprise. 'Longingly? You remembered that?'

He laughed. 'Sure! I did pay attention to you, Juliet.'

'You gave a good impression of barely knowing I was alive.'

Alec reached out and ran a finger along her chin. 'When I came to live with your family, you were a child. I went away to Ohio State when you were just thirteen, and you were still too young when I came back for visits. But I always liked you – you were funny and interesting. Even as a self-absorbed teenager, I was listening to you. And, of course, you blossomed into a beautiful young woman.'

'And you had a girlfriend in Columbus.'

'I had several girlfriends. Not all at the same time. But nothing serious.'

'Well, I never asked about your romantic life.' Juliet lifted the lid of the music box and played 'The Blue Danube' waltz. 'The music quality is wonderful! I never expected to get a box so beautiful, so expensive. Oh Alec, you shouldn't have!'

'Oh yes, I should have and you know it.' He laughed. 'Or would you rather have had a new curling iron or a pair of jeans?'

'I have plenty of jeans and I use hot rollers, thank you.'

'And I thought those long, smooth curls were natural.'

'The curl is natural, the smoothness isn't.'

How different Alec looked, Juliet thought, when he smiled and his dark eyes gazed at her with a mischievous twinkle. His face lost its hard, serious angles and showed humor and even joy. Had he looked like this before the car wreck that killed his family? She'd only seen him four or five times before then. She'd been so young and he was quiet, the opposite of his boisterous sister Brenda. All she knew now was that she never wanted to forget this moment or the delight and flirtatiousness in his expression.

Her face was so close to his she could feel his warm breath on her skin. She gazed into his ebony eyes and for a moment felt lost in their darkness, their beauty and depth. She realized how her feelings had changed from a teenaged crush to something much deeper, more profound – something she'd known for years now but hadn't dared to admit to herself. 'Alec, I . . .' *I love you*, she wanted to say, she almost said. But her throat went dry and her nerve deserted you. 'Thank you,' she whispered, then picked up her music box and hurried down the hall to her bedroom, closing the door softly behind her.

FIVE

Juliet had not been wrong when last night she told Davis Dawson that her mother's mood would quickly change. When Davis left after telling them that perhaps Owen hadn't killed himself, Sera had been almost ebullient. The next morning she'd emerged from her bedroom alarmingly pale and clearly miserable. Juliet fixed her a mug of coffee, which Sera held with shaking hands.

'Did you sleep well, Mom?' Juliet had asked.

'I woke up at three. I've been awake ever since.'

'What do you want for breakfast? I could fix French toast—'

'I'm not hungry, dear.' Sera had smiled weakly. 'I couldn't eat a bite. But maybe Alec would like French toast. He's awake – I heard the shower running.'

Juliet turned away from her mother, her cheeks flaming as she remembered last night. She'd almost told Alec she loved him. She knew he was aware of what she'd been thinking, what she'd nearly said. How could she have let her emotions run away from her? Was it fear, grief, or merely pent-up love that had almost caused her to completely lose her dignity? She cringed. How would Alec act this morning? Embarrassed? Overly kind because he thought she was pathetic?

'Oh, God,' she moaned softly.

'Is something wrong?' Sera asked.

'No. I dread today.'

'Good morning, lovely ladies.' Juliet glanced up. Alec was dressed in navy-blue khakis, a light blue shirt with the long sleeve rolled up to his elbows, and his black hair still wet from the shower. She quickly looked down. 'Good morning.'

'How's everyone?'

'Depressed,' Sera said promptly. 'Juliet wanted to fix me French toast, but I can't eat. Would you like some?'

'I'd love some.' He poured a mug of coffee and sat down at the table with Sera. 'You look tired.'

'I didn't sleep, darn it, and I have things to do this morning.'

'Have some more coffee. Juliet, you don't have to make French toast just for me.'

'I'd like some, too.' She poured milk in a bowl then added eggs, cinnamon, and vanilla and began stirring vigorously, not looking at Alec. 'I haven't had French toast for months.'

'No one makes it as well as you do,' Sera said.

'Thank you.' Juliet went on stirring.

'Dear, you're going to break the bowl. I think those eggs are beaten well enough.'

'I got carried away, Mom.'

She put butter into the electric skillet, dipped thick slices of bread into the milk, then put them in the pan. They sizzled and when they were done, Juliet sprinkled them with powdered sugar.

'Looks delicious,' Alec said, reaching for the maple syrup. 'Sera, have at least one slice. You'll feel better.'

As soon as they finished eating, the doorbell rang. Sera stiffened. Alec opened the door and ushered Davis Dawson into the kitchen. 'Hello, everyone. Sorry to interrupt breakfast, but we wanted to get an early start on the tree house.'

'Oh dear.' Sera quavered as her eyes filled with tears.

Juliet cast Davis a look that said, *I told you so.*

'We'll work fast and not trouble you.' Davis looked miserable. 'Well, except for Juliet. We need to get her fingerprints and swab the inside of her cheek for DNA.'

'You take care of that, Juliet, and I'll do the dishes.' Alec looked at Davis. 'She's made us some delicious French toast.'

'Sounds great.'

'Do you want some?' Juliet asked.

'No, thanks. I had plain old toast and jelly at home. Sera, Marcy loved the cake last night. I don't think I've ever seen her eat anything so fast.'

Finally Sera smiled. 'I'm glad. I remember that when I was expecting, I couldn't get enough sweets. I think Owen was afraid I'd put on about a hundred pounds with each pregnancy.'

'Well, she certainly appreciated your thoughtfulness in sending her some birthday cake. And she says happy birthday to you, Juliet.'

After Juliet's fingerprints and DNA had been taken, she took her shower and dressed in jeans, a pale-yellow blouse, and gold stud earrings. When she came back into the living room, her mother stood at the sliding glass doors watching men putting up fresh yellow crime scene tape and carrying evidence containers.

Tears streamed down Sera's face and Juliet put her arm around her mother's shoulders. 'Why don't you come away from the windows, Mom? It's upsetting and there's nothing we can do.'

'I know. When they came right after we found your father, I didn't watch. I was so stunned I think I just collapsed on the couch. I really don't remember. But now . . . having to do it all over again because maybe someone *murdered* Owen—' She made a tortured, bleating sound. 'Oh God, I never thought something like this could happen.'

'None of us did.'

'Kyle Hollister is out there. Do you remember him, Juliet?'

'Yes. I used to date him but Dad didn't approve.'

'Oh, I remember.' Sera frowned. 'Owen said something vague about Kyle not being right for you.'

'Did it have anything to do with Gary's drug use? Did he think Kyle was doing drugs with Gary? Or that Kyle was supplying drugs to Gary?'

'He never said so to me, dear. I only know Owen thought Kyle was very good-looking and didn't want you to fall for him because you were so young. I was also surprised when you didn't put up more of an argument about breaking up with him.'

'We only went out for a few months. I doubt his feelings for me went much beyond friendship. Mine didn't for him, in any case. I cared more about pleasing Dad than I did about dating Kyle. I didn't tell him Dad didn't want me to see him. I just let things drift. It was an easy break-up. Hardly even a real break-up.'

'Well, he's had some girlfriends, but he never married,' Sera said.

'I don't think that's because I broke his heart. Besides, he's only twenty-eight and great-looking. There might be hope for him yet, Mom. Alec's even *older*!'

Finally, Sera grinned. 'Maybe Kyle will be like Davis Dawson and wait until he's in his fifties to marry.'

'Davis was married for a couple of years when he was in his late twenties.'

'Oh, that's right, I forgot. I only met her a couple of times. I didn't care for her. Now what was her name?'

'Mom, I don't mean to be rude, but I think we should go out, get away from here for a while. It would be good for us.'

'Should we leave? What if they need us?'

'What would the police need us for, Mom? We're not crime scene analysts. They know what they're doing.'

'They might get thirsty.'

Juliet immediately thought of Belle Maddox offering her Lipton's iced tea. 'Please, Mom. *I* want to leave. I don't want to see them processing the tree house.'

Finally, Sera nodded. 'You're right. This is upsetting.'

'Good. And wear something pretty.'

In a few minutes, Sera returned wearing a short-sleeved, pink-patterned A-line dress. 'Does this look too happy under the circumstances?' she asked Juliet.

'It looks beautiful. So does your hair. I like it best loose.'

Alec strode into the room. 'What's the agenda for today?'

'The funeral home,' Sera said reluctantly. 'I know – that's even more depressing than here and I dread it, too, but we have to make arrangements for Owen. Let's get it over with as soon as possible.'

When they walked outside, Eddie was already at work trimming the box hedges. 'Eddie!' Sera exclaimed. 'I didn't know you were coming today and you're here so early!'

Juliet knew Deke Nevins had probably driven the boy out of the trailer as soon as the sun rose to earn money. She hadn't mentioned her visit to Belle's home yesterday or the dismay she'd felt at what she'd found. Eddie looked at her uncertainly for a moment.

'I asked Eddie to come today,' Juliet said quickly. 'The lawn should look perfect for any visitors we have after Dad's funeral. He'd want that,' she ended lamely.

'Yes, ma'am.' Eddie smiled although he looked sad. 'Mr Reid was real particular about his lawn.'

'The police are here, Eddie. They're inspecting the tree house one last time,' Juliet explained. 'If you have any trouble – if Wendell comes back – let them know. If they've already left and you're still working, I want you to call me.'

'Um, I don't have a cell phone, Miss Reid.'

'It's Juliet. And here's mine.' She handed it to him. 'We'll leave the garage door open. Go in there, close the door, and call the police, anyone who can help. I mean it, Eddie. We don't know what Wendell might be capable of and I don't want you at risk.'

'Thank you, ma'am. Juliet.' Eddie took the phone. 'I'll be real careful with it.'

'Has Wendell really been such a problem for Eddie?' Sera asked as they walked toward the cars.

'He thinks Eddie is his brother and . . . well, shouldn't be working for you.'

'His brother! The one who died?'

'I guess,' Juliet said.

'Benny – Benjamin. He was cute and smart and loved Wendell. Wendell worshipped him. Benny was only six when he died. A bad case of measles. The Booths didn't believe in vaccinations, not even for smallpox and polio, and Benny's measles followed a bout of the flu. Wendell changed after Benny died. He was often angry with people before, but *after* Benny died . . . well, you know what he was like.'

Juliet remembered years ago Wendell walking around the neighborhood talking and laughing with a darling little blond-haired boy who gazed at Wendell as if he were a god. Then the boy was gone and Wendell walked endlessly and cried. One day months after Benny's death, as she walked to Leslie's, she'd passed Wendell. She'd met his swollen eyes and said, 'Wendell, I'm so sorry about Benny.' Wendell had glared at her and snarled, 'You leave me alone or I'll . . . I'll do some-thing *awful* to you!' She'd never looked directly at him again.

'Oh, my,' Sera fretted. 'Wendell's dangerous. I don't understand why Wendell is allowed to wander around like an innocent man.'

'Because in the eyes of the law, he *is* an innocent man,' Alec said tautly.

Sera closed her eyes. 'That makes me sick, like it did Owen.'

'Me, too. But that's the way it is.' Alec looked at Sera. 'We have to accept it, no matter how hard it is to swallow.'

'I guess so.'

'I think it's best that we take two cars,' Alec said, changing the subject. 'I'll follow you to the funeral home and then on to the church to make arrangements. I'll come back here to keep an eye on Eddie.'

'Oh, my lord,' Sera moaned. 'How I wish Owen were here to help me deal with this. But that's a good idea, Alec. Don't you think so, Juliet?'

'It's an excellent idea. We'll see you in a few minutes, Alec.'

Alec tried to remain calm and stalwart during their time with the funeral director, but it was an effort. His office was heavy and ornate; he was short, round, and rosy-cheeked and talked non-stop. Alec had noticed Juliet's hands clenching and Sera's beginning to shake when the director's wife came in with a kind smile and a tray with a tea service. Everyone except the director had a cup of hot tea. Afterward, they looked at caskets. When Alec's parents and sister had been killed in the car wreck and his grandfather had died of a stroke on news of the deaths, there had been no one to call on except Owen. He'd been Alec's father's friend since childhood and legal guardian of his son since there were no other living family members. Owen had made all the funeral arrangements, including selecting the caskets. Now, although he was a man, when the person lying inside the beautiful, padded box would be Owen, Alec could barely bring himself to inspect caskets, much less ask questions. At last Sera had chosen an oak model and the director's face took on a pinched expression because it was less expensive than the mahogany model he'd been pushing.

Next they had gone to the church. The minister was kind and comforting without being melancholy. The Reids had been members of the church for many years and the minister recalled how they'd helped with picnics in the summer, how one year Fin had written the Christmas church play, and how Owen had always made himself available for spring and fall fairs. They decided on the church reception hall for the gathering afterward because Sera was afraid their house would be too crowded. Owen had many friends.

When they left the church, Sera's mood seemed to have improved. She even smiled, looked up at the cerulean sky, and said, 'What a beautiful day.'

'Mom, I didn't bring home anything suitable for a funeral,' Juliet remarked gently. 'Would you go downtown with me to get something?'

'Oh. I don't think I have anything, either,' Sera said. 'I have a black dress but Owen hated it. I won't wear anything he hated to his funeral. He wouldn't know but . . .' Her chin trembled slightly. 'Maybe navy blue? Or lavender? Lavender used to be considered half-mourning.'

Juliet smiled. 'I think that would be fine.' She looked at Alec. 'Are you coming with us?'

He glanced at his watch. 'I think I'll go back to the house and keep an eye on things.' He put on his black wire-framed sunglasses. 'Maybe they've finished with the tree house and Eddie is there alone.' He grimaced. 'Anyway, I'm not in the mood to try on clothes, but you two take your time.'

When Alec arrived home, Eddie was gathering hedge trimmings and putting them in a trash bag. He looked up and smiled when Alec got out of the car and walked toward Eddie. 'Are the cops still here?'

'They left about half an hour ago. I know it's none of my business, but I wondered why they were back. Did something else happen?'

'No, thank God.' Alec began gathering clippings and adding them to the bag. 'They're just being thorough.'

'Oh.' Eddie was silent for a moment than burst out, 'I can't figure out why Owen killed himself! Gosh, he had *everything*! Everybody loved him. *I* loved him!' He wiped a hand quickly across his face, smearing tears. 'I'm acting like a baby. I'm sorry.'

'It's all right. I loved him, too, Eddie. My parents were killed when I was sixteen and Owen took me in and treated me like a son. My folks had left me enough money to pay for my college tuition, but I spent all of my school vacations here with Owen and Sera. This became my home. I'm baffled by what Owen did. Baffled, horrified, and . . . well, mad. There. I said it. I'm mad at him for hurting so many people.'

'Wow.' Eddie looked at him wide-eyed. 'You feel exactly like I do.'

'And like Juliet does. Don't blame yourself. It's a natural reaction.' He gave Eddie a wry smile. 'At least I think it is. You, Juliet, and I can't all be awful people for being angry with Owen as well as loving him.'

Eddie seemed to relax. 'I don't know you and Juliet very well but you seem like nice people, so I guess it's OK. My mom's boyfriend Deke's been asking me a hundred questions about it. He used to know Fin.'

'So Deke says he and Fin were friends?'

'Well, I don't know about that. Deke said he was older than Fin and they had some kind of fight over a band – Fin's band. Deke said Fin was mean to him.'

'But he still liked Owen?'

'I don't think so.' Eddie immediately froze. 'Uh, he didn't say why. Besides, Deke gets drunk and rambles about how nobody likes him. Please don't tell anyone what I said.'

The boy had an anxious look in his eyes. *He's scared to death of Deke*, Alec thought, *and he's lying to protect him.* He smiled easily. 'It's already forgotten, Eddie. Don't worry.' The boy relaxed slightly but Alec could tell he was still upset. 'I'm going inside and I'll let out Hutch. He's probably in need of a bathroom break. We were gone longer than I expected.'

'OK. I'll get the hose and water all the shrubs and the flower beds.'

'I think the hose is curled up on the patio. After you're finished, we'll have a Coke.'

Eddie grinned. 'That sounds good.'

Not long after, flower beds watered and soft drinks finished, Alec said, 'I'll take you home, Eddie.'

Eddie stood up. 'Oh, that's not necessary.'

'Sure it is. Why pass up a free ride?'

On their way to Eddie's, Alec asked, 'Would you like to go to Owen's funeral the day after tomorrow?'

Eddie looked surprised. 'Well, sure I would. Can I?'

'We talked about it last night. Sera and Juliet want you to come, too.'

'Gosh. I don't have a suit to wear or money to buy flowers—'

'None of that matters. I'm sure Owen would want you to be there. He thought a lot of you, Eddie. I hope you know that.'

Tears rose in Eddie's eyes. 'I thought a lot of him, too. I don't remember my father very well – he died when I was six – but I like to think he was like Owen.' After a moment, Eddie said, 'I know your dad and Owen were friends. Was he like Owen?'

'Well, sort of. He wasn't as outgoing as Owen. He was a lawyer with a very busy practice. He wasn't home a lot, but he always took my mother and little sister and me on great vacations. Once we went to Aspen in Colorado, and I learned to ski. Another time we went to Hawaii. He could be a lot of fun but he was stricter than Owen, especially with me. He wanted me to be a success.'

'You are.'

Alec laughed. 'I'm not sure being a security guard is what he had in mind for me.'

'But Sera told me you're a supervisor with a really big company in New York. That's an important job.'

'I'm an assistant supervisor but I hope to be the supervisor one day. Do I turn left here?'

'Right. We live about a half-mile down the road.' Alec saw six mobile homes, all well-maintained with nice wooden porches surrounded by trimmed shrubs. 'We live in the tan-and-brown one at the end.'

When Alec saw the place, he would have described it as a tan, brown and heavily rusted trailer. Its two broken windows were covered with cardboard and there was no skirting from the trailer's bottom to the ground. As soon as he pulled up, Deacon stepped out on a tiny, shabby wooden porch dressed in cut-offs and a ripped T-shirt.

'Is Eddie getting chauffeured from work these days?' he called as they climbed from the car.

'It was on my way,' Alec lied. 'How are you?'

'Fine. You're Alex Wainwright, aren't you?'

'*Alec*. Alec Wainwright.'

'Whatever.' Deke looked at Eddie. 'Is my boy doing a good job over at the Reids' place?'

'I'm not your boy,' Eddie mumbled.

'What was that? What did you say to me?'

'I'm not your boy. I mean your son. You don't have to worry about me.'

'I have to worry about you because you're Belle's kid and don't you talk smart to me!'

Belle appeared behind Deke, her straw-like hair hanging to her shoulders, her face creased and worried. 'What's wrong?'

'I'm takin' care of it,' Deke barked. 'Go on inside.'

'Eddie, are you hurt?'

'No, Mom. I'm fine. Mr Wainwright just gave me a ride home.'

'Oh. Well, that was nice of him. Thank you, Mr Wainwright.'

'I heard Wendell Booth's been a pest,' Deke said.

Belle looked alarmed. 'Yes. He's not a danger to Eddie, is he?'

'Not so far. We're talking to the sheriff about the situation.'

'Maybe Eddie shouldn't work for you anymore,' Belle fretted.

'Now we don't have to get all riled up over nothing,' Deke said to Belle, then looked at Alec. 'Belle gets emotional, downright hysterical, like all women.' He gave Alec a man-to-man dismissive smirk.

'But I'm worried.'

'Belle!' Deke snapped. 'I said it's fine for Eddie to work for the Reids.'

In other words, Alec thought, *you don't want to lose a dollar of Eddie's income.*

Belle seemed to shrink behind Deke, but she said, 'I guess if Deke thinks it's all right, Eddie can keep working for you if he wants to. Do you, Eddie?'

'Yes, ma'am.'

'I remember you, Alec,' Deke said suddenly. 'I hadn't left Fin Reid's amateur band yet when you came to live at the Reids. You weren't all that friendly. The guys thought you acted better than us.'

Alec didn't think the boys in Fin's band had thought much about him at all, but he tried to be agreeable. 'I'm sorry they felt that way. I didn't think I was better than them – if I was quiet and distant, it was because I was depressed. My family had just been killed in a car wreck.'

'Oh, that's a shame,' Belle said sympathetically. 'I'm sorry.'

'Thank you, Mrs Maddox. I appreciate that.' He smiled at the woman. 'I have a request. Eddie would like to attend Owen Reid's funeral day after tomorrow. The family would like for him to be there. May I pick him up at one thirty?'

Alec could tell Deke badly wanted to say no just for the hell of it, but he stayed quiet. Belle smiled back at him. 'That's nice of them. He doesn't have a suit, though.'

'I know. It doesn't matter. Slacks and a shirt will be fine.' Alec turned to Eddie. 'See you at one thirty.'

Eddie smiled and nodded, then turned and walked slowly to the small, dilapidated trailer he called home.

While Alec was gone, Sera and Juliet arrived home, Sera flushed and flustered, tossing her shopping sacks on the couch. 'I think I got on Lillian's nerves.' She referred to the owner of Longworth Style. 'She's a great salesperson and has wonderful taste in clothes, but I didn't like her being so determined I should wear black. When I told her Owen didn't like me in black and she kept showing me one black outfit after another, and I tried on a couple and I *did* look dreadful and I *told* her . . .'

Sera's voice went on and on as she drew clothes from sacks and recounted nearly every single thing that had happened on the shopping trip. Finally, Juliet said tiredly, 'I know, Mom. I was there.'

'Well, didn't you think Lillian was being pushy?'

'Yes, but she *can* be pushy, which you know after shopping there for years. How about a cocktail to calm your nerves?'

Sera dropped onto a chair. 'That sounds wonderful.'

Juliet could hear Hutch scratching on the basement door. Maybe Alec and Eddie had gone down to look at something and Hutch had gotten trapped. 'I'm sure Hutch needs to go out by now. I'll take him then fix you something good to drink.'

Juliet opened the basement door and Hutch lurched through it then ran through the living room to the sliding doors over-looking the back lawn, chuffing and growling ferociously, pawing frantically at the glass. 'What's wrong with him?' Sera asked.

'Something more serious than needing a bathroom break.' Juliet slid open a door and the dog charged outside, rushing to the woods. 'Hutch!' she called then ran after him.

The dog stayed ahead of her, barking frantically. Juliet caught sight of Frank Greenlee standing in his backyard, cell phone in hand, as he watched them. In moments, Hutch had entered the woods and was racing up the stairway to the tree house. Juliet kept running, calling, 'Hutch! Stop!' But the dog was on a mission.

Hutch had reached the platform of the tree house, barking and snarling by the time Juliet caught up with him. She reached for the dog's collar and tried to pull him back from the door, but the dog was strong and frenzied. Finally, she heard a loud, human voice inside jabbering crazily and saw that the handle on the door hung uselessly, beaten free of the wood. Still holding Hutch's collar, she pushed the door open.

Inside stood Wendell Booth, with his hands over his ears. He looked at her and began screaming.

SIX

'Wendell!' Juliet yelled. 'Wendell, be quiet! No one's going to hurt you!'

Wendell screamed again and again, flailing his arms and kicking. 'You gotta leave! This is my place. Boys only. You're not allowed!'

'This is not your place,' Juliet said loudly. 'You're trespassing!'

'Trespassing, you devil! Now that *he's* gone it's *mine*. I won't let *you* have it!' He threw back his head and screeched.

Every one of Wendell's shrieks sent shockwaves through Juliet's nerves. She was terrified. She wanted to pull Hutch out of there and run, but she could barely hold onto his collar to prevent him from attacking Wendell. What would happen if he bit Wendell? Would they put him down? She leaned back on the collar with all her strength as the dog struggled to drag her forward toward an enraged Wendell.

'Wendell, stop screaming,' she persisted. 'Calm down.'

'I won't! I *can't*!'

'I'll call the police.'

'No, you can't! Where's your phone? I don't see a phone.'

'It's in my pocket.'

'Liar, liar, pants on fire!' He picked up a wicker chair, crashed it against the floor and shattered it. Juliet shielded her eyes from flying shards of rattan. 'Get outta my *house*, *devil*!'

Hutch snarled, saliva dripping from his jowls as he lunged toward Wendell. Juliet clutched his collar, which was chaffing and burning her weakening hand.

'Wendell, you're upset and mixed up. This isn't your house. You've never even been in here.'

'I *have*! I was lookin' around and Fin came in and he didn't do nothin' to me except talk about music. That shows he didn't care if I shared his house. It *shows*!'

It showed that Fin knew better than to get into a fight with Wendell Booth, Juliet thought.

She heard steps pounding up the wooden staircase. 'I've got a leash!' Frank Greenlee called. 'Juliet, let me help with the dog.'

'Frank!' Juliet gasped over her shoulder. 'Thank God! We need the police!'

'I called nearly five minutes ago when you were running across the backyard with Hutch. I saw someone going up the stairs earlier, but the tree limbs were in the way.' He took hold of Hutch's collar and managed to attach the leash. 'OK, boy, it's time for you to back off.'

The dog still jumped and barked but didn't growl at Frank, who led the strong, agitated dog down the steps to the yard. 'Juliet!' he called. 'Get out of there!' But Juliet stood frozen, looking at Wendell hunched over, sobbing, stomping his feet like a child. Then she heard the police siren and Wendell screamed again.

'Don't be frightened, Wendell,' she said, amazed at how calm her voice was now. 'Go along with the police. They won't hurt you.'

'They'll put me in jail like they did before! They don't understand that I was Fin's *friend* until he didn't like my music. I practiced and practiced. Deacon helped me.'

'Deacon did?'

'Yeah. He taught me how to play "Enter Sandman" by Metallica and "Satisfaction" by The Rolling Stones on the recorder and got Fin to listen to me. I was good but Fin said I couldn't be in the band and then I hated him.'

For the first time in ten years, Juliet felt a twinge of sympathy for Wendell. 'Enter Sandman' and 'Satisfaction' on a recorder. Deacon had been having fun with Wendell. Petty, cruel fun with someone who already had serious mental problems. That's what had turned the man into Fin's mortal enemy.

The siren had stopped a few seconds earlier and Juliet heard two sets of feet coming carefully up the steps. Juliet took two slow, small steps out the door. 'You're a good guy, Wendell. All you have to do is keep being a good guy, being calm—'

Wendell caught sight of Davis Dawson and let out a howl. 'You *tricked* me! People are always *trickin'* me! I want my mom! I want Benny!'

'If you come with us, you can see your mom,' Davis said. 'You'll take me home?'

'I'm afraid we have to take you to police headquarters first.'

'You'll throw me in jail!'

Davis stepped farther into the room. 'Come with me, Wendell,' he said, 'you aren't under arrest now.'

'Yes, I will! You've got it in for me! My dad told me so!'

Davis took a step closer to Wendell, Kyle Hollister following him. 'Wendell—'

'You!' Wendell pointed at Kyle. 'You talked about me at my trial! You're a liar!'

'Wendell, I didn't lie . . .'

Davis stepped closer to Wendell. 'We'll sort this out later. Right now we want you to come with us peaceably. No harm will come to you—'

'*Liar! Judas!* Followers of the witch Sera! You're under her spell. I know all about her. She'll get what's comin' to her!'

Muscular, six-foot-seven, two-hundred-forty-pound Wendell stomped his feet and jumped up and down. Juliet heard an ominous pop followed by the creaking of wood. Then the tree house slanted slightly. Her heart pounded as she and the men braced themselves.

Wendell picked up the small table, swiping the legs at Davis.

'Stop it, Wendell!' Davis shouted. 'The house is going to crack. Dammit, *stop* it!'

Wendell, holding tightly to the table, lunged at Davis, barely missing his abdomen and chest. Davis pulled out a taser and aimed it at Wendell. Although Davis didn't fire, Wendell immediately wailed and dropped the table. Davis and Kyle charged with incredible speed and grabbed Wendell's shoulders. They wrestled his arms behind his back and snapped on handcuffs. Wendell shrieked one last time, then began crying. 'Don't hurt me! Don't hurt me!'

Wendell went limp and the two police officers had to nearly drag him carefully down the steps. When they reached the lawn, at first he refused to stand. They pulled him along, Juliet and Frank following them, Frank still holding back Hutch. At last Wendell decided to use his feet to shamble along. Frank chained Hutch to a post on the patio where Sera stood rigid, her face white, her mouth open, and her eyes wide and horrified.

Alec arrived home in time to see Davis and Kyle putting a weeping Wendell Booth into the back of a patrol car. He rushed to the car. 'What in the name of God happened?'

'Wendell decided to visit the tree house,' Davis said, circling the car and climbing into the driver's seat. 'Juliet and Sera are here. No one got hurt. Ask them what happened. I'm in a hurry.'

Alec went in the house to find Sera standing in the living room looking stunned while Juliet hugged her. 'It's all right, Mom. He's gone now. Everything's fine.'

'You're not fine,' Sera quavered. 'Your hand.'

Juliet lifted the hand that had held Hutch's collar. 'I'm just scuffed up a little bit.'

Alec led Juliet to the kitchen sink, gently rinsed her hand and gave her two ibuprofen. Then he said, 'Now tell me what happened, Juliet.'

By seven o'clock, Alec, Sera, and Juliet had eaten a light dinner then settled down for the evening. Sera asked Juliet, 'Are you sure you're all right, honey?'

'I'm fine. Bullets bounce off me.'

'I could tell by the way you were trembling after Wendell's visit,' Alec said dryly.

'Can you play the piano, honey, or does your hand hurt too much? I haven't heard you play since you've been home.'

'My hand is fine, Mom. I'd love to play the piano.' Juliet took her seat and Hutch, who'd finally calmed down after his exciting afternoon, came to lie beside her. The room was dim with only soft lamplight turned on near the piano. Sera lay on the couch in a long, pink satin robe while Alec sipped a glass of white wine. Juliet was two minutes into the Chopin's 'Raindrop' Prelude when the doorbell rang.

'Oh, hell,' Alec muttered. '*Now?*'

It rang again. And again.

'All right, give it a rest!' Alec nearly snarled and opened the door to see Mr and Mrs Booth, Wendell's parents.

'I'm Hannah Booth. Who are you?' Mrs Booth had a round face, lashless light blue eyes, a wide nose, and jowls. She was thick and muscular and stood at least six inches taller than her husband.

'I'm Alec Wainwright, Mrs Booth.'

'You're that orphan the Reids took in 'cause no one else wanted you.' She paused, clearly waiting for an enraged reply, but Alec merely stared at her. 'Me and Micah want to talk to you about what you did to Wendell this afternoon.'

'No one did anything to Wendell. He was in the tree house and wouldn't leave. A neighbor called the police. Wendell got . . . agitated . . . and the police had to take him away.'

'They *arrested* him!' Micah shouted. His brown eyes were magnified by the thick lenses of his glasses. The top of his head was nearly bald, a few strands of white hair slicked down with oil, and dark age spots speckled his face and scalp.

'They didn't arrest him, Mr Booth, because Mrs Reid wouldn't press charges – even though he was trespassing and badly damaged property.'

'They took him away. After all he's been though!'

'Mrs Booth, from what I understand, they're only detaining him for forty-eight hours so they can do an evaluation.'

'Evaluation my ass!' Micah boomed. 'They're going to give him shock treatments and shoot him full of experimental drugs!'

'I doubt if he'll get a shock treatment and he won't be given experimental drugs. If we're lucky, he'll be prescribed proven drugs that will help to control his behavior.'

'There's nothing wrong with his behavior!' Hannah retorted.

'Oh no? Ask the people who witnessed his behavior this afternoon. He almost brought down the whole tree house! He thinks the tree house is his. He thinks Eddie Maddox is his brother, Benny. He needs medication to keep him calm and rational. And he needs *you* to keep him home and out of trouble!'

In spite of all of Micah's bluster, it was Hannah with her

bulging, light eyes who gave Alec the impression of barely suppressed fury.

Sera, dressed in her pink satin robe, appeared behind Alec. 'What's the problem now?'

Both of the Booths gasped and stepped backward when they saw her. 'The witch!' Micah exploded. 'She practices black magic and you've set her on us!'

'This is Sera Reid. She is not a witch and she doesn't practice black magic,' Alec said coldly. 'You're standing on *her* porch. If you can't be polite, get off her property before she has to have you removed.'

Micah looked horrified. 'She'll put a curse on us if we don't get off her property!'

'Oh, dear,' Sera said in dismay. She began to tremble as she looked at the Booths. 'I don't want trouble with Wendell—'

'*Witch!*' Hannah hissed. 'You'll pay for your evil doings.'

Juliet came to Sera, put her arms around her mother and gently urged her away from the doorway. Meanwhile, Alec stepped onto the porch, pulling out his cell phone.

'Either you leave right this minute or I'm calling the sheriff. His patience is wearing thin with the Booth family. If you don't want some real legal trouble, you should go home and don't *ever* come back here. That goes for your son, too.'

Alec slammed the door and locked it. He looked out the window and saw the Booths head to their car, get in and drive away, but the evening was ruined.

Six hours later, Alec was slipping into the familiar dream about Afghanistan when barking dragged him back to the present. His partially closed bedroom door flew open and a heavy weight landed on the bed, licking his face. 'Wha . . . what? Hutch?' he managed as the dog trampled around the bed, barking relentlessly. 'What's wrong?' Alec demanded, as if the dog could answer.

Hutch jumped off the bed and dashed to the bedroom window, nosing aside the curtains. Alec got up and looked out to see—

Fire! He pushed the curtains wider, looking in horror at the entire span of the tree house being hungrily devoured by flames that darted upward, catching the branches of overhanging trees, sending flickering sparks into the night, ferociously lighting the quiet darkness. After a few moments of frozen shock, Alec flung himself across his double bed and reached for his cell phone on the nightstand. He'd just dialed 911 when Juliet appeared at his open doorway in her nightgown, her thick hair falling around her face.

'The tree house,' she whispered in dread. 'The whole thing's burning.'

He held up a hand while he gave their address to the 911 operator and said urgently, 'There's a big fire in a structure at the back of this house and including the woods bordering Argent Creek.'

'Oh my God,' Juliet breathed as Hutch jumped up and put his front paws on the windowsill, parting the curtains and barking again. Wood crackled loudly before the tree house crashed to the ground. 'Did someone deliberately set fire to it?'

'I have no doubt,' Alec said grimly, wrapping his arm around her nearly naked shoulders and kissing the top of her head. 'Maybe to destroy evidence.'

SEVEN

J uliet turned on the coffeemaker, emptied a can of food into Hutch's bowl and slowly walked to the sliding glass doors of the living room. Outside lay trampled grass, wrecked flowerbeds, and the charred remains of trees that had supported Fin's tree house. Although firefighters had fought hard, flames had destroyed the entire tree house and the staircase as well as a few of the smaller trees that had surrounded it. 'I'm sorry, Fin,' Juliet murmured. 'Your fairy-tale house is gone. You're gone, your tree house is gone, your basement studio is damaged—'

'Juliet, are you all right?'

Juliet turned to face Alec, who was white with exhaustion. For hours she'd made coffee for the firefighters and offered soft drinks and iced water. Alec had helped her, then stayed up the rest of the night keeping watch over the backyard in case latent flames took life or anyone came back to do more damage. Juliet and her mother had gone to bed an hour after the fire trucks had awakened half the neighborhood and left the woods a sodden, acrid-smelling mess. 'I can't believe that this time yesterday, the lawn looked so beautiful,' she said dismally.

'The damage could have been worse if Hutch hadn't set off the alarm so quickly.' Hutch pawed at the door. 'I'll take him out on the leash,' Alec said. 'We don't want him nosing around too much in all the burnt rubble. Besides, we don't know what set off the fire. The arson investigator won't be here for about an hour. By the way, starting tonight we're staying at the Heritage Inn. Frank has arranged it. I don't think it's safe for us here. Is that all right with you?'

'The Heritage?' Juliet asked. 'God, yes! That sounds wonderful.'

Juliet watched Alec walk Hutch around the backyard for a few minutes, then poured a cup of coffee and went in search of her mother. 'Mom?' she called.

'Out here.'

Juliet went to the room the Reids had added as an office for Sera. Juliet loved the cream-colored carpet and soft yellow couch and chair for people who came to see her mother for tarot readings and also for the small classes she held teaching about edible and poisonous plants and fungi. Boston and lady ferns grew in hanging pots and a crystal fan light was suspended from the ceiling. Sera sat at the antique honey oak roll-top desk that had belonged to her father. A table with a computer and printer stretched along one wall and windows with yellow draperies faced the front of the house. A sheer, ivory curtain panel hung over a tall, twenty-five-inch-wide window beside the door at the back of the room. A panel oak door with blue-and-yellow stained glass led out the front to a winding stone walkway edged with lush violets.

Sunlight filled the room and gleamed on her mother's long gold-and-silver hair. Juliet placed her hand on Sera's shoulder. 'Whatcha doin', Mama?'

Sera looked up and smiled. 'You haven't called me "Mama" since you were ten.'

'I know. This morning it seemed right.'

'I'm making a to-do list. So much has happened that I need a reminder of the things I should take care of in the next few days. And I want to do something else.' Sera pushed aside her notepad, reached into one of the desk's pigeonholes and pulled out a deck of tarot cards wrapped in a square of magenta silk. Juliet knew the deck and the silk square had belonged to her grandmother and Sera cherished them. She'd taught Juliet and Leslie with this deck. 'I'm so upset after the fire. I've decided to read the cards.'

'Is that a good idea?'

'Do you mean I might get a reading that says disaster is on the way? You know the cards don't predict death or illness.'

'Those aren't the only bad things that could happen.'

'Then I'd rather be forewarned. If you're worried, you don't have to stay.'

'No. I'm curious, too.' Juliet sat down on the couch. 'I'll be quiet and let you concentrate.'

Sera unwrapped the deck of cards. With them was a cherished honeymoon photo of Owen and her on a beach at sunset and a two-inch-long antique gold-and-garnet cross pendant – another possession of Sera's grandmother. She shuffled the cards, sorted them, then shuffled them again and picked up the card she'd chosen to represent herself, which Juliet knew was the Queen of Cups. She closed her eyes, forming her question, then she laid out ten cards face up and across each other. After she'd looked at the tenth card, revealing the final outcome, she shook her head and muttered, 'No. No.'

Sera gathered up the cards and went through the whole sequence again. Once more, at the end, she shook her head.

'What's wrong, Mom?'

'Umm . . . nothing.' Sera gathered up the cards. 'Nothing at all. I'm just not in tune with them today. I'm too distracted, I guess.'

Juliet had never heard her mother say she wasn't *in tune* with the cards, but Sera quickly placed the photo and the gold cross on top of the stack and rewrapped it in the silk, turned, and smiled brightly. 'Too much excitement, too much caffeine.' She pushed the cards aside. 'Let's start packing for the Heritage Inn.'

'I just called to see how you're doing this afternoon,' Leslie said.

'As well as can be expected seeing as Daddy's being buried tomorrow.'

'I'm so—'

'You don't have to say it again. I know how you feel.' Juliet looked out the window at a bright red cardinal streaking past the house. 'Tell me something to lift my spirits.'

'OK. Hell has frozen over.'

'Really? When did it happen?'

'This morning when Jon suggested we go out for a romantic dinner this evening. I think we're going to a place out of town called Pascal's. I already have a babysitter lined up and I'm trying to decide on a dress.'

'Les, that's great! Did you have to threaten him? Did Danielle?'

'No. He came up with it all on his own. He said he's been neglecting his wife. He's right, but I thought it would be rude to agree with him right then.'

Juliet laughed. 'It *would* have been. I'm just so glad—'

'Oh damn,' Leslie interrupted. 'Call waiting. If this is Jon cancelling on me—' She clicked off and in a moment was back. 'Well, it was a cancellation, all right. The babysitter. She's eighteen and I trust her. Everyone else available is about fifteen and I'm not leaving Tommy with a little girl. I won't leave him with Danielle, either. She'll stuff him full of sweets and he'll be on a sugar high until tomorrow. I can't believe this!'

'I'll babysit.'

'What? No, Juliet. That's very kind but I couldn't ask it of you.'

'You didn't ask. I'd like to get out of this house tonight, frankly, and I know you and Jon will be home before dawn.'

'*Way* before dawn.' Leslie giggled.

'Then let me do this for you. Please?'

'Great. You talked me into it. And you're the best friend anyone ever had.'

Juliet arrived at Leslie's at 6:45, never having mentioned that she, Sera, and Alec were now installed at the lovely Heritage Inn. She knew part of the reason Leslie had agreed to let her babysit was because she believed Juliet wanted to escape her home for the evening. Leslie opened the door dressed in corn-flower blue dress with a full skirt. Her complexion bloomed and her eyes sparkled. 'Hello! And thank you so much!'

'Spending time with Tommy is always a pleasure,' Juliet said, stepping inside. 'What are my instructions for the evening? Are we going to make prank calls, toilet-paper houses, blow up mailboxes?'

'I'm having second thoughts about you as a babysitter.' Leslie grinned. 'He can watch TV until eight. Then you can start trying to get him to bed. If he's in before eight thirty, you're a success.'

'Got it.' Jon walked into the room. 'My, you look handsome!'

'Thank you, kiddo. I have to look like I'm worthy of my beautiful wife.'

'I've never been to Pascal's,' Juliet said.

'Neither have we, but I've heard it's good. Don't let Tommy wear you out tonight, kiddo, and thanks for helping us out.'

Three hours later, Juliet peeked into Tommy's room. The glow from his nightlight showed he was sound asleep, clutching his giant stuffed polar bear named Rufus. She smiled, relieved that their evening had gone well and Tommy had been tired by eight from playing earlier in the day with a friend.

Now it was ten fifteen and she was alone for the first time in days. Juliet paced around the family room then turned on the television and sank onto the couch, idly flipping through channels to find something interesting. All the shows that started at ten were partly over. She wasn't in the mood to watch a news channel. Finally she settled on an older movie she'd seen before, *The Ring* with Naomi Watts.

Halfway through the movie, Juliet decided she wanted hot chocolate. She went to the kitchen that faced the back lawn, poured milk, and set the mug in the microwave oven. While the seconds ticked away, she opened the blinds and peered out one of the vertical windows surrounding the breakfast nook. A westerly breeze moved the ground-sweeping limbs of the giant weeping willow beyond the house. Tommy loved hiding in its shelter then bursting out, yelling, 'Surprise!' She smiled at the memory. Then she froze.

When the skinny limbs blew aside, she saw someone standing stone still a few feet from the tree trunk. She caught only the image of a tall, bulky form wearing a jacket and hood. And a ski mask.

The microwave 'ding' sounded like a gong. Juliet let out a cry, then dropped the blinds back into place and stepped away from the window. She waited a minute before slightly parting the blind again and peeking out. Once again the breeze blew, the branches swayed to the side, but no one stood by the tree.

Did I imagine that? Juliet asked herself as she removed her mug from the microwave. Was it a trick of the light? What light? The soft landscape lights around the terrace glowed but the tree stood at least twenty feet away from the lights. And there was a new moon – no moonlight to illuminate the lawn. *Yes, I imagined it*, she told herself.

Then the locked handle on the kitchen door slowly moved, then jiggled. Hot milk sloshed over Juliet's hand, but she didn't feel it. Her only reality was the doorknob. Why wasn't the security system screaming? Because Leslie had told her the security system had shut down yesterday. The maintenance men were swamped and couldn't repair it until the day after tomorrow. Leslie said Jon had been angry at the manager and told him yesterday, 'Wendell damned Booth is wandering around here free as a bird and we can't get our security fixed for *days*!'

Jiggle, jiggle, jiggle. Juliet's gaze was fixed on the door-knob. Then it stopped. She didn't bother wiping up the spilled milk. She slipped into the family room, glancing at all the windows with their shut draperies, then taking small, frightened steps toward the side door and, sure enough, within seconds the knob began the same turning, shaking movements as the kitchen knob. Then she remembered Leslie telling her all the doors leading to the outside of the house had deadbolts. Jon and Leslie would have not only locked the doors but shut the bolts before they left. She and Tommy were safe.

Suddenly the room seemed to shake with the loud thud of a boot kick. Juliet jumped and clapped a hand over her mouth to stifle a scream. She couldn't wake up Tommy – he'd be terrified. Another kick. Then another.

While *The Ring* rattled on in the background, she ran to an end table, picked up her phone and dialed 911. Her voice shook and for a moment she went blank when asked the address. Another blow hit the door. 'Did you hear that? Please, *please* send someone as fast possible!'

She was asked to stay on the line until the police arrived. Holding the landline handset, she went to the fireplace and picked up a poker. She'd never struck anyone in her life – certainly not with a weapon – but she'd seen so many movies in which the heroine defended herself with a fireplace poker, she was almost certain she could do it. She was absolutely certain she would do anything to protect Tommy. *Tommy*. The little boy was now slowly crouching down the stairs, his eyes wide, asking tremulously, 'Mommy, what's goin' on?'

'It's not Mommy, it's Juliet. Go lock yourself in your room, baby.'

Tommy cringed as another blow hit the door. 'Who's that? Is someone comin' to kill us?'

Tommy darted across to her and she pulled him behind the wide arm of the couch farthest away from the door. Time seemed suspended as they hunkered in terror, Tommy whimpering, Juliet breathing heavily as she gripped the poker in one hand and the phone in the other. At last, she heard the blessed sound of a siren in the night, coming nearer, nearer, then screeching to a halt right outside.

Tommy looked up at her. 'Police?'

She nodded.

'Good.' Then he started to cry.

In less than a minute, the doorbell rang and someone knocked on the door. 'They're here,' she said into the handset as a man yelled, 'Leslie, it's Kyle Hollister. Please open the door.'

'Kyle?' Juliet murmured. 'Kyle Hollister?' She raised her voice. 'Kyle! Kyle, just a minute!'

She held onto the poker and Tommy held onto her shirt tail as they rushed to the door. Juliet peeked out the sidelight, saw Kyle standing on the porch, unlocked and threw open the front door. 'Oh Kyle! Thank God!' She threw herself into his arms, crying and laughing at the same time.

'Juliet? What are you doing here?'

'I'm babysitting.'

'Well, it's OK now.' Kyle held her. 'Hi, Tommy. What's going on around here?'

'A man! A man's in the backyard,' Juliet jabbered. 'He was standing beside the weeping willow, staring at the house. Then he tried the kitchen door, then the family room door, then he started kicking it *so* hard! He still might be hiding.'

'Officer Sanders is circling the house. May I come in?'

'Yes! Oh, yes, sure!' She stepped aside, although she and Tommy still clung to each other.

'Where are Jon and Leslie?'

'At Pascal's for dinner. Their babysitter canceled at the last minute and I volunteered.'

Kyle looked at her with his handsome, concerned face. 'You're safe now,' he said calmly. 'Let's go in the kitchen and you can show me the tree where you first saw the man. You didn't recognize him?'

'He was beyond the terrace lights. He was tall. He looked big, bulky, and he had a hood and a mask, something like a ski mask, not a Halloween mask.'

They saw another officer with a high intensity flashlight walking behind the house. Kyle pecked on the window and motioned toward the tree. Officer Sanders walked to the tree and circled it, then looked up and shook his head. As he came back toward the house, Kyle pointed to the kitchen door. Sanders kneeled and after inspecting it carefully, stood and raised his shoulders. Kyle then stepped outside and said, 'It was the door to the family room to the right that he tried to kick in. Let's take a look.'

Juliet and Tommy walked back to the family room, still holding hands as Juliet clutched the fireplace poker. At that moment, she heard a noise at the front door, something that sounded like the rattling of the doorknob. She screamed and raised the poker and in an instant Jon stood only feet away from them. Tommy whooped joyfully, 'It's Daddy!' and Jon shouted, 'What the hell?'

Tommy threw himself at his father and Leslie stepped from behind Jon, looking aghast. 'What's going on?'

'Someone was here, trying to break in, but we're safe,' Juliet babbled. 'When the trouble started, I called the police . . .' Tears began streaming down her face. 'Oh, Leslie, I'm sorry.'

Kyle and Officer Sanders came in the front door and stood quietly as Leslie hugged a shaking Juliet then lifted Tommy. Finally, Jon turned to Kyle. 'What happened?'

'You had a prowler. Well, more than a prowler. He tried to get in the kitchen door and the family room door. He kicked the family room door hard a few times. There's some damage. Do you want to see it?'

'Hell yes, I want to see it! Someone tried to kick their way in? Why?'

'We don't know, Jon,' Kyle said patiently, 'but Juliet saw someone tall in a ski mask standing under the willow tree. Apparently, he'd been watching the place before he decided to come in or act like he was.'

'Was it Wendell Booth?' Jon demanded of Juliet.

'He had a mask on. The terrace lights aren't strong enough—'

'Was he as tall as Wendell?'

'I couldn't tell his exact height in the dark, Jon.'

'And our security system is on the blink! Of all the damned luck! Well, the system had better be fixed tomorrow or the company can forget the job on our new house, that's all I have to say,' Jon blustered. 'Kyle, show me the damage the bastard did.'

As Jon went outside with Kyle, Juliet, Leslie, and Tommy huddled close on the couch, Juliet quickly turning off the end of *The Ring*. Tommy's face and hair were still damp with perspiration and tears, and Juliet felt as if everything inside her were shaking.

Half an hour later, Juliet walked into her room at the Heritage Inn. She and Sera had taken the room with two double beds and Alec the one next door with a king-size bed. They'd brought Hutch's doggie bed and he slept in Alec's room. Juliet took off her jeans and top and fumbled over to the empty bed, not turning on any lights to disturb her mother. She'd just settled under the sheets when her mother mumbled, 'How was your evening, dear?'

'It was a night I'll never forget,' she answered truthfully.

EIGHT

Who had tried to break into Leslie and Jon's house? Had they known Jon was gone and thought they would give Leslie and Tommy a fright? Why? The questions echoed through Juliet's mind while the minister spoke at her father's funeral service. She was oblivious to his eulogy. The words had no meaning, stirred no emotion, evoked no memories. She felt numb and unnaturally calm, as if this experience were happening to someone else.

Flanked by Juliet and Alec, Sera, wearing a short-sleeved dusky blue jacket over a matching sheath dress, had linked her arm through Juliet's. She kept dabbing her eyes and nose with a tissue and occasionally patted Alec's arm. They stood for the hymn 'Amazing Grace' before Owen's casket was carried out by Davis Dawson, Frank Greenlee, Jon Tresswell, and Kyle Hollister.

Julia thought the church basement had been decorated beautifully for the reception with pink roses, daisies, and lavender chrysanthemums. Eddie had arrived with Alec for the funeral and had been glued to Juliet and Sera ever since. He wore khaki slacks and a light blue dress shirt, the pants and shirt sleeves two inches too short, with comb tracks in his sandy hair slicked down for the occasion. He was very quiet and watchful, clearly being careful about his manners and demeanor. Juliet was touched and she knew her father would have been, too.

While they sat, Jon and Leslie stopped by to express sympathy once again and compliment them on the loveliness of the service and the reception. They'd left Tommy at home with a sitter but said he'd sent his love. They drifted away to be followed by Danielle and Carole, Danielle wearing forest green and Carole golden brown, both looking beautiful. Danielle was especially warm to Eddie, which brought color to his cheeks, while Carole concentrated on Alec. Juliet wondered if he knew he was being singled out for special attention. Was Carole looking for husband number three?

At the reception, they were served cherry cheesecake at the end of a meal of ambrosia salad, baked chicken, mashed potatoes, and French green beans. Eddie finally spoke up, saying, 'Gosh, people sure eat a lot at funerals!' Alec, Sera, and Juliet laughed quietly for the first time and some of the heaviness lifted from their mood.

When guests were beginning to leave, Davis Dawson approached them with his very pregnant wife. 'Marcy said she hasn't gotten a chance to speak to you.' He clasped her arm, smiling.

'This has been such a sad time for you and you know you have Davis's and my sincerest sympathy.' She stood nearly a foot shorter than her husband, and her voice was soft and gentle. She had short, lightly curled ash brown hair and candid, velvety brown eyes set in a heart-shaped face with wide lips and a small, turned-up nose. She wore a dark tan wrap dress and tiny pearl stud earrings. Marcy was not a beauty like Carole or Danielle or Leslie, but she was unassumingly pretty and had an easy charm. 'If there is anything I can do for you, please let me know, even if you just need someone to talk to. I might be pregnant, but I'm not helpless.'

'That's sweet of you, Marcy,' Sera said. 'I have Juliet and Alec here to help me, but Alec will be leaving in a few days, so I might be calling on you.'

Marcy turned her attention to Eddie. 'Hello, Eddie. How nice that you could come today. I know how close you and Owen were.'

'I was glad I could come,' Eddie said softly. 'Mr Reid was awfully good to me.' He smiled. 'How are those impatiens doing?'

'Oh, they're beautiful!' She looked at Sera and Juliet. 'Eddie talked me into planting a small bed of them. Or rather *he* planted them. They're white, red, violet, pink – lovely. And he taught me how to take care of them, so they're thriving.'

Juliet glanced up to see Danielle watching them fixedly, her eyes moving between Marcy and Davis, her expression severe. Was she another one of the people who disapproved of Davis marrying a woman sixteen years his junior, or did she envy the pride in Davis's eyes when he looked at his young wife?

'I should have at least a preliminary report from the arson specialist by tomorrow, maybe this evening,' Davis was saying to Sera.

'Please let me know as soon as you learn something!' Sera sounded almost pleading. 'I'm just sick about my son's beautiful tree house being burned to the ground and I know it wasn't an accident.'

Another man walked up to say goodbye and Davis took Marcy's hand, nodding to Sera, Alec, and Juliet. 'I'll be in touch.'

Alec dropped off Juliet and Sera at the inn and immediately left to take Eddie home. Without speaking, they went to their bedroom, took off their dressy clothes and slipped into robes. 'I may never wear that dress again,' Sera said.

'That blue looked beautiful on you, Mom. It really brought out your eyes.'

'Thank you, but the memories . . .' Sera put her hands over her face. 'Maybe I'll just put it in the back of my closet and not look at it for at least a year.'

'Good idea. I'll do the same with my beige dress.'

'Lillian called it "spun sugar."' Sera looked around. 'I'm glad I decided on a catered reception at the church rather than having all those people at the house, staring out at the ugly remains of the tree house. Of course, I'll probably faint when I get the bill.'

'You got estimates and they weren't bad.'

'I know I got some cost cuts, especially from Pauline on the flowers. I worked there until four days ago, for heaven's sake. I feel awful for deserting her. Hollisters' restaurant also cut their bill. Pauline and the Hollisters are old friends but I feel like I took advantage of them.'

'You made the right choice, Mom. I'm just relieved it's over. We held it together well during the funeral, though,' Juliet said as she curled up in a chair.

'Yes. No hysterics, even from me. I actually feel calm, but I know what I've been through the last few days will hit me tomorrow. I was happy Belle let Eddie come.'

'Deke rules the household so I'm sure it was with his permission that Eddie was allowed to attend. He probably thought Eddie would lose his job if he didn't come. The boy needs some new clothes. Belle and Deke seem unaware that Eddie is growing.'

'Or they don't care. Poor Eddie. I'm afraid he's going to quit school and run away, especially now that your father is gone.'

Juliet's cell phone rang. It lay on the table beside her and in a moment, Frank Greenlee said, 'I didn't want to disturb your mother. Are you two all right?'

'Yes. Tired but OK.'

'I was glad Eddie came to the funeral.'

'We were, too, although we didn't know if his mother and that lout she lives with would let him. Do you know Deke Nevins?'

'I met him years ago when Gary was in Fin's band. So was Nevins although he didn't last long. I'm surprised he's still alive, but his kind seems to have a talent for living while the good guys like Gary and Fin . . .' He swallowed hard. 'Anyway, I wanted to check on the two of you and let you know that Nancy called from Miami.'

'She *did*?'

Frank's ex-wife had left him nearly ten years ago, a month after Gary's death. The divorce was amicable, although Frank had begun drinking to the point that Owen had worried he might lose his job at the inn. Nancy hadn't kept in touch with any of her Parrish friends.

'I was surprised, too, Juliet,' Frank said. 'I haven't heard from her for years, but someone emailed her about Owen. She wanted me to tell you and Sera how sorry she is about him.'

'We appreciate her concern.'

'I'll let you relax now.'

'Thanks for calling. Bye, Frank.' She hung up and looked at her mother. 'Nancy's in Miami but she says her thoughts are with us.'

'Oh, that makes me feel so much better,' Sera said sarcastically. 'Nancy and I were never good friends. She came from a fairly affluent family in Florida and always gave the impression

she thought she'd married beneath her. She wasn't happy with
Frank but she loved Gary and while he and Fin were growing
up she was always pleasant to me. She changed several months
before Gary died. She wasn't mean – just distant. After Gary
died, she went utterly cold and left Frank immediately. First
Gary's death then Nancy leaving – I thought he was going to
have a complete breakdown. Nancy was already back in
Florida when Fin died and she only sent flowers and a brief,
chilly condolence note. She didn't even call.' She huffed in
remembered anger. 'I know I must have asked you this at the
time, but did you know Gary was using drugs before he
overdosed?'

'No. But when Carole was here, she told me she thought
Fin was suspicious. Gary's guitar playing and his behavior got
erratic.'

'If Nancy knew there was a problem, she would never have
said a word to me. But Frank? I'm sure he would have told
Owen, who didn't say anything to me. Of course, Owen wasn't
as open with me as I was with him. He never wanted to worry
me. He shielded me from so much. But I knew something was
wrong . . .' Sera shook her head. 'Several months before Gary
died, he changed. At first, we just didn't see much of him.
Then, when we did, he wasn't as nice or polite. And he looked
sloppy. Not even very clean.'

'Well, Gary's death was a terrible surprise to me and a
tragedy for Fin.'

'I got the feeling that Nancy held Frank responsible,' Sera
said. 'That's ridiculous, but the way she looked at him . . .
like he'd done something wrong. She was mad at him.' She
paused then asked abruptly, 'Do you believe Carole is interested in Alec?'

'I believe she's interested in flirting with him. Why? Don't
you like Carole?'

'Yes. I always have. But she's been married twice and
she's not even thirty. That's not a very good track record.
Hmmm . . . I hope she and Alec don't fall in love. He's so
hard-working and responsible, and she's a wild child. That
could be a *real* mess.'

Juliet was giggling when Alec came to their room, looking

tired. 'Deke insisted I have a beer with him. I didn't want him thinking I believe I'm too good for him, so I ended up having *two* beers while he held forth on what a glamorous and adventurous life he's had.'

'Oh, lord,' Sera said.

'I was trying to separate the lies from the truth,' Alec said. 'I'd like to know exactly how much of a threat he is.'

Juliet looked at him. 'A threat?'

'Yes. There's a look in his eyes and an edge in his voice like he wants to start a fight – he's just itching to start a fight.' Alec shook his head. 'And what's with his "I'm just a hick who don't know much" act? He didn't used to talk the way he does now or pretend he's not smart. I know he's not an intellectual but he's shrewd. I couldn't go to the police with any of that, but I don't like the idea of Eddie and Belle living with him.'

Sera said, 'Eddie has an aunt – a very nice lady, I'm told – who tried to get custody of him a few years ago. The court, in all of its wisdom, decided he'd be better off with his mother. She wasn't as bad then as she is now, but she neglected Eddie.'

'Carole told me Deke used to take drugs,' Juliet said.

Alec nodded. 'I'm sure he still does. Maybe Belle does, too. That might be why she keeps him around. He's her supplier.'

'Maybe, but why does he stay with *them*?' Juliet asked. 'It can't be for love.'

Alec scowled. 'That's what I'd like to figure out. What's his game? Belle doesn't earn a fortune working at that crummy bar Rocco's six nights a week and even though Eddie's doing fairly well with his lawn business this summer, school starts in the fall. Deke isn't being kept in style, at least not on Eddie's and Belle's incomes. There must be another reason.'

'You're sweet to care so much about Eddie.'

'You said Owen loved him, Sera. I barely know him, but I like him. I'm not sweet – nobody has ever said I'm *sweet* – I'm concerned about his situation.'

'You *are* sweet, even though you seem to think it isn't manly to admit it.' Juliet grinned, feeling a surge of warmth for him. 'It sounds like you've had a stimulating hour with Deke.'

'Stimulating isn't the word. I'm going to change out of this suit.' Alec went next door to his room and returned in jeans. He fixed everyone a drink from the minibar and for the next half an hour they talked about anything except the funeral.

Finally, Alec's phone rang. 'Hello, Davis,' he said.

Juliet and Sera watched him intently as he nodded and said 'Uh huh' and 'I see' and frowned. Finally, he clicked off and looked at them. 'The arson investigator found gasoline on the debris left from the tree house as well as four wooden matches.'

'Gasoline?' Sera quavered. 'That means the fire was set deliberately.'

'I think we already knew that.' Alec's dark gaze moved between Sera and Juliet. 'Now we have proof.'

NINE

'It's a beautiful day,' Juliet said the next morning.

'Isn't it?' Her mother beamed, standing and going to the window. 'How nice for the Fourth of July. The evening will be lovely for the fireworks.'

'Do you feel like going to the park to watch them or would you rather stay here?'

Sera smiled sadly. 'I always go to the park. I want to sit with you and Alec and Leslie and Tommy. He absolutely loves all the lights and noise just like Fin did when he was little.'

Alec asked, 'Who are we picking up to take to the park and at what time?'

'I think it'll be just the three of us,' Juliet said. 'Leslie said she's going with Jon and Tommy and Carole and Danielle. Frank says there's a party here and he'll be stuck. Davis will be with Marcy, of course.'

'Eddie?'

Juliet shrugged. 'I didn't ask. Besides, I don't want Deke thinking we want to take *his kid* away from him.'

'Even though we do.' Alec looked down at the dog. 'And Hutch?'

'He'll be staying here watching TV. He's terrified of fireworks.'

'Don't worry, boy. I think there are some good television shows on tonight,' Alec told Hutch.

'I'm glad I remembered to bring something for us to sit on tonight,' Sera said that evening as she tossed a gray-and-red wool blanket into Alec's car.

Juliet held up a can of insect repellent spray. 'We smell so strongly of lemon eucalyptus that no one will come near us.'

'Neither will fleas, mosquitoes, gnats, or ticks. It's safe for the whole family, even children.' Sera skimmed across the car's back seat. 'I hope they have concession stands. I already feel thirsty.'

'The city isn't going to pass up a chance to make money from permit fees by not having as many concession stands as possible.' Alec laughed as he got behind the steering wheel. 'You can have anything you want to drink.'

'Except a margarita, Mom. Unless you brought some mix and tequila.'

'Don't put it past me. Well, are we ready? It's getting dark.'

'We'll be there in time for the first firework, Sera,' Alec said, starting the car.

Many people had already gathered when they reached the city park. Alec slid the car into a space Juliet knew she could never have managed and they squeezed out, carrying their insect spray and bulky blanket. It was almost nine o'clock. The sky was a mix of gray-blue with streaks of peach and the sinking remains of a dull gold sun. People milled around the four-acre park, standing in groups talking, settling down on blankets, and walking toward the concession stands.

Sera picked a spot on the freshly mown, raked grass and spread out their wool blanket. Juliet and Sera sat down. 'What would you ladies like to drink?' Alec asked. They both asked for Cokes and he headed for a concession stand.

In a few minutes, Leslie and Tommy passed by them. Leslie didn't see them, but Tommy called, 'Juliet! Sera! Hi!'

Leslie turned and smiled, joining them. 'Where's Jon?' Juliet asked.

'Some problem came up at the plant about an hour ago. He said he'd try to join us before the end of the fireworks.'

'Oh, what a shame,' Sera said. 'He works a lot, doesn't he?'

'Too much.' Leslie's voice was sharp. 'I think he could delegate some of the work, but he's so hands-on and he thinks he needs to supervise everything.'

Sera smiled. 'That's what makes him a good leader, Leslie. The men at Tresswell Metal respect him like they did his father.'

'I guess, but I get frustrated.' She seemed to suddenly become aware of Tommy's serious expression, as if he was afraid she was angry. 'But we're not going to let his being late bother us, are we, Tommy? We're going to watch the fireworks and take pictures and stay up *really* late!'

Tommy looked at Juliet. 'Where's Hutch?'

'He's afraid of fireworks so he's at home. Or rather the Heritage Inn. We moved in there because of the fire in our backyard.'

'You think someone's gonna set another fire?'

'We don't want to take any chances.'

'It looks like the gang's all here!' Everyone looked up to see Carole and Danielle. 'Can we join you?' Danielle asked, smiling at Tommy.

'Sure, Grandma.'

Danielle winced and Carole winked at Juliet. Everyone knew Danielle hated being called *Grandma*.

'Hutch is staying at the Heritage Inn.'

'Oh yes, I heard something about your family leaving home,' Danielle said as she and Carole spread their blanket. 'I don't blame you. I would have left the day after the fire too.'

Carole sat down on the blue blanket. 'Alec's such a great guy. Where is he?'

'Getting us Cokes.'

In five minutes, Alec sauntered up holding two large plastic cups. 'I see our crowd has grown. Can I get anyone else something to drink?'

'I'd like something,' Carole said quickly. 'Mom?'

'I don't know. Lemonade. Leslie? Tommy?'

'Sweet iced tea for me and lemonade for Tommy, please.'

'I'll go with you, Alec.' Carole jumped up, her skinny jeans flattering her long legs and her embroidered chiffon tank top cut low. 'Everyone, get settled. We'll take care of the drinks.'

After they'd left, Leslie muttered, 'She couldn't wait to be alone with Alec.'

'He has that effect on women,' Juliet whispered.

'What are you girls muttering about?' Danielle asked. 'Keeping secrets from Sera and me?'

'Deep, dark secrets, Danielle.' Leslie laughed.

'I'm gonna take pictures,' Tommy said. He held up a 35mm disposable camera with flash. 'Dad told me to take pictures of all the fireworks until he gets here.' He leaned close to Juliet and whispered, 'Mommy's really unhappy about him working tonight. They almost had a fight.'

'Oh, really? Well, I wouldn't worry about it. She's just sad he's not here and married people have quarrels all the time.'

'*Quarrels?*' Tommy scrunched up his face. 'I don't know that word but I'm gonna start using it.'

'Who's quarreling?' Danielle asked.

'Mommy and Daddy,' Tommy announced. 'But married people do it all the time. That's what Juliet says.'

'Juliet who isn't married?' Danielle asked tartly. 'Well, I guess she would know.'

So Danielle wasn't in a good mood either, Juliet thought. Leslie and Danielle. She wondered how Carole felt this evening.

'Do you need some bug spray?' Sera held up her can to Danielle who cringed away. She was drenched in expensive perfume and wearing what looked like a designer top.

'I think I'm all right.'

'I'd like some,' Tommy piped. Sera began dousing him before asking Leslie first. 'Wow, I smell . . . weird,' Tommy said when Sera finished. 'I don't think bugs would like this. Hey, here come Carole and Alec!'

'I hope we got everyone's order correct.' Alec stooped and gave Danielle and Leslie their drinks then Tommy his. 'It's hot tonight.'

'I don't know why it always has to be hot on the Fourth of July,' Danielle fretted. Juliet and Leslie looked at each other, barely able to control their laughter. 'Oh my!' she exclaimed acidly, her eyes narrowing. 'The sheriff and his child bride have arrived.'

Davis Dalton, tall and trim, walked with his arm around Marcy's shoulders. She wore a blue-and-white sundress with a lightweight white shrug. Davis spread a blanket on the ground, then helped her gradually lower herself as they both laughed. He sat down so close to her they touched. Then he lifted her hand and kissed it. Juliet glanced at Danielle who looked as if she could chew nails.

'Do you believe she's too young for him?' Juliet murmured to her.

'It's ridiculous for a man his age to be parading around his wife who looks like she's ready to give birth on the spot. What are they thinking?'

'Maybe that she only has a couple of weeks to go before the baby comes and she'd like to see the fireworks?'

Danielle gave her a withering look. 'Juliet, you have *so* much to learn.'

Juliet had no idea what that meant so she gave up and turned to her own mother. 'Having fun, Mom?'

Sera turned tear-filled eyes toward her. 'I took half a tranquilizer so I wouldn't cry, but your dad and I loved the fireworks and I miss him so much right now I feel like someone punched me in the stomach.'

Tears stung in Juliet's eyes. Her head was beginning to hurt and she felt like putting it in her hands. This evening was supposed to be a relief from the earlier tragedy but nearly everyone was unhappy, especially Sera. She wanted to leave but Tommy would be disappointed. Then the first firework went off in a blaze of red, white and blue against the dark sky above the Ohio River, and people cheered. Even Sera clapped. Juliet turned her head and caught Alec's eye. He smiled so intimately at her it was almost like a caress. *We're the only people here*, that smile seemed to say, *and it's going to be all right*.

For the next forty-five minutes, people 'oohed' and 'aahed' as the night lit up with brilliant colors in various shapes. Tommy took pictures in between jumping up and down with glee. Sera's sadness seemed to fade and her tears dried. But Danielle's gaze kept floating back to Davis and Marcy, while Leslie fidgeted and sighed. Finally, Leslie said, 'I think I'd like some ice cream. Tommy, do you want some?'

'Sure I do! Chocolate!'

'I'll go to the concession stand with you,' Juliet said.

'I wanna go, too!'

Leslie smiled. 'OK, Tommy. Does anyone else want anything?'

Danielle and Carole shook their heads *no*.

'Not now,' Sera said. 'Thanks anyway.'

Alec stood. 'If you don't mind, I think I'll take a turn around the park. I'd like to get closer to the river.'

'Fine.' Juliet smiled, knowing how Alec had always loved seeing fireworks reflected in the river water. 'We'll see you soon.'

As Tommy skipped ahead, Leslie muttered to Juliet, 'I thought Jon would be here by now.'

'Maybe something serious is wrong at the plant. Call him.'

'He doesn't like for me to call him when he's dealing with a problem at Tresswell. You know, he thinks he has to oversee *everything*. He worries so much about the damned place. He's already getting gray hair. He dyes it. Oh, I shouldn't have said that.' She wiped a hand across her perspiring forehead. 'Never mind me. Our dinner the other night was wonderful – I loved Pascal's. But when we came home . . .'

'I know it was a shock. Do you have any idea who the prowler was?'

'Davis says there's not so much as a shoeprint – it hasn't rained for days. The marks on the door were left by what must have been a steel toe work boot. I don't know what he would have done if he'd gotten inside.'

'Is the security system fixed?'

'Oh yes. We'll be staying there tonight although Danielle wants Tommy and me to stay with her.'

'Why don't you?'

'I just can't bear it. She's domineering and makes me nervous anyway, but even before last night, I'd get mad or upset at the drop of a hat. I'll blow up – get in a terrible argument with her. I know it, especially since she's in such a lovely mood tonight and I'm hormonal and I can't explain why I am. We're going to tell everyone in two or three days.'

'Maybe you'd feel more relaxed if you went ahead and told people.'

'No. Jon and I agreed. Actually, I'm so superstitious. I'd really rather wait to announce the news until the baby is actually here.'

Juliet giggled. 'Well, friend, I don't think that's possible!'

'I know.'

'Then stop worrying and enjoy the pregnancy. Danielle will be over the moon although she isn't tonight. Does she have a crush on Davis Dawson or something?'

Leslie laughed for the first time that evening and spoke softly. 'Seeing him with Marcy certainly didn't make her happy, did it? They've been friends for over twenty years. Danielle likes the attention of handsome men and from what Jon has said, Nathaniel wasn't the jealous type. After he died, Danielle has only dated men who are important and have money. But her friendship with Davis cooled after he met Marcy.' Leslie shrugged. 'Marcy is the center of Davis's world and I believe Danielle's insulted that she's being nearly ignored for a woman who's not beautiful *and* a lowly bank teller. Also, she's worried about Carole.'

'Carole is nicer and more down to earth than I've ever known her. She's completely different than the Carole I knew when we were teenagers. She seems fine.'

'I know she's different. She's finally been humbled and she's not taking it well. She only *seems* fine. The last marriage took its toll. He physically abused her. I think she's ecstatic to be home and safe, but Danielle's afraid she isn't as calm and happy as she seems. She has terrible nightmares and she's seeing a therapist. Danielle feels guilty because she pushed the guy at Carole, pressured her into the marriage. But I'm telling tales out of school. Please don't repeat what I've said.'

'I won't, Leslie. For the first time in my life, I feel sorry for Carole.'

The three of them walked to the ice-cream stand, waited in line for ten minutes, then ordered chocolate cones. Leslie picked up enough napkins for twelve people and handed three to Tommy. 'Now try not to drip ice cream on your white shirt,' she said.

'I won't drip,' Tommy assured her just as a husky boy of around eight ran past him, swerved, and hit his shoulder hard, knocking him face-down on the ground.

A woman rushed past them shouting, 'Sorry!' then caught up to the boy, grabbed his arm, and delivered three smacks on his bottom.

Tommy was sobbing as Leslie handed her cone to Juliet

and began using napkins to wipe Tommy's chocolate-smeared shirt and face. 'I'm s-sorry,' he wept. 'It wasn't my fault.'

'No, it wasn't, honey. You're not in trouble,' Leslie said.

Tommy had gotten his tears under control although he looked thoroughly demoralized. 'It's OK, Tommy. We'll get you another cone.' She looked at the three melting cones in Juliet's hands. 'In fact, we need to throw these away and all of us will get fresh ones.'

Tommy looked down at the ground, picked up his camera and inspected it. 'It isn't broken!'

'That's lucky. You still have all those pictures you took for your dad,' Juliet told him. 'Now let's see about getting more ice cream.'

After standing another ten minutes in line, they started back with fresh cones wrapped in napkins but when they reached their spot, they found only Marcy sitting with her skirt spread around her and her shrug thrown over her shoulders. 'Hello. It took you a long time to get back.'

'We had an accident. Where is everyone?' Leslie asked.

'I'm afraid we've had a mass exodus. Davis got a call from headquarters asking him to come in. He told me he'd be back in half an hour and to just wait here. Then your mother left, Juliet.'

'She left?'

Marcy nodded, her short brown hair curls gone limp in the humidity. 'I saw her headed out of the park. A few minutes later, Carole came to me and said her mother was in a *foul mood*. Her words, not mine. She said she was taking Danielle home. She also told me that Sera wasn't upset. She said she'd left something at her house. I know you're staying at the inn, Juliet. Sera called an Uber because she didn't want to disturb your evening. She told Carole she'd be right back.'

'She's planning on coming back to the park, not going on to the inn?' Juliet asked. Marcy nodded. 'Where's Alec?'

'I haven't seen him since he went for a walk round the park earlier. Anyway, I've been left here as the messenger. I'm sorry everyone is gone – at least temporarily – but I'd love it if you'd all sit down and stop towering over me with your ice-cream cones.'

'Oh, of course!' Leslie sat down immediately. 'I don't really want mine. The cone is wrapped in a napkin and I haven't taken one lick of the ice cream. Would you like it?'

'Well . . . it does look good. It seems that these days I'm always hungry.'

'Me, too,' Tommy told her. Then he took a picture of Marcy licking her cone and she laughed. 'That's for your husband!'

'Thank you. You're a very nice boy.'

Tommy beamed and began eating his ice cream and taking pictures. Juliet couldn't imagine what her mother had left at the house that she needed immediately and her calls went to Sera's voicemail. She and Leslie looked at each other and shook their heads. If Juliet left now she'd have to take Leslie and Tommy with her since the two had come with Carole and Danielle in Danielle's car. So they sat down, side-by-side, to wait.

TEN

When Sera arrived at the house, she told the Uber driver to wait. She had left on a lamp that shone through the living room window, but to her it seemed obvious that no one was home. She took her keys from her purse, went to the front door and let herself in, closing and locking the door behind her. Standing still for a moment, Sera let the emptiness seep inside her. Owen wasn't here anymore. His essence was gone. For the first time, she felt the enormity of his death. A chill crept through her and she let out a deep, long moan. *I can't stand it*, she thought. *I simply can't stand the thought of losing Owen – my lover, my protector, my soul mate. But I have to. Juliet has already lost her brother and her father. She needs me.*

Shaking off the feeling of desolation wasn't easy, though. Sera had the eerie feeling that she would never be in this house again – the house she and Owen had bought six months after their marriage, the house where Fin and Juliet had grown up, all the Christmases and Easters and birthday celebrations as a family a thing of the past. Soon even Alec would stop coming back so often. It was over, she had to admit to herself. Her warm, lovely, happy home was a thing of the past and she had to say goodbye – alone – because she knew she could never live there again.

Sera walked through the soft light of the living room and concentrated on the other reason she'd come home. She knew Juliet and Alec wouldn't be happy, but she'd been even more shattered and forgetful than she'd let on to them. Still, she asked herself how she could possibly have left behind her tarot cards and honeymoon photo and gold and ruby cross. She'd always kept them near her, even taking them when she and Owen traveled. They weren't just physical objects to her – they had deep spiritual meaning. She wouldn't – *couldn't* – leave them behind, even if she was just a few miles away at the Heritage Inn.

At the door to the office addition, Sera stopped. She thought she smelled a man's cologne wafting through the house. She turned around, saw nothing in the dimly lit living room, and walked to the hall. Waiting for a moment, listening, she flipped on the overhead light. The hall was bright and empty but the smell was stronger. She moved slowly, walking the length of the hall, glancing into every bedroom, until she came to Alec's room. The smell was strong here and she went in, glancing around the room, moving onto the adjoining bathroom. She identified the scents of wood, citrus, and patchouli. In the sink she saw a few fragments of glass. The rest of a broken bottle lay in the wastebasket. Alec had broken a cologne bottle and the smell lingered. He'd probably been packing in a hurry and not cleaned up as well as he normally did. Funny that she hadn't noticed the smell before they left, but she'd been distracted. 'See, it was nothing, Sera,' she said aloud, just to hear a voice. 'Only some spilled cologne that was probably extremely expensive.'

On her way back to the office, though, she took time to part the draperies over the sliding glass doors in the living room and scan the backyard. The dusk-to-dawn light glowed on the patio. The Addisons' big tabby cat Cleo crept across the concrete, sat down for a few moments looking around, peering at the glass doors, ears twitching. Cleo and Hutch were friends. They usually gazed at each other through the glass around this time of night. Maybe she sensed her canine pal wasn't home tonight, Sera thought. Then Cleo cocked her head, tensed, and suddenly jumped up and ran away. Sera saw nothing on the patio that would have scared her. Immediately she whirled around and looked at the living room, thinking the cat had seen a figure standing behind her. But the room looked calm and empty. Too empty without Owen. Sera felt tears welling up and dropped the draperies back into place. All she wanted was to get her cards and photo and cross and leave this house where she'd once been so happy.

If she didn't stop wasting time, she thought, the Uber would leave. She rushed to the office and turned on the overhead fan light. The blades began spinning, fluttering the fronds of the Boston and lady ferns. She opened a desk drawer and removed the magenta silk-wrapped tarot cards, cross, and photo, kissing the silken package in her hand. Then she heard a cough coming from the nearby coat closet.

Sera went completely still, like a frightened animal. That couldn't be a cough, she told herself. That was . . .

A cough. A human cough.

Adrenalin raced through her and clutching the cards, Sera turned. 'Oh!' she uttered, surprised to her core as the closet door opened and someone stepped out.

'Why did you have to come back?'

'I – I wanted something. I don't understand but I won't say a word—'

'Of course you will.'

She darted toward the office door leading outside. She reached for the doorknob with her right hand. It didn't turn. She flipped the lock. The knob turned but the door didn't open. Damn! The deadbolt was on. She touched it just as she felt movement behind her. Frantically she turned the deadbolt latch but an arm circled her neck and wrenched her body away from the door. She dropped her cards and clawed at the arm with both hands, but it only clenched harder, cutting off her air. Then she felt the point of a knife at her throat.

Sera felt herself dragged backward, nearer the center of the room, beneath the whirling fan light. She kicked and thrashed, but she couldn't break free. She'd kept her eyes shut, somehow feeling that if she couldn't *see* what was happening, it *wasn't* happening. She managed to get enough breath to gasp, 'Please, no . . .'

The words came out as the knife cut into her skin. She felt blood dripping down her neck before a hand pressed hard on her chin, wrenched it to the right and upward. She heard a sickening crunch. Sinking to the floor, her last thought was faint and sad: *Just like Fin, just like Owen . . .*

Tommy yawned hugely and leaned his head against Juliet's arm. 'Where's Aunt Sera?'

'I don't know, honey.' Juliet looked at her watch. Her mother had been gone for forty-five minutes and the fireworks display would end soon. 'She should be back by now.'

'Maybe she went to bed.'

'She was supposed to come here first because we're staying at the inn.'

'Can't you call her?'

'My calls keep going to voicemail.'

'Oh, golly gee. Where can she be?' He suddenly beamed up at Juliet. 'That rhymed!'

'Yes, it did, you clever boy. Does your mother know you're a poet?'

'I don't know.'

'Who's a poet?'

'Alec!' Juliet beamed. 'That was a long spin around the park. Did you go to the river?'

'I got pretty close and stood for a while looking at it.'

'I like lookin' at the river, too, but I can't get close 'cause Daddy's afraid I'll fall in.' Tommy looked at Leslie, who was walking to Jon. 'There's Daddy!' Leslie's back was toward Juliet, but she could see her friend's head moving sharply and her hands almost waving. 'Uh oh, I think he's in trouble.'

'Well . . . maybe not,' Juliet hedged.

'Yep. He is.'

Suddenly Jon clasped Leslie's arms, pulled her to him, and kissed her on the mouth. By this time, Marcy and Alec were also watching them. When the kiss finished and Leslie lay her head on Jon's chest, Marcy, Alec, Juliet and Tommy clapped.

'Well, we have one little lost chick accounted for,' Alec said. 'Now we're only missing Sera, Danielle, Carole, and Davis.'

Marcy's cell phone rang. 'Where *are* you?' everyone heard her say before her expression changed from annoyance to alarm and she began speaking so softly no one could hear her. In a minute she clicked off and looked at Juliet, her face distressed. 'That was Davis. It seems there's been some trouble . . . Juliet, your mother . . . well . . .'

'What about Sera?' Alec demanded.

'Davis is at her house. She went back there and . . . something's happened.'

'*Marcy!*' Juliet nearly cried. '*What?*'

Marcy swallowed hard. 'Davis wants Alec to bring you home, Juliet. Only you. There's . . . bad news.'

Leslie and Jon had joined the group and heard Marcy's last words. 'We'll go with you.'

'No. Davis said *only* Juliet and Alec. No one else. He was emphatic. No one else.'

'Well, dammit!' Jon exploded. He looked exhausted. His face was flushed and his hair and yellow T-shirt were damp with perspiration. 'If Juliet needs us—'

'We'll do what Davis says. He must have a good reason.' Alec's voice was firm as he helped Juliet up from the ground and wrapped an arm around her waist. 'We'll call you later.'

'Why did she go home?' Juliet muttered as she and Alec nearly ran across the park to his car. 'What was so important that she had to go back there?'

'I have no idea.'

'Alec, I'm so scared. What if she's dead?'

'Don't even think that. She can't be.'

But even before they parked she knew something disastrous had happened to her mother. Two police cruisers and an ambulance with the lights flashing were waiting for them.

They went to the front door and stepped into a nightmare world. Officers milled around, two in white overalls, face masks, shoe covers and latex gloves. Juliet gasped when she saw them walking toward Sera's office and Davis Dawson hurried to her.

'What's happened?' she blurted.

'Your mother came home in an Uber. She told the driver to wait – she'd only be inside about ten minutes. She never came back. He rang the front doorbell but she didn't answer. He tried the door. It was locked. Then he called nine-one-one.'

'Davis—'

He continued in a coolly professional voice. 'One of the basement windows at the back of the house is knocked out. Somebody must have come in that way. Maybe they were robbing the place when Sera walked in on them.' He took a deep breath. 'I'm afraid your mother is dead, Juliet.'

'Dead?'

'Murdered.'

The room darkened and whirled. 'No. No, she isn't. She's fine . . . she's . . . *No!*'

'I'm so sorry,' she heard Davis say from what seemed far away.

Closing her eyes, Juliet tried to steady herself. 'Where is she?'

'In the small room with the overhead fan light—'

'Her office. I want to see her.'

'There's nothing you can do—'

'I want to *see* her!'

Davis looked helplessly at Alec, who clasped her arm.

'Come on, Juliet. Just hold onto me.'

They walked slowly to the door of the office. Juliet didn't step inside. She leaned forward, peering at the three people wearing latex and shoe covers gathered around something – someone – covered with a white sheet motionless on the light beige carpet. Then she saw a lock of her mother's long golden-silver hair and gasped. 'Oh, God. Mama.'

ELEVEN

Juliet approached her mother slowly, kneeled, and touched her hair. 'Will you pull back the sheet?'

A female crime scene investigator bent and slipped the sheet away from her mother's face, which still had the faint flush of life although her head was turned at an unnatural angle. Her eyes were closed, the long lashes dark against her skin. Juliet reached slowly for her mother's hand when the woman wearing a hairnet said sharply, 'Please don't do that, Miss Reid. There might be trace evidence on her hands or under her nails.'

'Trace evidence of the murderer.' Juliet spoke barely above a whisper. 'Of course. I'm sorry.'

'It's perfectly natural. Just . . . don't touch her. I'm sorry.'

'Don't be. I know better.' Juliet sat back and clasped her hands in front of her. 'Can you tell me how she was killed?'

'It appears that her neck was snapped.' Juliet winced. 'It's almost an instantaneous death, if that's any comfort,' the woman said gently. 'There's a cut on her neck, but it's not deep. She didn't feel much pain, if any at all.'

'Are there any other wounds?'

'Not external. When we get her to the hospital, there will be X-rays for any internal damage.'

So her throat hadn't been slashed like Fin's. She hadn't been shot like Dad, Juliet thought. *I guess that's a blessing.* But she'd known she was going to die. Juliet was certain she had and even if it had been for only a minute or two, that was *not* a blessing.

'Juliet?' Davis asked quietly.

She looked at him. 'Yes.'

'We think she made it to the door. She had on red nail polish and there are some small chips around the deadbolt. The door is unlocked. The deadbolt isn't.'

'She always wore red nail polish on Christmas and the Fourth of July,' Juliet said absently, then more sharply, 'The deadbolt kept her from escaping.'

'Maybe. It's more likely that she didn't have a chance.'

'I see.' She looked at the magenta scarf and the tarot cards spilled near the desk. 'She came back for her tarot cards. She always kept a photo of her with Dad and a gold-and-garnet cross with them. I don't see the cross.'

'The cross was probably stolen. Were the cards that important to her?'

Juliet nodded. 'The cards and the cross belonged to her grandmother and she treasured them. She was superstitious about them. She even took them with her on trips.' She pointed to a card lying face up beside Sera. 'That's the Death card.'

'So you think the killer was trying to send a message? That she was meant to die?'

Juliet frowned. 'Someone who doesn't know the cards might believe that, but the Death card doesn't necessarily mean literal death. It can mean physical death, but most readers think it represents change, transition, the end of one way of life and the beginning of another. That's what Mom believed. It's what she taught in her lessons.'

Davis said, 'Then you think the person who laid the card by her didn't understand the meaning.'

'Possibly.'

'Or the killer was giving us a message – Sera asked for death by reading the cards.'

Juliet looked up at him. 'The Booths think she practiced black magic.'

'I want to show you something. Are you up to it?'

Juliet looked at her mother's still face and felt a strange, deep calm wash through her. *There's nothing more I can do for you, Mama*, she thought. *I love you.*

She slowly stood. 'Yes, I'm all right.'

'Will you come with us, Alec?'

'Lead the way, Davis.'

Davis took them back the hall toward the bedrooms and Juliet immediately noticed a strong smell.

'What's that?' she asked.

'Cologne,' Alec answered. 'Men's cologne.'

As they followed Davis down the hall to the bedrooms, the scent grew stronger. He went into the bedroom Alec was using and flipped on the light in the adjoining bathroom. 'Please don't touch anything – you're not wearing gloves,' he said as he pointed to the single sink vanity. 'The odor is coming from the drain. Someone tried to wash it down.'

Alec sniffed. 'It's my cologne. I don't wear it often. I left the bottle on the vanity.'

'Did you spill it or break the bottle?'

Alec shook his head *no*.

'Then whoever was in the house did.' He pointed to the wastebasket beside the vanity.

'The remains of the glass bottle and the silver lid.' Alec's gaze shifted from the wastebasket back to Davis. 'Whoever was here knocked over the bottle, broke it, and tried to clean up the mess.'

Davis nodded. 'Which means he made a tour of the house. Most burglars don't look for valuables in the guest bathroom. I want to show you something else.'

They went to the basement. Davis led them to a broken window above a couch. 'This must be how he got in,' he said.

Juliet frowned. 'Isn't that opening a bit small?'

'Your basement windows were custom made and slightly larger than most basement windows.'

Juliet moved nearer the windows. 'But there are little pieces of jagged glass sticking out from the frame. Wouldn't he have cut himself?'

'We'll take DNA samples, but the killer could have been wearing heavy coveralls. The glass is on the couch. We might find something on it.'

Juliet looked at the window, the glass on the couch, and thought of the violation of her home. She started to picture her vibrant mother lying dead in her beautiful little office. 'I have to leave.' Her voice was abrupt and loud. 'I have to leave right now. I'm sorry.'

Alec reached for her arm. Davis looked at her with sympathy.

'I understand. There's nothing more I wanted to show you. And Juliet? I'm so *deeply* sorry.'

'Yes. Everyone is *deeply* sorry, but that doesn't do any good, does it?' She drew a breath. 'I'm sorry, Davis. That was unforgivably rude.'

But it was true, she thought. No amount of sympathy could bring back her parents.

During the ride back to the Heritage Inn, neither Alec nor Juliet said a word. When they walked into the lovely, brightly lit lobby, she winced. 'Are you OK?' Alec asked.

'Yes. I just want to go to my room.'

When Alec opened the door to the ivory-and-gold room, Juliet walked straight to one of the beds and collapsed, placing a hand over her eyes. In a moment, Alec said, 'If you're hungry I could order room service. Or maybe you'd just like a drink.'

'I don't want a drink.'

Alec ordered a vodka tonic for himself. When it arrived, Juliet hadn't moved from the bed or removed her hand from her eyes. Alec sat down on a chair near her bed. 'Are you all right?'

'No. I'll never be all right again.' She looked at Alec for the first time. His eyes were sunken, his face blanched. 'I should be crying right now but I don't feel like I have one tear left in me.'

'You're in shock, Juliet. The tears will come later, not that they really mean anything.'

'They don't mean anything?'

'You can grieve – deeply, heart-wrenchingly – without crying.'

'Did you cry for your family after the wreck?'

Alec took a sip of his drink. 'I don't remember.'

He doesn't want to talk about it, Juliet thought. She couldn't blame him – the woman who was his second mother had just been murdered. 'I'm sorry.'

'For asking or because I can't remember?'

'For asking.' She stood up and walked around the room, stopping at the other bed. 'Just a few hours ago, Mom was sitting on this bed. I think she was relieved to be out of the house for a while. She didn't think she'd be out of it forever. If only she hadn't gone back!'

'But she did.'

'It wasn't just for her tarot cards or the cross. She wanted to see her house again.'

'You don't know that.'

'Yes, I do, Alec. I knew Mom. That house stopped being her home when Dad died. She was saying goodbye.'

'Maybe.'

'Maybe? Definitely!'

'OK.' Alec raised his dark, tortured eyes to hers. 'Please sit down and stop trying to pick a fight with me. It won't help anything.'

'You're right. I guess I'm just looking for someone to get mad at. It should be the person who killed Mom, but we don't know who it was.'

'My bet's on one of the Booths.'

'Could they squeeze through that basement window?'

'Micah could. Maybe Hannah. I don't see how Wendell could have made it.'

'Whoever it was must have been there before Mom went home. But why would the Booths break into our house?'

'Curiosity? Maybe planning on doing something destructive, like burning the tree house?'

'And if it wasn't one of them?'

'Then I don't know.' Alec paused, clearly thinking. 'I have a two-week vacation. I planned on spending the first week here in Ohio and the second in Bali, but I'll cancel all of my travel plans. I need to stay here with you in Parrish. I won't leave you unprotected, Juliet.'

'Oh, Alec, I hate for you to miss your vacation—'

He smiled at her tiredly. 'Would you expect me to do anything else?'

She shook her head. 'Then it's settled. And now I'm afraid I'm going to nod off and slide right out of this chair. I have to get some sleep. Are you sure you don't mind being in this room alone?'

'I won't be alone. I'll bring in Hutch. I'll also take one of Mom's sleeping pills and be out like a light. I promise.'

Alec stood slowly. 'OK. I'm not much help to you in this shape anyway.' He stepped closer to her and kissed her lightly on the forehead. 'Goodnight, Juliet.'

Dimly, Juliet heard the sound of *Für Elise* playing over and over. She groaned and turned her head, burying it deeper in the down pillow. Then she felt something warm and soft and wet bathing her hand. She groaned again, lifted her face, and saw Hutch lovingly licking her hand that hung over the side of the bed.

'Hutch,' she murmured. 'Hi, boy.'

Für Elise sounded again. Her cell phone, she realized. She sat up in bed and looked at her unfamiliar ivory-and-gold surroundings. Then the night rushed back to her – going to the park to see the fireworks, the return to her house to find—

'Mama!' she cried, then covered her mouth.

The phone rang again and this time she answered. ''Lo?'

'Juliet! It's Leslie. I just heard. I can't believe it. Oh my God! Is there anything I can do?'

'Do? No. What time is it?'

'Are you all right?'

'I don't know, Les. I was asleep—'

'I'm so sorry I woke you. I didn't even think. It's nine-thirty. Danielle called us about fifteen minutes ago. Your mom! What happened?'

Juliet kicked off the covers and slowly sat up. She was wearing her blue nightgown although she didn't remember putting it on. Her clothes lay in a pile by the bed. 'Mom was murdered.' Her voice was slightly slurry, her mouth dry. 'In her own house. Someone broke her neck.'

'Broke her neck—' Leslie let out a sob.

'And cut it – just a little – I don't know why.'

'You sound odd.'

'I took a sleeping pill last night. It's the first one in my life. I didn't think I could sleep at all – even with the pill – but I guess the last few days have caught up with me. Nothing feels real. It's all far away, like it happened a long time ago. Or maybe not at all. Maybe it didn't – not really. Oh, I sound crazy.'

'No, you don't. You sound dazed. How's Alec?'

'I haven't seen him this morning. When he left me last night, he was beyond exhausted. I hope he's sleeping late.'

'I'm sure you both were beyond exhausted. There must be something I can do to help you.'

'Thank you, but no. At least not now. I'm not even really awake. I need coffee. And to see Alec. Davis might have called him and he knows more than I do.'

'OK. I don't mean to be a pest, but you will at least call me later and let me know how you're doing, won't you?'

'Of course. And thank you, Leslie. You're the best friend in the world.'

After she ended the call, Juliet thought of putting on her robe and going next door to Alec's room. He might still be asleep, though, and he certainly needed rest. Instead, she called room service and ordered coffee, and English muffin with butter and jam. While she waited, she brushed her hair and teeth, washed her face, and slipped into her robe.

When the tray arrived, the cheerful young man who delivered it asked if she'd like him to take the dog out. 'Oh my, yes!' Juliet exclaimed. 'I forgot all about him. Here's his leash and his name is Hutch. Thank you so much.'

Ten minutes later someone tapped at her door. She opened it to find Alec with Hutch. 'I sent him out with the guy who delivered my breakfast—'

'And I ran into them in the hall.'

'I didn't tip the guy.'

'I did.' Alec and Hutch came into the room. 'I also brought Hutch's kibble and bowl from my room. I know he's hungry.'

'He prefers moist food but he'll eat anything in a pinch.' Juliet watched Alec pour kibble in Hutch's bowl. 'Did you sleep last night?'

'Yes, surprisingly. You?'

'Yes. Either that or I passed out. Leslie called about half an hour ago.'

'So the word is out.'

'She's horrified and kept asking if there was anything she could do for me.'

Alec stood, looking at her seriously. 'Davis called me.'

'Do they know anything yet?'

'Not much, but he'd like to see us this afternoon.'

'Oh. Maybe they'll know more then.' She sat down on the bed. 'Do you want some coffee? There's a little bit left or we could order more.'

'I already had some.'

Another soft knock on the door. Frank Greenlee stood outside looking worn and unutterably sad. 'Juliet,' he said. 'I can't believe what's happened. I'm not going to say I'm sorry – you already know it.'

Juliet hugged him. 'I do know it, Frank. Come in.'

'Hello, Alec,' Frank said with a faint smile. 'And here's Hutch, hungry as always.' He looked back at Juliet. 'I feel like if I'd been home, I could have done something – prevented what happened – but I was here. There was a party in the ballroom and I stayed until almost midnight. When I got home—'

His wrinkled face crumpled and he covered his eyes. 'There was probably nothing you could have done if you'd been home,' Alec said. 'Someone came in a basement window. We think they were robbing the place and Sera walked in.'

'Someone came in because they thought the house was empty – that you'd left after Owen—'

Alec nodded.

'Well, you had left temporarily. At least that's what I thought. Why did Sera go back?'

Juliet spoke up. 'We're not sure. We were at the park watching fireworks and she disappeared. She told Carole she was taking an Uber home and would be right back. We think she went to the house for her tarot cards and her grandmother's cross. She was superstitious about them and she'd left them. We found the cards scattered around. The cross was gone.'

'Good God,' Frank moaned. 'To die because of some cards and a cross . . .'

'And a photo taken of her and Dad on their honeymoon, which is missing, too. Those things were precious to her but she must have come back for more than them. Before we left for the park, she asked me if I thought we'd ever see home again,' Juliet said. 'I'm afraid she thought she might not. Maybe she thought it would be burned to the ground like the tree house . . . I don't know. I think she wanted to say goodbye to our old life in that house.'

Frank drew himself up and took a deep breath. 'I'm not being any help at all. I know you'll have things to do, so why don't you let me take Hutch for the day? We're good friends. I'll walk him all around the grounds, introduce him to everyone, let him watch the ducks in the pond.' He smiled. 'We'll have a fine time, won't we, boy?'

The dog let out a little 'woof' and Alec attached his leash and handed it to Frank. 'Don't you two have *too* much fun, today.'

Frank smiled. 'We'll try to behave ourselves.'

TWELVE

Carole pulled up to the Tresswell's two-story French Provincial-style home, shut off the car and sat still. She'd delayed coming home by driving five miles north and crossing the cantilever bridge spanning the Ohio River into West Virginia, before turning around and heading toward home. She wished she had somewhere else to go – she didn't want to see her mother – but her mind was blank. It was only 11:20, too late for breakfast out and too early for lunch. As soon as she walked into the house, though, she thought *certainly* she could have come up with a different destination. She put her head on the steering wheel and drew a deep, steadying breath.

Her mother was waiting for her, seated on a couch pretending to read a magazine, and jumped up as soon as she saw Carole. 'Honey! How was your therapy session?'

This was what Carole had dreaded – the weekly grilling about what she'd talked about with the psychiatrist this morning. This session had been worse than usual because the doctor had concentrated on the events surrounding Fin's murder and the death of Owen Reid. 'It was all right,' she said, carelessly dropping her handbag on an end table.

'Just OK? Does she think you're doing better? Did she prescribe any new medicine?'

'I'm taking a tranquilizer and an antidepressant. Isn't that enough?'

'Well, I thought maybe a sleeping pill. I hear you up at all hours.'

'In this big house? How could you?'

'Maybe I'm awake, too.' Danielle was dressed in sleek light gray pants and a green silk top, her hair and make-up perfect, but Carole saw the worried look in her eyes. 'Dear, Robert called this morning.'

Carole went rigid at the name of her husband. 'What did he want?'

'To see you. He was very abrupt. I said you weren't home. He asked where you were. I told him the grocery store.'

'Mom, I never go to grocery stores. Couldn't you have come up with something better?'

'I panicked. I thought of saying you went to see Leslie but I didn't because he knows where she lives.'

'What difference does that make? He's in Chicago.'

Danielle's hands twisted. 'While he was on the phone, I heard the bells on the courthouse clock.'

Carole's heart beat a bit faster. 'I'm sure the Parrish courthouse clock isn't the only chiming clock in the United States.'

'I've heard those bells ever since I moved here. I know how they sound – not exactly resonant, rather flat and clanging, although I wouldn't say that to anyone who lives here. Anyway, I'm sure it was them.' Danielle choked back a combination of a cough and a sob. 'I'm so sorry. This whole mess is my fault. I encouraged you to marry him. I nearly forced him on you.'

Carole felt like screaming and crying and throwing something – anything – at a wall and shattering it. She'd been trying to escape Robert Reynard Monroe IV for months and lately she thought he'd backed off. Apparently, she'd been wrong. She clenched her hands and forced down her rage and fear. 'Did he say why he wants to see me?'

'He said he wants to talk to you.'

'Why couldn't he do that on the phone?'

'I don't know. I asked and he said he wanted to talk to you in person. He said he *will* talk to you in person. There was a threat in his voice.'

'He doesn't love me but he's never lost anything in his life. His ego won't allow it.' Carole's hands clenched. 'We have to tell Davis.'

'I already have.'

'And?'

'Right now he's busy but he'll look into it—'

'Certainly he's busy. Sera Reid was murdered last night.' Carole closed her eyes. 'Oh, God.'

The doorbell rang and both women jumped then looked at each other in alarm. Danielle clutched Carole's arm. 'Let Martha get it.'

In a moment, tall, stocky, beaming Martha walked in with Leslie and Tommy. 'Hi!' Leslie burst out shrilly. 'I'm sorry we came without calling first but I just had to get out of that house. The cleaning woman who comes twice a week quit this morning – that's fine, I couldn't stand her anyway – but suddenly I realized we were alone and I kept thinking of the prowler. Anyway, here we are. Can we spend the day?'

Danielle drew her close. 'Oh, dear, you spend as much time as you like. After you had the prowler, I said you should come.'

Tommy, without his usual smile, stood close to his mother and held her hand. Danielle stooped and hugged him. 'How are you, darling?'

'OK,' he said in a small voice. 'I'm glad to see you.'

'And we're thrilled to see you.' Danielle hugged him again.

'Aunt Sera's dead.'

Leslie closed her eyes. 'He overheard me talking to Juliet on the phone.'

'She's in Heaven with Owen,' Danielle said gently. 'That's where she would want to be. You mustn't be sad. She wouldn't like for you to be sad.' He looked at her doubtfully. 'Are you hungry?'

'Not really, but maybe I could eat a blueberry muffin.'

'That's lucky for you. Martha made a fresh batch this morning. We were going to bring some to you when we came to visit this afternoon.' Danielle looked up at Martha. 'Will you take him into the kitchen for a muffin and milk? Leslie, would you like coffee, tea . . .'

'Some chamomile tea sounds good.'

Martha smiled. 'Coming right up. Anything to eat?'

Leslie shook her head.

'Carole?'

'Just decaf coffee.'

'For me, too,' Danielle said. 'Thank you, Martha.'

As Martha led Tommy toward the kitchen, the others went into the family room and sat on overstuffed, rust-colored couches facing each other across a large, hexagonal mahogany coffee table. To the right, four tall, wide windows looked out on a patio seating area with a grill and beyond it a big, bright blue pool – the pool where Nate Tresswell had died.

Leslie looked outside. 'It's such a beautiful day' – her eyes filled with tears – 'and Sera Reid has been *murdered*! I cannot believe it! Owen's death was bad enough . . . but *Sera*? I called Juliet this morning and she's doing better than I am – shock, I guess – but I can't stand to think that someone deliberately killed Sera. She's always been like a second mother to me and . . . and . . .' The tears began to flow and she wiped at her face like a child.

Carole pulled a tissue from her pocket. 'Here. I'll get a fresh box for you.'

Leslie sobbed into her single tissue. 'I'm making a fool of myself.'

'No, you're not, Leslie,' Danielle said gently. 'I wasn't close to Sera but hearing about her death hit *me* hard. I can't imagine how bad you feel.'

'I feel like crap!' Leslie burst out. 'What kind of damned world do we live in, anyhow?'

Carole returned with a small box of tissues and handed it to Leslie. 'We live in a world that sometimes is a really terrible place. This is one of those times.' She looked at Leslie with concern. 'Would you like a tranquilizer or just half of one?'

'No. I can't because—' Leslie froze and blinked rapidly. 'I mean . . . well, it's too early in the day.'

'But you're nearly distraught.'

'I'll get control of myself. I feel better already now that I'm not alone in our house with Tommy.'

'If you change your mind, let me know.'

'Thanks, Carole.' Leslie sniffled. 'I haven't called my mother. She and Bruce are on their second honeymoon in Venice. They've been planning this trip for months and were so excited. I haven't told her about Owen or our prowler or Sera and I'm not going to, although she'll be mad at me for not letting her know.' Leslie blew her nose. 'And then a while ago I thought I saw Robert Monroe parked outside my house! I believe I'm losing my mind!'

Danielle and Carole exchanged looks. 'How long ago?' Danielle asked.

'About half an hour. I looked twice . . . I could have *sworn* . . .' Leslie frowned. 'What's wrong? I can tell something's wrong.'

'Robert is in Parrish. Mom got a call from him this morning asking for me. She heard the bells on the courthouse clock. She told him I was at the grocery store.'

Leslie put down her tissue and almost grinned. 'The *grocery* store? That's the most unlikely place—'

'I see a psychiatrist once a week and I had an appointment this morning,' Carole said. 'Mom didn't want to say I was at your house because he knows where you live. She said the grocery store off the top of her head. Apparently, Robert didn't believe her because he must have been looking for me at your place.'

'Are you sure he's in Parrish?'

'During his call to me, I heard the courthouse clock clanging. I'd know that sound anywhere,' Danielle said. 'He didn't say he was here, but I thought he was and then you *saw* him—'

'I *thought* I saw him in a black Nissan Maxima. Does Robert have a Nissan?'

'He drives a Mercedes. He probably rented a Nissan at the airport,' Carole said. She frowned and nervously tucked her hair behind ears. 'I wonder how long he's been here.'

'Why would he come at all?'

'He told Mom he wants to see me.'

Leslie looked troubled. 'He and Jon have been on the phone to each other twice. I overheard – no, I was trying to eavesdrop but I didn't need to because Jon was shouting at him. He detests Robert.'

'The feeling is mutual. We don't know when Robert came to Parrish,' Carole said thoughtfully. 'What if he was the prowler and thought he was scaring Leslie? He's more than capable of something like that, especially if he's furious with Jon. Robert is all good looks and charm on the outside. Underneath, he's a vicious little boy with a piece of fungus for a heart. And he strikes back – *hard* – at people who make him angry. He hates Jon. He could be trying to torment him.'

'Maybe he's determined to have a face-to-face with you and he'll stop at nothing to get it,' Leslie said. 'I know how controlling he is. There's something deeply wrong with him.'

'Yes, there is.' Carole shook her head, her expression miserable. 'Maybe he's just not going to let me go.'

'I called the restaurant I worked at in Columbus and told them I won't be coming back.'

Alec looked at Juliet as they drove toward police headquarters. 'How long have you worked there?'

'Almost eleven months. Five evenings a week I played the piano from seven until eleven. They gave me a week off to come home for my birthday. I explained the circumstances and the manager said he'd give me an excellent recommendation even though I'm leaving a month early. He was very understanding.'

'He should be although he'll have trouble finding a pianist as good as you for his dinner crowd.'

'There are lots of other students who would like to have that job.'

'I'm sure there are, but not as good as you.'

'Are you trying to cheer me up before we see Davis?'

'Yes. Is it working?'

'It's nice, but it's impossible for me to feel cheerful. This has been one of the worst weeks of my life.'

'Mine, too, and I've had some bad ones. I wish to God Sera hadn't left the park and gone home.'

'She was sad at the park. I think she had a compulsion to go back to the house and she waited until we weren't around to call the Uber because she didn't want us to stop her. We *couldn't* have stopped her.'

'I could have gone with her,' Alec said flatly. 'She wouldn't be dead if I'd gone with her.'

'You don't know that.'

'Yes, I do.' They turned into a small parking lot. 'Here's police headquarters. Ready to hear what Davis has to tell us?'

'No, but we don't have a choice.' She smiled sadly at Alec. 'I'm glad I'm not alone.'

'You're never alone, Juliet.'

They walked side-by-side into the rectangular, two-story brick-and-granite building that had become so familiar to Juliet during her father's thirty-two-year career as a police officer. The interior had been remodeled four years earlier, but in spite of the new paint colors and updated furnishings, to her the feel of strength and authority of this place had not changed in the least. She'd always felt safe and welcome at headquarters and she'd been proud that her father was highly respected and liked here.

A young man working in Davis's office said Davis was waiting for them. They walked into a small, bright room painted beige. He stood up and circled his desk, shaking hands with both of them. On his desk sat an 8-x-10-inch picture of a smiling Marcy. Beside it was a sunset jade plant in a six-inch turquoise ceramic pot. 'Your mother gave me the plant,' Davis said when he saw Juliet looking at it. 'It's managed to flourish in spite of my inept care.'

'It was one of her favorite plants because of the reddish tips on the leaves.'

'So she told me. I don't know much about plants, but it's pretty.' He cleared his throat. 'How are you doing?'

'Not well,' Juliet answered. 'Neither of us is.'

'Marcy asked me to tell you how very sorry she is. And you know how I feel.' Davis took a deep breath. 'Please sit down.' They each sat on uncomfortable chairs and Davis retreated behind his desk. 'I'm not good at this. Your parents were my friends, Juliet, yet I have to tell you things that will be hard to hear.'

'I think I'm prepared,' Juliet said, although she was shaking inside.

'First of all, autopsies showed that both Owen and Sera died immediately. Well, Sera might have lived a few seconds, but she didn't suffer.'

Juliet managed, 'That's good. I guess.'

'Yes. That's a blessing.' Davis glanced down at a legal pad, on which he must have made notes. 'The basement window glass had no matter, blood or tissue. There was a partial boot print in the well beside the window. However, we did find twill threads under Sera's nails. We assume the . . . intruder, we'll call him, wore coveralls. We're still trying to find a match with the sole of the boot print and the material of the coveralls, although they both look common, which slows our database searches.'

'That's disappointing,' Juliet said in a monotone that surprised her.

'Yes, it is. Throughout the house we found a number of fingerprints that don't belong to the family, but considering the amount of people who were in your house after Owen's death, that's not unusual. Of course there's Alec's broken bottle of cologne in the bathroom. He says he didn't break it. We assume the intruder did, then tried to clean up, which seems puzzling. It wasn't as if he was trying to hide the fact he'd been in the house – the broken window in the basement, the fact that nearly all the drawers had been riffled, Sera's jewelry box and the antique cross were gone . . . it doesn't make sense. I'm sure you'll find that other things are missing.'

'Maybe,' Juliet said. 'I haven't actually lived there for a few years now. I'm just glad that when we went to the inn I took my birthday presents with me – a pin from Leslie, a brooch from Mom, a music box from Alec.'

'Do you have any information about the tree house?' Alec asked.

'No.'

'What about the missing photo of Fin's group?'

'We have no idea when that was taken away.'

'So that's it,' Alec said flatly. 'You're still ruling it a suicide.'

'I'm sorry, but the prosecutor's office says I don't have enough evidence to open an investigation. Officially, I'll let it go. Unofficially, I won't. I cared too much about Owen.'

'Thank you, Davis,' Juliet said sincerely.

'It's not much, and I have to be careful unless I want to lose my job, but it's all I can do. However, there's something else. Wendell Booth is missing.'

'*Missing?* Are his parents hiding him?' Juliet asked.

'I don't think so. They seem too worried.'

'Naturally they'd seem worried if they thought he murdered Mom.'

'It's more than that. Mrs Booth got hysterical. They begged

us to look for him. They wouldn't do that if they thought he'd killed someone and had any idea where he is.'

'They're so out of touch with Wendell they don't know what he'd do or what he might have done!'

'True. They've mishandled Wendell's problems since he was young. Still . . .'

'Still what? I think he murdered my mother and then ran off.'

'It's a theory. It's not the only one.'

'What *is* the other one?' Juliet asked.

'That he was in the wrong place at the wrong time. That he saw something that's frightened him and he's hiding.'

'You mean maybe he saw who *did* murder my mother?'

'Maybe.'

'I don't know what to believe.'

'You have to look at all possibilities, including Wendell's possible innocence.'

'And if he *is* innocent?" Juliet looked around. 'Who does that leave? Deke Nevins because of the burglary-gone-wrong theory?' She paused, her voice lowering in dread. 'Or . . . someone who disappeared from the park during the fireworks display? The same time my mother was murdered.'

THIRTEEN

'I haven't seen Eddie for two days,' Juliet said as she and Alec walked to the car after their meeting with the funeral director, the second one in less than a week.

'You've been at the inn.'

'Alec, don't you think he would have called me when he heard Mom is dead? Or you? You haven't heard from him, have you?'

'No. But maybe Deke hasn't let Eddie talk to us.'

'Eddie's strong-willed. He'd find a way to get in touch with us, even if he can't come to the funeral.'

Alec opened the car door for her. 'You shouldn't worry about Eddie right now. You have a lot on your mind.'

'But he cared about Mom. He has to be shocked. And with Wendell missing . . .'

Alec looked surprised. 'You think not hearing from Eddie has something to do with Wendell's disappearance?'

'I don't know what to think. Maybe we should go by the trailer and ask Belle if he's been around.'

'You mean ask Deke, which I believe might only get Eddie *and* Belle in trouble. Let's leave it alone for now. Eddie knows how to take care of himself. He'll turn up.'

'I wish I could be sure of that, but I have a bad feeling.'

'If we haven't heard from him in two or three days, then we'll worry.' Alec circled the car and got in. 'Where now?'

'The florist. Mom's favorite flowers were pink, blue, white, and purple asters.'

'Pauline Vevey will go along with anything you want and make beautiful arrangements. Lillian at Longworth Style might be more difficult.'

'I know. But I want Mom to wear something she loved.'

'The night we went to Danielle's party, she wore a long, deep pink dress made from some floaty material. I don't know much about women's clothes. Anyway, your father said she'd never looked more beautiful and she blushed. She got a lot of compliments at the party. She *did* look beautiful.'

'Then that's what she'll wear. Any shade of pink was my father's favorite color on her. We don't even need to stop at Longworth's. Mom will wear that gown. I'll wear my dress from Dad's funeral. I thought I'd never wear it again.' Juliet's eyes filled with tears and she tried to unobtrusively wipe them away. 'I can't afford another reception in the church.'

'Frank has something planned at the inn. He told me.'

'Oh, no! He can't do that!'

'Why not?'

'The expense, the trouble . . .'

'Leave that to him. He was almost as close to your mother as your father.' Juliet remained silent. 'Are you all right?'

'As all right as I can be right now. I don't know why I'm not in hysterics.' She looked at Alec. 'I don't believe someone broke into the house to rob it. Whoever came in had a different reason.'

'I think so, too.'

'Wendell?'

'He's missing.'

'That's not an answer to my question.'

Alec's face went still before he finally spoke. 'I think it's possible that Wendell went in the house but I don't know why he would want to rob it. As far as I know, he's never been accused of stealing. He wanted the tree house, but that's not the same as pilfering jewelry. So he would have had another reason.'

'Murdering Mom?'

'She probably wasn't home when the intruder entered. She hadn't been home the night before, either.'

'So breaking in to kill Mom doesn't make sense. I wonder what Davis really thinks.'

'He's being cautious, not jumping to conclusions, and he's not going to tell us exactly what he thinks.'

'Is not believing Wendell masterminded a plan to rob the house jumping to a conclusion?'

'I don't think so,' Alec said slowly. 'As for Wendell's parents . . . well, don't forget the tarot death card placed beside your mother.'

'Wendell thinks she's a witch.'

'True. But the card bothers me. Would he take the time to sort through the cards and find the one he thought belonged beside Sera?'

'I don't know what he'd do. I only know that he's missing and Davis doesn't think his parents know where he is. And I'm worried about Eddie.'

'You can't worry about *everyone*, Juliet. Concentrate on yourself right now.'

'I can't. I'm scared. I wonder who's going to die next.'

'No one.'

She looked at him. 'If only I could believe that.'

That evening, Frank had brought Hutch back to Alec's room and the two men began talking about Alec's time in Afghanistan. Juliet couldn't think of anything she wanted to hear about less and had politely excused herself, saying she wanted to watch her favorite television show. She didn't have a favorite television show and now, at nine o'clock, she sat slumped in a chair as her mind raced.

She would not allow herself to think about her mother lying dead on the floor of her office. As soon as the image flashed in her mind, Juliet shut it out. She couldn't do anything for her mother except grieve, and she had a lifetime for that. But there were other people – living people. Leslie had called again in the late afternoon to say that she, Tommy, and Jon were spending the night at Danielle's. Juliet was relieved – all too often Jon was called back to work and she didn't want Leslie and Tommy left alone in their house in case the intruder came back. Leslie mentioned that they thought Carole's husband Robert Monroe had come to town, which wasn't good. Juliet knew little about him except that he was bad news and tenacious. But if Robert decided to stop by Danielle's, he wouldn't have a chance of finding Carole alone.

Alec was occupied and had no plans to leave the inn tonight. She had a feeling Frank might stay at the inn as well. Going home to the house next door to where one of his closest friends probably had been murdered would fill him with dread. Juliet knew that sometimes he spent the night at the inn and this would probably be one of those nights.

So those people were safe, she thought. Who did that leave? Eddie Maddox.

Her parents had cared very much for Eddie and he'd cared for them. Yet she hadn't heard a word from him since Sera's murder. Maybe he was scared. Being around the Reid family didn't seem safe. But Eddie wasn't used to being safe, she reasoned. She didn't know what his life was like before his father died, but it couldn't have been pleasant since his death. His aunt had tried to get custody of him from Belle, her own sister. Throughout the years, how many sketchy men had preceded Deke Nevins, who was unsavory and probably dangerous? Eddie presented a strong exterior as if he was taking it all in stride, but Juliet was convinced that underneath lay a frightened boy who lived each day just hoping nothing bad happened. And even though she'd known him such a short time, she cared as much about him as her parents did, Juliet realized. She cared and she was deeply concerned at his silence the last few days.

She stood up and paced around the room. Could she go to Belle's trailer and ask about Eddie? She looked at her watch. It was 9:30. Deke might be home – Deke, a man she least wanted to visit alone at night – but Belle would be working at the bar Rocco's. Juliet briefly thought of asking Alec if he'd go to Rocco's with her, but she knew he'd discourage her, present a dozen arguments, maybe even start a quarrel. Besides, she was growing too dependent on him. Although her family and people like Carole Tresswell seemed to think of her as an adolescent, she was an intelligent, independent twenty-five-year-old woman more than capable of taking care of herself.

Still, she didn't want to run off and leave Alec worrying about what had happened to her. She thought about calling him, but that would bring on the resistance she wanted to avoid. So would texting. Juliet's gaze fell on a small pad of Heritage Inn notepaper. She found a ballpoint pen in the desk drawer and wrote *I was restless so I decided to go out and drive around for a while. Yes, I will keep the car doors locked. Don't worry. J*

Not the full truth but not a lie, she thought, rereading the
note. She looked in the mirror. She'd cut and ripped five holes
in the thighs of her good jeans, put on a tight white tank top
she always wore under a semi-sheer blouse, some large hoop
earrings, bright red lipstick and eyeliner she'd drawn into an
exaggerated wing. Juliet usually dressed more conservatively,
but she thought she looked appropriate for an evening in a
dive bar. Next she grabbed her purse, dug in the zipped inner
pocket, and pulled out her small canister of pepper spray and
alarm keychain. Finally, she folded the note, left her room,
and slipped it under Alec's door. How juvenile and old
fashioned, she thought, but the only way it wouldn't catch his
immediate attention. *I shouldn't have to go to such lengths*,
she thought absently. *I'm not a little girl sneaking out of the
house.*

Juliet pushed aside the thought as she passed a maid behind
a cart in the hall and gave her a friendly 'Goodnight.' The
lobby was fairly crowded and she forced herself to walk slowly
while avoiding the glances of staff behind the desk. Out in
the parking lot, she drew a deep breath and looked up at the
stars, wishing they weren't quite so bright. Maybe once she
drove out of the lot she would feel less like she was sneaking
around, afraid that Alec would come strolling out the front of
the inn, calling to her. *I'm being ridiculous*, she thought. *No
wonder everyone treats me like a child.*

Nevertheless, after she turned from the parking lot onto the
highway and headed toward town, she relaxed. Fifteen minutes
later, she pulled up in front of the bar Ike Rocco had built in
the eighties. It glared into the night with strings of red, blue,
and yellow lights as if someone had forgotten to take down
the Christmas decorations. A huge sign announcing LIQUOR
and COCKTAILS loomed in front of the bar. Neon signs
promoting various beers shone from the windows of the
long, low dark gray wooden building that had been built over
thirty-five years ago.

The parking lot was nearly full and Juliet had to pull into
a space at the far side of the bar. After she parked, she sat
still, gathering her courage. It wasn't as if she'd never been
in a bar before, even one like Rocco's, but tonight she had a

mission and she didn't want to seem nervous. At last she emerged from the car, locked it, and headed to the front door, watching as a couple came out. Both wore torn jeans and tank tops and the girl sported over-the-knee boots that looked more suited for winter than a July night. They clutched at each other, arms circling and twining and making Juliet think of two octopi in love. *You're just jealous*, she thought, making herself smile at the image of her and Alec in their place. Warmth rushed through her and she banished the thought quickly. This was not the time to be thinking romantically of Alec.

As the door closed behind the couple and they weaved toward a car at the side of the lot, Juliet braced herself. *Time to go, 'fraidy cat,* she told herself. *Pretend you're Lara Croft Tomb Raider.*

She walked into the bar and a deafening wave of AC/DC's 'Back in Black' hit her. How many times had Fin played that song? So many that finally even Owen had asked him to stop. 'I'm an old man with a weak heart,' he'd said.

Fin had grinned. 'You're not old and you don't have a weak heart. But OK.' The next day he'd started playing the song again.

Juliet looked around at the black walls, more neon beer and liquor advertisements, glowing red lights that showed a tile floor, old tables and chrome chairs with plastic seats, rock posters everywhere, three pool tables at one end, and an aged, crudely built stage where local bands sometimes played. Fin's band had never performed here because all of the members had been under twenty-one. Smoke floated in layers throughout the bar. Half of the people were laughing loudly, the other half arguing. Juliet made her way to the long, scarred bar, hoisted herself up on a stool, and over the noise shouted an order for a beer. 'What kind, miss?' the forty-plus bartender with deep forehead wrinkles, happy eyes, and a wedding ring shouted back.

'Anything as long as it's cold.'

He laughed. 'Not a connoisseur, are you?'

'No, I'm not.' She tried to smile back sweetly. 'I'll let you pick what you think I'd like.'

'Well, that's mighty trusting of you.' In less than a minute, he placed a mug in front of her. 'If you don't like that, let me know. I'll get you something else. It's on the house.'

'Aren't you kind!' Juliet sipped, wiping foam off her upper lip. 'It's delicious.'

'And you're a sweet girl . . .'

'Juliet.'

'That's pretty. I'm Cooper.' He looked down the bar where a man was calling 'Bartender! Bartender!' 'Excuse me,' Cooper said. 'One of our less mannerly customers is summoning me.'

Juliet sipped more beer and within five minutes a man who looked about thirty-five sat down next to her and grinned. 'Hi there. I don't remember ever seeing you in here.'

'That's because I've never come here,' Juliet said. 'The place looked interesting, so I thought I'd give it a try.'

'Interesting? Ha! Never heard it called that. What do you think so far?'

'It's fine.'

'Fine? You don't like it.'

'I didn't say that.'

He seemed offended and his grin faded. 'I think you're used to going to fancy bars. You have that *money* look.'

'Money look?'

'You come from a family with money. Lots of it. Shows all over you.'

'I don't know if that was a compliment or not, but you're wrong.'

His face turned hard. 'Got that money tone in your voice, too.'

'Now I *know* that wasn't a compliment. Have I insulted you somehow?'

'Nope. You just think you're a lot better than you are. I can tell. I can also tell you're capable of buying your next drink.'

He grunted, slid off the stool and strode toward the pool tables. 'Rude one who's had too many beers,' Connor said, standing in front of her behind the bar. 'Never mind him.'

'I didn't.' She smiled. 'But I would like another beer. And I'll pay for this one, although you were very kind to give me one on the house.'

In the darkness she wasn't sure, but it looked as if Connor

blushed. 'Rocco's is a real hospitable place, Juliet. We're not all oafs.'

'Juliet!'

She looked up to see Belle Maddox. 'Hello, Belle.'

'Well . . . well . . . what are *you* doing here?'

'Having some beer.' She glanced at Belle's black leggings, spike heels, translucent white top with her signature black lace bra underneath. Belle looked back at her from eyes heavy with glittery eyeliner and furry false lashes that aged her. 'Are you working tonight?'

'What? Working? Well, sure. I work six nights a week.' She leaned close and said softly, 'My feet are already killing me.'

'That's too bad. Maybe you could wear lower-heeled shoes.'

'No. This is how the boss likes me to look.'

Connor came back with Juliet's beer and Belle set a tray on the bar as she rattled off an order for five drinks. Then she looked back at Juliet, her green eyes sad.

'I heard about your mother. I'm *so* sorry. I swear, I don't know what the world's coming to these days. That's why I was surprised to see you in here because your mother just got—'

'Don't say it!' Juliet realized how sharp her voice was. 'I'm sorry. I didn't mean to snap at you. I'm upset. I'm trying to drink away my misery and my shock.'

'Oh, yes, I understand. I wasn't judging you.'

'Belle, I know how fond Eddie was of Mom, but I haven't heard a word from him – not for days, actually. Is everything all right with him?'

Belle's eyes filled with tears. 'That's why you're here, isn't it? You're worried about Eddie.'

'Well, a little. Is something wrong with him?'

'Nothin' is wrong – nothin' that concerns you, anyway.'

Juliet and Belle both stiffened as Deke appeared. He grasped Belle's arm and leaned over Juliet. 'What's wrong with you Reids anyway? You pretend to love Eddie, you put ideas in his head, you make him think he's better than he is. Are you tryin' to replace your precious Fin with our boy?'

Belle gasped but Juliet managed to look calmly into his

angry gaze. 'We like Eddie. Our feelings for him have nothing to do with Fin.'

'Yeah, sure. Try again.' His voice rose. 'You're nothin' but a conceited jerk like your dead brother!'

Connor had returned. 'Deke, I have a tray full of drinks for Belle to deliver,' he said stonily. 'Take your hand off her arm so she can do her job.'

Deke's nostrils flared as he breathed hard, but he released Belle's arm. 'Belle, get to work and stop blabbin' to Miss Juliet Reid about Eddie. He's none of her business.'

Juliet's heart rate had sped up, but her hands were steady. As Belle scuttled away with her tray, Connor said, 'I think you'd either better have a seat or leave, Deke. I don't want any trouble from you tonight.'

'And when do I cause trouble? I haven't started a fight for years.'

'You're being obnoxious. Now take a seat before I throw you out.'

Deke stood, glaring at Connor, then said truculently, 'All right, but I want another bourbon. Straight.'

'One.'

'Have Belle bring it to me. I have somethin' to say to her.'

Deke retreated to a nearby table and sat drumming his fingers and glowering around the room. 'You're going to get a terrible impression of our clientele,' Connor said to Juliet. 'But most of them are OK – nice and even well-behaved. I guess all the bad apples decided to turn out tonight.'

'It's fine. I can take care of myself.' She sipped her drink and asked nonchalantly, 'Was Deke here last night?'

'Last night? Yeah, for a while. I can't remember when he left but it was earlier than usual. Why?'

'I just wondered if he always came in to keep Belle company.'

Connor laughed. 'Not good company, if you ask me, but usually. He keeps a pretty close eye on her.' Someone yelled at him from down the bar. 'Duty calls. I don't know why I've worked here for twenty years. Guess I'm a glutton for punishment.'

'You're not the manager?'

He laughed again. 'No, thank God. I don't want to deal with all the finances that keep this dump running for Ike Rocco.'

Juliet sipped a third beer, listening to the music roaring from the jukebox and trying not to look in Deke's direction. After twenty minutes, Belle returned with an order for seven drinks. She smiled at Juliet but said nothing. When she left with her full tray, Juliet watched her and saw Belle swiftly dip and set two of the drinks on Deke's table before quickly moving on to another. Connor had limited Deke to one more drink. He was now starting on his second since then with a third waiting. Juliet had no idea how many he'd had before their clash, but she did notice that Deke didn't sit as straight and quiet as earlier – he bobbed his head and sang along with 'Welcome to the Jungle' by Guns N' Roses, smacking his hands on the table as if he were keeping rhythm.

At 10:45, Juliet felt tired and it was clear Belle couldn't talk to her. She wasn't going to learn more about Eddie tonight, so she told Connor it was close to her bedtime, paid for her beers, left a slightly larger tip than she usually would have, and slipped to the door while Johnny Cash and June Carter roared 'Jackson.'

Juliet had parked in the dimmest reach of the parking lot, so she reached in the zipper compartment of her purse and pulled out her pepper spray keychain along with her mini-flashlight. She shone the flashlight on the concrete until she reached the area of her white Ford then picked out her car key from her regular key ring and started to insert it into the lock. Suddenly, an arm wrapped around her neck and jerked her backward.

'You just can't leave things alone, can you?' a male voice rasped in her ear.

'Deke?' Juliet gasped.

'Where's your watchdog? The one with PTSD?'

'Alec? He doesn't have PTSD.'

'He never told you about it? He never told you about his time in the looney bin? Well, I guess that's no surprise.'

'He's a high-ranking security supervisor with a big corporation in New York City!'

'Sure about that? Did you ever check on him? All you know is what he's told you. And think about this, Juliet – there wasn't any trouble until *he* came home a week ago. Now both of your parents are dead. Even before he went off to war, he was home when Fin was murdered. What a coincidence! And here *you* are nosing around, upsetting Belle, trying to get your hands on Eddie. And Alec is helping you, coming to our home asking a dozen questions. He's dangerous, you're trouble, and don't think I won't do something to both of you to protect what's mine.'

A chill swept over Juliet in spite of the warm night but her thoughts stayed focused on her present predicament. 'Deke, don't to do this. Turn me loose right now and there won't be any trouble.'

'Trouble? *Trouble?* You've already started trouble – the emotional kind. That's all you can manage.'

'How have I caused trouble?'

'By not minding your own business.'

'Are you trying to hide something?'

'Oh, you're so sweet and innocent. *Are you trying to hide something?*' he mimicked in a high-pitched voice. 'I'm tryin' to take care of what's mine.'

'Eddie isn't yours.'

'That's what you think. He *is* mine and I'll do what I want with him. You can't stop me.' His arm tightened around her throat, constricting her air. 'You know, I haven't liked a lot of people in my life, but I hated your brother – *hated* him! And you're just like him, you smirking, sneaking, treacherous *bitch—*'

Juliet pressed the button on her keychain and set off the alarm. Deke's arm loosened for a moment as a few other people in the parking lot turned to look at them and yelled. 'You whore!' he shouted.

She was dimly aware of a hubbub a few yards away and a flash of light and music as someone opened the door of Rocco's and ran inside. Taking advantage of the distraction, Juliet wrenched around, grabbed the small pepper spray canister from her purse, flipped the trigger release with her thumbnail, and shot the mixture of pepper spray directly into his eyes.

Deke howled and stumbled back from her, his hands pressed to his eyes, weaving in his drunkenness and pain, cursing her at the top of his voice. Juliet, proudly horrified at what she'd had the presence of mind to do, edged away from him but he reached out and grabbed her arm, holding her hard, still alternately screaming wildly and threatening her. She sprayed the canister again, but it was empty. Wrenching her arm violently, she fought with all of her strength until at last someone jerked Deke backward, nearly pulling him off his feet. As Deke flailed and jerked, two others joined the fray and finally managed to subdue a now sobbing Deke.

'Are you all right, Juliet?'

She finally looked at the man who had pulled Deke away from her to see a man in jeans and an Aerosmith T-shirt. 'Kyle Hollister?' she asked, amazed. 'Kyle, is that you?'

'Yes.' He turned to the two men still holding a gradually fading Deke. 'Don't let him go.' He looked back at Juliet. 'Are you all right?'

'Yes. I think so. Just scared.'

'Where's Alec?'

'At the hotel. I ditched him. I got the bright idea of coming alone. Why are you here?'

'I come here sometimes. I'm not all work and no play.' He gave her his dazzling smile. 'You're lucky to be OK. Deke can be mean and he's got it in for you.'

She touched her neck, the adrenaline rush draining from her body. 'He grabbed me just like someone grabbed my mother and broke her neck,' she said just above a whisper. 'He could have—'

'Maybe you should go to the emergency room.'

'No. No. I just want to go home. Or rather, the inn. That's where we're staying.'

Belle came running out of the bar and made a beeline for Deke. 'Oh my! What happened? Deke, what did you do?'

'I gave her a little of what's coming to her!' He dropped his hands. The area all around his eyes was stained red from the dye in the pepper spray. 'She tried to blind me, the no good, shit-eating—'

'That's enough, Deke!' Kyle thundered.

Belle looked desperately at Juliet. 'I haven't seen Eddie since yesterday afternoon. I'm afraid he's run off. Anything could happen to him. I'm worried sick but Deke says—'

Deke shot out a hand and slapped her hard. She yelped and backed away. Kyle turned toward him. 'You got something to say, you rotten pretty-boy pretend cop?' Deke yelled in Kyle's face. He raised a fist. 'Go ahead and I'll give you what's coming to *you*, too!'

'All right, Deke, you've just threatened a cop on top of assaulting two women.'

'I didn't assault them!'

'You *did*.' He looked at Belle. 'Do you want to press charges?'

Her terrified, tearful eyes opened even wider. 'Oh! Oh, no. I couldn't. He didn't mean it.'

Kyle turned to Juliet. 'And you?'

She stared at the ragged, drunken, glaring bully with his stained, rage-twisted face. '*I* want to press charges,' she said firmly.

Kyle smiled and looked at Deke. 'Deacon Nevins, you're under arrest.'

FOURTEEN

As Deke was being taken away, Belle rushed to her car. Juliet caught up with her, grasping her arms and forcing her to stand still and talk to her. 'Belle, I know you're upset, but this is important. It's about your son. Where did you last see Eddie?'

'Home. I'd just woke up and I heard Deke and Eddie going at it in the living room. You know – arguing. Loud. I hate that.'

'What were they arguing about?'

'Oh, the usual,' she said vaguely. 'They just don't get along. I tried to settle them down, but I couldn't. Deke shouted at Eddie to get out and Eddie said the trailer was *his* home, not Deke's, then Deke really lost his temper and . . . well, I'm not real clear about exactly what happened next but Eddie took off.' Once again, Juliet was certain Belle wasn't telling the whole truth. Eddie didn't just run away – Deke had done or threatened something. 'Anyway, that was the last I saw of Eddie. I mean, he doesn't have a cell phone – he can't call me.'

'Pay phones still exist, Belle, or he could have called from someone else's phone. Mine, for example.'

'Well, he doesn't like to bother people. I don't know. He was mad and upset. Maybe he wanted to worry me.' She was crying and the tears dragged eyeliner down her raddled face. 'I wasn't too worried until this morning when I saw that he still hadn't come home – he hadn't slept at the trailer. Then all of today went by and . . .' She sniffed and wiped at her tears. 'Well, I wanted to call the police but Deke said no. He said Eddie would show up when he got hungry and tired and that he was a bad boy for worrying me so much.' She let out a little sob. 'But I'm scared. Eddie's not a bad boy, Juliet. He's just unhappy. His daddy was such a nice man and Eddie loved him like crazy. Ever since he died . . .'

'How long ago was that?'

'Four years. I'm doing my best, trying to keep a roof over our heads, but it's so *hard* and now I've lost Deke!'

'Is he more important to you than Eddie?'

'*No!* But I need him. *We* need him. Eddie doesn't realize what Deke does for us. He's saving up a college fund for Eddie.'

'A college fund! Oh, Belle, you can't be so stupid!'

Belle suddenly looked angry. 'You wouldn't understand. You don't care. It's because of you Deke got arrested.'

'He did that all by himself, Belle.'

'Says you! You caused all the trouble.'

'*I* did?'

'I don't have time for this. I've got to go to Deke.'

'To *Deke*! He just hit you!'

'He didn't mean to hurt me.'

'Yes, he did. What about Eddie?'

'I'll think about Eddie tomorrow. He's a smart boy. He'll always get by. That's what Deke says.'

'Well, if Deke says it, it must be true.'

'You can be sarcastic all you want, Juliet. You don't know anything about me or my life or my kid. So leave me alone. You've caused enough trouble tonight!'

Belle climbed into her aged compact car and tore out of the parking lot, screeching her tires. Juliet stared after her, feeling angry, exhausted, and empty.

When Juliet got back to her room at the inn, she texted Alec to say she'd returned, hoping that he was already asleep. When three minutes later someone rapped on her door, her hope plummeted. She opened it to an infuriated Alec clutching Hutch's leash. Even the stiff-legged dog looked angry, she thought.

'Hi. Sorry I took off without talking to you but—'

'Where the *hell* have you been?' Alec demanded loudly.

'If you two will come in, I'll tell you. And please lower your voice.'

Alec entered the room and stood glaring at her. 'Well?'

Juliet calmly closed the door. 'I wasn't aware that I had to answer to you.'

'I thought you would have the *courtesy* to tell me—'

'So we could get into an argument. I *did* leave a note.'

Alec looked at her with a mixture of anger and disappointment, then headed for a soft chair, still holding onto Hutch's leash. 'You shouldn't have left without telling me but as to an argument – well, that depends on where you went. I know Leslie is staying with Danielle but you weren't there.'

Juliet walked toward him and took Hutch's leash from his hand, unhooking it and letting the dog saunter around the room. 'I went to Rocco's bar and don't yell at me. I had a good reason.'

'What possible good reason could you have to go to Rocco's bar? Oh, you wanted to talk to Belle about Eddie.'

'Yes. I'm very worried about him.'

'*Why?*'

'Why? Because we haven't seen or heard from him for days.'

'He's not our child. I mean, either of us. He's not your son or mine and he's what – fourteen?'

'Barely fourteen. Neglected, mistreated, and God knows what else. Mom and Dad loved him. I've come to love him. I know you care about him. Do you blame me?'

'I blame your methods. You didn't have to talk to Belle at Rocco's.' She saw the anger in his eyes. 'How could you have gone there alone without even telling me?'

'I wasn't aware I needed your permission.'

'You owed it to me.'

'*Owed* it to you? Why?'

'Because I'm responsible for you now that your parents are dead. You're in my care.'

'I don't need someone to take care of me, Alec. I'm twenty-five. You're released from duty!'

'Maybe I don't want to be.'

'OK. You care about me. I get that. But enough is enough, Alec. You're not my dad.'

He shifted his gaze and pulled a pack of cigarettes and a disposable lighter from his pocket. 'When did you start smoking?'

'Afghanistan. What difference does it make?'

'Your health.'

'My health is fine. You're trying to change the subject.' He lit the cigarette and tapped off ashes into a small glass ashtray on the desk. 'Well, did you find out anything?'

'Yes. Do you care to hear it?'

Alec rolled his eyes. 'Juliet. Really? Are you going to get pissy?'

'Not that you don't deserve it, but I won't. First, I'll tell you exactly what's wrong with *me*. I'm tired of your attitude. I don't want to insult you or hurt you because I'm just as much to blame as you are. I know I've depended on you a lot – more than I should – and I appreciate everything you've done for me. But I'll remind you again – I'm an adult and I think it's time we both realized it. I'm not a child. I don't have to consult you about everything I do, nor do I need your permission.'

Alec took a drag on his cigarette, not looking at her. 'Is that all?' he asked coldly.

'No. I want to tell you about Eddie. Day before yesterday Eddie and Deke got into an "argument" according to Belle. I'd wager it was more like an all-and-all fight. Eddie left. Belle hasn't seen or heard from him since and we haven't heard from him, either. I'm really worried and I think you should be too – if you care about Eddie at all, that is.'

Alec scowled at her. '*If I care about him?* That's a low blow. You know I care about him.'

'Then show some concern instead of saving it all for me. I know he must be a fairly tough kid to live with Belle and Deke, but he's still a kid, Alec.'

Once again he tapped ashes off his cigarette. 'Is that why you're so white and your eyes are huge? You're worried?'

'A little more happened at Rocco's than I told you. Deke's been arrested.'

'Because Eddie is missing?'

'No, but I'll tell you about that later. It's actually a stroke of luck. I know Belle can't come up with bail for him. At least he's out of the way for a while. Maybe Eddie will come home.'

'If he knows that Deke's in jail, which I doubt.'

'Then we have to tell Davis Dawson about Eddie,' Juliet said firmly.

'There must have been trouble at Rocco's and I want you to stay out of this. I insist.'

Juliet glared at him. 'Oh you do, do you? Well, that's too bad. I don't take orders from you, Alec Wainwright, and you'd better get used to it. Now leave before I *really* lose my temper.'

Juliet tossed and turned most of the night. She fell asleep near morning and woke up three hours later in tears. She paced her room and cried most of the day, the reality of her mother's death finally hitting her. Alec checked on her twice. She asked him to find out if Deke was out on bail or still in jail and to tell Davis about Eddie in case Belle had not. He coolly asked if she needed anything and said he would work out the few final arrangements for her mother's small funeral, but otherwise he left her alone as she wished. He looked as if he'd had a bad night himself and she appreciated his consideration if not his lack of apology for the previous night's anger. His temper was infuriating. She may have accepted that she was in love with him, but he still looked at her as a child – a little sister. *Little Juliet.* 'How damned frustrating!' she burst out loud enough to startle Hutch. She stooped and hugged him. 'You're lucky not to have these problems,' she said softly. 'At least I don't think you do. Right now I'd swap places with you in a minute.' The rest of the day she lay in bed, not eating, alternatively crying over her mother and crying over Alec.

The next day Leslie turned up at Juliet's hotel room with clothes. 'I knew you hadn't brought anything with you to wear to a funeral and your house is still a—'

'Crime scene,' Juliet said flatly.

'Well, yes, so I brought some things from home. We're the same size except you're an inch taller, so here are some things of mine. I've brought matching shoes.'

'Thank you, Leslie. I really appreciate it. Come in. I've ordered coffee and pastries.'

'Pastries. Yummm.' She looked closely at Juliet. 'How are you?'

'OK, considering. This isn't the happy homecoming I'd pictured.' Her eyes filled with tears. 'Oh, Les, what am I going to do without Mom and Dad? I loved them *so* much. I'll never be happy again.'

Leslie flung the clothes on the bed and hugged Juliet tightly. 'I can't imagine how you feel. I know how much you loved them. But you're strong, Juliet. You're stronger than you realize. You *will* go on and you'll be happy – maybe not right now, maybe not for a while, but eventually. I promise, and you know I don't easily make promises.'

Juliet giggled in spite of herself. 'No, you don't. When we were little, wrenching a promise from you was like arm wrestling a bear.'

'Good heavens! I didn't know I was that difficult, but my mother told me to never make promises except to her. She didn't trust people.'

'Maybe she was right not to.'

'You can trust me and I can trust you. We've known that for a long time.' Leslie smiled. 'Now let's pick out an outfit for you to wear today.'

An hour later Juliet sat in a church pew with Leslie on her left and Alec on her right as the minister spoke about the exemplary life of Sera Reid. Juliet barely heard what he said. She kept picturing her mother moving around her house, singing, laughing, patiently teaching her daughter to cook, listening to Juliet play piano, listening to Fin play guitar. Sera had been a happy and loving soul, devoted to her husband and children, and now she was gone – brutally murdered in her own cherished home. Life wasn't fair, Juliet thought rebelliously. It just wasn't fair and she was deeply, smolderingly angry.

After church, they met in one of the Heritage Inn's dining rooms for a small reception arranged by Frank Greenlee. Pauline's had supplied the multicolored asters Sera had loved and Hollisters' restaurant had provided a lovely meal. Juliet's head throbbed and her eyes were swollen. As she picked at her food, she looked around at the people talking in muted tones. Kyle Hollister, Davis Dawson and Marcy, Leslie and Jon Tresswell, Frank Greenlee, Pauline Vevey, a few police officers that had served with her father, Danielle and Carole Tresswell.

After the meal, Marcy came up to her. 'I'm so sorry, Juliet.'

'Thank you. So am I.'

'I thought Eddie might be here with you.'

'I haven't seen Eddie since the day before Mom died.'

Marcy's brown eyes widened. 'Oh. He was supposed to do some work for us yesterday but he didn't come. I tried to call but I got his mother. She said he must have forgotten, but Eddie never forgets. Do you think we should be concerned?'

'Yes. I think Eddie is missing. Alec talked to Davis about it yesterday.'

'He didn't tell me. Davis is so protective.'

'Well, I feel like Eddie's all alone in the world except for you and Leslie and me. I hope Davis is checking around for him.'

'I'll see that he is. And once again, you have our condolences. Your mother was much loved in this community.'

'Not by everyone,' Juliet muttered as Marcy walked away.

After the reception when Alec and Juliet went back to her room, he told her that no one could find Eddie. 'I talked to Davis and because of the fight Eddie and Deke had before Eddie went missing, Davis isn't putting out an amber alert. There's a strong possibility that Eddie ran away. At least Deke hasn't made bail. He's still in jail.'

'Well, that's one piece of good news. I suppose Belle is distraught, although whether she cares more about Eddie or Deke is a mystery.'

'She's trying to raise Deke's bail. A fine citizen like him shouldn't be rotting away in a cell,' Alec said sarcastically.

'How *can* she?' Juliet demanded. 'What's wrong with her? Is it love?'

Alec shrugged. 'Who knows? I don't believe it's love. I don't think Belle is in a good place mentally, but she's not crazy. Still . . .'

'Still what?'

'Something's going on with her and Deke that doesn't have anything to do with romance. But she's not talking.'

'Maybe she will when her son shows up,' Juliet said slowly, then looked at Alec. 'And he will show up. I believe you think he might be dead – dead like your sister.'

Alec looked appalled. 'No, I don't! What in God's name are you talking about?'

'He's the age Brenda was when she was killed. You care about him. You're terrified of another tragedy. You are, aren't you? I *know* it. But he's not dead, Alec. He's *not*, no matter what you think.'

Alec glowered at her and slammed out of her room.

Hours later, Alec was aware of thrashing and mumbling in his sleep. It was hot – so hot. His throat was parched, his tongue dry. He heard the men's voices, loud and frantic: 'You're gonna be OK. Just hang on, Wainwright.' 'Bullet didn't go through the helmet.' 'Is it bad? It looks bad.' Searing pain burned in his abdomen. *I'm dying*, Alec thought. *This is the end.*

Then he'd heard the deafening blades of the helicopter slicing the scorching air. 'They're takin' you out of this hell-hole.' Alec felt as if he were floating away and the world around him began to dim. He closed his eyes and through a blaze of pain and dust beneath his eyelids, he saw his sister's dead blue eyes staring back at him as she lay in the snow after the car wreck. 'I'm sorry,' he rasped, half awake. Then, in dream light, Eddie's face looked bleakly back at him. 'I'm sorry, Eddie. I didn't protect you.'

FIFTEEN

'We have to talk,' Alec said.

Juliet sat on a bench in the courtyard of the inn, watching the ducks swim and play in the clear water of the large, stone-surrounded pond. At ten o'clock, the sky was clear and the sun bright, a soft breeze wafting the slender limbs of a tall weeping willow behind them.

'What about?' she asked, not looking at him.

'You know what about.' He sat down beside her, handing her a large paper cup of coffee and a film-wrapped cherry turnover. 'I come bearing gifts.'

'Good. I didn't eat breakfast.' She removed the lid from the coffee and took a deep swallow. Then she unwrapped the turnover and nibbled. 'I needed sugar and caffeine.' She took another bite of the turnover. 'I repeat – what do you want to talk about?'

'The distance I've been feeling from you since the night before last.'

'When you yelled at me for going to Rocco's without asking permission?'

'I didn't yell.'

'You came close to yelling. As if you had the right to get mad because I went somewhere without telling you.'

'I was worried. More than worried. Who can blame me after all that's happened lately?' He hesitated. 'Still, I was wrong to act the way I did. I was rude.'

'And arrogant and domineering.'

'Yes, I guess I was. I'm sorry. But I've looked after you for so many years . . .'

Juliet turned to him, anger flaring in her eyes. 'You have not looked after me for *years*, Alec. You've been considerate and caring and yes, lately, you've looked after me from time to time. But you aren't my parent or my guardian. You aren't even my brother. There are limits to how much authority

I will allow you.' She paused. 'Not that I'm not extremely grateful for all you've done the last week.'

'I hope I've done something right.'

'You have and you know it. I don't know how I would have gotten through my parents' deaths without you. You know it. Everyone knows it. Leslie has her own family to look after. I'm alone.'

'You're not alone. You have me.'

'You're not really family, Alec. You don't owe me anything.'

'Oh, will you stop it!' Alec burst out. 'I loved Owen and Sera like a mother and father.'

She turned to him. 'And me? Do you love me like a sister? Like Brenda?'

He looked at her steadily, his dark brown eyes depthless. 'I most definitely don't love you like Brenda.'

'I didn't think so.'

'You don't know what I meant by that.'

'Then why don't you explain it?' Alec stubbornly turned his gaze to the quacking, frolicking ducks and Juliet softened her tone. 'You've never talked about Brenda. Never. Please, Alec. *Please* explain to me how you felt about her – about her death.'

'Do you know how hard it is for me to talk about her?' Alec asked quietly.

'I can guess. You've talked about your parents but never her. It isn't hard to figure out that it's painful.'

'Too painful.'

'Painful but necessary. It's been thirteen years, Alec. It's time.'

He looked down at his hands, clasped on his lap. For a moment, Juliet thought he wasn't going to answer her. Then he began speaking in a low voice.

'You didn't know Brenda, but you were around her a few times. What was your impression of her?'

'My impression?' Juliet pinched off three small pieces of her turnover and tossed it into the pond where four ducks dived for them. 'She was very different from you.' She hesitated. 'To be completely honest, she annoyed me. She was an attention-seeker, loud and disruptive.'

'Disruptive. Yes. She was from the time she was a little girl. She was diagnosed as hyperactive when she was five.'

'I didn't know. Was she treated professionally?'

'Not at first. But by the time she was eight, she was getting out of control and my parents put her in therapy. She began taking medication a year later, but she wouldn't stick to it. She didn't like the way it made her feel. So a lot of the time, Brenda was a handful.'

'That must have been hard on your family.'

'My parents were happily married, just like yours, but Brenda did put a strain on things. There was a lot of arguing and she'd have temper tantrums when they'd force her to start taking her medicine again. After she did, her behavior would even out and things were fine for a while. Then she'd stop the meds and the whole cycle started again.'

'I'm sorry, Alec.'

'Oh, it wasn't something terrible. It could have been easily managed if she would have cooperated. That's why I got so frustrated with her. And my parents. When she didn't take her meds, she lost all impulse control, got aggressive and my parents were worried, but not angry. They didn't force her to do anything.' Alec looked at Juliet. '*I* was angry. By the time she was twelve, I'd almost completely lost patience with her.'

'You were a kid, too.'

'But I was her older brother.'

'Don't you think Fin would have lost patience with *me*?'

'Yes. But I also lost patience with my parents. I resented that they wouldn't take control of her. I know they felt sorry for her. They told me she couldn't help it. But she could have helped it by taking her medication. They could have helped it – by *making* her take her medication, not giving her free passes because they felt guilty.'

'Guilty for what?'

'They blamed genetics for her problem.' He lifted his head and gazed at the ducks on the lake. 'But you want to hear about the wreck.'

'Not out of curiosity—'

'Out of concern for me. I understand, Juliet. I *know* you.' Juliet couldn't think of anything to say. Silence spun out for a moment and then Alec began speaking in a low monotone. 'We were going to Burlington, Vermont, to spend Christmas with my mother's father. He was our last living relative and he'd already had one stroke. Brenda didn't want to go at all. My mother wanted to fly but my father insisted on driving even though it would take us two full days in the car. Anyway, things were tense and Brenda had decided to show her temper about the whole trip by going off her meds almost a week before we left home. She didn't tell anyone but I knew it our first day on the road.'

He drew a deep breath, still gazing at the ducks. 'We took our SUV and were an hour away from Grandfather's. Brenda and I were in the back seats. The third row of seats was down. She'd started the trip being annoying and by the second evening, she was awful – alternately singing at the top of her voice and arguing with everyone, especially me. Snow was really coming down. My parents were exhausted, mad at her, mad at each other, not talking to each other. They'd given up saying *anything* to her and left her to me. I'd gotten an iPod five generation for my birthday – Brenda was getting one for Christmas – but she didn't know that and she was jealous of mine. I was concentrating on it when she grabbed it and threw it in the back. I was furious. I . . . I felt like I *hated* her.' He frowned and a tear ran down his face. 'Anyway, I unfastened my seat belt and climbed in the back to get it. Dad told me to leave it and get up in the seat and fasten my belt. I didn't. Then we began spinning. I know now we'd hit a patch of black ice. Mom and Brenda started screaming as we turned over and over. Everyone else stayed in place but I was flung all over the back as we went down what felt like a hill. I remember crashing against the roof of the car and hearing something in me cracking. Finally we hit something hard.'

He looked at Juliet, his eyes tortured. 'No one made a sound. Juliet, I swear, and it was like I had only one thought: *Get out of this car*. I didn't think of my parents or Brenda or what had happened. It was just, *You'll die if you don't get out of this car.* I managed to raise up, grab the tailgate door handle, open it and push out into the snow. My left side hurt horribly and my left leg felt nearly useless, but I dragged myself a few feet away. The car was at a forty-five-degree angle smashed on the driver's side against a giant tree. Then . . .'

Juliet put her hand lightly on his thigh. 'You don't have to go on.'

'Yes. Yes, I do. I've never told you and I have to because I don't think you really know me.'

Juliet wanted to protest that she *did* know him, but she realized it was important for him to tell her about the wreck. Certainly he'd told officials at the time, but that wasn't the same as unburdening himself to someone close. 'Go ahead, Alec.'

'I heard the first burst of fire coming from the car. That's all I'd heard since the crash. The hood of the car was burning and then I saw fire inside the front of the car. I thought, *Mom and Dad are up there.* I started pulling myself through the snow back to the car when the whole interior burst into flames. I stopped. I just sat in the snow, gaping.' He drew a deep breath. 'Then I saw Brenda's face at what was left of the side window.'

'Oh, my God,' Juliet gasped.

'I remember her eyes. They were wild. Her hands clawed at the glass, red, burning. She screamed *Alec* again and again. I saw the flames leaping behind her. I started to crawl to the car. I was dragging one leg and every breath hurt. I was going *so* slowly – just creeping. And she began to shriek. *Alec, help me! Please, Alec! I'm sorry. Help me . . . help me . . .* And then her voice faded and there was nothing in the window except a wall of fire. Fire.'

Juliet choked back tears and managed to say steadily, 'There was nothing you could do, Alec.'

'I could have tried harder. The side doors wouldn't open, but I could have gotten to the car faster and dragged her out the back. I know Mom and Dad were already gone, lost in the fire, but Brenda was *alive*! I let her die!' His voice dropped to a whisper. 'I let her die.'

After Alec finished his story of the wreck, they sat quietly on the bench for nearly twenty minutes. At last, Alec said, 'I feel more tired than I have in my whole life.'

Juliet took his hand. 'You look more tired than *I've* ever seen you. Alec, you look shattered.'

He squeezed her hand. 'I am. I'm sorry.'

'Why?'

'It's been years. I should be stronger. I should have recovered.'

'From something like the wreck? Don't be foolish. You never completely recover from something so horrendous.'

'No? I think I should have. I think a stronger man would have.'

'You're wrong.' He said nothing. 'Why don't you go up to your room and lie down for a while? I doubt if you got much sleep last night. I didn't. And Hutch would be very glad for your company.'

'I don't think I'm fit company for anyone right now.'

'Yes, you are, but you're exhausted. You need sleep. Will you at least try?'

Alec nodded. 'Yeah, I guess. I don't have any energy left. I don't have any words left, either, but Hutch never minds. What will you do?'

'I think I'll go downtown and stop at Hollisters' and Pauline's to thank them for the reception. I'll insist on paying something for each bill, though. I won't take charity.'

'You've always been determined to earn your own way, even through college.'

'My parents had to pay for part of my tuition.'

'But you always had part-time jobs, even though it wasn't necessary. Anyway, that stubbornness of yours is a trait I admire.'

'You didn't last night.'

Alec winced. 'Last night. Forgive me. Juliet. I was out of line. You don't have to answer to me. And, well . . . I *never* want you to look at me as an authority figure. That's the last thing I want to be to you.'

Juliet leaned over and gave him a quick kiss on the cheek. 'That was exactly the right thing to say, Alec Wainwright. Thank you very much.'

Alec went to his room and Juliet to hers where she changed

into beige linen pants and a blue chiffon blouse. She hadn't
fully absorbed the agony that Alec had felt after the car wreck,
but she felt calmer, more understanding of his sometimes
smothering protection of her. She didn't need to be protected,
though. She thought of herself the night before, frightened
that he would catch her sneaking off to Rocco's bar, slipping
a note under his door like a child, nearly cringing when he
came to her door when she returned. The way she'd acted had
encouraged his attitude. She was as much to blame as him,
she told herself. Things would change, though. She would
never again act as if she needed his permission to live her life
the way she wanted.

Juliet was glad she took her umbrella with her. After a futile
effort to get Beau Hollister and then Pauline to agree to let
her pay for anything, she stepped onto the sidewalk and into
a gale. She opened her umbrella, which another gust of wind
promptly caught and swept out of her wet hand, sending it
skittering down the sidewalk before it banged onto the corner
of Pauline's and made a sharp turn into the alley between the
flower shop and the deserted Regal Cinema.

Juliet's chiffon blouse was soaked and her long hair hanging
limp and wet as she pursued the umbrella into the alley. Ahead
of her ran a tall, bulky man dressed in jeans and a black rain
poncho with the hood pulled up. The sight of him distracted
her momentarily from her umbrella, especially when she
noticed that he went to a side door of the Regal and pulled it
open. Surprised because the Regal had been closed and locked
for years, she watched. His hand slipped on the wet knob and
the door blew wide open. She was only about ten feet away
from him and heard a high-pitched frantic voice call 'Help!
Help me!' before the man slammed the door shut behind him.

Something about the voice had seemed familiar to Juliet
and, in spite of her fear, she crept closer to the door. She heard
nothing now, but someone was in the abandoned theater with
the big man – someone frightened and desperate. Her inner
voice told her to run, but she ignored it and instead leaned
against the building and reached in her tote bag, pulling out
her cell phone. Rain streamed down her face and she pushed

back her wet hair as she dialed 911. 'This is Juliet Reid. I'm at the Regal—' Before she got out another word, the door opened, a strong arm reached out, wrapped around her, and dragged her into darkness.

SIXTEEN

For what seemed like an eternity, Juliet felt as if all the air had left her body. She couldn't breathe. She tried to see but everything was black. She felt an iron grip pinning her arms against her torso. When she kicked, she was lifted off the floor. The smell of perspiration and stale body odor overwhelmed her and she heard deep, slightly wheezy breathing. She tried to calm herself, trying to suck in just one breath to keep her from passing out. As she quieted, a weak, hopeless cry floated to her: 'Is someone there? Please help me.'

Juliet's heart skipped a beat, sending a shudder through her but finally expanding her lungs enough to draw in air. She gasped but forced herself not to struggle or try to say a word. With all of her will, she managed to stay quiet and keep her body still, almost limp. And within seconds, the iron grasp loosened slightly.

'Hold still,' a deep voice finally rasped.

Juliet managed to swallow even though her mouth felt parched. 'I am.'

'Don't do anything.'

'I won't. I promise.' She took another breath. 'What do you want?'

'Want?' The voice sounded genuinely puzzled. 'I don't know.'

'Then why—'

'Is someone there?' came the weak and obviously young voice from far away. 'Who's there?'

'You be quiet,' her captor ordered her. 'You got to be quiet.' Seconds ticked by. 'How come you came here?'

'I didn't mean to. I was chasing my umbrella.'

'You were callin' someone. I saw your phone.' He reached in her tote bag and dug out the cell phone. 'Here it is.'

'I was just calling home because I was caught in the rain with no umbrella.'

'That's a lie. You were callin' the police. I know about

police.' He threw the phone on the floor and stomped on it. 'I know about you, Juliet.'

Wendell Booth! Why hadn't she guessed before? The size and strength, the voice gritty but still recognizable. 'You know me?' she asked innocently.

'Sure I do. All your life. And you know me. You want to hurt me.'

'I don't want to hurt anyone. That's the truth.' She waited a moment. 'Who's here with you?'

'You know.'

'No, I don't,' she said although an idea was beginning to niggle in her brain. 'Is it someone you're trying to protect?'

'Protect?' He'd been startled into sounding unmistakably like Wendell. 'How'd you know?'

'Because I think the person I hear calling out is Eddie.' She nearly shuddered, waiting for him to explode with rage, but he was quiet. 'You care about Eddie. You love Eddie.'

'He's Benny come back to me.'

'Yes, he's like your brother Benny.' Juliet's instinct was to win him, not antagonize him. 'You wouldn't hurt Benny. You'd only protect him. That's how I know.'

'Gee. You're smart. Smarter than Fin. Nicer than Fin.'

'I know you didn't like him, but I hope you won't hold that against *me*.'

'Well . . . my parents said I should hate you just like we hated your mom and dad.'

'Did *you* hate my mom and dad?'

'Yeah. They got a lawyer to put me in prison. It was awful . . . *awful*.' Juliet heard a catch in his voice. 'They did that to me. But . . . well, you were too young. The lawyer didn't work for you.'

'No, he didn't.' Juliet felt almost dizzy from fear, shortness of breath, and being cautious about every word she said. She knew she couldn't go on much longer. 'Wendell, do you think I could sit down for a few minutes? I'm wet and cold and tired.'

'Ummm . . . maybe it wouldn't hurt. But not here. Not by the door.'

Three camping lanterns lit the aisle leading toward the stage.

He picked her up and carried her past rows of seats to the front of the theater where he sat her on a wooden chair, wrapped a rope around her chest fastening it behind the back of the chair, then pulled her arms behind the chair and tied another piece of rope around her wrists. He tested the ropes twice, then grunted in satisfaction and stared at her, barely blinking.

Juliet felt as if she would scream. She couldn't stand that stare. 'Could I have some water, Wendell? I'm really thirsty.'

'Got no water. They turned the water off in here. I stole some Cokes, though. They're warm. You want one anyway?'

'Yes. Thank you.'

He lumbered off and Juliet whispered loudly, 'Eddie? Are you near enough to hear me?' Nothing. 'Eddie?' He didn't answer and she heard no more feeble cries. She was too far away from him.

Another camping lantern sat near her and she looked around in its light. The Regal Cinema had been built in 1965 in imitation of the magnificent atmospheric theaters of the 1920s. It couldn't compare with the Olympic Theater in Miami or the Carpenter Theater in Richmond, Virginia, but it was considered breathtaking in Parrish, Ohio. Juliet's parents had told her about having their first date in the theater. Years later, Juliet had seen for herself the domed ceiling with its myriad of twinkling stars, the magnificent gilt-edged balcony, the impressive opera boxes placed on the red brocade walls decorated with elegant, muted sconces, the towering pillars holding the intricate arch above the red velvet curtains that drew back with a flourish as someone played the three-console organ at movietime. And she remembered Wendell Booth, sitting near the front, either spellbound and silent or whooping with glee every Saturday night.

Shortly he returned with a can of Coke, which he opened and tipped to her mouth. Although part of it leaked down her chin, she still got enough of the fizzling sweet liquid to slightly ease her thirst. After a third sip, she asked, 'How long have you been here, Wendell?'

'Two, three days. I don't remember.'

'And you have food?'

'Why? You hungry?'

'No, but I wonder about you. And Eddie. You must be feeding him.'

'Sure I do!' Wendell sounded indignant. 'You think I'd let him starve? I steal things. God doesn't mind. He understands that we need food.'

'No, he won't mind, or you would have been caught by now.'

'That's right! God thinks I'm doin' the right thing.'

'Yes, but what about Eddie? Is he scared?'

'Why would he be scared?'

'His voice sounded scared. Why would he be afraid if you're protecting him?'

'He's just upset about his mom. He says she'll be worried. I don't think she'll care as long as she's with that Deke Nevins.'

'Did Deke do something to Eddie?'

'Yeah. Hit him.'

'And you're protecting him from Deke.'

Wendell didn't answer.

'Did Eddie come looking for you after Deke hit him?'

'Not exactly. But I got him. He's safe . . . from everyone.'

'Deke's been arrested. He can't hurt Eddie now.'

Wendell's gaze sharpened. 'Arrested for what?'

'For assaulting me, and Belle, and a police officer. He's in jail.'

Wendell huffed. 'That one's got nine lives. He'll get out real soon. Eddie won't be safe. No one will.'

'No one? What do you think Deke will do to someone else?'

'Something. He's a mean one.' He huffed. 'You want more Coke or are you just gonna to sit here askin' questions?'

'More Coke, please.' This time Juliet managed not to dribble and took a big swallow. 'It's good even if it's warm.' He stared at her. 'I remember seeing you here when the theater was open. You loved it here.'

'It was my favorite place.' He waited a few seconds before he continued, 'I'm gonna open it up again. Not now. But someday when I have money.'

'That would be wonderful. It was beautiful.'

'It was magic,' he pronounced, nodding slowly. 'Magic.'

'Did Benny come here with you?'

'Yeah. He loved it then, but he doesn't like it so well now.'

So Benny had liked the theater but Eddie didn't, at least under these circumstances.

'Are you sure he shouldn't go home?'

'Yes, I'm sure!' Wendell thundered. 'You don't know anything.'

'I know Eddie is afraid of Deke but he's afraid here, too.'

'He doesn't understand, that's all. But I've got him.' He wandered away muttering, 'But I've got him. I've got him.'

Oh my God, Juliet thought in despair. *Why did I follow that umbrella down the alley? But if I hadn't, I wouldn't have found Eddie. What do I do now, though? Eddie and I are both prisoners.*

She sat stiffly, listening for some sound from Eddie, but she heard nothing. Was he too sick to call out anymore? Had Wendell forgotten to feed him or give him liquids? Had he badly hurt himself struggling to escape? Had the blow Deke had given him been worse than he'd thought? He wouldn't have gone to a hospital for fear of Deke finding him. Damn it, she'd known Belle was lying to her at Rocco's. She'd said Eddie and Deke had an argument but she didn't know what happened afterward. But Belle *must* have known and she'd ignored any harm Deke might have done her son. Fretting didn't count. She'd taken no action and Juliet knew she would continue doing nothing. And Belle called herself a loving mother, Juliet thought in disgust. In his way, Wendell seemed to be more protective of Eddie than Belle did.

She kept listening and sat still, not wanting to do anything that might agitate Wendell. How long would it take to make him feel secure, though? She'd lost all sense of time and she couldn't see her watch because her hands were tied behind the back of the chair. Juliet twisted them in frustration and to her surprise, the rope was slack. Only slightly, but still loose.

Wendell abruptly returned. He opened a package of Twinkies, and began feeding her one. 'I love these things. So does Eddie. I just fed him two. He's fine for a while.'

Juliet chewed slowly and made herself smile. 'What else do you feed him?'

'I told you I have to steal things, mostly from those little stores that sell gasoline, too. I go late at night when the check-out people are tired and not paying much attention to the customers. I got us some meat slices in packages – baloney, pickle loaf. I got bread and some cheese.' When she finished hers, he began eating his own. 'And lots of Twinkies.'

'That's all you've had for at least three days?'

'And Cokes.' He glowered. 'What's wrong? You think I'm starvin' Benny?'

'Eddie. He's older than Benny was when he . . . when you last saw him. He needs more food than Benny did.'

'I'm lots bigger than Eddie and I feel fine. I feel great.'

'Really? You look sort of gray, like you're hungry or sick.'

'How can you tell what color I am in this light? You don't look so hot and you just got here.' He broke off and his vision seemed to turn inward. 'I saw you cryin'. You were sittin' on the steps of the tree house.'

'So you were out there by the creek?'

'I wanted to go into the tree house or at least look in the windows, but I couldn't because you were there. Later, I went up and the door was unlocked. I went in.' So it was Wendell that night Hutch had gone wild barking and Alec had run out to get them, Juliet thought. 'I really liked the tree house, but after I got in trouble there, my parents burned it down.' He paused and added sadly, 'I wish they hadn't done that.'

'Me, too. My friend Leslie and I used to play in the tree house when Fin wasn't there.'

Wendell looked up at the dark ceiling. 'Remember the stars that used to float around and blink up there?'

'Yes. They were beautiful.'

'They sure were. My parents said whoever built this place was tryin' to imitate Heaven, which was a sin, but I liked them anyway, even if they were a sin. But in general, I don't approve of sin,' he informed her seriously.

'Oh. Well, neither do I. That's something we have in common.'

He looked at her suspiciously. 'You're bein' awful nice. How come you're not mad, not fightin' and callin' me names?'

'You haven't hurt me. You've been very nice to me.' Juliet

swallowed. 'You've treated me like a friend. I'm not afraid or angry.'

'Huh. Well, I didn't mean to scare you, but you took me by surprise. I figured you'd carry on somethin' terrible when I dragged you in and tied you to a chair. You've been OK, though.' He looked confused. 'Maybe you're not really bad.'

'I'm not.'

'Then how come you wanted me to go to prison?'

Juliet's heart fluttered as she tried to think of an acceptable answer. Finally she said truthfully, 'I thought you killed my brother, Wendell. I loved Fin like you loved Benny.'

'Like I *love* Benny. And they aren't alike. Benny is the sweetest person that ever walked this earth.'

'Fin could be sweet.'

'Not to me.'

'Because he didn't think your music was right for his band? "Enter Sandman" is an odd choice to play on a recorder. I know Deke Nevins told you to play it.'

Wendell's face sharpened. 'You and Deke are friends?'

'Absolutely not. I can't stand him. *He* talked you into playing that song because he knew Fin wouldn't like it. He tricked you, Wendell. Fin just gave you an honest opinion.'

'Fin said it was *all wrong*.'

'It was. But you could have learned some different songs.'

'Deke said after I left my audition that Fin nearly died laughing at me.'

'Deke told you that? You can't believe a word Deke says. You *know* that, Wendell.'

'Well . . . well, it's all water over the bridge – way over, the way water goes. I was awful mad at Fin but don't care about him anymore.'

'Well, that's good because he's *dead!*' Juliet realized how harsh she'd sounded, which was the wrong path to take with Wendell. She immediately made her voice kinder. 'He's been dead a long time and we're all getting over him. Even me.'

Wendell stared at her. 'You're depressin' me. I'm gonna go talk to Benny.'

He wandered away, heading to the back of the theater. Juliet heard no noise and counted to three hundred before she began twisting her hands again. They were rigid with tension and she forced herself to relax, to alleviate the tightness in her muscles. After a few moments, her hands seemed more flexible, although the rope was chaffing her skin. She ignored the stinging, continuing to work her wrists gently, patiently. After a minute, the rope felt slightly looser, but she thought she might be imagining it. She closed her eyes and kept up a slow, deliberate rhythm, refusing to let herself get upset or frustrated.

Finally her right hand slipped free of the rope. She drew a deep breath and dropped the rope off her wrists, then wriggled her hands, restoring full blood flow and dexterity. Then she reached for the knot that held the rope binding her to the chair. She worked at it with fingers grown strong and agile from years of almost daily piano practice and when Juliet finally felt a sheen of sweat forming on her forehead from intense concentration, the knot fell open.

Jubilation rushed through her as she leaned forward and drew a deep breath for the first time since Wendell had tied her up. She'd done it! She'd managed to free herself from the clumsy bond that had kept her nearly immobile for what seemed an hour.

But what should she do next?

Don't jump up and run, Juliet told herself. *You don't know where Wendell is. You don't know what he might do. You need to be careful, and shrewd, and above all, quiet.*

Her gaze shot around the theater, lit only by camping lanterns – one near her at the stage, three spaced along each wall, and two on the high balcony. They were just spots of glowing light in a sea of shadows. She looked to her left toward the door Wendell had used to drag her inside. She couldn't see it, but she knew it was about halfway up the outer aisle.

Juliet slid from the seat of her chair and went down on her hands and knees. The carpet smelled slightly moldy but it cushioned any sound and she crept across it slowly, heading left and skirting around the camping lantern. She wished she could move it, so it didn't illuminate the now-empty chair, but she didn't dare. Any transfer of light could draw Wendell's attention. What if he were looking at her now, slinking along like a pathetic worm just waiting for him to come and stomp on her like he had her cell phone? *Well, there's nothing I can do about that*, she thought. *I can only go forward, hoping he's distracted, praying I make it to the door and freedom where I can get help for Eddie.*

She made the turn and started up the far-left aisle, feeling along the wall until at last she reached the metal door frame. Taking a few seconds to absorb the surge of triumph she felt, Juliet then raised up and found the doorknob.

It was locked.

Of course, you fool, she thought as she needlessly again tried turning the immovable metal knob. *Did you think Wendell would leave the door unlocked so anyone could wander in or you could escape? He's not stupid. He's careful and canny and determined to keep this an impenetrable sanctuary for Eddie and him.*

Juliet knew there were other exit doors throughout the theater but she had no idea where to find them. The ornate theater entrance still faced Main Street with the round, gold-painted metal box office locked behind glass doors and an old-fashioned folding metal security grille beneath a marquee that had gone dark years ago. She had no hope of getting out that way. But she couldn't give up. If she kept going, she might find a way out.

She finally stood up and inched along the wall, staying as far away from the glow of the camping lanterns as possible. She wished she'd been in the 1,500-seat theater more recently and better remembered the interior. The last time she'd been here had been with Leslie to watch *Inception*, which neither of them had understood and laughed about later. 'Oh well, at least we got to see Leonardo DiCaprio and Tom Hardy,' Leslie had giggled. That was at least ten years ago, and less than five years later, the theater had closed.

At last Juliet reached the wall that separated the theater auditorium from the lobby. Her clothes were still damp from the rain and clung to her, making her uncomfortable and chilly. Already, she was tired and miserable. But she had to keep going, she told herself as she felt her way along slowly until she found the double doors and stepped out onto the marble floor. Dim daylight shone through the glass front doors and she saw that rain still poured so hard the drops bounced off the sidewalk. Thunder rumbled in the distance muting any noise she might be making by opening doors. In the gray light, she saw the winged stairways on either side of the lobby leading to the balcony. She stayed to the left and began climbing, holding onto the railing. She didn't count steps, but for some reason, she remembered that the balcony was thirty-seven-feet high. Maybe Kyle Hollister had told her that on one of their long-ago dates. It was the kind of thing that interested him and once they had sat up there eating popcorn and watching a movie she didn't remember.

When Juliet reached the top of the stairs, she stood still for a moment, listening. She heard a faint moan near one of the camping lanterns located near the balcony railing. Beside the lantern, she saw a long bundle on the floor. She moved toward it slowly, puzzled. Then she realized it was a comforter tied with ropes at the foot and around the middle. At one end of the comforter, she saw a thatch of dark blond hair. 'Eddie?' she whispered cautiously. 'Eddie, is that you? It's Juliet.'

'Juliet.' His voice was a low, raspy moan. 'Help me.'

She rushed toward him. His face was alarmingly pale, his lips chapped, his eyelids swollen. 'What has he done to you?'

'I'm not hurt.'

'You have a bloodstained cloth stuck to your head with tape.'

'Wendell didn't hit me. Someone else did.'

'Deke.'

'He hit me enough to hurt in the evening, and later that night someone else knocked me out. Wendell put that bandage on me. Then he wrapped me in this comforter because he said it's soft and thick and then he tied the ropes to it. He said he knew I'd try to get away because I didn't understand.'

'Understand what?'

'Why I'm here. Oh, God, I'm so hot. And hungry and thirsty. A while ago my stomach started cramping and . . . I have diarrhea.'

'Where's Wendell?'

'He goes into a room off the balcony. There's a couch in there. It's where he sleeps. I think he's asleep now.'

Juliet was already working at the knots in the rope, her fingers sore from her earlier bout with untying knots. 'How long have you been here?'

'I don't know. It seems like forever.' He swallowed. 'Is my mom OK?'

'Yes. I saw her last night. Deke's in jail.'

'For what?'

'Assault. Anyway, you're safe from him.'

'No, I'm not,' Eddie said dully. 'She'll get him out.'

'Why? I know he hit you. He hit *her.*'

'It doesn't matter.'

'Because she loves him?'

'Maybe. Or something like that.'

'There!' Juliet said triumphantly as she loosened the knot near Eddie's feet and slid off the rope. 'One more to go.'

'Hurry. He could wake up any time.'

'I know. I'm going as fast as I can. I'll get us out of here – I promise.'

He tried to smile and failed. Then tears rose in his bloodshot eyes. 'How did you find me?'

'Accidentally, although I've been worrying about you.'

'I'm sorry Wendell caught you.'

'I'm sorry he caught me, too, but if he hadn't, I wouldn't have found you, so it was worth it. You mean a lot to me, Eddie Maddox. And to Alec. You meant the world to Mom and Dad, too, God rest their souls.'

'*Their* souls? Your mother?'

'She dead, Eddie. Murdered.'

Tears began streaming down Eddie's face and Juliet felt her own eyes stinging. This poor boy, she thought. What a bad hand life had dealt him. He knew his mother didn't love him, no matter how many times she told him she cared. He was too smart not to know better.

'Ha! Success!' Juliet almost chortled before lowering her voice. She began pulling off the rope before helping Eddie unwrap himself from the heavy comforter. Once free, he began clambering up on shaky legs. 'Can you walk?' she asked.

'I can in a minute. My legs are asleep.' He stamped them quietly. 'Pins and needles.'

'They'll go away in a few seconds.'

'How are we going to get out?'

'I'm not sure. I figure out something—'

'What are you doin'?' Wendell roared. Juliet and Eddie went rigid as his voice boomed in the darkness. 'You're not leavin' here! Neither of you! I won't let you!'

He rushed at them from the right, his big body suddenly swift and agile. Juliet pushed Eddie behind her as Wendell grabbed her shoulders and glared at her with enraged pale blue eyes. Then he began to shake her.

'Wendell, stop!' Eddie shouted. 'Leave her alone!'

'Trouble, trouble, trouble! I knew she'd be trouble!'

Eddie came out from behind Juliet, took a few steps back, and lunged at Wendell, hitting him in the side. Wendell staggered but didn't release Juliet. 'Stop it!' Eddie screamed. 'Wendell, don't!'

Wendell seemed beyond hearing and Juliet felt like a rag doll in his strong grip as she whipped back and forth. 'Nobody hurts Benny!' he said in a guttural monotone.

'She's not trying to hurt me but you're going to hurt *her*. You don't want to hurt a girl, Wendell. If you do . . . if you do I won't love you anymore. I *won't*! Stop shaking her!'

'Benny will always love Wendell. *Always*.'

'No, he won't. *I* won't! I swear it on the Bible!'

'She'll tell people who'll come and take you and you'll be hurt—'

The sound of metal grating floated up to them. Juliet registered it through the ringing in her ears as she struggled to escape Wendell's grasp, but she didn't know what it was. More pounding and rattling. Then came the distant sound of glass shattering on marble. Juliet suddenly realized that the grating metal had been the security grille opening and now someone was crashing through the glass entrance doors into the lobby. A man shouted, 'Juliet! Juliet Reid! This is the police!'

Eddie screamed, 'Up here!'

Wendell's eyes widened at the word *police*. 'How?' he

gasped. 'You . . . you . . . *you* . . .' His lips drew back over his teeth and he lifted her high, shaking her harder.

'No, Wendell! It's too late! Don't hurt her!' Eddie shrieked. Juliet's legs kicked, her arms flailed, but Wendell's grip on her shoulders only tightened as his gaze went eerily blank.

'You'll *kill* her! If you do, you'll go to hell! You'll never see Benny again!' Eddie cried, but Juliet knew Wendell didn't hear him. Dots started to spark behind her eyes as Eddie backed up, then charged at Wendell, throwing his whole body weight against the man's side.

Wendell staggered but regained his footing. 'Juliet, you have to help!' Eddie ordered.

Her mind questioned, *how*?

'Fight him with me! *Now*, Juliet!' Eddie shouted. He lunged at Wendell. His words roused her and Juliet used the last of her strength to fling herself to the left. This time Wendell teetered. Eddie thrust himself against Wendell relentlessly until the big man's feet in their clumsy work shoes got tangled. Wendell grunted and, dragging Juliet with him, stumbled toward the railing where he completely lost his footing. He blinked at her, seeming to see her again. Eddie kicked at Wendell's legs until he finally landed a blow to the man's knee. Wendell whimpered in a high, strange voice and his body swayed over the ornate gold-painted railing that topped at his hip. Juliet frantically grasped the railing with her left hand as Wendell, still holding her, bent double over the edge. Eddie plunged at him again and threw him completely off balance.

Juliet screamed, desperately clutching the railing with one sweating, weak hand, as Wendell tipped over and fell thirty-seven feet to the seats below him, landing with a sickening crash, his face turned toward the ceiling of the theater where the stars he'd loved once twinkled magically in the heavens.

SEVENTEEN

Eddie grabbed Juliet and pulled her away from the railing. They both collapsed onto the floor of the balcony, completely spent. She looked at Eddie, almost too exhausted to speak.

Remarkably, he grinned at her. They'd done it – they were free. She didn't want to think about anything else, particularly Wendell. She lay nearly motionless, trying to draw deep breaths and orient herself until suddenly a face appeared above hers. 'Kyle?' she asked in surprise.

'Yes, Juliet. Are you all right?'

'I'm not sure. Wendell seemed to just lose it. Eddie saved me. If it weren't for him . . .'

'I didn't do much,' Eddie said weakly.

'The paramedics are on their way,' Kyle said. 'Don't try to sit up.'

'I have no desire to sit up, Kyle Hollister. How did you know we were here?'

'We didn't know Eddie was here. You called nine-one-one. You gave your name and said, "I'm at the Regal," before the call ended. Then we lost your phone – we couldn't trace you. We knew you were around the theater, though, and luckily we went into Pauline's. She said you'd been there over an hour earlier then left in the pouring rain, but your umbrella had come blowing up the street the opposite way past her shop and she'd retrieved it. We checked the parking lot and your car was there. We were almost certain you were in the theater and in trouble. The owner of the Regal lives a block away. He's at least a hundred years old. He had the keys. He got the security gate open but he kept fumbling with the key to the entrance doors so we just broke the glass.'

'Thank God. Please don't ask me the exact details of what happened right now. I'm a little fuzzy. I'll tell you everything in a few minutes.' Juliet turned her head. 'Eddie, are you OK?'

'I'll do.'

'You'll *do*? That's not good.'

'I'm awfully tired but I'll do.'

Juliet smiled up at Kyle. 'He's the bravest boy in the world. Wendell has been holding him in here for days.'

'Why?'

'I'm not sure. It was something about protecting him. Maybe Eddie can tell you more later.'

'That's all right. Don't worry about it now. Just relax.' Kyle raised his head and gazed around the balcony. 'I always knew I'd get you back here again someday. I just didn't dream it would be under these circumstances.'

'I hate to say this, but I don't remember what movie we saw when we sat up here.'

He grinned. 'I have no idea. I only remember that it was awful.'

Juliet grinned back. 'Yes, it was. I guess I'm not meant to enjoy this balcony.'

A man and woman appeared announcing they were the emergency technicians and Kyle moved out of their way while one began examining Juliet and the other Eddie. She heard him moan softly once and cough twice. She wondered if he'd suffered broken ribs or internal injuries. She was certain Wendell wouldn't have intentionally hurt *Benny*, but he didn't know his own strength and he'd been rolling up and binding Eddie with ropes for days.

The woman took Juliet's pulse and announced it slightly elevated. She listened to her breathing, which was now normal. Juliet had a temperature of 97.8 and just-above-average blood pressure. Eddie, however, had a fever of 101.2 and showed signs of dehydration. His stomach was slightly distended, and he had soreness in the right rib area. He would have to be immobilized before being carried to the ambulance. Both he and Juliet were headed to the Emergency Room.

As they were loading Juliet into the ambulance, Pauline appeared, coatless and trembling. 'Oh, Juliet, *ma chére*! I was so worried! What happened? Oh, you can't tell me now. Are you hurt?'

'No. Just scared. They insist on taking me to the hospital for a routine check-up, though.'

'That's good. Bless you, my girl.'

'Everything will be all right,' Kyle assured Juliet before they closed the ambulance doors.

'Wendell *is* dead, isn't he?'

'Yes. His neck is broken.'

'I see.' For some reason she didn't understand, Juliet's eyes filled with tears. 'Could you call Alec?'

It was 8:30 when Jon arrived at his mother's home. Leslie was going to be upset. *Very* upset, which was the last thing he wanted, but there was nothing he could do except try to keep her as calm as possible under the circumstances. He braced himself before he walked in, full of apologies.

'I'm sorry. I'm late. Very late,' he got out in a rush. 'I'm a complete jerk.'

'You called almost three hours ago and said you'd be a bit late,' Carole said tartly. 'A *bit* late. We know what a *bit* means to you so we didn't bother waiting dinner on you – Tommy was hungry.'

'OK, Carole, I'm awful. But something's happened and I wanted to find out all the details before I came home or I knew the three of you would be on your phones until midnight.'

'Thank you for that explanation, darling,' Danielle said calmly. 'We had a lovely dinner. All of your favorites. Tommy cried because you weren't home at bedtime. Now what is your big news?'

'You haven't gotten any calls?'

'No, Jon. We turned off our phones before dinner.'

'Then I couldn't have called you again anyway, so I don't know why you're mad.'

'Jon, will you please stop and announce your bulletin?'

'Juliet Reid was attacked and held prisoner by Wendell Booth in the Regal Cinema.'

'What?' all three women cried at once.

'Juliet—'

'Is she hurt?'

'No, Leslie. But Wendell has been keeping Eddie Maddox for days and Eddie's in the hospital.'

'Is he critical?' Danielle asked.

'I talked to several people who didn't know anything definite. I just know he needs to stay a couple of days at least. I think there are some cracked ribs and . . . I don't remember . . . complications of some sort. Nothing too serious.'

Leslie had been sitting on the couch but she jumped up, facing her husband. 'How could you know this and not tell me? What's wrong with you?'

'You turned off your phones—'

'Oh, damn the phones! You could have come home as soon as you heard. Where's Juliet?'

'I think she went back to the Heritage Inn. That's where she and Alec are staying.'

'I *know* where she's staying. I took clothes there for her mother's funeral!' Leslie abruptly burst into tears. 'Oh, dear God!'

'Les, please settle down,' Jon implored.

'I don't *want* to settle down!'

'Juliet is all right, I tell you. The hospital wouldn't have released her if she wasn't OK.'

'What in the world did she do to deserve all of this?' Leslie was sobbing. 'I don't understand. Why is this happening to her?'

Danielle rose from her chair, grabbed a tissue, and went to Leslie, hugging her. 'Sweetheart, none of us understand. It's terrible. But you falling apart isn't going to help her. You're *so* emotional lately, dear. You're worrying me.' She handed Leslie the tissue. 'Blow your nose and dry your tears. I'll get you some sweet, white port.

'I hate port! Besides, I'm pregnant!' Danielle, Carole, and even Jon gaped at her. 'Yes, I have a bun in the oven, I'm preggers, I'm knocked up—'

'I think everyone has the idea,' Jon interrupted.

Danielle looked utterly shocked. 'Why didn't you tell us?'

'We were waiting for the three-month mark, Mom,' Jon said. 'We're a little past that but with everything that's been going on, we held off telling you. But now you know and it's important that Leslie stay calm because of the miscarriage—'

'Don't you dare mention that!' Leslie ranted. 'How *could* you?'

Jon looked stricken. 'I'm sorry. Honey, please . . .'

'Leslie needs to calm down and you need to be quiet,' Danielle said firmly. 'Leslie, dear, sit on the couch. Carole will get you water or a soft drink or some of that chamomile tea you like.'

'Tea. It's calming.' Leslie thumped down on the couch and Danielle sat beside her, wrapping an arm around her shoulders.

'Just cry gently. Jon, give us more tissues. Carole, get her tea.' Jon grabbed a handful of tissues and Carole turned toward the kitchen. Danielle called, 'Be certain it's *chamomile* tea. We have several kinds.'

'I can read the tea bag boxes,' Carole muttered while Jon hovered over Leslie.

'Jon, you sit down, too. Over there in my chair.'

'Yes, ma'am.'

Leslie unexpectedly giggled. 'You sound like you're five, Jon.' Then she hiccupped. 'Did they catch Wendell?'

'He's dead. He was struggling with Juliet on the theater balcony and he fell.' Jon rubbed a hand over his forehead. 'Thank God. He should have died a long time ago. Of course his parents will raise holy hell, claim he was innocent, *murdered* by Juliet who should die for ending his useless life—'

'That's enough for now, Jon,' Danielle said sternly. 'Leslie has heard enough.'

'Will you stop giving me orders?'

'When you stop distressing your *pregnant* wife. Really, Jon, you should know better.'

He looked coldly at her. 'I think we should go home, Mother.'

'*Home!*' Leslie cried. 'Are you joking? It was probably Wendell who was prowling around the other night, trying to get in, nearly scaring Tommy and Juliet to death. I'm staying here with your mother and Carole. You can go home if you want to, Jon Tresswell.'

'Oh, dear lord.' Danielle's voice quivered. 'The other night must have terrified you and you're *pregnant*. I didn't know. It was even more dreadful than I thought. I'm so sorry.'

'It's not your fault. But Jon should have told me about Juliet as soon as he heard.'

'I didn't want to give you partial or incorrect information and that's why I waited to tell you. My judgment was bad, but I meant well.'

'You always *mean* well.'

'Leslie, darling, I don't think you're really mad at Jon. You're upset about Juliet, and with good reason, but you must relax. I mean, if you're expecting a baby. A baby!' Danielle smiled then said regretfully, 'I wish you'd thought enough of me to tell me weeks ago.'

'Here's the tea.' Carole walked in carrying a silver tray with a tea bag tag hanging out of a china cup. 'And it's chamomile, I promise.'

'Where's the sugar bowl and the creamer?'

'For chamomile tea?'

'For all teas.'

Carole groaned softly. 'I'll be right back.'

'I made a big mistake by not teaching that girl her way around a kitchen,' Danielle said. 'I tried to teach her to cook and Martha tried, but she simply refused.'

'She was spoiled.'

'So were you, Jon. And I don't want to hear any more talk about Leslie and Tommy going home – or you. You're staying here with your wife and son and mother and sister.' She looked compassionately at Leslie. 'Now, dear, what can I do for you?'

'I n-need to talk to Juliet.' Leslie sniffled. 'I have to hear from her own lips that she's all right.'

'Then after you've had your tea and stopped crying, you certainly should call her,' Danielle pronounced. 'I agree that it's the only way you can reassure yourself about your best friend, who's a *very* good girl. The best, except for you.'

'I'm not sure you should have come home from the hospital this evening. You look feverish.'

Juliet lay on the bed in her beautiful room at the inn and Alec had pulled an armchair beside her. He kept looking at her anxiously. 'I'm fine, Alec. Really I am. And I don't think I'm feverish. You've piled too many blankets on me plus Hutch won't move off my stomach.'

'I'll move him if he's making you uncomfortable.'

'He's not. I want to hold him. Besides, he's sound asleep. We don't want to wake him.'

'Because he'll *never* get back to sleep, the poor thing.' Alec frowned. 'We were supposed to move back into the house tomorrow, but I think we should delay it another day.'

'No. There's no use in putting off the inevitable.'

'After all you've been through today?'

'It's been a day I'll never forget but at least everything turned out well. If Eddie had died . . .'

'But he didn't. And he won't because of you.'

'I didn't track him down, Alec. It was pure chance that I found him.'

He smiled into her eyes. 'You never stopped thinking about him. You even went to Rocco's last night to ask his mother about him.'

'And found out nothing helpful.' Juliet grinned. 'Last night I was giving you hell for being overprotective, telling you how well I could take care of myself, and today I went out and got into all sorts of trouble.'

'And got out of it with no help from me. I was here sleeping all afternoon. What a hero.'

'I believe I sent you to your room for nap. I thought I was going to do only errands, not get taken prisoner by Wendell Booth.' Her light tone vanished. 'Alec, I had the strangest reaction to his death. You would have thought I'd be triumphant – he murdered my brother and probably my parents – but I felt anything except triumphant. I cried.'

'Nerves. You were having a nervous reaction. You look absolutely drained.'

'So do you.'

'But I didn't do anything—'

'To help me? Stop feeling guilty. I mean it, Alec. I think feeling guilty has become a way of life for you. That was harsh but it's true. You have no reason to feel guilty about Brenda and no reason to feel guilty about me, or Dad, or Mom. Do you hear me?'

'Yes. You're nearly shouting.'

'Maybe that's what I have to do to get through to you.'

'No, it isn't. You're probably the only person I've ever really listened to,' Alec said softly, hesitantly. 'It's been that way since you were around twenty.'

Juliet stared at him for a moment then almost whispered, 'I don't know what that means.'

'I didn't either at first. And then I realized I had feelings for you – feelings that have nothing to do with you being like a sister.'

Juliet went still and quiet inside. 'Your feelings are romantic?'

'Yeah, I'm afraid they are.'

'Afraid?'

'For a long time, I didn't want to get too romantically involved,' Alec said. 'Ever. I intended to avoid it.'

'Why?'

'I didn't want to risk the pain.'

Although he was looking at her steadily, Juliet didn't believe him. 'I don't think that was the reason, Alec. I believe you think you don't deserve love.'

'Are we talking about my feeling guilty being a way of life again?'

'Yes. Am I right? *Do* you think you deserve love?'

'That's a complicated question.'

'It seems fairly simple to me.'

Alec stood up and began slowly walking around the room. Juliet thought he wasn't going to answer when he finally said, 'I loved my family. Yes, even Brenda. Maybe her most of all, believe it or not. And look what happened.' He stopped walking and looked at her. 'And Fin.'

'You didn't love Fin.'

'No, I didn't love him, but I liked him. We'd actually become friends when he was murdered. I didn't realize how much I liked him until he was gone. And I didn't do a damned thing to prevent his death.'

'What could you have done to prevent it?' Juliet asked in disbelief.

'I knew he had enemies. I could have looked out for him.'

'Fin was good-looking and talented and arrogant. He'd had enemies since he was a kid. And at the time he was murdered, you were only home on Christmas break. Were you supposed to follow him around twenty-four/seven?'

'Maybe.'

'Now you're being ridiculous.'

Alec turned to face her, his expression angry. 'Ridiculous? Thank you, Juliet.'

'Well, you are.'

'I don't think so. Fin may have had enemies all of his life, but he didn't die until I came home. Your parents didn't have any enemies except the Booths, but *they* didn't die until I was back here! Wherever I go, death follows.'

'Alec Wainwright, that is the silliest, most melodramatic thing I've ever heard you say!'

Alec's lips tightened and then he said coldly, 'Are you trying to demean me, to make me sound like a fool?'

'If I can shake you out of this box of self-pity you've shut yourself in, then yes! Alec, you're too sensible to believe any of this stuff you've been spouting. Death follows you. Good God!'

Sensing tension, Hutch finally lifted his head, looked from Juliet to Alec, then slowly crawled from Juliet's lap, dropped to the floor and crept under the bed.

'My parents and sister died horrible deaths. Hopper, my best friend in Afghanistan, was killed just a few feet away from me.'

'So what?'

'So *what*?' Alec thundered.

'Oh, I didn't mean to sound flippant. I'm upset, my head hurts—'

'After all you've been through today, we shouldn't be talking about any of this.'

'It doesn't have anything to do with what happened today except that maybe I'm more raw – not tiptoeing around trying not to say anything offensive. But right now, I'm going to tell you exactly what I think. I know all of these deaths have hurt you deeply – scarred you – but you're not the only person who's suffered loss, Alec. I've lost my brother and my parents. When you were away in college, one of my closest friends drowned on a summer vacation to Miami with her parents. But I didn't wrap myself up in Fin's death or her death and say, "That's it! Death is all around me!" Death happens in *everyone's* life, Alec. You're not omnipotent. You didn't cause the car wreck or Fin's murder or the murders of my parents.'

He looked at her stubbornly.

'Or maybe you did. Deke Nevins said you had PTSD. He said you'd been treated for it. People with PTSD – well, I know they have nightmares and flashbacks and they can exhibit aggressive behavior—'

'Stop right there!' Alec shouted. 'Let me get this straight. Deke Nevins told you I have PTSD and have been treated for it?'

Juliet nodded.

'Where was I treated for it?'

'He didn't say.'

'I'm sure he didn't because I don't have it and I certainly wasn't in a treatment center.'

'So you say.'

'I'm an assistant head of security at Bernard-Widmere, one of the biggest investment houses in the world. Do you think I could have gotten a job like that if I'd undergone treatment for PTSD?'

'I don't know.'

'Well, I do.' Alec neared the bed. 'Do you have any idea of the stigma that goes along with having PTSD? Do you know anything about the job exclusion people who have PTSD endure? It's deplorable! Advocating for them is one of my passions. But I don't have it. I have nightmares, yes. I don't have flashbacks, I'm not antisocial, I'm not aggressive, I don't have bad thoughts about myself.'

'I have to take issue with that last one. You think death follows you? What the hell do you call that except having bad thoughts about yourself?'

'Well, maybe I exaggerated.'

'I'll say you did. Alec, the man I'm in love with is too smart to think like that!'

Alec turned slowly and looked at her, his eyes disbelieving. 'The man you're in love with?'

'Yes. I've loved you for a long time.' She went silent and tapped her fingers on the blanket. 'If you haven't realized that, maybe you aren't as smart as I thought you were.'

'You're in love with me?' he repeated.

'Yes. How many times do I have to say it?'

'Maybe you just love me like a brother—'

'I *don't*. I'm *in love* with you. You said you didn't love *me* like a sister. You said your feelings are romantic. Does that mean you're in love with *me*?'

'Well . . . yes.'

'Could you stop pacing and come sit beside me on the bed?'

He came without a word, kicked off his shoes, propped himself on the bed and took her hand. Then he looked deep into her eyes. 'I think this might be the most honest talk we've ever had.'

'Talk or moment?'

'Moment sounds too short.'

Juliet stroked his arm. 'How long have you known you're in love with me?'

'Years. And you with me?'

'Years. I was about to give up hope that my love would ever be returned.'

Alec's face was only a couple of inches from hers. He ran a finger down her cheek. 'We've been such fools.'

'I know, but I blame the circumstances. Because you came to live with my family when you were a teenager, you believed you had to think of all of us as family. And even when I became a woman, I still tried to think of you as a brother, or at least make everyone think I did. But I didn't, Alec. I realize now that I haven't for a long time. I thought you might have known it.'

'I didn't. Well, I suspected it, but thank God,' he murmured, bending his head to kiss her tenderly on the lips, then the tip of her nose, then each cheek, then her lips again.

'Alec?'

'Yes, sweetheart.'

'If we're to have a true, out-in-the-open love affair, I have only one demand.'

He pulled back slightly and looked at her with troubled eyes. 'And what is that?'

She grinned. 'Don't ever call me *little Juliet* again.'

Alec threw back his head and laughed. 'It's a deal, *darling Juliet.*'

EIGHTEEN

'Are you sure you're up to this?'

Juliet was putting faux pearl studs in her ears. She stepped back from the mirror and looked at her pale green straight leg pants and white blouse. 'I feel fine, Alec. I want to see Eddie.'

'You don't look fine.'

'Thank you.'

'Your outfit is nice. Lovely. But you're pale, you have a bruise on your left cheek and circles under your eyes.'

Juliet didn't tell him that twenty minutes after she'd reached the hospital yesterday, she'd had a panic attack and been given a five milligram Valium. The doctor had sent her home with nine more. She didn't want to worry Alec any more than he was already worried. She now felt sore all over and had taken three buffered aspirin for the pain and a Valium for her nerves. Instead, she picked up her concealer and lightly applied more to the bruise and the circles then stepped back from the mirror. 'There. Almost as good as new and I feel fine. I'm ready.'

Alec sighed hopelessly. 'You might be the strongest woman I've ever known and I know better than to argue with you when you're determined. Let's go.'

Yesterday's rain had moved westward and the day was clear, the sky blue, the sun shining. The world looked entirely different than it had yesterday with its overcast skies and pouring rain. They said nothing on the way to the hospital and once there, had to wait fifteen minutes before they were admitted to Eddie's room. He sat up in bed, his face pale and marred with a few bruises and two small bandages, one on his forehead and another on his cheek. 'Hi!' Eddie said brightly. 'I'm glad both of you came. I thought you might never want to see me again, Juliet.'

'Why on earth wouldn't I?' she asked in surprise.

'Because of what Wendell put you through because of me.

But I want you to know how grateful I am. If it weren't for you . . . well, I don't know what would have happened to me.'

Juliet quelled an impulse to run over and kiss him. 'I'm just happy you're OK.' She looked at him. 'You are OK, aren't you?'

'Yeah. The doctors say I have a couple of cracked ribs. They hurt when I take a deep breath. I got a knock on the head that needed three stitches. And I take antibiotics for a parasite called *giardia* I probably caught by swallowing water in Argent Creek.'

'How did you swallow water from Argent Creek?' Alec asked, moving closer to Eddie's bed.

Eddie's lids dropped over his bright, green eyes. 'It must have happened the night Mrs Reid was . . . killed.'

'You were there?' Juliet asked, aghast. Eddie nodded slowly and she fumbled her way over to the chair beside his bed and sat down heavily. 'You were at my house the night Mom was murdered?'

'I must have been.'

'You're not sure?'

'I was just out there, wandering along the creek. Earlier Deke and I got in a fight. He slapped my face so hard I think my teeth rattled. I ran off. I didn't know where to go.'

'Why not the police or the hospital?' Alec asked.

'The people at the hospital would have called the police.' He looked away. 'I knew that even if the cops arrested him, he'd get out and then I'd pay. Or Mom would. Probably both of us.'

Juliet leaned close to him. 'Eddie, please tell us what happened that night.'

'I already told the police – Sheriff Dawson and another cop – but OK.' He took a deep breath. 'Deke hit me around six o'clock. My nose was gushing blood, but he came after me again. I took off and he chased but I'm faster. I hid around the high school – I knew it was the last place Deke would look for me. When it got dark, I went to the woods behind your neighborhood. I thought I'd sleep there but I couldn't sleep. Way in the distance I could see the fireworks in the park and I wished I was there. I started wading in the creek, feeling really sorry for myself. I stopped behind your house. I knew you were gone, but I saw a light moving around inside.'

'Like a flashlight?' Alec asked.

'Yeah. A real powerful one. It went all over the house, stopping in some places. Once I caught sight of a silhouette. Someone tall.' His face turned red. 'I thought the place was being robbed, but I didn't do anything. I was scared. I'm sorry.'

'Don't be,' Juliet said. 'You did the smart thing considering that you don't have a phone. You couldn't call nine-one-one.'

'No, I couldn't, but I moved a little closer to the house and huddled in the trees. After a few minutes, I didn't see the flashlight anymore. It vanished all at once, like someone clicked it off. Then a bright light came on inside – I could see it from the dining room window. I didn't think a burglar would turn on overhead lights. I waited and the light in your mother's office came on. So I moved closer.'

'Did you see my mother?'

'No. I didn't see anyone inside then – not even the tall person – but I thought I saw someone outside. Someone big. I thought it could either be someone spying or a look-out for whoever was inside. I wasn't even sure it was a *him* at first, because the light was so bad and the person was crouching around, peeking in windows. I stepped on a twig and I swear it sounded like it was hooked up to an amplifier when it snapped. The person looked around at me.

'Right then the back door to your mother's office opened, Juliet, and someone came running out – someone I hadn't seen inside. The one from outside ran after him and both were running toward me. I started running, too. Then someone picked me up. I was fighting and yelling and when we reached the creek, all at once, the one who held me cracked me on the head. I saw a flash of light and then felt cold water. The next thing I knew, I was somewhere dark with Wendell. He kept calling me Benny and muttering about how he was going to protect me, drying me off, taping a cloth on my head. I struggled some and ended up wrapped in that comforter with ropes holding me in. Then it was nothing but Twinkies and baloney and Cokes. For days.' He started coughing. 'I'm sorry,

Juliet,' he choked out. 'There's nothing more until you found me.'

Alec came to Eddie's bedside. 'Two people were at the house – one outside, one inside.'

'Yes.'

'Wendell was obviously one of them.'

'*One* of them!' Juliet burst out. 'He was inside!'

'We can't know that for certain.' Alec looked at Eddie. 'Did the person outside look as big as Wendell?'

'He was crouched over. It was dark except for that dusk-to-dawn light but he was never near enough to it for me to see him clearly.'

'But it was a man.'

'Yeah. I knew that for sure when he started running toward me. He ran like a man.'

'And the person who ran out of the house?'

Eddie scrunched up his battered face. 'It would have been a tall woman – taller than anyone I know.'

'Hannah Booth is about five-foot-ten. Was this person taller than Hannah Booth?'

'I've never seen her run and the person running out of the house was *fast*.'

Juliet clasped her hands and bent her face.

'Are you OK, Juliet?'

'Yes, Eddie. I realize the person who ran out of the house had just murdered my mother.'

'Oh, gosh. Yeah. I *am* sorry.' He hesitated. 'That person was carrying something. A bag. A plastic bag with stuff clanking around inside it. I guess that was stuff from the house.'

'It must have been,' Alec said, 'although Juliet hasn't gone through the place to see what's missing. We're fairly certain a gold cross with garnets belonging to Sera was taken –she kept it with her tarot cards.'

'I've seen it. Are her tarot cards gone?'

'No. They were scattered around her. The death card was lying beside her.'

Eddie blanched. 'Oh, that's terrible. And it sounds like the Booths, although, if you don't mind my saying so, Juliet, a lot of people thought Miss Sera reading the tarot cards was evil.'

'Like who?' Juliet asked sharply.

'Deke.'

'Oh. He'd say that even if he knew better. Deke was in jail, though.'

But when Juliet and Alec said goodbye to Eddie and left his room, they found Belle and Deke Nevins waiting outside. They both looked shabby and swollen-eyed with Belle slightly shame-faced and Deke defiant.

'Shoulda known you two would beat us here to see Eddie,' Deke almost snarled. 'Busybodies.'

'What are you doing out of jail?' Juliet demanded.

He smirked and put his arm around Belle. 'Do you think my little sweetie would let her man stay in jail? She bailed me yesterday after *you* had me arrested!'

Juliet looked at Belle incredulously. 'Belle, how could you? He assaulted me. He *hit* you!'

'You claim he assaulted you. And what he gave me was nothing more than a little tap.' Belle sounded as if she didn't believe herself. 'You just like causing trouble. I don't want Eddie around you anymore.'

'You do realize she saved Eddie's life, don't you?' Alec asked coldly.

'You'd better quiet down, Alex.' Deke tightened his arm around Belle's shoulders. 'Come on, sweetie. Don't you listen to them. Eddie's *your* boy. *You* make the rules for him.' And together they swept into Eddie's room hearing Eddie ask almost fearfully, 'Mom? *Deke?* You're here?'

'Now where else would we be?' Deke boomed.

Alec took Juliet's hand and started urging her gently down the hall. 'There's nothing we can do. Belle is Eddie's mother. We can't keep her away from him.'

Juliet's eyes narrowed. 'Or Deke, either.'

Alec unlocked the front door to the Reid home and opened it. Juliet took a step in then faltered. 'I don't know if I can face taking down all the crime scene tape and whatever the police have left.'

'You don't have to,' Alec said. 'Davis called me last night. He asked if it was all right for Marcy and Leslie to use the house key and come in to clean up for you. I said yes.'

'Marcy and Leslie? Oh, how sweet of them. How considerate.' She walked farther into the living room. 'So far, no trace. But Mom's office . . .'

She strode to the once-cheerful office that had always been filled with plants and light. Her gaze scanned the floor. The last time she'd seen it, spots of blood from the cut on her mother's throat had dotted its creamy pile. Now a yellow-and-blue patterned area rug covered the spots. Juliet stooped and lifted the rug. Under it on the pale carpet were light brown stains. Clearly Leslie and Marcy had tried to clean the carpet, but the blood wouldn't come out completely. It never would, Juliet thought. Eventually, she would have to replace the carpet in this room, especially before she tried to sell the house, but for now the rug was a lovely and thoughtful addition.

She went to the living room, opened the draperies and looked out at the backyard. 'Two murders have been committed here – one in the house, one in the tree house, although it no longer exists.'

'We don't know that your father was murdered.'

'Yes, we do. So does Davis, although he hasn't committed himself to that conclusion.'

'Can you stay here?' Alec asked, standing behind her.

Juliet stood. 'Yes. For now. I don't have much choice. I can't afford the Heritage Inn forever.'

'I'll take care of the Heritage—'

'You've done that for long enough. Besides, I'll be going back to my apartment in a few weeks. It's fine.' Alec looked at her doubtfully. 'OK, I'd run straight out the door and never look back if I could, but I can't. There are so many things I have to take care of – I'm not sure about all of them, but I'll find out.'

'You have to contact your parents' lawyer.'

'I'll do that tomorrow. Right now, I need to start looking around to see what's been stolen so I can give Davis a list.'

They toured the house slowly, Juliet scrutinizing every counter, dresser top, and drawer while Alec walked behind her taking notes with a pen on a legal pad and Hutch padding along after them. 'The candlesticks they got for their wedding,' Juliet said. 'How could I have guessed a burglar would take candlesticks? It's right out of a book.'

'Candlesticks,' Alec repeating, writing. 'Anything distinctive about them?'

'They were Lennox china. Ivory with gold around the base and the top. Maybe nine inches tall? About that. They're over thirty years old.' Juliet went into the living room and looked on the mantle top. 'Two porcelain mallard ducks. About seven inches high each. Not too valuable, but Dad loved them. And a foot-high Polynesian teak wood carving of a fisherman.' Alec followed her into her parents' bedroom. 'Mom's jewelry box is gone. I think the only valuable pieces she kept in there were a necklace of cultured pearls and matching studs. She had a couple of other more valuable necklace and earring sets along with a natural emerald and gold bracelet that belonged to her mother in the safety deposit box.'

Juliet continued around the bedroom. 'A photo of Dad's parents in an ornate silver frame. The lockbox with the gun Dad kept for home protection.'

'What kind of gun?'

'A Taurus Ultralight. It had never been used.' She rummaged through the dresser drawers. 'Nothing else seems to be missing in here.'

Her bedroom and Fin's and Alec's old bedroom looked untouched except for some open drawers. 'Well, I guess that's it,' Juliet said. 'The robber didn't make a very big haul.' She frowned. 'I don't remember if when we found Mom, she was wearing her engagement and wedding rings. They were gold and the engagement ring had a one carat diamond.'

'I'll ask Davis if they recovered them.'

Juliet trudged back to the living room and sat down on the couch. 'I'm so tired. Maybe I've tried to do too much after yesterday.'

'You certainly have. I'll get you a drink. What would you like?'

'Anything we have.'

After a few minutes he returned with two drinks and held

out one for her. 'Rum and Coke for you, Scotch on the rocks for me.' He sat down on a chair opposite from her. 'You look like something's on your mind.'

'Isn't just being back here enough?'

'Not for *that* look. What else is bothering you?'

'You know me too well, Alec.' Juliet sipped her drink. 'I keep thinking about what Eddie said – that whoever he saw running out of this house was tall and fast.'

'That could be Wendell.'

'I don't know how fast Wendell is. I'm sure the person in the house wasn't a woman, though. There were two men – one inside the house and one outside. What if the one inside wasn't as big as Eddie said?'

'Why would he lie?'

'Because Wendell is dead. Eddie has nothing to fear from him.' She looked apprehensively into Alec's dark eyes. 'But he's scared of Deke and with good reason – who knows what he's capable of doing? In the theater, Eddie said Belle would get Deke out of jail and that he'd never be safe from him. Alec, Deke could have been the person in this house the night Eddie saw *someone*, or so he claims. Deke could have murdered my mother. And if he thinks Eddie saw him . . .'

'Then maybe in order to keep himself safe, he'll murder Eddie.'

Juliet and Alec stayed up late that night talking, reminiscing about times they'd had in the house, each reluctant to go to bed. At one in the morning, Juliet couldn't hold her eyes open and had given up, crawling into her familiar double bed too tired to think. At eight o'clock, the phone rang.

'Juliet?' Davis Dawson asked when she picked up. 'I'm sorry to bother you so early, but I need to talk to you.'

'Oh my God!' Juliet sat up in bed and Hutch, lying on the floor beside her, let out a bark of distress. 'What's happened now?'

'No one has died. I didn't mean to scare you. Marcy says I can be a bull in a china shop when it comes to words—'

'*Davis!*'

'Sorry. There was a drug raid on Rocco's around midnight.

We've had our eye on it for quite a while. Anyway, part of the staff was selling drugs. We arrested two young guys and Belle Maddox.'

'Belle! Selling drugs supplied by Deacon Nevins,' Juliet almost whispered.

'Right. Kyle Hollister says Deke left about an hour before the bust. Maybe he has a sixth sense. Other people have given him up, but Belle won't say a word, even though she was arrested.'

'So Kyle Hollister had something to do with this?' she asked.

'He's been hanging out at the bar a lot. We have a true undercover agent from another area, but Kyle convinced us that because he's gone there from time to time for years, people's guard would be down around him.' Davis paused. 'He's also the youngest, handsomest, and coolest-looking of us,' he said with a chuckle.

'So that's how I happened to run into him there.'

'Yes. He was on business. Thank goodness. Hard to tell what Deke would have done to you if Kyle hadn't interrupted. But it also might have given him the tip-off that something was wrong.'

'It wasn't. I mean, *I* had no idea I was stepping into a drug den.'

'Well, *drug den* is a slight exaggeration. Anyway, Belle is carrying on about Eddie. He's due to be let out of the hospital tomorrow, barring complications, and there's nowhere for him to go except into the system unless she finds someone to bail her out.'

'And she wants *me* to bail her out?'

'I believe she thinks there might be a slight possibility.'

'There isn't,' Juliet said coldly.

'That's what I told her. So, she's asking if you could take him in. Just for a little while – maybe a couple of hours. Until her sister Pamela Alder in Cincinnati can come get Eddie.'

'The one who tried to get custody of Eddie three years ago?'

'Yes, Belle says she'll turn over custody to her.'

'Do you believe her?'

'I'm not sure but last night she was pushing cocaine and methamphetamine. There's no way out of this for her. She'll be doing years in prison. She cannot hold onto Eddie anymore.'

'Does Pamela know the whole story?'

'Yes. We called her to make certain Belle even called at all much less told Pamela the whole story. Belle had. Pamela said she won't bail out Belle but she and her husband will be more than happy to take Eddie. Her husband is a successful accountant with a big company, they have a sixteen-year-old daughter, and they all care for Eddie.'

'And he cares for Pamela. He's told me so. She's kept in touch with him for years.'

'Then the situation is perfect. She'll get here tomorrow afternoon, though we don't know when exactly. If Davis could bring him to your house first . . .'

'Of course. He knows Alec and me. I'm sure we could make him comfortable for a few hours – more, if necessary. But only if that's all right with him.'

'I'll talk to him. It's my place as sheriff. You can speak with him later. And Juliet?'

'Yes.'

'Thank you.'

NINETEEN

'I saw Robert this morning,' Jon announced as they sat around the family room in Danielle's home.

'On purpose?' Carole asked.

'Oh yes.' He half-smiled at her. 'How would you like to have your freedom?'

Carole drew deeply on her cigarette then blew out the smoke in a thin, swift stream. 'Is this your idea of a joke?'

'Not at all. You are my sister, after all, and you deserve my protection. This scum has made you miserable for long enough and I won't tolerate it anymore. So I had a talk with him.'

Danielle said, 'From the look on your face, I'd say this talk went your way.'

'Carole's way. He's willing to give her a quiet divorce.'

'*What?*' Carole, Danielle, and Leslie exclaimed at once.

'It's true.' He paused. 'But there are certain terms.'

'Oh, here we go,' Carole groaned. 'What are they?'

'First, you will never say anything about him hitting you or mistreating you in any way.'

'That's easy. I never had any intention of letting people know how stupid I was to stay with a man who physically abused me. Besides, I was dumb enough at the time to not get any photos, call the police, anything. I have no proof.'

'Second, you will file for divorce on the grounds of irreconcilable differences. Robert will give you a generous settlement and a monthly stipend for five years as long as you stay away from the US. Immediately after the papers are drawn up and signed by both of you, you will go overseas. If testimony is needed, you may come home for that only; otherwise, you'll stay away from Parrish, Chicago, and the United States.'

Carole waited a beat. 'Why?'

'It's what Robert demands. He doesn't care where you go. The yearly stipend will be generous and you can live just about anywhere. Also, if you have any romances, they'd better be low-key. Nothing tabloid-worthy. And no lovey-dovey post-ings on Instagram. The only pictures that can appear are of you alone. If you disobey, he'll take you back to court and cut off the stipend.' Jon looked at her. 'I think the five-year absence from the US is because he wants you out of the press. The more you're seen the more digging reporters will do. Maybe some things that Robert would rather keep hidden will appear, which could be disastrous for him since he's lately been linked to the twenty-four-year-old daughter of a man worth millions, and I mean that with a capital M.'

'Who?'

'He didn't say and I didn't ask but I'm sure that's why he's done this one-eighty. Four months ago, he was dead-set against a divorce. Oh, I did forget to mention that your yearly stipend will end if you marry before five years.'

'How much money will I get?'

'We'll talk about that tonight, but I promise you, Carole, I'll drive a hard bargain.'

'Jon, I'm . . . I'm flabbergasted. Not that I'm complaining, but what made you decide to talk to him?'

'He came here to Parrish. He's been lurking around like some creep in a crime novel.' Jon paused. 'And I think he attacked my house the other night. If he'd been watching, which I think he has, he would have known I wasn't home, that only a babysitter was there with Tommy. I can't let him get away with that.'

'May I ask what you threatened if he didn't let me go?'

Jon grinned. 'No, you may not. But I didn't threaten to hurt him physically, if that makes you feel any better.'

'It makes *me* feel better!' Leslie rushed to him and sat down on his lap. 'Oh Jon, this is wonderful! I'm so proud of you!'

Carole looked at him and smiled. 'And I'm so grateful.'

Davis and Marcy Dawson sat side-by-side on the couch with a baby name book while Marcy wrote with a ball point pen on a spiral notebook. 'I don't need to look at the book. How about Davis Darby Dawson II?' she asked.

'I *hate* my name, Marcy. Do you want our son to hate us, too?'

'Not particularly.' She picked up the book and began flipping through. 'Vladimir Dawson. Vlad for short.'

'Great. His middle name can be Dracula. Vlad Dracula Dawson.'

'No. Hmmm. My grandfather's name was Ebenezer.'

'His middle name wasn't Scrooge, was it?'

'You're being a grouch. This is fun.' Marcy tapped her pen. 'I had an uncle named Woodrow.'

'Ugh.'

'Owen?'

Davis was quiet for a moment. 'I think Juliet might want to name any future son Owen.'

'You're right.' She frowned. 'Wasn't Danielle's husband's name Nathaniel? That's nice.'

'Yeah, but Nathaniel Tresswell wasn't a great guy.'

'Really? You two were good friends.'

'We were friendly. That's not the same as being good friends.' Davis looked at her seriously. 'When I came to Parrish, I was in my twenties. I was ambitious and Nathaniel Tresswell was a big deal. So I made a point of getting to know him and Danielle. I'm not proud of that, but it was almost thirty years ago. I became their go-to guy and it paid off. But even when I was young, I didn't think highly of Nathaniel.'

'And Danielle?'

'I liked her. And I felt a little sorry for her. She'd gotten herself into a marriage that shouldn't have happened. Her father and Nathaniel were friends and business partners. Tresswell was having a downturn. Nathaniel needed the money that Danielle's father had and her father wanted the prestige of the Tresswell name. It was an arranged marriage – at least on Nathaniel's part – but even once she realized he didn't love her, she stuck by Nathaniel, even when he got his diagnosis.'

'Some people say *you* were in love with Danielle,' Marcy said quietly.

Davis laughed. 'I told you I *liked* her. I guess I admired her as a good wife and a strong leader of Tresswell Metal when Nathaniel got sick. But there's only one woman in my life I've been in love with and her name is Marcy Lynn Baxter

Davis.' He kissed the tip of her nose. 'We only have two weeks left. Next name.'

The doorbell rang. 'I don't suppose that's the baby who's decided to give his mom a break and arrive in a more gentle and elegant fashion than usual,' Marcy said. Davis laughed as he headed for the door. As soon as he opened it, his laughter died. Standing there were Hannah and Micah Booth.

'We want to talk to you,' Hannah announced.

'Then you can do so at headquarters,' Davis said. 'I'm off duty.'

Micah stepped forward aggressively. 'We came by your office earlier this afternoon and they said you weren't in.'

'I wasn't.'

'Where were you?'

'I don't see how that's any of your business.'

'It is when our boy's been murdered,' Hannah barked.

'Murdered?'

'We want to come in and sit down.'

'Well, you can't, Mr Booth. This is my home. I've told you that you can see me in my office. You can sit down there. I have chairs.'

'Nice that you can make jokes when our boy's been murdered.'

'You keep saying that Wendell was murdered. He was not murdered.'

Hannah took two steps closer to Davis. He could smell her powdery sweet cologne. 'Juliet Reid picked up our son and threw him over the balcony of that old theater. She *threw* him and she broke his neck.'

Davis looked steadily into her pale blue eyes. 'Are you claiming that five-foot-four, one-hundred-twenty-pound Juliet Reid *picked up* Wendell and *threw* him off the balcony?'

'Exactly.'

'Mrs Booth, have you lost your mind?'

'You're not allowed to talk to me that way!'

'Call the police.'

Hannah glared at Davis. 'You think just because Wendell was in prison, you can get away with ignoring his murder.

But he was wrongly accused. He never hurt anybody and people are going to realize that he didn't. Then they'll go after the person who put him in prison, who protected his murderer, who's ignored the law.' She narrowed her eyes and stepped even closer to him. 'And Micah and me will lead the charge, Mr Sheriff. So you'd better take good care of all those people you care so much about, like Juliet Reid, like your own child bride and that kid inside her, 'cause me and Micah have had enough.'

Davis shut the door and walked slowly back to the living room. Marcy had laid aside the notebook and stared at him with troubled brown eyes. 'Is there anything you can do about them?' she asked.

Davis sat down on the couch and took her cold hand in his. 'Not until they break the law.'

'I can't believe they're saying Juliet Reid killed Wendell,' Marcy said.

'They're crazy. They shouldn't be walking around free. I'm not sure it wasn't one of them who killed Sera Reid.'

Marcy was quiet for a moment. Then she asked in a lighter tone, 'Davis, how do you know Juliet is five foot four and one hundred twenty pounds?'

'She's just about your size.'

Marcy looked down at her stomach beneath a yellow tunic. 'One hundred twenty pounds? I feel about two hundred pounds.'

'I think you're overestimating, but even if you were two hundred pounds, I'd still love you.'

'They said you'd better take care of your wife. They threatened me, Davis, and our baby.'

Davis's hand tightened on hers. 'I will kill them before I let them hurt you. I swear I will.'

'And Juliet?'

Davis's face tightened. 'I'm going to put her under protective surveillance. After all, she's living at a house where at least one murder was already committed. I'll be damned if I let another one happen.'

TWENTY

Moving men tramped through Leslie's and Jon's new one-story home. 'Sure this is gonna be big enough for you?' one of the men jovially asked Leslie.

She smiled. 'My husband made me memorize this. It's three thousand and eighty-eight square feet. Big enough for Jon, me, Tommy and one on the way.'

The man whistled. 'I'll say. Think I might move in here myself!'

'Be careful not to scratch these hardwood floors,' Danielle told him. 'They're natural hickory, *not* veneer!'

Juliet saw Leslie roll her eyes at the moving man. She knew Leslie hadn't wanted Danielle here today, but Danielle had insisted on coming to help. 'To supervise,' Leslie had told Juliet in private. 'She's dragged Carole along and I know Carole couldn't care less. She's worried about how Jon's talk with Robert will go later.'

'And how do you think it will go?' Juliet had asked.

'It all depends on how much money is involved. If Robert tries to fob off Carole with a pittance, it won't happen.'

'Isn't Carole desperate enough to get away from Robert that she won't ask for a lot of money?'

'Oh, definitely. She's not trying to get a fortune out of him – just enough to live comfortably. Overseas.'

'Why does Robert want her out of the country?'

'He says it's because he doesn't want her appearing in the US news, as if the press is following around Carole like they did Princess Diana. But you know Robert's ego. In his mind, he's as famous as Prince Charles.' Leslie shook her head. 'My God, were the Tresswells fooled by him. He seemed so nice, so charming, so modest, *so* in love with Carole. All he loved were her looks.'

'Leslie, I don't know how we're going to be ready for a housewarming in two days,' Danielle called from across the room.

'Well, you picked the day,' Leslie returned. 'We could have made it for a week later but it's too late to change the date now.'

'Then we'll just have to get the house ready. You, there,' Danielle said sharply to the moving men, 'that sofa goes two feet south. It sits directly across from the fireplace, you see.'

'Yes, ma'am,' they chimed together.

'Do you have the coffee table that goes in front of it?'

'I don't think so, ma'am.'

'The table will be arriving tomorrow, Danielle,' Leslie said.

'Oh. Well, make sure it's placed correctly if I'm not here.'

'This would be so much easier without her,' Leslie muttered to Juliet.

'But she's having the time of her life,' Juliet whispered back.

As soon as the men set down the couch, Danielle looked at it critically, then nodded. 'Fine. Where are the other two men?'

'Getting more furniture out of the truck, ma'am.'

'Well, there's not much. My son and daughter-in-law bought mostly new furniture for this house. The old furniture simply wouldn't do.'

'Yes, ma'am.'

Leslie looked at Juliet and cringed. 'God, we sound like insufferable snobs.'

'Gee, aren't you?' Juliet teased and Leslie scrunched up her nose at Juliet.

Actually, Juliet was enjoying the activities. Last night had been difficult, sleeping in the house where her mother had been murdered. She hadn't slept much and she'd heard Alec up pacing through the house. They'd gotten another call from Davis earlier telling them that the Booths had come to see him and made threats. Davis said he was having surveillance placed at the Reid home and Juliet thought Alec was making sure he could see a patrol car parked unobtrusively on the street. She hadn't told Leslie about the Booths. Between her distress over the recent deaths, her pregnancy, and worrying about the move into the new house, she had enough on her mind. Juliet only hoped the move and the housewarming party would go well.

Carole walked in holding a large box. 'It's marked "This 'n That." Where do you want it?'

'Oh, I found it in the attic of the other house,' Leslie said. 'Put it in the room next to Tommy's, please. I'll sort through it later.'

'OK.' Carole headed back to the hall, then stopped. 'Hey, Les, am I getting paid by the hour?'

'Minimum wage. Now get a move on.'

'When is the rest of the furniture coming?' Juliet asked.

'Some tomorrow, some the next morning. I don't know why I let Danielle talk me into the party.'

'Because Danielle can talk just about anyone into just about anything.' Juliet put her arm around Leslie's shoulder. 'I won't be able to help for long tomorrow. You know that when Eddie's released from the hospital, he's coming to my house. His aunt will pick him up there.'

'How does he feel about going with her?'

'I haven't seen him since the day after Wendell's death. Eddie was sick and needed to concentrate on getting well, not talking about leaving his mother. In spite of everything, he loves her.'

'But in getting away from her, he'll also be getting away from Deke Nevins. They haven't caught him yet, have they?'

'Not that I know of. That guy has nine lives.'

'Let just hope this is the end of his ninth,' Leslie said.

Deke worried that he'd waited too long to leave Parrish. True, Rocco's had only been busted the night before and thank the powers that be he'd decided to play poker with friends instead of hanging out all evening in the bar. When he'd heard the news, he'd taken off and hid in a deserted shack he always kept ready for emergencies. He'd stayed put, eating canned foods, drinking colas, munching crackers, knowing that although Belle would never tell that he was her supplier, the two other young men who sold Deke's wares at Ike Rocco's bar would blab their damned heads off.

Outside of the trailer Deke never handled the drugs himself, but in the bar, he always gave them to Belle, who sold most of them and gave some to two other people to sell. Unfortunately,

one of them wasn't Connor. Deke hated him and would have
loved to see him arrested, but he was too *honorable* to sell
drugs. Anyway, Belle wasn't smart enough to talk her way
out of this one and Deke was screwed in Parrish, Ohio.
Everyone would know where she'd gotten the drugs. He had
a reputation – he'd just never gotten caught. But he felt like
his luck had run out. He had to get as far away from this town
as possible. That took as much money as he'd saved within
the last few months, though, and he'd hidden it in the trailer
he'd shared with Belle. The police had already searched it.
They'd found the money but Belle had claimed it was hers.
She'd bailed him out when that Reid bitch had gotten him
arrested but been afraid the police would seize the rest of it,
so she'd given the rest to one of her friends – a 'friend' who
wouldn't return it to her when he told her how stupid she'd
been. Now he had nothing.

Thoughts of the sleazy tin can he'd shared with Belle
depressed him. He'd done her a favor to live there so long,
especially with that smart-alec kid underfoot. But he didn't
have to worry about that anymore. He would no longer be
sleeping with her skinny, cigarette-reeking body anymore and
God knew where the kid would land. Someplace good. People
like him always did. *It's people like me – hard-working, clever
people like me – who always get the raw deal*, he thought
resentfully.

He paced around the shack. He'd been in the tumble-down
building for hours and he was so restless he was tempted to
retrieve his car from the stand of trees where he'd hidden it
and take a spin around back streets. But that wouldn't be
smart. He knew there was a police BOLO out on him. If he
drove around, he might find a car whose license plate he could
steal and replace his own, but that could be chancy. Maybe
he could wait until after midnight and take a walk, but he was
two miles out of town. That would be a four-mile walk, a lot
of it in open country where he could be easily spotted. And
that still didn't solve the problem of having only twenty-two
dollars in his pocket. 'Where the hell can I get money?' he
asked aloud. 'I can't go back to the trailer. The cops are
watching it. They'll pick me up. Can I rob a convenience

store? No, that would only make the search for me hotter. Besides, I don't have a gun. So what other choice do I have? Think, Deke. *Think!!!*' He stuffed stale crackers in his mouth then followed them with his last can of soda, which he hated. He burped twice then looked at the canned foods he had left. Some sliced peaches. Two cans of spaghetti. Cream of mushroom and cream of celery soup. Why the hell had he bought them? They must have been on sale. Another box of stale crackers. One ancient joint. That was it.

And then it hit him. A theory – a theory he'd had for a long time about a death. When he'd first thought of it, he'd been afraid to say anything. After all, he was involved. Not directly, but close enough to get himself in trouble. That had been years ago, though. He was safe from any crimes he'd committed then – at least he thought he was safe. He could get himself in a world of hurt if what he had to say now was taken seriously, but he had no intention of hanging around Parrish long enough to suffer any fallout from information he intended to pass on soon. In any case, he needed money *now*. Staying here was too risky.

He must take some kind of action soon.

'Jon, did you eat at the Parrish Hotel?' Carole asked nervously.

'I did.' Jon waited a moment. 'Room service in Robert's room. Do you want to talk in private?'

'No. We're all friends here. Just tell me if Robert and I have a deal.'

Jon looked around the family room of his new house where his mother, Leslie, Juliet, Alec, and Frank Greenlee had all gathered. 'All right. I had to haggle a bit, but you have a deal.'

For the first time in her life, Jon thought his sister was going to faint. She paled, swayed, extended her hands as if she couldn't see well, and moaned. Danielle rushed to her and enfolded her in a hug. 'It's OK, darling. You're free.'

Carole opened her eyes and batted away tears. 'I'm sorry, but I'm so relieved.' She went quiet for a moment, looking troubled. 'You don't think he'll back out, do you, Jon?'

'No. This afternoon I had our lawyer draw up divorce settle-ment papers. Robert signed them. Now you have to sign them.'

'He can still change his mind, back down, tear up the papers.'

'There are copies of the settlement, of course, and if he backs down, I'll turn loose the papers to the press. That won't bring publicity Robert will like, not to mention that he'd be breaking the law.'

'Thank God,' Carole murmured. 'How long will the divorce take?'

'I have no idea. You have to talk to our lawyer, but I don't think it will be long. Then you'll be leaving the United States.'

'Leaving?' Frank asked.

'It's one of the conditions,' Carole said. 'Robert wants me to go abroad for five years.'

Frank looked amazed. 'Five *years*? What the hell?'

'I don't know why, Frank. I just know my leaving is the only way I'll get the divorce. It's worth it. And everyone can visit me, wherever I end up.'

'Well, at least that nightmare is over,' Danielle said, hugging Carole. 'And dear, I promise to never pick a husband for you again. I have the *worst* taste!'

Everyone laughed, especially Carole. 'I think I'll stay single for at least a few years,' she said. 'I'm ready to have some fun. Marriage, for me at least, hasn't been fun.'

'Not all marriages are made in heaven,' Jon said, pulling Leslie closer to him. 'I've known since I was seventeen I wanted to marry this wonderful girl and she did me the greatest favor in the world by accepting my proposal.'

Juliet felt tears in her eyes. She remembered so well how much Leslie had loved Jon since she was just fourteen and Jon three years older. And Carole had loved Fin. What would have happened if she'd married him instead of two handsome, wealthy men without kindness or ethics? Would Fin still be alive? Would they still be married?

Alec must have known what she was thinking because he looked at her tenderly and stepped closer to her, although he didn't touch her. They hadn't announced that they were in love. Their relationship was too new, too fragile. But Juliet knew she'd loved Alec for a long time and apparently he'd felt the same way. Her tears dried and she felt warm and comforted inside.

'It's so nice of you to cater this party,' Danielle said to Frank Greenlee. 'I know the inn doesn't usually cater, but Hollisters' has been scheduled to cater an anniversary party for three months and they can't cancel.'

'It's no trouble at all. The owners don't like to cater big parties – they'd rather hold them at the inn – but we won't have more than twenty guests—'

'Make that twenty-five,' Jon interrupted. 'Mom has thought of some more people who simply must see the house. It will probably be more than thirty by the day of the party.'

Frank shook his head. 'No more than twenty-five, Danielle. Don't forget that we need to know how much food to prepare.'

'And how much liquor to bring.' Jon laughed.

'No one will be getting drunk in this lovely home.' Danielle looked around. 'You all do think it's lovely, don't you? I mean, I've never lived in a one-story house myself with an open floor plan and a wrap-around porch and called—'

'A modern farmhouse,' Carole said. 'Would you feel better if they stopped calling it a farmhouse?'

'Oh, *much.*'

'OK, Mom. From now on, it won't be referred to as a farmhouse. Is that all right with you, Les?'

'Fine, but Tommy loves calling it the farmhouse.'

'He'll get used to calling it *our* house instead. And he loves that big bedroom of his. It will make him forget everything.'

'Except how much he wants a swimming pool.'

Jon suddenly turned stern. 'No pool. Absolutely not, no matter how much he begs.'

Leslie nodded meekly. It seemed that Jon would never get over his brother Nate's death in the family pool. If Tommy wanted a pool, he would have to wait until he grew up and had his own house.

Frank Greenlee's phone dinged. 'Excuse me,' he said. 'Might be business.'

He read a text message then his expression changed, first to disbelief, then to anger. Everyone was watching him and he turned around as he texted an answer.

'Now you said the rest of the furniture will be here tomorrow morning?' Danielle asked Leslie for the tenth time, obviously just to break the tension.

'Before noon.'

'I'll send Martha over to help clean.'

'I've hired a cleaning service, Danielle. Martha can keep Tommy company.'

'Oh, yes. A cleaning service. I hope they're good.'

'They will be. If they aren't, the guests will just have to step over the mess.'

'*What?*' Danielle burst out. Then she smiled. 'Oh, one of your jokes.'

'Yes, I'm a laugh a minute.'

Frank turned around, his plump face sweating, and gave them a tight smile. 'I'm sorry. I have to go back to the inn now.'

'No trouble, is there?' Jon asked.

'Trouble? No, no. Just the usual hassles.'

'I'll be stopping in this afternoon to take care of the bill,' Jon said.

'There's no need. I'll send the bill later.' Frank shook everyone's hand and Juliet noticed that his was trembling slightly. 'I'll see you all soon. Leslie, Danielle, I promise it will be a party to remember.'

TWENTY-ONE

D eke Nevins stopped and drew a deep breath. He'd waited until ten p.m. to start out, then parked his car two miles away in a cluster of trees that couldn't be seen clearly from the highway. He wished he had a can of cola with him, but the shack was empty and he didn't dare go into a convenience store. He'd reached Argent Creek and thought about stooping down and taking a couple of gulps, then remembered hearing something about Eddie catching something from the creek water – a parasite. Served him right, the little creep. He hoped it went to the kid's brain and ate it. But thirsty as Deke was, he had come this far. He wasn't going to let some parasite take him down now.

He walked along the edge of the creek, carrying a low-powered flashlight that he turned on once a minute and kept the beam pointed down. He'd never played in this area with the other boys when he was a kid. They waded and some-times took off their jeans and tramped to the middle of the stream, which only came up to their waists. But Deke was smaller than all of them with legs like sticks and it would have taken torture for him to admit he couldn't swim and actually feared bodies of water. His father had called him a sissy and laughed at him, saying he was no son of *his*. Deke knew that he wasn't the son of his so-called father. He had no idea who his father really was, but occasionally he saw his mother look at an old photo of a teenaged boy who looked like Deke.

But keeping a picture of someone Deke's mother had cared for didn't mean she loved him. She seemed to resent him, look at him as a millstone around her neck, the end of the wonderful dreams she'd had for herself when she was young. Deke was certain she'd fooled her husband into thinking Deke was his baby, although as he grew, even that stupid man real-ized he'd been tricked. Now Belle, although Deke couldn't say much in her favor, had loved her husband and loved Eddie.

But she was the helpless, self-destructive type. She didn't know how to take care of herself much less that boy of hers who was ten times smarter than she was. He'd met Belle's sister Pamela once. He'd hated Pamela, but he could see that she'd gotten all the brains in the family. Certainly Belle would lose Eddie now, and Pamela would take him and turn him into something successful. The very thought made Deke feel sorry for himself again. Why was it always the little shits like Eddie who made good?

Deke thought at last he'd reached his destination. He flicked the flashlight around, raising the beam higher than he had earlier, until he could see the trees, the sloping bank, the white vinyl picket fence that enclosed the backyard. Yes, this was the place and he was about to come into some money.

He stepped carefully over the rocks near the creek. Then he slowly climbed the bank covered with dew-laden grass. He opened the gate of the picket fence and walked on the wide flagstones until he reached a stand of four full-grown, wide spruce trees.

The trees made him nervous and Deke picked up his pace, tripped on a flagstone and hit the ground hard on his hip. 'Goddammit!' he burst out, then immediately smacked a hand over his mouth as if he could retrieve the loud word. He held perfectly still, his small, dark eyes darting wildly around the backyard. No sign of anyone. Not even the back porch light flipped on. Maybe no one had heard him. Maybe he hadn't been as loud as he thought.

He was rubbing his hip, trying to stand up, when a voice behind the trees said softly, 'Hurt yourself, Deke?'

His heart nearly banged out of his chest. For a moment he couldn't get his breath and the landscape whirled around him. Then he blinked and tried once again to get up, but pain stabbed down his leg and he sat flat again.

'Don't think you broke that hip, do you?'

'Look, I ain't doin' nothin'.' Deke's voice was high and weak.

'You ain't? You were going awfully fast for a man doin' nothing.'

'I'm just out for a stroll. I don't know these parts and got lost. Just tryin' to find my way back to the street, that's all.'

'Hmmm. You don't know these parts? Well, your voice sounds familiar although you're trying hard to change it.'

'I don't know what you're talkin' about. I got to be on my way.'

'Where?'

'The street! I told you—'

'I know what you told me. I just don't believe it.'

'Well what the hell else would I be doin' at this time of night?'

'Going to visit someone?'

'You're nuts.' Deke finally managed to clamber to his feet although the pain in his hip was excruciating. 'I'm goin'.'

'I don't think so.'

Deke expected someone to step in front of him, but instead he heard a movement behind him. He jerked to attention, ready to run the best he could, when he felt something sharp penetrate his lower back. 'That's the right kidney,' the voice said. Another stab. 'That's the descending colon.' A third stab. 'That's the gall bladder.' At last, Deke's attacker turned him around. Deke's eyes widened. 'Surprised, are you? No wonder.' A fourth, powerful stab. 'And that, Deacon Nevins, is the heart.'

Juliet was awakened by the sound of Hutch barking frantically. She jerked up in bed and listened. He wasn't in the house. He was outside, his bark rising and falling as he ran up and down the bank from Argent Creek to the backyard.

She got out of bed, put on her robe and slippers, and started toward Alec's room. He met her in the hall wearing jeans and pulling on a T-shirt, 'Something's wrong with Hutch,' she said.

'I know. It just started. Maybe he spotted a squirrel.'

'You've tried that squirrel bit on me before, Alec. He's used to seeing squirrels. How did he get out of the house?'

'Dog door. I forgot to close it last night.'

They rushed out the kitchen door as Hutch topped the bank again and ran to them. 'What is it, boy?' Juliet asked. 'Did someone scare you?'

The dog made a chuffing sound, barked again, and took off

over the bank. 'Something's around the creek that has him upset. I guess we'll have to investigate.'

Alec wore sturdy boat shoes and moved faster than Juliet in her dainty ballet-style slippers. He ran ahead of her, passed through the white fence gate that had been left open and hurtled down the bank. As Juliet picked her way carefully over the sloping earth, Alec yelled, 'Stop there, Juliet. Don't come any farther.'

'Why?'

'Just don't come down here.'

Juliet stopped for a moment. Hutch kept barking. She couldn't stand here because Alec told her to, she thought rebelliously. She had to see for herself what was wrong.

When she reached Argent Creek, she saw why Alec had told her to stop. A man lay floating face-down, his white T-shirt mottled with large pink splashes. His long dark hair floated around his head and an arm had caught on a rock and kept him close to the shore of the creek.

'Oh, my God!' Juliet burst out. 'Whose?'

'I don't know.'

'Turn him over!'

Alec made a move toward the body, then stopped. 'I'm sure he's dead. We shouldn't touch him. We need to call the police.'

'What's going on?'

Juliet and Alec looked up to see Frank Greenlee peering at them from the top of the slope. 'We've – or rather Hutch – found a body,' Alec called.

Frank stiffened and swayed slightly. His expression went rigid as he stared past them at the remains of a man in jeans, a stained T-shirt, and floating dark hair. 'Who . . . who is it?'

'We don't know. We shouldn't touch the body. We'll call the police.'

'Yes. Yes, I guess that's the right thing to do.' Frank kept staring at the man. 'How long do you suppose he's been there?'

Alec shook his head. 'We have no idea. Hutch woke us up just now.'

'Me, too.'

'We didn't hear anything last night. Did you?'

Frank shook his head. 'No. Nothing. I didn't even have

on the TV. I had a long call with Nancy. I don't really know why she kept talking. She wants as little to do with me as possible . . .'

Frank had a wandering, confused air that puzzled Juliet. He was usually a take-charge kind of person, which made him a great manager for the Heritage Inn. But this morning, he seemed oddly at sea, almost helpless.

'I don't have my cell phone,' Alec said. 'I'll go inside and call nine-one-one. Juliet, why don't you come with me? You look like you could use a cup of coffee.'

'We have to get Hutch. I don't want him trying to drag the body out of the water.'

But Hutch seemed to have no such inclination. As soon as Alec tapped his thigh and said, 'Come on, Hutch,' the dog raced toward the house. He even ran through the dog door instead of waiting for Alec to open the larger kitchen door.

Juliet wanted to go back into the house with Alec and Hutch, but Frank simply stood looking stunned and gray-skinned, and she didn't feel she could leave him. Finally, he said, 'Do you remember that this is exactly the spot where we found Gary's body?'

So that was what was wrong with him, Juliet thought, as her mind filled with the memory of Frank's wife Nancy letting out a cry and running to her house and then next door to the Reids'. Juliet's father hadn't left for work yet and he'd raced to the scene, then held back a hysterical Nancy and overwhelmed Frank who wanted to drag his son from the creek. Sera had hurried Juliet back to their home and not let her go out again for the rest of the day. Sera had tried to stifle her tears, tried unsuccessfully to make Fin go to school as usual in spite of the death of his best friend, and to comfort Nancy, who'd soon lain in a deep sleep induced by sedatives prescribed by the doctor. Only three months later, the Reid family would be devastated by Fin's murder.

'I'll never understand why he came down here to overdose.'

'It was an accident, Frank,' Owen had said.

'Was it? Or was it suicide?'

Juliet didn't have an answer and she didn't think it was good for Frank to talk about Gary's death so she changed the subject. 'You said that Nancy called you last night?'

Frank looked at her blankly for a moment, then blinked and seemed to come back to the present. 'Yes. It was . . . odd.'

'Is she all right? She didn't call because she's sick or something's wrong?'

'No. She told me she's getting married again.'

'Oh.' Juliet didn't know what to say and blundered through the next sentences. 'Well, at least she told you. It might have been worse to hear about it after the fact. I mean, if it would upset you.'

'She left *me*. I was hurt at the time, but we've been divorced for nine years. I'm past it. I wish her well. She was a good wife and a good mother.' He looked into the distance. 'Yes, she deserves happiness. Happiness that I didn't give her.'

But it hurts, Juliet thought. *After all this time, you still regret that divorce, even though you and Nancy didn't share the kind of love my parents did.* 'How long did she talk?'

'What? Oh, I don't know. Forty-five minutes. She told me about her husband-to-be, but I don't remember much of what she said. I was so surprised. I shouldn't have been. I thought she'd remarry a long time ago. That's why she went to Miami – for a fresh start in a different atmosphere.' He looked at Juliet. 'She's never been back to Parrish.'

'I know,' Juliet said gently. 'I guess it was just too painful for her.'

'Yes, maybe. And she was angry. *So* angry.'

'Frank, why don't you come in and have some coffee with me? You look like you need it.'

She'd expected him to decline, but instead she thought she saw a hint of pleasure in his eyes. 'Really? I won't be a bother?'

'You? A bother?' Juliet extended her hand. 'Never, Frank. Never.'

'I'm surprised Deke Nevins made it as long as he did,' Davis said as Deacon Nevins' body was being loaded into an ambulance. 'He's been trouble since he was a teenager.'

'At least he won't be causing any more now.' Alec shook his head. 'I wonder how Belle will take this.'

'Not good. She might be the only person in the world who cared about him, although he didn't care about her. Eddie won't lose any tears over him, though. He doesn't have to worry about Deke anymore.'

'But who murdered him? How many stab wounds did you say there were? Three?'

'Four. And no random slashes. Deke wasn't armed, unless whoever killed him took away his weapon. What I wonder was why he was in this area.'

'He was stabbed in Frank's backyard. That's where most of the blood is. A blood trail leads to the creek.'

'Why would he go to Frank's?' Alec asked. 'I'll bet he hasn't been there since Gary died.'

'Do you think Deke had anything to do with Gary's death?'

'That was almost ten years ago. I wasn't in on what everyone on the force thought, but I know nothing pointed directly toward Deke besides that he might have been supplying some of Gary's drugs. And I'm saying *might*. There was no proof. He even had an alibi for the night Gary died. A girl, of course. No one could shake her story.'

'I'm sure he didn't stop by last night for a chat with Frank about Gary.'

'Hardly,' Davis said. 'Frank says he didn't hear anything even though he wasn't watching TV like he was the night Owen died. Also, when Owen died, Frank was nearly dead drunk. But last night he had a long phone conversation with his wife. We'll have to establish the time of Deke's death and the time of Frank's call, not that the call eliminates him as a suspect. He could have been standing right in front of Deke and talking to his ex-wife while stabbing Deke to death.'

Alec couldn't help smiling. 'That doesn't sound very likely.'

'Not likely, but not impossible. If there's one thing I've learned in doing this job for thirty years, it's that nothing is impossible.'

Davis left to question other neighbors. So far they had not located Deke's car and had found nothing on his body to indicate why he'd been in the area. Juliet offered to fix breakfast, but no one had any appetite. Frank went home and Juliet took a quick shower, planning to spend the rest of the morning helping Leslie move into her new home. The party would be tomorrow night and Juliet knew there was a lot left to do.

Leslie wasn't looking forward to the party – she still wished she'd had another week to get ready – but Juliet hoped Leslie had hired more people to help with the preparations.

'Don't forget that Davis said he'd be here with Eddie around two o'clock,' Alec told her before she left.

'We could have picked up Eddie at the hospital.'

'Davis thought having the sheriff handle the transfer of Eddie to his aunt would seem more professional. No one would question that we'd just hidden Eddie somewhere and kept him for ourselves.'

Juliet laughed. 'You're right, although I'd like to keep Eddie for myself. He seems like one of our family, Alec.'

'*Our* family.' Alec put his arms around Juliet and looked deeply into her eyes. 'I like the sound of that.'

'So do I.' She kissed him lightly on the lips.

Alec grinned at her. 'All right – the sooner you go, the sooner you'll be back. Don't wear yourself out.'

'I can't guarantee that. Leslie will probably have me down on my hands and knees scrubbing floors and climbing ladders knocking cobwebs out of the rafters.'

'Well, don't hurt yourself. I'll want you looking good for the party.'

'My gosh, you're romantic, Alec Wainwright! I had no idea.'

Twenty minutes later Juliet found Leslie sitting on the floor of a large storage room in the bedroom area. 'The cleaning crew in the front of the house told me you were back here,' Juliet said. 'What are you doing?'

Leslie looked up with large, troubled eyes. 'Just going through some boxes we had hauled over from the other house and haven't unloaded yet.'

'What's wrong?'

'Nothing. Just memories.' Leslie quickly closed the lid on a medium-sized cardboard box and smiled, but Juliet had never seen a worse excuse for a smile. 'How are you this morning?'

'In shock.' Juliet sat down on the floor beside Leslie. 'Hutch found a body floating in the creek this morning. It was Deke Nevins. He's been murdered.'

Leslie's pale lips parted. '*Murdered?* Are you sure?'

'He had four stab wounds, one through the heart. I don't think there's any doubt.'

'But . . . *who*?'

'Who killed him? The police have no idea. Someone like Deke must have had a hundred enemies just here in Parrish. And after Rocco's was busted the other night—'

'What did Deke have to do with Rocco's?'

'Leslie, everyone knows he must have been one of the drug suppliers. He's been hiding ever since the bust. Who knows what kind of hell he let loose on himself with his involvement?'

'I guess you're right. He's always been bad – even back in the days when he was in Fin's band. That's why Fin kicked him out.' She clutched Juliet's hand. 'My God, what a morning you've had! You poor thing. Let's get out of this dreary storage room and into the kitchen where it's bright. Are you hungry?'

'I wasn't earlier but now I'm famished.'

'Good. I stopped at the bakery and bought doughnuts and turnovers and muffins.'

'*You* must be hungry!'

'Me and the people working here today. Thank goodness Danielle had something else to do this morning. I know she means to be helpful but she's so bossy. Carole went with her.' They entered the beautiful, large robin's-egg blue kitchen with cream-white ceramic counter tops and a wall of windows looking out onto the emerald back lawn. 'There's half a pot of coffee left or would you like fresh?'

'Unless it's three hours old, I'd love a cup of what you have. I've already had four. I'll probably shoot through the roof after one more. Alec, Davis, and Frank were at my house drinking coffee, too.'

'Frank? Why?'

'The body was between our houses. Actually, it was in the same spot where Gary's body was found.'

'Oh no!'

'Yes. It really shook Frank up. Me, too. Well, not as much as Frank but . . . oh, Les, I remember that morning so well. Fin had gone out to his tree house to get something and he spotted Gary. I'd never seen him so upset. He went wild – Dad had to hold onto him to keep him from dragging Gary out of the water. Fin and Gary had been like brothers all their lives.'

'Do you think Gary was getting his drugs from Deke?'

'Yes. They knew each other – it would have been easy for Gary to reach out to him.'

'But why? *Why* did Gary start taking drugs?'

'I don't know. I have a feeling other people knew – even Fin – but no one ever told me.'

Leslie poured coffee into two mugs, spilling a bit of one. 'Milk?' she asked.

'Yes, if you have it.' Juliet had taken milk in her coffee since she was a teenager and wondered how Leslie could have forgotten. Leslie opened the refrigerator and stared. 'It's right in front of you.'

'Oh, sure! I don't know what's wrong with me this morning. I didn't sleep much last night.'

'Why couldn't you sleep?'

'Worrying about getting the house in shape. We aren't moving in until day after tomorrow, but I have things at Danielle's and a ton of stuff at our house.'

'Not everything has to be here for the party, Les. Maybe you're overdoing it. Are you feeling all right?'

'Yes. Oh, you mean the baby. Everything's fine. I see the doctor at ten in the morning. I'm at fourteen weeks.'

'That's wonderful. Does Tommy know yet?'

'We told him last night.' Leslie placed an apple turnover on a plate and handed it to Juliet without asking if she wanted one or a doughnut or a muffin. 'We were going to wait another week, but when he heard he's staying at Danielle's with Martha instead of coming to the housewarming party, he started crying so we broke down. He was so happy that the tears stopped.' She smiled. 'He wants to name the baby Spike.'

'Spike?'

'Spike the Dragon. It's the name of a preteen dragon on *My Little Pony Friendship is Magic.*'

'I'm blank. I'll have to start watching more television. What if it's a girl?'

'Rarity. Spike has a crush on her. We told him we'd think about it.'

'I don't know how Danielle will feel about having a grandson named Spike.'

Leslie smiled. 'She loves Tommy so much she'd probably champion any name he chose.'

TWENTY-TWO

Juliet got home just before one o'clock, prepared to straighten up the house before Davis and Eddie arrived, but Alec already had everything looking perfect. 'I didn't know you were such a good housekeeper!' Juliet exclaimed.

'I've kept that talent a secret.'

'So you wouldn't have to do it. Now I'm onto you, Alec. Have you heard any more about Deke?'

'No.' Alec plumped two throw pillows on the couch, placed them and administered a karate chop in the top of each. 'Is that right?'

'Perfect if you're staying in a five-star hotel. We're a bit more casual around here in case you've forgotten.'

'I haven't forgotten anything.' He hugged her then ran his hand along a strand of hair trailing down her face. 'Leslie didn't work you too hard, did she?'

'Hardly at all. I think she just wanted company. She seemed sad today. Troubled. I asked how she's feeling and she's not sleeping well, but something else is wrong. I know her too well.'

'Maybe she's overwhelmed by this party.'

'She's not excited about it but it would take more than organizing a party to dampen her spirits, especially when she has a cleaning crew and caterers. No, that's not it. Maybe I'll hear more in the next few days.' She glanced at her watch. 'In the meantime, we're having guests in half an hour.'

Forty-five minutes later, Juliet looked at her watch again. 'They're fifteen minutes late. Maybe they forgot to stop by here.'

Alec, who was looking out the front window, called, 'They didn't forget. Davis and Eddie are coming up the front walk right now and Marcy's with them.'

Juliet jerked open the front door before they had a chance to ring the bell. 'Eddie!'

He blushed. 'Hi, Miss Reid. Juliet.'

'How do you feel?'

'Good. Well, fairly good. I'll be fine in a week.'

'That's wonderful.'

'I hope you don't mind that I tagged along,' Marcy said. 'I'm friends with Eddie, too. I want to spend as much time as I can with him.'

'Of course I don't mind. Please, everyone come in. Davis, I didn't even say hello to you.'

'That's all right. I'm used to people not saying hello to me – part of the joy of being the sheriff.'

'The house looks lovely, Juliet.'

'Thanks, Marcy. That's due to Alec. I think he should quit his security job in New York and become a professional housekeeper. Now, what can I get everyone to drink?'

'I'll have a boilermaker,' Davis announced.

Marcy made a face. 'Oh, you will not and neither will I. Do you have some iced tea, Juliet? If not, water will be fine.'

'I have iced tea. Would you like mint in it?'

'Oh, yes. That sounds great. And lots of sugar.'

'Me, too!' Eddie said.

'I guess me three,' Davis added.

Juliet quickly fixed five glasses of iced tea and mint and carried them in on a tray along with a lemon tea cake she'd baked last night. As she served, Alec asked, 'Does it feel good to be out of the hospital, Eddie?'

'It sure does. They were really nice to me, but it's hard to just lie in bed and watch TV all day. I never thought I'd say that until I didn't have any other choice. I like working outside more, even in winter.'

'Well, you've been sprung,' Alec laughed, 'and by the sheriff himself.'

'Yeah, no one could argue with him.' Eddie's laughter died. 'He also took me to see my mom. I was afraid I might not get to see her before I leave.'

'How is she?'

'OK, I guess. I mean, how OK can you be in jail? She's real unhappy but she didn't cry. Well, once there were tears in her eyes but they didn't roll down her face . . . even when she talked about Deke.'

'She already knew he was dead?'

'Yes. She said she knew I didn't like him and maybe I was glad he was dead.' Eddie looked at each of them with his beautiful green eyes. 'Sometimes I thought I hated him. But I only wanted him out of our lives. I really didn't want him to get murdered.'

'I believe that, Eddie,' Alec said.

'Do you? Because when I told Mom, I don't think she believed me.'

Marcy, who sat by his side, touched his arm. 'Eddie, your mother is very upset. None of us understood how she could care for Deke, but perhaps she saw something in him that the rest of us didn't. Anyway, she knows you a lot better than she knew Deacon Nevins. She knows she has a fine, admirable son and she loves you more than anyone in the world. She won't forget that, Eddie. She will *never* forget that.'

Marcy's low, compassionate voice touched all of them but Eddie the most. He gazed at her gratefully, and Davis looked at his wife with boundless love and pride. Theirs was a match meant to be, Juliet thought, no matter what Danielle's opinion.

They talked for ten more minutes and Eddie had another slice of cake when the doorbell rang. Juliet opened the door to see an attractive, slender woman dressed in tailored white pants and a coral-pink silk blouse. She had shining, dark blonde hair, flawless skin, and remarkable green eyes like Eddie's. 'Hello, I'm Pamela Alder. I'm Eddie Maddox's aunt and I was asked to meet him here.'

'Oh! Mrs Alder—'

'Pamela, please.' The woman had a broad, friendly smile and dimples.

Juliet knew she was older than Belle, but she looked so much younger and fresher, Juliet caught herself staring. 'And I'm Juliet. Eddie is right here. Please come in.'

When Pamela entered, Eddie stood and smiled at her. 'Hi, Aunt Pam.'

'Hello, young man. My goodness, you've gotten tall. And *very* attractive.'

Juliet introduced Alec, Davis, and Marcy, then went into the kitchen to fix Pamela an iced tea. When she came back,

Pamela was sitting in Owen's chair, talking easily. 'I had a nice drive from Cincinnati. It's a beautiful day and I love to drive. My daughter's taking her driver's test next week. I'm not worried about the written part, but she's not great at parallel parking.'

'I am!' Eddie piped up. 'Maybe I could help her.'

'You're barely fourteen,' Pamela said.

'Yeah, but I've been practicing for a year. Do you think Jessica would let me help her?'

'I think she'd be delighted.' Pamela turned to look at Davis. 'So you're the famous Sheriff Dawson.'

'Famous? Where would that be, ma'am?'

'I've heard of you from Eddie. And Alec Wainwright? You work at a huge business in New York City.'

'Bernard-Widmer. It's an investment house. I do security.'

'He's a senior supervisor,' Marcy said. 'He doesn't just prowl around looking down hallways.'

'And Marcy, the beautiful Mrs Dawson. You're absolutely blooming. I looked like a blimp when I was expecting Jessica.'

'I think *I* look like a blimp, but Davis hasn't complained. Still, I'll be really glad to lose the pregnancy pounds. Goodness, I'd be glad to lose *half* of them!'

Pamela turned her green eyes to Juliet. 'And the concert pianist.'

'Just pianist. I've given a few *very* small concerts, but I'll never make Carnegie Hall. I finished my Master's degree in music a few weeks ago. I plan to teach.'

'That's what I do! English at our local junior college. I enjoy it but I'm glad to have the summer off. We're planning a trip to Ireland next month. We're so happy that Eddie will be able to go with us. You haven't been there, have you, Eddie?'

Juliet knew asking Eddie if he'd ever been to Ireland was like asking if he'd ever been to the moon, but Pamela was being polite, pretending to not be acutely aware of his impoverished childhood.

'No! Where in Ireland?'

'Dublin. County Donegal. Some castles. Are you interested in history?'

'Gosh, yeah. Only I don't know a whole lot about it.'

'No matter how much you learn, there's always more.' Pamela laughed.

Half an hour later, Pamela said, 'Well, if we're to make it to Cincinnati before dark, we'd better be going, Eddie.'

'Oh, so soon!' Juliet said louder than she meant to. 'I mean, time flies,' she ended lamely.

'I'm afraid so.' Pamela picked up her leather handbag and stood, smiling at Eddie. 'Are you all ready to go?'

'I've got some stuff in the sheriff's car – stuff from the hospital, stuff from the trailer. I don't have a whole lot of clothes. I won't take up much room.'

'We'll have plenty of room.'

'OK.' Eddie looked around sheepishly. 'Juliet, can I use your bathroom before we go?'

'Oh, sure, Eddie. Good idea, especially after all that tea you drank!'

As soon as he left the room, Pamela looked at all of them and spoke in a soft voice. 'I'm afraid you think I'm terrible for not bailing Belle out of jail, but I believe she needs time to think about the terrible effect she's having on Eddie's life. Also, I'd like to give Eddie a chance to settle in at our house, to be able to rest and have some fun. He certainly deserves it. But if I bail out Belle, she'll immediately start trying to get Eddie back. She'll be on the phone to him, crying, acting pitiful. Oh, she's my little sister and I sound like I don't have an ounce of sympathy for her, but in the past I've seen where sympathy gets me with her. The only chance Belle has is to not be mollycoddled – to pull herself up by her bootstraps. She's not stupid although she's done some stupid things in the past. She's just convinced that she's weak, that she's not capable of leading a worthwhile life. But she is. It's just not going to be easy to make her try.'

'We all understand, Pamela,' Davis said. 'No one is judging you for not getting Belle out of jail. Frankly, I think it's the best place for her right now, especially after Deke was murdered last night.'

Pamela shivered. 'You told me earlier. That man was despicable. I'm not sorry he's gone. I wish he'd disappeared years ago before he could do so much damage to Belle and Eddie.'

'We have no idea who killed him, but our investigation has just started,' Davis told her. 'Do you want me to keep you apprised?'

'Only of my sister's well-being. I hated Deke. It would be hypocritical of me to act as if I care who killed him. Also, if you don't tell me and Eddie should ask me, I can truthfully tell him I don't know anything.'

Eddie returned to the living room. For a moment he looked nervous, almost panicky. Then he focused on Juliet. 'Miss Reid, I haven't been completely honest with you.'

Juliet was surprised. 'You haven't? About what?'

'Well, it was something that I promised your father. You know how much I liked him – well, loved him, really – and when he asked me to do something for him, I wasn't sure I should do it. It was after he'd started acting strange and unhappy and he *begged* me and I just couldn't say no, even though I thought I might be doing something wrong—'

'Eddie, I'm sure you didn't do anything wrong.' Juliet tried to keep her voice calm. 'Just tell me what it is.'

Eddie reached to his neck and pulled out a silver dog tag ball chain. He pulled it over his head and handed it to her, two small keys dangling from it. 'He didn't tell me what the keys open. He said it was a secret and that if there was trouble – if something happened to him *and* Sera – I was to give them to you.'

Juliet turned the keys over in her hand. She had no idea why her father had given them to Eddie to keep them in case of *trouble*. What had he been expecting? Had he thought something might happen to him *and* his wife?

'Why didn't you give them to me after Mom died?'

'Wendell got me. And then I was sick and I didn't really forget but I didn't really remember, either,' Eddie said abjectly. 'I'm awful sorry. I hope I haven't done anything terrible.'

'You haven't.' Juliet stared at the keys. 'What on earth could they open?'

'A safety deposit box,' Marcy said abruptly. 'I know your parents had their accounts at Ohio One, Juliet, but I worked at First Parrish Bank. About a week before your father died, he came in and rented a safety deposit box. I'm absolutely certain because I took all of his information. He brought someone with him as a joint renter.'

'I don't understand,' Juliet said slowly.

Marcy looked at Juliet soberly. 'He must have put something in the box that he wanted to keep secret from you and your mother because it could be dangerous, but someone else had to know so that they could get into the box.'

'Then who was the other person he signed in on it?' Juliet asked in bewilderment.

'Kyle Hollister.'

'Juliet, staring at those keys isn't going to tell you what's in that safety deposit box,' Alec said an hour after Eddie and Pamela had left.

'I know, but I can't imagine what my father would have hidden. He and Mom told each other everything, but I'm sure she didn't know about this box. She went to the box at Ohio One and got out everything she needed after his death, but she wasn't even signed in as a joint renter on this box. Eddie said Dad told him to tell *me* about it only if something happened to him *and* Mom.'

Alec looked at her intently. 'All right. He had a second safety deposit box where he kept something he didn't want your mother to see.'

'Well, *what*? A photo of his mistress?'

'Juliet, don't be ridiculous.'

'I'm frustrated. I know something bad is in that box. Maybe he'd discovered information.' She lowered the keys and closed her eyes. 'Why did the bank have to close ten minutes after I got the keys?'

'Because it was closing time. Same time every day. You'll have to wait until tomorrow morning to get into the box.'

'The first thing I have to do is call Kyle Hollister. *Kyle* of all people, not Frank. I don't get it. I didn't think Dad particularly liked Kyle. He didn't want me to date him.'

'That was years ago. Your father could have changed his mind about him.'

'Maybe, but he never mentioned him. They didn't become pals.'

'That you know of.' Alec looked at her tenderly. 'I don't want to hurt your feelings, but your father changed in the last few months of his life, particularly the last few weeks. There was a lot going on with him that you didn't know about – that none of us knew about, sweetheart. Please don't let it hurt you – just accept it.'

Juliet waited until evening to phone Kyle. She began haltingly, asking him if anything stolen from the house had been found.

'Yes. I'm surprised you haven't heard already. We found a large plastic garbage bag in the theater. Everything you put on your list was in it except for the gold-and-garnet cross.'

'Oh!' Juliet didn't know why she was surprised. Had there ever really been any doubt that Wendell had robbed the house? Which must mean that he'd murdered her mother, too. 'Well . . . that's good.'

'I know how precious your mother's rings must be to you. We'll be returning them as soon as possible. I wish we knew what Wendell did with the cross.'

'We'll probably never know,' Juliet said tiredly. 'It's a shame – the cross meant so much to her. But I really called about something else. Eddie Maddox left with his aunt this afternoon. Before he did, he gave me two keys.'

'Keys?' Kyle asked cautiously.

'Safety deposit box keys. Davis and Marcy Dawson brought Eddie here. Marcy said Dad had rented a box with you at One Parrish Bank about a week before he died. Dad gave the keys to Eddie and told him to not give them to me unless something happened to him *and* Mom. Eddie had forgotten because he was sick.' She swallowed. 'Kyle, I'm very confused. Is this true? Did Dad rent a box with you?'

After a beat, Kyle said softly, 'Yes, Juliet, he did.'

'I see. I don't mean to sound insulting, but I wasn't aware that you and my father had much of a relationship. I know his own wife didn't know anything about this box and . . . well, all I can think of is, *why?*'

She heard Kyle take a deep breath. 'Juliet, this has been

tearing me apart. I was going to tell you about it in a couple of days. I'm sorry about the way you found out but I'm so relieved that you know . . .'

He trailed off but she could still hear him breathing harder than normal. 'You and I have always been friends. This doesn't change anything for me. Honestly. All I want is for you to please tell me how and why it happened.'

'OK. Here goes.' He took another deep breath. 'A little over two weeks ago, your father asked me to have lunch with him at your house. Your mother was working at Pauline's. I haven't been to your house for years, so I was surprised but pleased. He served grilled cheese sandwiches.'

Juliet couldn't help smiling. 'The only thing he could cook.'

'Well, they were damned good. And he was friendly. Beyond friendly. Jovial. After lunch, he took me to the basement. I haven't been down there since Fin died. He showed me the damage the flood had done and explained how he was renovating it into a studio for you.'

'Yes, Mom told me he was. Frank was helping him.'

'I know. At first I thought he was going to ask me to help him, too, but instead he asked me to sit on the couch. Then he brought a notebook to me – a notebook sealed in a plastic zip-lock bag. He said it was Fin's and he'd only found it a couple of weeks earlier when he was tearing down one of the damaged walls. It was stuck in a crack that had been in the wall even before the water had done more damage.' Juliet realized she was holding her breath. 'He told me he'd expected it to be full of music, but instead it was a journal. You know, like a diary.'

Juliet still said nothing.

'He didn't let me read it or even hold it. He said he hadn't even told your mother about it.'

'Why?'

'He said he didn't want her to know about it much less read it because it's hard for your mother to hide her reactions and he felt the journal contents required some thought, some restraint, before any action was taken and Sera is impulsive. He also didn't want to upset her and . . . well, he didn't want to put her in danger.'

'In danger? How could knowing about Fin's journal put Mom in danger?'

'Because of what Fin wrote. Your dad believed it and he was protecting your mother from any knowledge of the journal or its contents. She couldn't talk about something she didn't know about – not even with you.'

'This sounds crazy, Kyle.'

'I know. It did to me, too. But your father was so intense about it – and I don't mean irrationally intense. I didn't get the feeling there was anything wrong with him mentally or he was imagining things. He said he knew I care about you – I think of you like a sister – and I wouldn't do anything to put you in harm's way. He needed someone to know about the journal but keep it a secret for a while until he could try to "work things out." Those were his exact words. Anyway, he chose me as the only other person to confide in about the journal. And he asked me to take care of you. That's why you've been seeing me everywhere.'

'Oh. Well, thank you, but this still sounds absurd. The contents of Fin's journal were a deep, dark secret that had to be kept from Mom and me for our safety. What about Alec? Couldn't he tell him?'

'He said he thought Alec was too close to the family. If Alec gave the slightest hint of knowing about it, he'd be in danger, too. No one would suspect me. Still, he kept both keys to the deposit box and I didn't know where he put them.'

Juliet was getting impatient. 'Kyle, can you please give me at least a hint about what was in the journal?'

'As I said, I didn't read it. He wouldn't let me. He just said, "It tells about what could have been a murder."'

'A murder?' Juliet asked incredulously. 'Of whom?'

'Gary Greenlee.'

Juliet sat frozen on the living room couch. Alec sat down beside her. 'Darling, you have to stop thinking about this tonight.'

'I know,' she said woodenly. 'But there must be someone I should call and ask about this.'

'Kyle said Owen hadn't talked to anyone else about it.

Besides, what Fin wrote may not be true. I mean, maybe Fin's imagination ran away with him. Or maybe your father thought what the journal says is truth, but he misunderstood, misread what Fin had written. After all, he didn't let Kyle read the journal or keep one of the safety deposit keys so he could get the notebook and read it later. All we know is what your father told Kyle. Anyway, there's nothing you can do until tomorrow.'

'I don't think I can wait that long.'

'You have to. Let's go out and get some dinner.'

'I'm not hungry.'

'Your stomach just growled.'

'That was habit. It always growls at dinnertime.'

'You're a terrible liar, Juliet, which is not a bad quality.' Alec grasped her arm and gently pulled her up. 'You have to get out of this house. It's time for food. If you're not hungry, you can get a salad and a glass of wine.'

Reluctantly, Juliet went with Alec to a small Italian restaurant just out of town and surprised herself by eating half of a pizza and drinking three large glasses of Chianti in record time. 'I feel like I'm going to explode,' she said as she took her last sip of wine.

'Well, you don't look like it. For the first time since this morning, you have some color in your face and your eyes have lost that wary expression.'

'Did I look wary?'

'Yes. Who wouldn't be after seeing the body of Deke this morning and having to say goodbye – maybe forever – to Eddie.'

'It won't be forever. I won't let it be, even if Pamela would rather I didn't see him.'

'Why wouldn't Pamela want you to see him? She seemed like a lovely, smart, caring woman. She knows what you mean to Eddie and you've certainly shown what he means to you. Don't confuse her with Belle.'

Juliet smiled at him. 'You've always been so perceptive, Alec. It was one of the first things I noticed about you. Well, maybe not one of the first. First, I thought you were cute.'

'*Cute?*'

'I was a little girl. Give me a break.' She winked with woozy flirtatiousness. 'But now you're even cuter.'

'Gosh, thanks. That's always been my life's ambition.'

'Don't knock it. You look like Colin Farrell in *In Bruges*.'

'Colin Farrell? Well, that's good. Better than good. But you're the most beautiful woman in the world.'

'Oh, I know. It's such a trial, drawing gasps of admiration wherever I go, having young girls want to grow up to look like me, doing endless hair and make-up tutorials on YouTube.'

Alec was laughing. 'Sweetheart, you drank far too much wine too fast.'

'I know. I think you'll have to help me to the car.'

Darkness had fallen when they arrived home and Hutch was ecstatic to see them. 'What's up with you?' Juliet asked. 'I didn't forget to feed you before we left.'

But the dog seemed energized and happier than he'd been since before Owen's death. Juliet sank to the floor and sat playing with him, holding his squeaking stuffed lion cub above his head, tossing his squeaking red ball, waving around his squeaking ground hog toy while Hutch barked joyously.

'Good lord!' Alec finally laughed. 'You two are going to deafen me!'

'Dad's mad,' Juliet mock-whispered to Hutch. 'Looks like we've got to cool it.'

'Juliet, would you like a cup of coffee?' Alec asked.

'No.'

'Please?'

'OK. Make some. I *might* have a cup. Meanwhile, I'm going to change into something more comfortable.'

Juliet went into her parents' bedroom, opened one of her mother's dresser drawers, and searched the neatly folded contents. Then she took off her clothes and slipped on a pale blue jersey chemise and a long, azure blue kimono decorated with white orchids. She crossed the hall into Fin's room, retrieved the boom box and a CD by Linda Ronstadt. When she reentered the kitchen, the coffeemaker was on but Alec had disappeared. Juliet took advantage of his absence and hurried out to the terrace where she set up the boombox then ran back into the kitchen for four fat cream-colored candles. When Alec returned, she was sitting on the terrace sofa with her legs tucked up, candles glowing and music playing.

'Wow,' Alec said. 'I'm taking you to that Italian restaurant more often.'

'It does seem to have had a liberating effect on me, although I think it's really that this day is over.' She patted the sofa. 'Won't you join me?'

'Do you want me to bring out coffee?'

'OK. I know you made it just for me. I'll take a cup – with milk.'

'I know how you take your coffee.'

'Leslie didn't this morning. After all of these years, she had to ask. But she wasn't herself.'

'We'll continue this conversation over coffee before Hutch drinks it all. He's so hyped up tonight, I don't know what he might do.'

When he returned, Alec carried a tray with one cup of coffee and one big mug. 'The mug is for you,' he said, grinning. 'You and Hutch seem to be in the same mood.'

'Then he needs a chew toy. Where is he?'

'Passed out in his doggie bed. I think he's been partying all evening. Do you think he has a girlfriend?'

'I did see him with that attractive golden retriever Gigi down the street.' Juliet sipped her coffee. 'It's good. I'm surprised you didn't make espresso.'

'I thought about it but the espresso maker is broken.'

'That happened in the spring. It broke Dad's heart. I'm surprised Mom didn't get him a new one before—' She broke off and Alec reached over to stroke her shoulder. 'I'm not going to cry. I guess the alcohol in the wine has dried up my tears for now.' She laughed. 'Thanks for making me go out. I really didn't need to sit around here all evening and brood.'

'No, you didn't. But aren't you worried about being out on the terrace at night after what happened to Deke?'

'Not at all. I should be but I can't even think about him or what happened to him. I'm thinking about you going back to New York and your life—'

'What life?'

'What do you mean? You must have friends, a girlfriend.'

'I have acquaintances. Sometimes I go out on a date – usually no more than two or three with the same woman. Is that a life?'

Juliet stared at him for a moment. 'I suppose it's a life of *your* making, Alec. There's absolutely no reason in the world that you should be so isolated. You're smart and great-looking and ambitious and kind and—'

Suddenly he leaned over and kissed her passionately, holding her tightly in his arms, which were trembling. When he pulled away from her, he looked as if he expected to be slapped.

'Well!' Juliet gazed at him in surprise, then uttered another, 'Well!'

'There's only one thing I want in my life, Juliet. You.'

Juliet put down her legs and scooted closer to him, taking his darkly handsome face in her hands. 'Alec, we already talked about this. I told you how much I care about you. I love you. You love me.'

'Then why did you just mention my having a girlfriend?'

'Why? I don't know. This is all new. We've only been truly open with each other for a couple of days much less open with anyone else. For all I know, you *do* have a girlfriend—'

'I don't.'

'OK. And I don't have a boyfriend. I love *you*, Alec Wainwright. I've loved you for years – not just lately because of all the things that have happened. I'm not turning to you out of need. *I am in love with you.* Now. And I will be in the future, too. I know that. I've known it for a long time. I just thought you were out of my reach.'

Alec pulled her close and hugged her with a mixture of tenderness and desire. 'If only you knew how many times I've dreamed of you saying that to me.'

'All you had to do was ask me how I felt.'

'That would have taken a lot more nerve than I ever had.'

'More nerve than going to Afghanistan?'

'*Much* more.'

'Well, I wish you'd just asked instead of marching off to the desert and getting yourself shot.'

Surprisingly, Alec laughed. 'Yes, I should have. I suppose I'm a coward.'

'Oh, no, you're not. You're strong like my father – not that

I think of you as a father-figure. But you're a brave man, Alec. A brave, ethical, loyal man. And I adore you.'

They kissed again. Then a special song came on the boombox. '"Blue Bayou,"' Juliet murmured. 'My parents loved this song. They danced to it.' She stood up, bathed in the light of the solar torches and holding Alec's hand. 'Will you dance with me, Mr Wainwright?'

He smiled gently. 'It would be my pleasure, Miss Reid.'

And so they ended the evening, holding each other close and dancing to the beautiful strains of music floating up through the jasmine vines and into the warm July night.

TWENTY-THREE

J uliet awakened at eight a.m. with a strange sense of fore-boding. At first, she attributed it to having drunk too much wine last night, but half an hour later, as she sat sipping coffee and smiling at Alec across the kitchen table, she knew the feeling was not physical. Something in her mind waited with a dismal expectancy.

Alec finally said with concern, 'You don't look in the mood for a party.'

Juliet tried to look at him brightly. 'I don't? Well, we had a late night. And I have to get Fin's journal.'

'Do you want me to go with you?'

'No. I'm meeting Kyle at nine. He has to sign in, show them a key . . .'

'I get it. This is something you want to do alone without feeling I'm there to bolster you into womanhood.'

'Yes. Exactly. You're as wise as the sphinx.'

'I thought I was Colin Farrell.'

'You're even better. I adore you.'

'Then I'll stop hovering over you.'

Juliet forced herself to be calm as she showered and dressed to go to One Parrish Bank. Before she left home, she called Leslie. 'Hey, girl,' she greeted her friend, trying to sound as lighthearted as possible. 'How are you today?'

'Fine. Well, tired. I haven't really worked very hard – Danielle's seen to it that I have plenty of help – but I'll still be glad to have this party over.'

It wasn't like Leslie to let a simple unwanted party drag her down, leaving her voice flat and her spirits clearly low. Perhaps the pregnancy was affecting her, but Juliet thought there was more to her friend's obvious unhappiness than being three months pregnant. Whatever it was, she wasn't ready to open up to Juliet.

'I'm calling so early because I want to know if I can do

anything for you today,' Juliet said. 'I have some errands to run, but if you need help—'

'I don't. Thank you for asking, Juliet, but you've helped enough. Everything is going smoothly. Just be sure to come tonight.'

'Of course I'll come! Les, where else would Alec and I be but at your party?'

'I don't know. I simply want to make sure . . . well, I might need you. Uh, for moral support or . . . I don't know what I'm talking about this morning. See you at seven?'

'On the dot. Earlier if you need us.'

'Seven will be fine. Thanks, Juliet. Thanks for everything.'

Leslie hung up without saying goodbye. Juliet was bewildered by her tone but there was nothing she could do. She couldn't make Leslie tell her what was wrong *now*, but clearly she thought she'd need her best friend later at a party that was only meant to be fun.

When she arrived at the bank, Kyle was standing outside, waiting for her. He waved and smiled, then took her hand as soon as she walked up to him. 'Good morning. Did you sleep well?'

'No.'

'Neither did I.'

'Then let's get this over with. And, Kyle, no matter how it turns out, we'll always be friends.'

His beautiful smile suddenly looked less tentative and his blue eyes a bit merrier. 'You don't know how glad I am to hear that, Juliet.'

Before they entered the bank, Juliet handed him a key. Inside, they stated their business, Kyle signed his name as co-renter of the box and produced his identification. A bank official took him into the back. Juliet sat in the lobby, trying not to look jittery. Within ten minutes, Kyle returned and handed her a notebook in a sealed zip-lock bag, just as he'd described. On the front of the notebook, Fin had written, 'The Journal of Finian McQuire Reid.' Juliet smiled. 'That was Fin – dramatic to the end.' She looked up at Kyle. 'You said my father wanted you to know about this notebook because it was about Gary Greenlee. Why?'

Kyle looked at her somberly. 'Because since I was seventeen years old, your father knew Gary was the love of my life.'

'You are stunning.' Alec's gaze traveled over her sapphire-colored flared cocktail dress with a plunging neckline, delicate faux sapphire necklace and dangling earrings.

'Thank you. The dress was on sale at the Longworth Style. I keep buying clothes there I'll probably never wear again.'

'Oh, you might.' Alec studied her face. 'Can't you fake a smile?'

'Not when I don't have to,' Juliet said, thinking of the afternoon she'd spent sitting in the basement reading Fin's diary twice, thinking about everything he claimed, drawing in on herself in horror. Her father had been too dubious to take the journal to the police and perhaps damage someone's life. Yet something deep inside Owen had believed Fin's accusations and his belief had resulted in his death. And he'd feared for his wife's life, a fear that had been justified. Now Juliet was the only one left who knew what Fin and Owen thought. She wouldn't risk someone else's life with what could very possibly be the awful truth.

'Are you sure you don't want to tell me what was in Fin's journal?'

'I don't want to tell you *now*.' She closed her eyes. 'Alec, I have no proof that anything Fin wrote is true. I need to show the journal to the police. They have to decide if it merits an investigation. All of that can't be done within the next few hours. I have to face it – deal with it – tomorrow. But right now, we have to get through tonight, and if I tell you, I'm not sure we can.'

'It's that bad?'

She nodded and he pulled her close.

'OK, my darling, I'll smile and act silly and we'll pull off tonight in style.'

'Thank you.' Juliet looked up at him appealingly. 'What kind of person do you think Fin was? And be honest. Please. I trust your judgment more than anyone's, so you have to be truthful, even if he was my brother.'

'All right.' Alec led her to the couch and they sat down. 'I used to think your brother was an arrogant jerk. I couldn't believe that such a sweet girl as his sister had been raised by the same parents in the same house. After I came to live here, things were tense for a while. He didn't want me here, especially sharing his bedroom. Then, over a course of months, we began to talk, especially late at night. He gradually opened up – I mean the real Fin opened up, because what most people saw wasn't the real Fin. He knew he was talented but the showmanship – the charisma – was an act that he could stop performing at any time. Fin was scared of himself, of the image he'd created of himself. But it wasn't an image – he was just as talented and charismatic as everyone thought he was – everyone except himself. And he wasn't self-centered. Maybe that was the biggest surprise to me. He cared about people, although he tried not to let on how much he cared. He loved his parents and he loved you. He loved his friends, especially Gary. He worried about them.' Alec bent his head and closed his eyes. 'Fin was a good guy, Juliet. A truly good guy. And I cared about him deeply.'

By the time Alec finished, Juliet's eyes had filled with tears. She'd thought Alec had at first tolerated Fin and then came to mildly like him. She'd had no idea how he really felt and apparently he'd never been inclined to tell anyone. 'Thank you for telling me that, Alec.'

'It's the truth.'

'I know.' She kissed him gently. 'I know you'll always tell me the truth. And now we have to go to a party.'

When Juliet rang Leslie's doorbell, she asked Alec what time it was. He glanced at his watch. 'Seven-oh-seven.'

'We're late.'

'Yes. They've probably already called off the whole thing and sent everyone home.'

Danielle, resplendent in a metallic gold jumpsuit, flung open the door. 'Well, at *last!*'

'We're sorry we're late,' Juliet began quickly. 'Hutch ran out the front door as we were leaving. He has a crush on a girl in the neighborhood—'

'A girl *dog?*'

'Well, of course,' Alec said, pushing Juliet in ahead of him and past Danielle. 'The only female human for him is Juliet. For me, too.'

'Really? Am I getting late breaking news? Are you *finally* announcing you're a couple?'

'Where's Leslie?' Juliet asked.

'In the family room. That's where everyone is for now. You both look lovely.'

'I tried extra hard,' Alec said. 'Do you think I look like Colin Farrell?'

'Well . . . now that you mention it—'

'Juliet!' Leslie rushed to her and gave her a hug. 'I'm so glad you're here!'

She wore a tiered-skirt mesh dress with delicate pink flowers on a black background. Her long hair fell in graceful waves, her make-up was perfect, and she looked just about as unhappy as Juliet had ever seen her. 'Hi. We're a little late—'

'It doesn't matter. Only half the people are here. Please come in and have a drink. Jon's putting on some music.'

'No DJ?' Alec asked.

'Oh, I don't think so. I'm sorry.'

'He's joking,' Juliet said. 'I don't know what's gotten into him tonight. He'll probably have two drinks and do a stand-up comedy routine.'

'Well, that sounds like fun,' Leslie murmured vaguely. Juliet looked at Alec who shrugged. 'Are you feeling well, Les?'

'Yeah. Sure. Why? Do I look bad?'

'You look beautiful. I love the dress.'

They walked through the foyer to the large family room with its dramatic vaulted-ceiling, wooden beams and skylights. The yellow-and-rust color scheme was punctuated with the same robin's egg blue of the kitchen and complimented the tall limestone fireplace. Waiters from the Heritage Inn were serving around twelve guests and the sounds of laughter mixed with 'All Night Long' by Lionel Richie.

'I haven't heard that song for a while,' Alec said.

Leslie nodded. 'I know. I think Jon put on an old playlist.'

'Everything looks great,' Juliet told Leslie.

Leslie's eyes trailed vacantly around the room. 'I suppose it does.'

'I guess Tommy is at Danielle's.'

'Yes, with Martha and not happy about it. I promised him he could have his own housewarming party later and he asked me if the house wasn't warm already.'

Juliet laughed and heard the brittleness in her voice. Alec asked her if she'd like a cocktail. 'I'd kill for one,' she whispered. 'Anything. I don't care.'

As he headed off in search of liquid courage for her, Carole sauntered up. She wore a deep green sheath dress that showed off every curve of her beautiful body. 'Hi, Juliet. You're looking especially pretty.'

'Thanks. Last-minute buy. And as always, you look fabulous.'

Carole's mouth quirked. 'Listen to us making that phony party chatter I used to bask in. Now I hate it. From now on I'm going to do exactly as I please.'

'Good for you,' Juliet said sincerely. 'You deserve happiness, Carole.'

'As do we all.' Alec handed Juliet a piña colada. 'I hope you like these.'

'I love them. They're also fattening. I'm glad I wore a flared skirt.'

'You don't need to worry about your figure,' Marcy said, appearing in front of Juliet wearing wide-leg white pants and a white jacket over a sparkly blue tunic top. 'I didn't think I was going to find a tunic large enough for me. I swear I'm the biggest pregnant woman who ever lived.'

'That's because you have a small frame.' Juliet laughed. 'Anyway, the top is beautiful and fits perfectly.'

'It won't in a week. I swear, if I don't have this baby soon, I'll have to become a recluse. I have nothing left to wear.'

The doorbell rang again and Leslie started to move away, but Danielle was ahead of her, rushing to welcome more guests. 'I might as well not have come,' Leslie huffed. 'This is Danielle's party.'

Carole smiled. 'I know she can be maddening but thinking about moving away from her for five years pains me.'

'You'll see her,' Alec said. 'If you move somewhere exciting, you might see more of her than you'd like.'

For the next fifteen minutes, Juliet was aware of more people arriving, the laughter growing louder, and Leslie growing quieter. Davis and Kyle seemed to be having a serious conversation and for once, Davis didn't devote most of his attention to Marcy. Frank Greenlee came alone and Juliet thought about the things she'd read in Fin's journal just that afternoon. Were all of his observations accurate? More and more, she was certain they were exactly on point. She looked at certain people in the room with uncertainty and dread and unutterable sadness.

Suddenly, as if an alarm had gone off, guests began to depart. Danielle looked disappointed, as if she wanted to go on and on, but there was nothing she could do. Leslie floated around, seemingly in a distracted haze, while Danielle stood at the door, bidding people goodnight. In a little while, only a few of the partygoers remained.

'There's plenty of food left,' Danielle announced. 'I, for one, want another drink. Who else wants one?'

Frank Greenlee was the first to laugh and say he never turned down free drinks. Carole was second to accept another gin and tonic. She'd seemed downhearted ever since the party began. After he got his drink, Frank struck up a conversation with Leslie. Earlier, Juliet had seen Davis talking with Kyle and then with Jon. Now he and Marcy sat on a couch, Marcy looking tired and pale although they made no move to leave. However, a handful of stragglers ambled over to the bar and put on another play list, this one of even older music than had played earlier.

Leslie came up to Juliet and Alec. 'I think Danielle wants the party to go until dawn. I'm exhausted.'

'Would you like Alec and me to leave?' Juliet asked kindly.

'No! Please stay with me!'

Juliet heard the edge of hysteria in Leslie's voice. She hadn't wanted this party. She was tired. She'd been frightened ever since someone had tried to break into their other house. Juliet wasn't going to leave her and she knew Alec wouldn't push, either. He was still trying to act like the life of the party – for her sake – and he wasn't going to give up.

'I wish I knew some party games for us to play, but I don't. I've never liked them anyway,' Danielle said, sitting down on a chair and holding her fresh martini. 'Maybe you'd each like to say what your favorite room in the house is?'

Leslie and Carole groaned. 'Oh lord, Mom, not *that*. What if no one likes any of them?'

Danielle looked stunned. 'Well, they're all . . . lovely. How about a game of strip poker?'

'I'm out,' Marcy called.

Jon grinned and laid a hand on his mother's shoulders. 'It's OK. You don't have to entertain everyone.'

'No, you don't. I think everyone wants to go home,' Leslie said. Her voice rose. 'Marcy is half-asleep. Ready to drop. Literally ready to *drop*—'

'Leslie?' Danielle cried, standing up. 'Why . . . how rude, dear. What on earth is wrong with you?'

'I . . . I . . .' Suddenly, 'California Dreamin' resonated through the room. The Mamas and the Papas sang that they'd been for a walk on a winter's day. Abruptly, Leslie's hands began to shake before she started trembling all over. She dropped her glass of apple juice, the glass shattering on the hardwood floor beside the area rug. Her face blanched and she cried, 'Oh God, *Fin*!'

Carole looked at Leslie in shock. 'What's wrong with her?'

Jon was beside her in an instant. 'Leslie? What's wrong?'

Her head whipped toward him. 'What's *wrong*? How could you play that song?'

'It was on the playlist.'

'It was *Fin's* song!'

'OK. I'll turn it off if it upsets you.'

'Don't. *Don't*! We should all remember it. You *deserve* to remember it! Because of *you*, he never went to California! Or anywhere else!'

Jon took a step away from his wife, looking at her guardedly. 'I think we need to call a doctor. Or nine-one-one. You're not well—'

'Oh, I'm well! I wish I weren't – I wish I were crazy as a loon – but I'm not!' She looked at him venomously. 'You know I'm OK and you know I'm about to tell the truth.'

'You're not OK.' Jon turned around to the waiters cleaning up and pretending not to listen. 'You should go home. We have a family crisis here. The fewer people, the better. Please. Go *now!*'

No one had to be asked twice. Within five minutes, the last of the three caterers were gone, the front door shut firmly behind them.

'You can't send *everyone* home, Jon. They won't go,' Leslie said. 'You *murdered* Fin Reid!'

Jon gawked at her. 'I *what*?'

'Don't play dumb. I know it.' She looked around. 'And your mother knows it!'

Danielle spilled her martini on her gold jumpsuit. She looked horrified – and scared. 'Leslie, dear, Jon is right. You're not well. You don't know it but everyone here does. Please do as he says.'

Leslie whirled to Carole. 'You must know it!'

'Me? You believe Jon killed Fin? Leslie, how could you even say such a thing?'

'Because I have proof.'

Davis stood. 'I'm not sure what's happening here. Alec?'

Juliet looked in surprise at Alec.

'I don't know exactly, either,' Alec said. 'I only know that something isn't right – something that goes beyond Leslie being . . . upset.'

'Alec, I didn't tell you anything!' Juliet snapped. 'Shut up!'

'I don't know what you're trying to hide, darling,' Alec said, 'but it's coming out. Not tomorrow – tonight.'

'What she knows?' Danielle asked. 'What the hell are you talking about?'

Juliet didn't mean to speak but when she saw Leslie and Alec looking at her imploringly, the words rushed out. 'I found a journal of Fin's. He wrote about everything – everything up until his death, that is.'

'Fin's journal!' Danielle's voice was high and tight. 'What *everything* did he write about, for God's sake? And what does it matter? He had more imagination than anyone I ever met. He didn't know fact from fiction. He was an attention-seeker. He wanted everyone to look at him!'

'Then why did he *hide* the journal in the basement walling?' Juliet asked steadily. 'That wasn't any way to get people to look at him.'

'Hide a journal?' Danielle echoed. 'What are you talking about?'

'He wrote a journal telling what he thought had happened to Gary. He hid it. My father found it almost ten years later.'

'And you're bringing up Fin's accusations *now*?'

Davis came around the couch and stood closer to Jon. 'That's enough. I want to know what you're talking about, Juliet.'

'I guess you already know about the journal. Alec told you.'

'He called about an hour before the party and told me you'd found a journal of Fin's and the things he'd written about people who'd be at this party shook you to the core. He asked me to be sure to come and not leave until Jon and Leslie had gone back to Danielle's. I don't know what the trouble is but I've stayed, even though my wife is exhausted. I'm here and I'm not leaving. Now tell me what you know, Juliet.'

'Davis, don't be ridiculous,' Danielle snapped. 'Take Marcy home. She doesn't look well.'

'I'm OK.' Marcy came to stand by her husband. 'This is important. I can tell. Davis, go on.'

Jon looked furious. 'I don't know what you're talking about, Davis, Juliet. A journal about *me*?'

'And your brother Nate and Gary Greenlee.'

'My brother *Nate*?'

'Yes. That was supposition.' Juliet glanced at Carole, whose face was white, her head hanging downward. 'You know something about Nate, Carole. What is it?'

Silence spun out before Carole said, 'I don't *know* anything. I was just a little girl when Nate died.'

'You were nine,' Juliet went on relentlessly. 'You had eyes.'

Danielle's fists clenched. 'Don't say another word, Carole.' She turned on Juliet. 'Who do you think you are? What trouble are you trying to start?'

'I'm Finian Reid's sister and I think Jon murdered him. And Fin wasn't the first of Jon's victims.'

'You bitch!'

'That's enough, Danielle,' Davis said calmly. 'We're in the

mess – let's hear what she has to say. If we don't hear it now, I'll be hearing it in my office tomorrow.'

'Davis, how can you indulge a poor, deluded girl this way? I know she's been through a lot these days, but to allow her to go on—'

'Danielle, shut up.' Davis turned to Juliet. 'Go ahead.'

'I think Leslie should speak first,' Juliet said. 'She's the most upset.'

Leslie stood beside her, clutching her arm, sobbing. 'Jon has been acting strange for a couple of weeks. I knew something was wrong, and not just with Tresswell Metal. Then two days ago I found a box when I was packing. It was taped shut but I opened it. I found a gold keychain with FMR engraved on it. Finian McGuire Reid. Fin's missing keychain. I found a cowrie shell bracelet just like the one Gary Greenlee used to wear—'

'Gary's bracelet?' Frank echoed in disbelief.

'There are thousands of shell bracelets floating around,' Jon said.

'With small turquoise beads?' Kyle retorted.

'Gary's bracelet disappeared after his death,' Frank said emptily. 'It wasn't on his body, not in his room, nowhere.'

'So what?' Jon asked belligerently.

Kyle's voice seemed hollow. 'I gave that bracelet to him.'

Jon shot him a surprised look. 'What the hell for? Some kind of love symbol? Oh, you weren't out of the closet – you still aren't – but I knew about you two.'

Kyle merely stared at Jon.

'He probably sold it for drugs.'

'A nearly worthless bracelet?' Kyle asked.

'Oh. You knew about the drugs, Jon?'

'Yes, Davis, I knew Gary was dabbling in drugs.'

'He was doing more than *dabbling.*'

'And that's my fault? Or that he somehow lost his bracelet?'

Juliet felt a tremor go through Leslie. 'I also found a framed photo of all of you guys in the band.'

'Juliet told you the picture was missing,' Jon said to Leslie.

'It had dried blood on the frame, Jon. And there was a six-inch tall wooden carving of a lion.'

'Nate's,' Carole gasped.

Danielle glared at her. 'Be quiet, Carole.'

Leslie went on tonelessly. 'And a thin silver hoop earring with dried blood on the wire.'

'Deke Nevins's earring,' Kyle said.

Leslie kept looking at Jon. 'And a gold-and-garnet cross. Sera's cross. And a photo of Owen and Sera on a beach. There was blood on it, too.'

Her mother's blood on her cherished honeymoon photo. Juliet felt a wave of nausea rise in her as Jon moved threateningly toward Leslie.

Leslie said, 'I don't know anything about the lion. But I'd seen Gary wearing that bracelet. And Fin's keychain – the one they couldn't find after his murder. It had all of his keys on it. I told you, it was engraved FMR.'

'I found it later but the Reids had gotten their locks changed.'

'Why didn't you turn it over to the police?'

'Wendell was already in prison. The investigation was finished. It was a keepsake.'

'And was Gary's bracelet a keepsake? And Sera's cross?'

'That's not Sera's cross!'

'Then whose was it? Why do you have it?' Leslie screamed at him.

Jon's lips narrowed. 'Leslie, you're pregnant. You're imagining things.'

'Being pregnant doesn't make me delusional!'

Juliet put her arm around Leslie and held her tight as she shuddered and wept. Frank moved closer to Leslie, his face etched with concern.

'That's enough of all this,' Davis said. 'I'll need to see that box full of items, Leslie, and the journal, Juliet.'

Jon suddenly turned aggressive. 'What the hell for? A box full of junk, the ramblings of a teenage boy?'

'A box with Sera Reid's cross in it, Jon.'

'A box with *a* cross in it! Who says it was Sera's?'

'Juliet can say when she sees it.'

'It was made in 1925,' Juliet said softly. 'The date was engraved on the back.'

'Have you seen this cross Leslie claims to have found?' Jon demanded of Juliet.

'No. But I will.'

'Oh, that's convenient.' Jon looked around. 'You're all accusing me of something so ludicrous and I *cannot* believe it! What's wrong with you?'

'I saw you,' Carole said in a small voice. 'When you were diving with Nate. I was looking through the windows. He jumped in. He didn't come back up. You walked around and looked down in the water. You stood there for a while, smiling. Then you just left.'

'You were always a lying little bitch!' Jon snarled. 'You told that story to Dad and he believed you. Didn't he, Mom?'

Danielle had her head in her hand. 'Y-yes.' Her voice quivered. 'But he wasn't well . . . and Nate was his pride and joy . . .'

'Maybe it was because you aren't Nathaniel Tresswell's son,' Kyle said coldly.

Jon looked stunned. And enraged. 'What are you saying?'

'You aren't Nathaniel Tresswell's son. Your mother had an affair. You're the result. He knew it.'

A small moan came out of Danielle and everyone turned to Davis. He looked blank for a moment, then said loudly, 'Oh no. Not me. I *never* had an affair with Danielle.'

Kyle's handsome face seemed carved out of stone. 'Gary knew. He told me as soon as he found out. Jon's father is Frank Greenlee.'

TWENTY-FOUR

Frank's face froze, then the creased red cheeks turned even redder. Sweat popped out on his forehead. He looked at Danielle, who didn't look back. 'Gary was mistaken,' Frank said unconvincingly. 'He didn't know . . . he was so mixed up. The drugs. It was his imagination. I mean, look at me.'

Everyone's gaze slid up and down his doughy body, his thinning hair, his puffy eyes, the loose skin hanging at his neck. But he hadn't always looked that way. Juliet remembered when he was young and slender with thick dark hair and long-lashed dark eyes. He'd been charming and happy and even better looking than Kyle Hollister was now.

'That is absurd,' Danielle strangled out. 'I was . . . content with Nathaniel.'

Carole looked at Danielle. 'No, you weren't. You didn't love Daddy. Only *I* loved Daddy. That's why I told him about Jon leaving Nate in the pool.'

'Be quiet, you stupid little girl,' Danielle snapped.

'He was so mad. I never saw him that way. But he said, "I'm not surprised. Jon's always hated Nate. He let him lie in that pool, unconscious, and drown."'

Danielle looked murderous. 'You can't possibly remember what he said to your lie!'

'I do. And he never forgave Jon. He didn't like him anyway. Kyle says Jon wasn't his – I believe him. Daddy wasn't Jon's father and he knew it. I know that now. The way Mom acted around Frank—'

'Stop it!' Danielle shouted.

'You're the one who always hated me,' Jon said to Carole. 'That's why you lied to Dad. That's why you're lying now.'

'I didn't like you back then! You were mean to me. But so was Nate. I didn't like either of you. But I didn't lie and Daddy knew I wasn't lying.'

'And do you think Frank is *your* father?'

Carole blanched. 'I . . . I don't know.'

Danielle stood up. 'No! No, you are the daughter of Nathaniel Tresswell. I married him in good faith but he didn't love me – he never loved me. I was so unhappy with him.' Her gaze fell. 'I was only unfaithful for a year.'

'So it's true?' Juliet asked. 'You had an affair with Frank?'

'I . . . I loved him. We had so many parties at the inn and he was always there – good-looking, fun, attentive . . . loving . . .'

'Mother!' Jon barked. 'You're drunk! Stop talking!'

'Why? Frank knows he's your father. Nathaniel knew Frank was your father. *You* know he's your father.'

'Go home.' Jon's voice was icy. 'Go home and cry out your guilt and sober up.'

'Did you know you were Frank's son?' Leslie asked tremulously.

'If I were, would you have married me?'

'Of course, Jon. I love *you*.'

'You've certainly sound like you love me tonight,' he snarled.

'Jon, the stuff I found in that box and the way you've been acting—'

'Stop talking about that damned box!'

'Why, if the stuff inside is harmless? But it isn't, is it, Jon?'

Jon went rigid. 'I won't take this. I am the President and CEO of Tresswell Metal and I will not take this.'

'That's it, isn't it?' Danielle asked. 'Tresswell. You've always been obsessed with Tresswell and wanted it to be yours.'

'Certainly I did. So did Nate.'

'You didn't know you weren't a Tresswell when you were eleven. But you knew Tresswell Metal would go to Nate because he was the oldest. So you let him die.'

'It was an accident!'

'No, it wasn't. You showed no genuine grief when Nate died,' Danielle said. 'Oh, you said over and over you were sorry you left him and he'd promised not to dive anymore. You even cried. But they were crocodile tears. And your voice didn't hold a note of sincerity. I knew, Jon. I *knew*.'

'If that's what you thought, why didn't you say so?'

'Because I loved you so much!'

'Why didn't Dad say so?'

'He already suspected you weren't his son. And then
murder?' Danielle laughed roughly. 'But that damned pride
of his kept him silent. Not love, Jon. Pride. He could not let
himself be humiliated.'

'Nancy and I were having a fight.' Frank's voice seemed to
come out of nowhere. Everyone looked at him and seemed as
if he were talking to himself. 'It was a vicious one, even for
us. She knew Gary was doing drugs. She blamed it on me.
"It started when you got involved with Danielle," she screamed.
"Then she had your bastard Jon. What kind of husband were
you? But I stuck with you. All these years. And now look at
Gary. A drug addict and a . . . a homosexual! Him and that
Kyle! God! I hate homosexuals and I hate you and Gary."'
Frank finally gazed at them. 'All I wanted was a healthy, happy
child. I didn't care if he was gay, but Nancy was violently
homophobic, you see. She didn't understand Gary – she never
wanted to even acknowledge it that he was gay much less try
to understand him. He knew how she felt. That's why he got
into drugs. Anyway, during the fight, Gary was in the basement. We didn't know. But he'd heard us. He told me later he
had and he knew I was Jon's father.'

'You two had a fight and Nancy hurled accusations at you,'
Jon fumed. 'So what? She was always mad. Nasty.'

'She was right about Gary taking drugs and you being my
son,' Frank said. 'Why did you have to kill him?'

'I *didn't* kill—'

Juliet cut Jon off. 'Fin's journal says Gary was in debt to
his supplier – Deke Nevins. Gary was going to ask you for
the money and say that if you didn't give it to him, he'd tell
everyone that Frank was your father. He was going to black-
mail you, Jon. That wasn't the Gary that Fin had grown up
with, but it was the Gary at the end of his life. The day after
Gary told Fin what he was going to do, Gary was dead of
an overdose.' She paused. 'Fin began to wonder about that
overdose.'

'Then Fin was insane!'

'Fin said you also turned up with two songs you'd supposedly written. They were very good. They also had Gary written

all over them. Fin had seen parts of them. You stole his music, too. Fin said he was going to confront you about everything – the theft of the music, Gary's overdose. It was his last entry. Then two days later, he was murdered. He told you what he suspected the day after he wrote the entry. You needed a day to set up Wendell and you did a fine job of it – very dramatic – and it worked.'

Jon suddenly smiled and shook his head. 'Juliet, you should have been a murder mystery-writer. What about all the DNA evidence against Wendell?'

'You buried the knife in the Booths' garden and you used his rope. He said in his testimony he'd touched Fin's body when he found it tied to the tree.'

'Oh, sure.' He grinned. 'The jurors thought that was a bit too convenient from Wendell. He was convicted.'

'But he wouldn't have been if one juror hadn't been bribed.'

'And I suppose I bribed that juror. Where would I have gotten fifty thousand dollars? Isn't that how much she said she got from some "middle man"?'

'I attended the trial frequently and I told Danielle I thought there was a juror who didn't seem *right*. She was obviously concentrating more on a guy sitting next to her than on the evidence being presented,' Davis said softly. 'It was just an observation. I knew – or thought I knew – that Danielle wanted justice for Fin.' He looked at all of them miserably. 'Now I'm not so sure.'

Danielle burst out, 'What an awful thing to say, Davis! Wendell murdered Fin! Of course I wanted justice. I cared deeply about Fin.'

'But not as much as you did your son. You'd also been afraid Carole would run off to California with Fin. She wanted to, no matter what she says now.'

'I . . . I didn't,' Carole stammered.

'You *did*,' Jon sneered. 'You begged him but he wouldn't take you. So you rewrote history to save your ego.'

'Oh, what does that matter now?' Danielle cried. 'Fin wouldn't have gone to California and been a success. And Carole certainly wasn't meant to be a groupie.'

'No, she wouldn't have lasted if she had gone. But that's

not important now,' Davis said. 'What is important is that y*ou* bribed that juror, Danielle. Or you got someone to do it for you. Surely not Frank.' She stared at him unflinchingly. 'You knew he would never do it. But you know people . . .'

'You can't prove I did *anything*! The woman who took the bribe is dead.'

'I can't prove it, but I know it. Who gave her the bribe? Who was the "middle man?"'

'I never knew. Someone else dealt with him.'

Danielle was lying but Juliet could tell she had no intention of giving him up, whoever he was.

Davis still stood next to Jon. Marcy moved to him and clutched his arm. She was alarmingly pale and her colorless lips were pressed together. He distractedly rubbed her hand. 'It's all right, honey. Just a little while longer.'

Meanwhile, Jon's body had gone rigid and he stood at an odd angle, his hazel eyes narrowing and taking on a strange, threatening look. *He's unraveling*, Juliet thought.

'I suppose I drove Owen Reid to suicide, too.'

'He didn't commit suicide,' Alec said. 'He'd found Fin's journal. He'd read it. He was dumbfounded but he almost believed it. To give you a chance, he asked to see you.' Juliet knew Alec was guessing, but Jon's expression said Alec was right. 'I was at your mother's party. That night you acted nervous, edgy. You disappeared for a while. Then you were back, acting more jittery than ever. Leslie noticed it. I saw the way she was looking at you. And so was your mother. Danielle had a bad feeling, didn't she? After all, she'd dealt with your work earlier – Nate. I don't think she knew about Gary.'

Suddenly, Jon smirked. 'No one except Fin suspected Gary's overdose was anything but a suicide. When he called me, demanding money or he'd tell who my father is, I knew I had to get rid of him. We set up a meet on the creek bank at night. I came with a syringe – I told Gary it was a weak mixture of morphine and he probably really needed it if Deke wouldn't sell him anymore. If he hadn't been so strung out, he wouldn't have let me inject him, but he was and I did – with two hundred milligrams of heroin. His heart stopped. That was his mistake and my salvation.'

'Jon, don't say anymore without a lawyer,' Danielle begged.

Jon tilted his head cockily. 'I don't need a lawyer, *Mother*. I'm through listening to what you say.'

'You've *never* listened to what I say,' Danielle sobbed. 'Never!'

'I wasn't a Tresswell. All I ever was to you was the accidental son of a fat, alcoholic motel manager!'

'You fool!' Carole cried. 'You were the only one of us who really mattered to her! Don't you remember how she used to fight with Nate? He was so insufferably arrogant. And me? I was just someone to marry to a rich man. Look at her last choice for me. He beat me and he wouldn't let me go!'

'I made him let you go!' Jon shouted at her. 'I had photos of you with Kyle. They were harmless until they were photoshopped. I told him if he didn't give you the divorce, I'd turn them loose to the news.'

'And you think he wouldn't have discovered you'd tampered with them?'

'By then it would be too late. He'd be a laughingstock. There's no rich girl in the wings – his gigantic ego just couldn't take humiliation, sister dear.'

'Why did you do that for me?'

'Have you forgotten the caveat? You had to leave the country and keep your head low, not draw any attention.'

'Because?'

'Because after Owen's death, after Sera's death, you began giving me the same look you did after Nate drowned. I saw it again the night I came to Mom's house hours after Juliet was kidnapped. I said I'd been making calls to see that she was all right. I was really making certain Wendell hadn't said anything about seeing me at the Reid house when Sera was murdered. If he had, I would have run. And that isn't the only time I've seen suspicion in your eyes. You have an uncanny way of seeing through me. You nearly destroyed me once when Nate died and I was afraid you'd do it again. Your gaze is too sharp, Carole, especially when it's directed at me.'

Danielle's eyes were closed. 'Son, please, shut your mouth,' she said tiredly. 'You're destroying yourself.'

'It seems I've already been destroyed – by you and your

uncontrollable libido. I should have been Nathaniel's. Why couldn't you be faithful to him?'

'I fell in love with a man who adored me. Nathaniel didn't. He didn't even like me. My father gave him a loan for his company in exchange for me – the trophy wife with a big bank account that I turned over to Nathaniel.'

'You're a whore!'

'Jon!' Frank shouted. 'Don't say that to your mother!'

'That's what she is! She traded herself for prestige; she cheated on her husband with *you*!'

Leslie held onto to Juliet's arm so tightly that Juliet felt her arm going numb. Leslie's face was distorted from crying and she trembled. 'The night someone tried to break into our house and nearly frightened Tommy and Juliet to death – did you do that, Jon? Did you terrify your own son?'

'No. I thought it was Robert or Deke,' Jon said.

'I did. Jon knew nothing about it,' Danielle's voice was desperate as she still defended her son. 'I hired someone to scare you – not hurt you or Tommy – but to make you leave that house and come stay with me. I knew something was wrong with Jon. I'd known since shortly before Owen . . . died. I was afraid it wasn't suicide and I didn't think you were safe with Jon.' She looked at Jon. 'I'm sorry but I had to protect my grandson. I wanted to keep him with me until . . . until you were all right again.'

'You?' Leslie gasped. 'You hired someone to do *that* to us? And I'm pregnant—'

'I didn't *know*!'

'What about Tommy? He's still having nightmares.'

Danielle shook her head. 'He's young. He'll get over it.'

Leslie said acidly, 'You just wanted what you wanted. Who did you hire? Deke?'

'No, I didn't hire Deke. I hired someone you don't know. He was just some guy who needed the money. He's left town.'

'My father,' Juliet said to Jon. 'You murdered him.'

Jon looked as if he were weakening and diminishing in front of them. 'He called me. He said he had to see me – it was about Gary and Fin. He said Fin had made allegations against me in a journal he'd just found. He didn't want to believe them. I'd been friends with the boys since childhood. He owed it to me to talk it out, he said, the sentimental fool.' He smiled tiredly. 'But I could tell he did believe what Fin had written. I knew he had to go. So I waited until he didn't turn up at Mom's party and I paid him a visit.'

'And my mother,' Juliet said softly. 'Why did you murder my mother, Jon?'

His head turned slowly toward her, his eyes flaring wide then narrowing again. 'I didn't plan to. I'd gone to so much trouble to make Owen's death look like suicide, do you suppose I'd barge in and kill your mother, stir up another murder trial like Fin's? But I couldn't search the house for Fin's journal after your father died. I didn't have time. So I went back the night of the fireworks, when it was empty. I'm very good at picking locks and I got in easily. I did knock over that cologne, but I cleaned it up and I thought you'd believe Sera or Alec did it. Then your mother came in. I hadn't found the journal. I was waiting for her to leave. Then she heard me and I had to do something. I was going to slit her throat but there would have been so much blood and I was already late. So I snapped her neck. I'm sure it didn't hurt. Then I made the house look like it had been robbed. I thought I'd throw suspicion on someone scared of her tarot readings by putting the card next to her.'

'But someone saw you,' Davis said.

'That damned Wendell Booth. I'd gone to the basement and broken a window then found a trash bag and loaded it with stuff to make the burglary look real. I went out the door and there he was. I ran through the backyard. He couldn't keep up with me, but he chased me, the fool. I went tearing to the creek where I banged into Eddie Maddox – knocked him clean out and dropped my bag. I guess Wendell dragged him out of the water and took the bag. But he'd seen me. He must have thought Eddie did, too. That's why he took him.' Incredibly, Jon started laughing. 'For safe-keeping. Wendell is *so* dumb. He should have died in prison.'

'Wendell wasn't dumb,' Juliet said. 'He knew you'd kill him *and* Eddie. He kept himself – and Eddie – hidden from *you.*'

'Oh God,' Frank moaned. 'Jon, tell me none of this is true. Tell me you're not a monster!'

Jon tensed and looked as if he were going to lunge across the room at Frank before Leslie burst out, 'What about the earring? That was Deke's earring, wasn't it?'

'No!'

'Yes, it was.' Frank spoke in a flat, hopeless voice. 'Deke texted me when I was here with Jon and Danielle and Leslie. Deke said he needed to see me – urgently – that night at ten o'clock with information about Gary. I told him to go to hell. He texted back that he was coming to my house anyway.'

'I knew something was wrong,' Jon said. 'You put your phone in your jacket pocket. I came to your home an hour later. Your jacket was on the back of a chair. I kept talking, lingering, until you left the room, then I got your phone and read the text message. I hadn't bought that dose I gave Gary from Deke, but I knew he thought I'd killed Gary. He'd gotten high and shot off his mouth once a long time ago. He was too slick for me to take him out then, but I knew what he wanted to tell you and I was waiting for him when he was on the way to your door, Frank.' Jon shrugged. 'Deke had lived longer than he should have. Much longer. Good riddance.' He looked at all of them. 'I did you *all* a favor. Don't you see that?'

'Deke was no great loss,' Kyle said, 'but what about Nate and Gary and Owen and Sera?'

'Threats! They were all threats to my family!'

'Nate *was* your family.'

'*No!* He was a Tresswell – by name at least. I'm a Tresswell by spirit! Look at my mother. Look at my grandfather. Do you think they climbed their way up into the world and held on because they were *kind*? Danielle is as selfish and calculating as they come. So was her father and her grandfather. I was protecting *my* family!'

'Tommy and me?' Leslie asked pitifully. 'Look at the carnage you've left in your wake. What kind of legacy is that for Tommy and the new baby? Huh, Jon? Is that something to take pride in? Are you pleased with yourself? Do you think *they* will be proud of you?'

'They'll never know if you keep your mouth shut,' Jon

hissed. 'Just keep your simple-minded, sanctimonious mouth shut and do what you do best – follow my orders, adore me, and look pretty. Oh, and keep pushing out my kids, only don't screw up like you did last time.'

Leslie looked like a switch had been turned on in her. She drew herself up, glared at Jon, and snarled, 'You are a lunatic.'

Jon surged forward and Davis grabbed for his arm. Like lightning, Jon whirled, grabbed Marcy, whipped a switchblade knife from his pocket, snapped it open and held it against her throat. Marcy's brown eyes flew wide. Davis moved toward her again and she gasped, 'No!' A tiny trickle of blood ran down her neck to her shoulder. 'Davis, *no!*'

Juliet's gaze was fastened on the blade that she estimated was nearly four inches long and serrated. The handle was black and Jon's hand trembled slightly. 'I will use it, Davis,' he said ominously. 'I won't hesitate to use it on this delicate white throat.'

Marcy whimpered. Davis stepped back. Leslie sagged and Frank caught her, gently lowering her to the floor.

'Jon, *no!*' Danielle sobbed. 'Jon, please don't do this.'

'Do what? Protect myself? Save myself? Or should I let you do that for me? You've been doing it nearly all my life.'

'Yes, because I *love* you. You've been my darling, my precious boy, the child of the only man I ever loved—'

'Frank *Greenlee*,' Jon spat out. 'You *loved* Frank Greenlee? That middle-class drunk? You let him seduce you when you had Nathaniel Tresswell?'

'You didn't know Nathaniel. Not the real Nathaniel. He was another Robert Monroe. Worse.'

Jon slowly smiled. 'You wanted Carole to marry Robert.'

'I thought he was a nice man. He played me. You know how tricky he is, how unscrupulous.'

'Just like me. Robert and I are two of a kind. Only I'm smarter. And more ruthless.' Still smiling eerily, Jon started walking toward the family room entrance, dragging Marcy along, the blade at her throat. 'I think we'll be leaving now, folks. I don't believe I'm wanted anymore.'

Juliet knew that the tightrope Jon had been walking since he was a child had finally broken. He was free-falling. He didn't know where he'd land and he didn't care. He was just following those merciless impulses that had been in him forever. And poor Marcy was caught in the crossfire.

'Jon, please let me go,' Marcy pleaded. 'I feel terrible.'

'I'm sure you do, my dear. You're as big as a whale.'

Davis drew his gun. 'Jon, I swear if you hurt a hair on her head—'

'You'll shoot me?' Jon pulled Marcy closer in front of him. 'You'll have to go through her, first.'

Davis and Kyle began edging toward Jon. 'Don't try to rush at me and take me down,' Jon ordered. 'I can slash her neck in an instant. Try to kill me and I'll kill her. You know I won't hesitate. Stop them, Davis. She's *your* wife, full of *your* baby.'

'You son of a bitch.'

'Oh, Davis,' Marcy whispered as Jon dragged her past Alec and Juliet and Leslie, who was lying limp on the floor. 'Don't move. Please don't move.'

Jon moved out of the family room and headed for the front door. In spite of Marcy's pleas, Davis inched forward, gun drawn, face drawn taut and eyes burning. He held his service revolver by his side. Behind him, Kyle crept along, weaponless but looking relentless. Ten seconds after Kyle began trailing Jon and Davis, Alec said softly, 'Stay with Leslie,' as he started to follow Kyle.

Juliet looked at her best friend. Frank sat on the floor beside her, stroking her face with one hand, holding his cell phone in the other. 'I'm calling the paramedics. Let me take care of her, Leslie. I owe it to her. Please.'

Juliet paused. Frank looked old and broken and heartsick. He needed to help the wife of his son, she realized. 'All right, Frank. Thank you.'

Juliet ran after Alec and the four of them watched as Jon managed to get the front door open without moving the knife from Marcy's throat. She was whimpering and crying pitifully, clearly frightened beyond speech, beyond reason. Then water gushed between her legs. She groaned as water splashed over the door seal, soaking through her white slacks. She bent over, and groaned again.

'Ah, good try,' Jon said. 'But it won't save you, Marcy. You're coming with me.'

He yanked her out the door and pulled her, crying and moaning, across the driveway to his large silver Dodge Durango.

'Jon, for God's sake,' Davis yelled. 'The baby!'

'An inconvenience. That's all.' He opened the car door and shoved Marcy roughly onto the front seat. 'Did you think I'd give her back to you out of pity? I have no pity.'

Jon ran around the front of the car, keeping low as Davis aimed at him, and jumped in. Marcy had disappeared, no doubt doubled over in pain. Jon pulled the SUV out of the driveway and screeched the tires as he tore down the street. Davis and Kyle ran toward Davis's car and jumped in, Davis behind the wheel. Then Alec went for his car. Juliet caught up with him, grabbing his arm. 'You're *not* going!'

'I am. They may need me.'

'You're not even armed!'

'Neither is Kyle.'

'Then I'm coming, too.'

'Juliet   '

'You can't stop me.'

Juliet hopped into Alec's car and they took off, following Davis who was going at least twenty miles above the speed limit. Juliet fastened her seat belt and held onto the arm rest. 'We're going to wreck.'

'No, we're not. I know how to drive, Juliet.'

Ahead, they saw Jon's SUV racing along at breakneck speed. They closed in on Davis and Kyle. Davis was not in his patrol car so there were no lights or sirens. Juliet had no doubt Kyle was calling in the chase on his cell phone, though. Meanwhile, Jon was sticking to back streets, clearly not wanting to draw the attention he would on main streets where patrol cars waited for speeders, and keeping up with him was harder than it would have been on a straightaway. They screeched around turns, ignoring stop signs, racing against time.

'Alec, what's Davis going to do if he catches up with Jon?'

'I'm sure backup is on the way.'

'But what if backup is too late? What if Jon kills Marcy as soon as he's stopped?'

'Don't think about that. It won't happen. It *can't.*'

But it could, Juliet thought dismally. Jon was crazy. He could strike out at Marcy, take her life out of pure rage. The same thoughts must be going through Davis's mind. She couldn't imagine his agony.

They were passing north through town. They reached the highway running parallel to the river. Juliet looked behind her and saw no patrol cars. What was going on? Couldn't Kyle or Davis raise someone on their cell phones? Couldn't the police catch up with them? She wanted to cry but she wouldn't let herself. It wouldn't do any good. Alec might even make her get out of the car.

'I know what you're thinking,' Alec said. 'Where are the cops?'

'Well, where *are* they?'

'Coming. Do you think they're going to desert Davis? They just haven't caught up with us.'

'And Davis hasn't caught up with Jon. I can see Davis's car but Jon's is long gone.'

'Not long gone. Just temporarily out of sight.'

'God, what an optimist.'

'Would being a pessimist be better? Would that help, Juliet?'

'No,' she said miserably. 'It wouldn't help a bit.' She twisted her hands. 'Where is he *going*?'

'I doubt if he knows himself. He's just running.'

'And Marcy's in labor. What if he doesn't stop? What if she gives birth in the car?'

'She won't.'

'Oh, how do you know? Under the circumstances, she could lose the baby. Oh God, Alec . . . Oh *God*—'

'Stop it, Juliet!' He looked in the rearview mirror. 'The cavalry's coming.'

'What?' Juliet craned around and saw lights flashing behind them.

'I have to slow down so they can pass me. They want to be behind – or maybe in front of – Davis.'

They slowed and two patrol cars passed them, sirens screaming, lights flashing. The night had come alive with blasting sound and garish color. Juliet felt almost dizzy as

Alec picked up speed again, following them. She closed her eyes, imagining Marcy terrified and in pain. She'd been torn away from Davis by a madman; the stress was probably causing her baby to force its way out of her body in a speeding car, and she had no idea if she would live or die.

Alec's face was grim and sharp-edged. 'Damn, Jon's moving fast. That model has great acceleration.'

'Where do you think he's going?'

'Maybe the bridge across the Ohio River into West Virginia. He was always drawn to that bridge. Don't ask me why.'

They whizzed past houses with lights glowing from windows and two brightly lit convenience stores. The moon wasn't full but shone enough to clearly illuminate the night. She felt as if they'd gone fifty miles when she knew it had only been a few. Then, up ahead, Juliet saw lights on the bridge arching above the river. She was fixated on the bridge when Alec burst out, 'What the hell?'

The trail of cars following Jon slowed. Suddenly, a mass flew out of the right passenger door and landed on the berm of the road. 'Is that Marcy?' Juliet gasped. Before Alec could answer, one of the cars ahead pulled to the side of the road, and two men jumped out and rushed to the figure. A man stooped over the collapsed body.

'Is that Davis?' Juliet asked, leaning forward and squinting. Alec nodded. 'Pull over next to them and let me out of the car. The patrol cars are chasing Jon. I want to see about Marcy.'

Alec slowed and swerved to the right. They came to a stop a few feet away from the two men with a huddled, moaning Marcy. Kyle was on the phone and Davis stooped beside her, tears running down his face as he rubbed her back and murmured to her. 'It's going to be all right, sweetheart. Kyle's calling nine-one-one. Just hold on.'

Juliet cautiously approached Marcy and bent at the knees. 'Marcy.'

'Oh, Juliet.' Marcy reached up and clutched Juliet's hand. 'He just screamed at me to get out of the car. He didn't even fully stop. He *pushed* me out! I'm so scared for the baby.'

'Just breathe.' Juliet didn't know if breathing really helped, but it's what they always told women in labor on television. 'Deep, slow breaths. Try to be calm.'

'*Calm!*' Marcy shouted. 'How can I be calm?'

'Juliet's right. Breathe, sweetheart,' Davis said desperately. 'Breathe.'

'Why did he let you out of the car?' Juliet asked.

'I don't know. Maybe I was making too much noise.' Marcy cringed and let out an air-shattering cry, bending forward, squeezing Davis's hand. 'Oh, my God, Davis! This baby is going to die. Our baby is going to die!'

'It *isn't*! You just have to get through this part. The EMS will be here in a minute.'

The sirens screamed in the distance. They turned onto the bridge, climbing the arch, chasing Jon. Juliet watched as the lead car, which she knew was Jon's, raced down the left-hand lane and swerved right. 'Davis, what's happening?' she asked.

Davis turned toward the bridge. Suddenly, the lead headlights pointed toward the side of the bridge and the SUV surged through the side barrier. Juliet, Davis, Alec, and Kyle watched open-mouthed as the car arced, its headlights shining brightly against the night sky, then plunged downward into the deep, dark depths of the Ohio River.

'Oh my *God*,' Kyle gasped as police ran to the side of the bridge and looked into the water. 'Unless he had a window open—'

'The devil is trapped inside,' Davis said flatly.

EPILOGUE

The next day, Jon Tresswell's SUV was raised from the Ohio River, his body inside. Juliet was with Leslie when Davis told her that Jon was dead. She promptly burst into wild sobs.

Juliet wrapped her arms around Leslie. 'I'm so sorry, Les. I know how much you loved him.'

Leslie raised her swollen face. 'No, not anymore. I'm crying because I'm so relieved. I've been terrified that he escaped and he'd come back here for Tommy and me and make us go somewhere with him. I thought I loved Jon Tresswell, but I didn't know him at all. He was a monster, Juliet. A *monster*. He murdered—'

'Don't,' Juliet said sharply. 'Don't think about the awful things he did. Not now. Just be glad he's gone. You and Tommy are free.'

'And the baby. It was a miracle I didn't lose it. I will be such a good mother to Tommy and it – I'll make up for everything.'

'I know you will and both children will be so lucky to have you.'

'And Marcy,' Leslie rushed on. 'Thank God she and her son are all right. It was touch and go. If the EMS hadn't gotten there in time—'

'But they did. She's fine. And happy.' Juliet hesitated. 'Leslie, Jon didn't lose control of the car – he committed suicide. Why didn't he take Marcy with him? He didn't care anything about her.'

'I don't know,' Leslie said slowly. 'She told me she kept begging him for her life. Then, unknowingly, she said the one thing that pulled him up short. She told him if he didn't stop, if he killed her, it would be the end of Tresswell Metal. The horrible publicity, the ruined reputation, would destroy it. If he stopped, maybe Tresswell would survive and someday go to Tommy.' Leslie sighed. 'She knew from Davis that Tresswell meant everything to Jon. It had since he was a kid. That's why he let Nate die – so Tresswell would be his. I'd like to think that maybe he realized whether he lived or died, Tresswell was gone for *him*. His reason for living was gone and that's why he decided to do one last good thing before he died – let Marcy go.' She shrugged, looking crushed. 'Maybe he did it for Tommy so people would remember that his father had spared Marcy. I don't know what he was thinking. I didn't know Jon, Juliet. Not ever. I wonder if anyone did.'

'Perhaps Danielle.'

'She probably knew him better than anyone did, but I don't think at first she realized how twisted he was. It would be a hard thing for a mother to admit even to herself. By the time she couldn't hide from it anymore – after Fin – it was too late. So, she started covering for him. God knows how she excused herself.'

The next evening, Juliet and Alec sat in the living room sipping brandy as Debussy's 'Claire de Lune' played softly in the background. Hutch lay on his back beside them, sound asleep. Alec looked at Juliet. 'I love you.'

'I love you, too.'

'So what are we going to do about that, darling?'

'What are you suggesting?'

Alec took her left hand. 'I suggest I put a ring on your third finger. A nice ring with a great big diamond. Do you like white or yellow gold?'

'Yellow, and a ring sounds lovely, but the diamond doesn't have to be big.'

'I want it to be.' Alec's dark, intense eyes gazed into hers. 'Then I suggest we get married and you come back to New York with me.'

Juliet clasped his hand. 'Alec, I want to be your wife. I've wanted that for years. But I can't go to New York with you now.'

Alec's smile faltered. 'Is it because we don't have time to arrange a wedding before I have to go back to work?'

'No. I don't care about a formal wedding. A ceremony in front of a judge is fine with me. It's the timing.'

'The timing?'

'We've only just admitted our feelings for each other. Our new relationship is . . .' She laughed. 'New.'

'You think it'll change in the next few weeks or months?'

'Maybe. Not that we'll fall out of love with each other, but we need to get used to each other *this* way – as lovers, as a *couple*. We've never been that, Alec. We've kept a distance between us.'

He frowned. 'I see. And much as I hate to admit it, I understand.' He grinned at her. 'But you're not being impetuous, Juliet Reid.'

'No. Fin was the impetuous one, not me. Besides, I can't leave Parrish now.'

'I'd think this is the last place you want to be after all that's happened.'

'I know. And in a way, it is. But things have to be done. I have to sell this house.'

'You can get a realtor here in town to handle the details.'

'Yes, but there's something else. Or *someone* else. Leslie.'

'Won't she go to her mother?'

Juliet shook her head. 'Leslie's mother isn't like mine. Her child isn't the center of her life. She loves Leslie, but right now she's . . . well . . . besotted with her new husband. I'm sure she'll come here to see Leslie, but she really doesn't want Leslie and Tommy crowding in on her new life. Besides, Leslie has at least one house to sell, plus she's expecting another baby. She can't turn to Danielle. I don't think they can prove Danielle bribed that juror during Wendell's trial – she won't be arrested – but after everything that's happened—'

'Leslie won't turn to her for help. Besides, she'll have to take over Tresswell Metal. That won't be easy after the scandal caused by Jon.'

'And Carole has to leave the country. She signed the divorce papers – they're binding. Anyway, Leslie wants to solve her own problems. Before, Jon handled everything. I think she wants to show Tommy that she's a strong woman.'

'With another strong woman to help her.'

'And myself to look after. I have this house to sell and my parents' estate to settle. I want to help Leslie, even if I can only give moral support. I've known her since she was six – I can't run off and leave her.'

'She'll also have Frank, if she'll accept his help. And Kyle. He's very fond of her.'

'Yes. She can depend on them.' Juliet smiled. 'I finally know why Dad didn't want me to date Kyle. He knew Kyle was gay. Dad was afraid I'd fall for him and get hurt.'

'Well, his sexuality is now common knowledge. I suppose he hid it because he wanted to be a police officer. I know attitudes have changed a lot, but he still wasn't taking any chances.'

'And I understand it. But back to Leslie. She needs me.'

'What about the teaching jobs you've applied for?'

'I wasn't excited about any of them. And yesterday, Pauline offered me a job at the Flower Garden. I won't make a fortune but enough to maintain myself for a few months.'

'A few months. That's how long you're delaying our marriage?'

'If it's all right with you.'

Hutch rolled over, snorted loudly, then began snoring again. Alec laughed. 'I guess it's all right with him!'

'He doesn't care as long as he's with one of us.' Juliet looked at Alec appealingly. 'I can come to see you every few weeks in New York. You can make quick trips here. And there's always Skype.'

'Hallelujah! How could I forget Skype?'

'I know it's not ideal, but . . .'

'But wanting to stay here, to take our time, to help your friend – that's all part of why I love you, Juliet. You've always been realistic and unselfish, even back in the days when you gracefully stepped aside and let Fin have the spotlight. It's charming, it's unbelievably kind, and it's the stuff dream girls are made of.'

'So I'm a dream girl?'

Alec smiled at her tenderly, then moved closer and murmured, 'You are *my* dream girl, darling Juliet. Now and forever.'